To Shaman
Best Wishes
Elizabeth Scott.
August 2011

3

CONTENTS

Preface 7
Map 1 – War in Poland 8
Map 2 – War in Germany and Lorraine 9
Chapter 1 – The 7th July 1636 11
Chapter 2 – Athelstaneford 17
Chapter 3 – School at Haddington 23
Chapter 4 – St Andrews University 29
Chapter 5 – Poitiers 35
Chapter 6 – Recruited by Gray 45
Chapter 7 – Getting to Leith 55
Chapter 8 – Journey to Prague 69
Chapter 9 – Captain of the Palace Guard 81
Chapter 10 – Battle of the White Mountain 89
Chapter 11 – Frankenthal to Alsace 101
Chapter 12 – Fleurus and Bergen op Zoom 111
Chapter 13 – To King Gustavus Adolphus 119
Chapter 14 – War in Poland 131
Chapter 15 – Pitched Battle with Sigismund 139
Chapter 16 – Dirschau 145
Chapter 17 – Relief of Mewe 151
Chapter 18 – Knighted by Gustavus Adolphus 161
Chapter 19 – In Action with Monro 167
Chapter 20 – Taking Gartz 175
Chapter 21 – Destruction of Frankfurt on Oder 181
Chapter 22 – Landsberg to Berlin 189
Chapter 23 – Breitenfeld 195
Chapter 24 – Frankfurt on Maine 207
Chapter 25 – Mainz 217
Chapter 26 – Munich 227
Chapter 27 – Escape from Gustavus Adolphus 237
Chapter 28 – Marshal de Camp 245
Chapter 29 – Taking la Mothe 251
Chapter 30 – Moving into Lorraine 261
Chapter 31 – Metternich of Trier seized 269
Chapter 32 – The Retreat of 1635 279
Chapter 33 – Paris. Winter 1635 289
Chapter 34 – Return to Winter Quarters from Paris 295
Chapter 35 – Retaking Lorraine and Siege of Saverne 1636 301
Chapter 36 – Burial in Toul 311
Acknowledgements 317

PREFACE

Sir John Hepburn, first Colonel of The Royal Scots, the only Scotsman to become a Marshal of France, and, in the words of Cardinal Richelieu, "The best Soldier in Christendom, and therefore the World".

Born at Athelstaneford, the site of the inspiration for Scotland's Saltire flag, he died far from home in Lorraine, but his name lives on, in his native land and in France where he lies buried in the Cathedral of Toul.

I visited many of the sites associated with him and have researched in depth, drawing on family materials, Sir John's letters, the National Archives, literary sources (including his friend and fellow soldier Robert Monro's history of Mac-Key's Regiment) and the historical framework and participants are based on fact.

This is not a biography. Instead, I hope that I have breathed life into the memory of a man who bestrode the military world of his day but has fallen somewhat from view in modern reckoning.

If, after reading about Sir John Hepburn, you are interested in finding out more about the Royal Scots and the men who led them, visit their website at www.theroyalscots.co.uk

Elizabeth Scott
Edinburgh. 2011

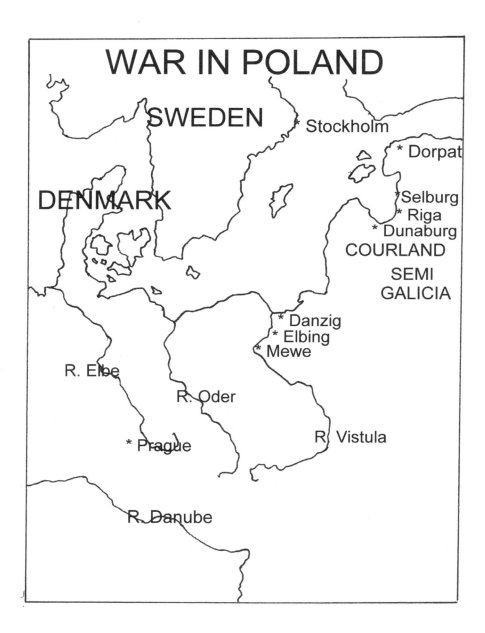

WAR IN POLAND

SWEDEN * Stockholm

* Dorpat

DENMARK

*Selburg
* Riga
* Dunaburg
COURLAND
SEMI
GALICIA

* Danzig
* Elbing
* Mewe

R. Elbe

R. Oder

* Prague

R. Vistula

R. Danube

WAR IN GERMANY AND LORRAINE

SWEDEN

DENMARK

* St Andrews
* Athelstaneford

* Hamburg * Greifswald

* London

* Berlin * Stettin
Gartz

* Bergen op Zoom

* Fleurus

* Breitenfeld

R. Rhine * Erfurt

* Paris

R. Elbe R. Oder

LORRAINE * Mainz

* Trier

* Prague

* Mannheim

* Donauworth

* Toul
* Saverne

ALSACE

R. Danube

* Munich

CHAPTER 1
The 7th of July 1636

In Spring 1636 Sir John Hepburn, first Colonel of the Royal Scots, led his regiment, as part of the army commanded by Cardinal la Valette, to subdue Lorraine and annex it to France. Hepburn's regiment, recruited by him in Scotland by warrant of King Charles and now on loan to King Louis XIII of France, were trained soldiers from all over Scotland and in many cases veterans of the Swedish wars against the Hapsburg menace in Germany.

At the end of the previous year, their campaign in Lorraine had been thwarted by an all-out Spanish attack. But Cardinal Richelieu had ordered their return in greater force and now only the red-walled city of Saverne stood between them and the narrow pass that led to the rich lands of Alsace.

In command of this phase of the campaign, Sir John Hepburn had besieged Saverne so tight that no one came or went. But still the town resisted. Their commander, Colonel Mulheim, hoped that his fellow Spaniard, General Galas, would come to their aid as he had done the year before. Sir John Hepburn knew from his scouts that he would not. With English and Dutch ships harrying the treasure galleons from South America, Spain was no longer rich in bullion. Galas was fully involved repelling the renewed campaigns mounted against him by Swedish and Dutch troops.

Saverne's garrison and townspeople starved and died. Yet the plain in front of those high, blood spattered walls remained a killing ground for attacking troops and Saverne still had huge stores of ammunition as the piles of dead around the walls attested.

It was time for a new approach and on that evening of the 7th July 1636, Sir John Hepburn had given orders that, come night-fall, a unit from his regiment would quietly clear a path through the mass of dead bodies to allow him to reconnoitre the walls for a final attack the next day.

Dusk had brought welcome respite from the summer heat. Sir John, clad in shirt-sleeves, breeches and thigh boots, was thankful for it. He made his way past the half-ruined cottages of Phalsburg, the small village beside Saverne where his regiment was quartered, and down to a stream that wandered through trampled, blackened fields. The mouldering hay reminded him of those last autumns at Athelstaneford, his family's home in East Lothian where year after year storms had destroyed their oat harvest. Here the carnage was caused by a retreating Spanish army, intent on burning their French pursuers' supplies. Bodies had lain rotting in those fields until he had ordered a clear up and now at last the sickly smell of putrefaction was out of his nostrils, hidden in mass graves.

"Not for long," he muttered to himself with a sigh. They had taken dreadful losses on the plains before the walls of Saverne. The scent of death was already on the wind and he would be glad to see his men decently interred. The defending garrison would pay for their stupidity in resisting when they could have capitulated and marched out with banners flying days ago. Now it was too late. Blood lust was in his soldiers' eyes. French and Scots alike had friends to avenge. Saverne's townsfolk as well as the military would suffer. He had seen it all before. There would be women raped and slaughtered, men and children lying naked in the streets, their mouths agape in their last agony as their throats were slashed or they felt a pike's steel rip their abdomen open. Houses would be looted, then set on fire, like as not with their occupants still in them. There would be no prisoners. Saverne would be destroyed and left a bloody, smoking desolation. Even the garrison commander, Colonel Mulheim, would be lucky to escape. The man who got to him first would have to decide whether his blood lust was stronger than his greed for ransom. If it was one of his Scots it would be a close call, he thought with a wry grin. "Incorrigible Border dastards", the Edinburgh Privy Council had called the first company of jailbirds he had led to the defence of the Scottish Princess Elizabeth who had married Elector Frederick of the Palatinate. But they had fought like fiends for him whenever he had asked it of them. This regiment, The Royal Scots, veteran soldiers whom he had recruited from all over Scotland and whom he now led, were no less tough and valorous.

He remembered his sick horror after his first skirmish. Those limp white throwaway puppets had become so much a part of his life now that he no longer turned away as they were tossed into pits. But a sick sense of loss tightened his throat as he thought of his younger brother James being treated that way. James Hepburn had been his loyal lieutenant colonel, a magnificent administrator and above all his safe courier to Rex Chancellor Oxenstierna, his long-time friend and now Sweden's military commander. James had ridden into an ambush while on skirmish in the last stages of this campaign to subdue Lorraine. A few survivors had straggled in to report the disaster. Hepburn had wanted to kill them himself for being alive while his brother was dead but in his heart he knew James was no tactician, just brave and loyal and foolhardy. There was no dignified burial for losers.

That evening as he had looked down the dinner-board at his senior captain and cousin, another James Hepburn, who looked so like the sandy haired brother he loved, his heart had felt heavy with loss. How happy he would have been to tell James the good news, the amazing news that he had just received from Cardinal Richelieu. In his mind he could see his brother's face light with delight. "Marshal of France!" he would have said as he embraced him. "There is no higher honour, John. I am so proud of you!"

He nodded to the few soldiers that he met. They all knew the huge, red haired Colonel Hepburn whose piercing blue eyes missed nothing. They ducked their heads respectfully, or if they were one of his own, raised a hand in salute. Most soldiers would be thronging the small stone houses that still had intact thatch roofs, or filling the tents they had set up. Some of his Scots would have preferred to set up their own tents of turf and branch and be sitting round a fire watching a stew of cabbage and whatever meat or fowl they could scavenge to supplement their evening meal. His musketeers would be heating their ration of lead and fashioning musket balls for use the next day. Twelve balls to each pound of lead was the recognised yield but each musketeer had his own way of pouring it and finishing the cooling ball. Their lives might depend on a ball not sticking in the barrel. It was a serious business and his men gave time and care to the process as they had been trained to do.

Dusk was well established and the sun hung, a great blood-red ball, over the dark pines that clothed the jagged cliffs to the west. July was hot as Hades, but by the stream a crouching willow, its fat old trunk evidence of many years pollarding, gave a small canopy of shade. It reminded him of the squat willows beside the Peffer burn below the farm at Athelstaneford where he had grown up. As he sat, settling his back against the gnarled tree trunk, and felt at last the cooling breeze of evening coming off the ripples beside him, he let his mind run free.

His thoughts were too chaotic to suppose sleep was at hand. To be "Marshal of France!" The highest military honour! A deep feeling of contentment pervaded his mind. But it brought decisions. How could he influence the Swedish Command without a safe pair of hands to carry his letters to Rex Chancellor Oxenstierna?

"His Royal Majesty and especially Cardinal Richelieu are not only inclined to assist your Excellency in everything but also to make a continuous alliance" he had written to reassure the Swedish Rex Chancellor, and later "How much your Excellency is obliged to his Royal Majesty and especially the Cardinal who to myself honoured your Excellency's virtue, quality and assurances."

From his first meeting with Cardinal Richelieu he knew he had found the leader he would follow for the rest of his life. Oxenstierna, now the power behind the Swedish attack on the Hapsburg menace, would always be a revered friend. If that friendship could benefit France, Hepburn was happy to encourage him to trust and co-operate with the Little Red Cardinal who held his heart, his loyalty and for whom he would gladly lay down his life.

Looking back it seemed his whole life had been an up and down preparation for this final honour. Recruited by Sir Andrew Gray and later abandoned in Holland after the campaign in Bohemia with the rump of his Scottish regiment, that first command decision he had taken to march his Scots to join the Swedes had been risky. He had been lucky to impress the King of Sweden.

"The King can do nought without ye!" his friend Robert Monro had said years later, and Hepburn had been thankful for it. He had learned to lead and he had become rich.

When King Gustavus Adolphus of Sweden had tired of the Scottish Colonel who won his battles for him, Hepburn had been experienced enough and famous enough to be chosen by Charles I to recruit and lead a Regiment on loan to Louis XIII of France and know he had a welcome waiting for him.

A smile crossed his face as he remembered his first Sergeant, Andrew Armstrong's aggrieved tones, "I aye thought the Privy Council were a mite hard calling us "incorrigible Border dastards" just for a bit o' rieving, Sir!"

Some of those border Scots from his first command were still part of this regiment of veteran soldiers. "Le Regiment d'Hebron" Cardinal Richelieu had called them, but Hepburn had insisted on them being named the "Royal Scots" and they had become all the family he needed, sharing hardships, finding food from sources he did not want to know about, but obeying him utterly, and brave as lions when it came to a fight.

Now, notified in a despatch that he had been promoted to Marshal of France, he could ask for no further honours for himself or them and was deeply grateful to Cardinal Richelieu who had undoubtedly pushed the award through. This was an evening to savour.

Settling his back against the willow, he stretched his long booted legs comfortably on the grass of the river bank and was content. So many struggles, so many dead, but at last he had reached the top and could look back. As he sat listening to the slap, slap of the little wavelets moved by the evening breeze, he wondered if he had just wanted to outdo his elder brothers. But then he shook his head. He had craved a finer life than mucking out a cow byre.

CHAPTER 2
Athelstaneford

The lad with the flaming red hair tore down the hill towards the ford over the Peffer burn that gave its name to the East Lothian village of Athelstaneford, a sickle held aloft like a sword. In his imagination he was Fergus McErk, grandson of the King of the Scots who, long ago, had gone on a raid with the Pictish King, Angus. The two leaders did not often combine but times were hard, their harvest poor and the Angles to the South were rich in cattle.

Fifteen year old John Hepburn knew all about poor harvests. His two older brothers, George and Andrew, growled that their farm at Athelstaneford was mismanaged. His mother held the reins and beat them all for not working hard enough, and her brother Edward Hepburn, the minister of Haugh, told them in his unctuous voice that affliction and suffering was God's call to true repentance.

John Hepburn hated that bitter, harassed woman they called his mother. With every beating he loathed her more. He could not recall a single kindness from the woman they said gave him life, only pain. He abhorred his uncle who loved to see him beaten and he was racing away from the house that day because he had been told they needed more rushes for the mud floor of their dining hall and if he went fast he would escape their God's encouragement upon his back.

He waved his sickle-rapier at old William Watnoun and Johnne Borthwick, already bent over their scythes trying to salvage the oats that lay blackened and rotting, laid by the storms that had once more ruined the harvest. Neither paused in their stroke but William Watnoun's leathered face creased in a grin as the third son of his old master tore past him at full charge.

"Happen we're fighting the battle o' Athelstaneford again," he muttered.

"We could aye do wi' winning summat," replied his companion.

Every one in the village knew the story about the battle over their land that had determined the flag of Scotland. It had been handed down, mother to child, and lost nothing in the telling.

Marie, John Hepburn's eldest and dearest sister, had told it to him often enough at his insistence.

"It was eight hundred years ago," she used to begin, "there in our fields just below the house. Angus, King of the Picts, turned to face the Angles led by their chief, Athelstan. That Athelstan and his band of warriors had come from Northumberland to plunder us. It was just unfortunate that King Angus was returning from the south with a herd of English cattle when he met them. He had joined up with a raiding band of Scots and together they had been very successful.

Athelstan saw a way to quick booty and came after them with all speed. Angus could see no escape. He sent the Scots on with the cattle and, outnumbered as he was, turned his weary men to fight."

She would shake her head sadly at that point.

"There was no use hoping that the sea mist, the haar, would creep in to blanket the land and offer a chance of escape. When King Angus looked up the sky was azure bright, highlighting his puny forces. Sensing victory, Athelstan spurred his men across the Peffer marsh down there where our cows graze."

John Hepburn would follow her pointing finger with his eyes as his mind drew the pictures.

""We have them!" was their shout.

But as he gazed skywards, Angus saw the wispy white clouds come together in a diagonal cross. His heart lifted.

"St Andrew is with us. See his cross above. We will triumph!"

He launched his force down the hill, unaware that once the cattle were over the brow of the hill behind, the old Scottish chief had sent his grandson back in support. Fergus McErk, leading his grandfather's men, poured down the hill in a wild screaming charge. Angus felt the power at his back and his men responded. Mired in the marshy ground,

Athelstan's mounted men were powerless to charge. They were slaughtered to a man and Fergus McErk remembered that day when, many years later, he was crowned King of Scotland and he named St Andrew as Scotland's saint and his white cross on sky blue, Scotland's flag.

You're not far off the age of McErk, young John," she would finish. "What a boy he must have been."

John Hepburn and his younger brother James often played it out, sometimes alone, sometimes with their cousins from over the hill at Waughton Castle. He was always King Angus, James the young Scot, and Marie, watching over them, had obligingly died innumerable times as Athelstan. But when he was alone he was McErk in his wild charge to victory.

His family had partially drained the boggy land round the Peffer burn to grow grass for their cattle so John Hepburn was able to run free, leaping the burn as he went, without recourse to the ancient ford that carts used as they came and went to North Berwick. He crossed the field, still called the Field of Blood, where Athelstan and his men had died and had been trampled into the marsh, and headed towards the sea.

There, behind the dunes, he knew he would find huge swathes of green coarse grass that came up to his waist and covered the bents. Those bent grasses had a smell all their own and, spread on the beaten earth of their hall floor, scented the room. He knew that if he worked fast he could cut enough in a few hours and leave time to strip off and rush into the waves.

The sea was cold, numbingly cold, but the exhilaration of swimming in that clear blue water would over-ride his shrinking nakedness and in September he hoped the water still had some of the warmth of summer left. Come October, he knew that he had to return to school. All winter his life would be a long hard grind, split between schooling at Haddington and keeping his chores going at home lest he reap his mother's stick across his shoulders for backsliding.

His childhood had finished with his fifth birthday. The Reformed Church decreed that all children from five to eight years old must learn to read and write and do sums.

"All children must read the bible," said his uncle Edward Hepburn, Rector of Haugh. But once he was eight, his mother saw no reason for him to waste time in further education when he was old enough for hard labour. The dominie of his first school had reasoned with her to no avail.

"The boy is clever, Mistress," he had begged. "He maun get the chance o' an education."

"I need men to work the farm. We're poor enough as it is."

"But the burgh will pay." Gathering courage to face the sour woman glowering at him he finally shouted, "It is my right to name him, Madam, and I canna' see past that!"

"He'll not need to neglect his work at the farm then," was her grudging acceptance.

It had been hard going. John Hepburn paused in his strokes with the small hand sickle to wipe his brow. His mind went at once to his eldest sister, Marie. Without her he would never have managed.

"If ever I had a mother," he said to himself, "it is Marie; my little mother, my eldest sister, who helps me by keeping candles so that I can work at night through the winter dark, who mends my clothes and keeps me right for school. She loves me and I love her."

Looking up at the sun he saw that it was still mid-morning and set to cutting again, stacking the grass in great heaps and tying them round with rope made of woven grass so that he could carry them home. He could picture his four sisters sitting sewing together, Marie helping poor Alisoun who was always sickly, and encouraging Isobel and Helen to keep their stitches small. Together they sewed shirts and trousers for their men-folk, dresses for themselves and their mother, as well as knitting the coarse wool spun from their own sheep into stockings. Mostly, as today, John Hepburn went barefoot, the skin of his feet toughened against stones in summer and snow in winter, though for the High School he drew on stockings and square toed shoes like the other scholars.

This year was going to be particularly hard, he thought with a sigh. This year he faced examination in Rhetoric, Philosophy and higher Latin to see if he could apply to St Andrews University. There he could study law. Lawyers were rich men and lived in comfort. Farming was not for him. He had no wish to fight the land to yield its harvest. That was for George, his eldest brother. George tolerated his mother's savagery because he loved the land. Andrew, the brother between them, wanted to get away. He had a promise of help from his uncle, a Burgess of Haddington, but had sworn his brothers to secrecy. It would not do to let his mother know. James, two years his younger, seemed but a child to all of them.

John Hepburn, well aware that if he excelled at his studies he could escape his mother's domination, studied long into the night. While his brothers and his mother slept, the candles Marie hid for him were burned to their stumps. So far he was the top of the class. He whispered his successes to Marie alone and she took his hands exclaiming in delight.

"Dinna' tell our Mother," he had begged. "She'd put an end to it."

They agreed on that. He wished he could take Marie with him when he left home but he knew he could not. She and her sisters were sentenced to sew and manage the house until such time as some man would offer marriage. "And who that might be when Mother will not give up the money Father left to us to be our dowries I know not," was her sad remark when John Hepburn had talked about her future. He could only hope to make enough money one day to be able to keep her too. When he suggested it, she smiled a little sadly.

"Save yourself, John. I'll manage somehow, you'll see."

 The piles of grass had mounted as his thoughts had run on. Looking around he thought he had done enough and eased his back, stretching to the still blue sky. Now he could swim.

In the fields William Watnoun was stretching in much the same way. He and Johnne Borthwick nodded to each other and moved off to sit snug beside a willow tree that grew by the burn. It screened them from their mistress whom they could hear shouting at one of her sons.

William shook his head. "A right torment, so she is. I miss the master. This was a happy farm, despite bad harvests and his being away so often."

They shared the bannock that Borthwick's wife had put up for them.

"Your wife's the best baker o' them all," Watnoun muttered as he chewed. "Do ye remember being called in to witness the Master's last testament, Johnne? Our John must have been about two then."

"Aye, William, May the ninth it was, and the first year o' the 1600's and a bad century it's been since for all o' us."

"Great strapping red-head the master was, wi' a temper to match. He should have been the eldest son of the Laird and that's for sure, not the eldest of the second son."

"Aye, he couldna' stand the failure of his farm year after year when he'd worked so hard."

"It takes people different, the bad luck. Some thole it better. He couldna' and that woman he married, Helene Hepburn, is a right harridan. She didna' make him welcome at home so he went carousing in Edinburgh. I'm heart sorry for her children the way she drives them."

"A right hard wumman!" Johnne Borthwick got slowly to his feet. "I aye thought the master was better content to meet his God than face up to his wife. We'd best get back to work and show willing or she'll be at us o'er the dinner table."

"Aye, she's a wicked, shrewish, grasping wumman, that she is. But it's in my mind that our young John will not be denied his birthright for ever and one day she'll rue the weals she's put upon his back."

CHAPTER 3
School at Haddington

His final exams taken, John Hepburn faced his headmaster "Ye're a linguist, John," The hunched dominie crouched in the high-backed chair fixed him with a sharp glance. "Ye've surprised me."

"I'd a great need to learn Latin, Magister. Those Romans were amazing soldiers. Agricola could have marched across our farm!"

School year finished in late Spring. From then on he rose with first light, grabbed a bannock and joined his older brothers in back-breaking, endless drudgery. Their mother kept them at it, ploughing, harrowing, planting, weeding, driving the cattle to pasture and scything the meadow for hay. The short noon dinner hour, when his sisters set the board upon its trestles in the hall and brought in the steaming bowls of stewed cabbage and meat, seemed but a breathing space.

"Better to thank our ain father than the Lord," Marie used to mutter as they sat hungry through their mother's interminable grace. "He built our doo-cot. He used to joke it would last a thousand years the way he'd built it and we'd all live there when our house fell down. With out it we'd aye be short o' meat."

His mother sat in his father's chair at the head of the table. He had known no different way but he knew his elder brother George coveted the place.

"Take it then!" John had said.

"How? She has all the money and all the power? I'm wanting her rod on my back as little as you, daftie!"

"But she canna' make the farm pay!"

"Na', she makes the wrong decisions year after year. Right enough the harvests have been poor but she makes it all worse. I could get a living. I ken it fine."

John Hepburn had kept his head down, done his chores and then as his young brother James snored beside him in the bed they shared, he had read and learned and read again. It meant he was tired the next day but by thirteen he stood as tall as his elder brothers and a lifetime's work had given him enormous strength. Being tired was a part of life. Nothing would stop him studying.

High School terms ran through the winter. With few chores awaiting him, his mother was pleased enough to lose one hungry mouth to her sister-in-law Marion who had married John Robeson, a Burgess in Haddington.

Helene Hepburn considered her sisters-in-law had married below themselves but both Marion and Agnes, who had married Musselburgh Burgess Alex Wright, lived comfortable lives in town houses. John Hepburn loved his Aunt Marion and, childless, she spoiled him all winter. He returned home on Friday to face a mountain of work stored up by his mother. But mucking out the byre and grooming the horses was a small price to pay for freedom to study the rest of the week.

All Sunday morning he stood in the Kirk at Haugh, listening to their Uncle delivering a hell-fire sermon on the punishments awaiting backsliders and watching his mother's uplifted face as she drank in her brother's words.

"Oh God I'd better not die!" he muttered to George beside him, "I'm doomed to hell fire the way I feel about my mother. Do ye think father is there already?"

"He'd make it a brighter place if he were," William Watnoun growled behind him and his younger sisters turned away to hide their giggles.

In the evening the family listened to bible readings. This was John Hepburn's task and by Monday he was often hoarse. In the afternoon, however, he and his sisters might walk out together, warmly wrapped in winter and revelling in the sun-bright blue sky in summer: it was the only time he could get Marie to himself.

"It's as if that witch kens you've been the only caring mother I've had, Marie, and she's trying to spirit ye away," he said once but she shook her head.

"Dinna' say that, John. I'm aye here for ye. But you're a man, grown now. You'll manage fine without me."

"No I won't! It would be great to be put forward to be a Bursar, Marie, but I've no money at all. None o' us do."

"Aye. I ken it isna' right, John. Isobel and Helen lost their dowries. If Alisoun had lived she'd be the same way."

"You too, Marie. You'd be married long since if you'd had a groat."

She smiled a little sadly. "I ken. But I feel while you are still home I should stay. You'd never manage without. None of you would."

John nodded. "We'd fair miss you."

"You'd get no candles to read by and no good new shirts, young man. It's cupboard love, so it is."

He grinned down at her. "No it isna'. You're the only one that understands. You've the brains for the rest o' them."

"You and me, John," she sighed. "We'll get you to the University some way. Why don't you ask our Uncle Robeson in Haddington. He knows everyone."

Now when he stood facing the hard face of his headmaster whose lessons in Logic and Rhetoric he had struggled with for the last two years, her words came unbidden to his mind.

"It all depends on the next few minutes," he thought and took a deep breath.

Five minutes later he reeled into the icy corridor sweating as if it were high summer.

"I am to go to St Andrews! I can get away!"

"Dinna be sae full o' yourself, Hepburn," his Headmaster had growled as he had turned to leave, a huge smile on his face. "Ye'll have to satisfy the Regents o' St Leonard's College that your Latin is as sound as we think and ye and I ken just how well founded your Logic and Rhetoric are, do we not?"

But that was all tomorrow. Today his prison gates lay open.

They celebrated at his aunt's house. His aunt from Musselburgh and her husband were visiting and dinner was festive. Afterwards the older men swept him off to his aunt's bedroom to sit round the fire by the great four-poster bed while they questioned him closely about his next step. Both merchants soon had his problem with funding out of him.

"The rights of the children to a third of their father's leavings are well kent." His uncle Robeson shook his head. "I ken a good solicitor who helped me get my dues frae other merchants who wouldn't pay. I'll have a word wi' him, young John, and when you're next in Haddington I'll have his advice."

"But he will charge too, Uncle."

"Aye, Aye but the cause is good, laddie." Robeson patted him on the shoulder. "Away now before the dark sets in and tell your family the good news. Your mother should be proud o' ye."

A week later his elder brother George drew him aside.

"I was in Haddington to pick up more seed and our Uncle Robeson asked me to visit and bring you too. What is it about, John, lad?"

"It's about getting our leavings frae father," John whispered looking over his shoulder to make sure his mother was not about. "I told him that we were all penniless and he said it wasna' right."

"Nor it is." His brother nodded. "Better tell no one or our mother will hear somehow."

"I've already told Marie, George. She'll join with us. I'll tell mother I've to return a book to my Latin master and Marie can be wanting the shops for summat. You can drive us all in the gig."

Their uncles were waiting for them with a younger, stern-faced man who they introduced as Mr Watson, Writer to the Signet.

"It's this way," Watson said. "If ye wish the Privy Council to pronounce for ye in this case ye'll need to lodge a joint action as a family, to demand your rightful leavings frae your father. I've perused his will and it is quite clear. Your mother has withheld what is rightfully yours." He paused and raised a pair of sharp and rather frightening eyes to scan the three young people. "Mind ye, what ye propose is a serious matter. There's folk who will term it right unfilial and ye should know it may have consequences."

"Consequences?" They looked at each other in some alarm.

"Aye. Folk may look sidey-ways at ye, your mother's friends and relatives for one."

George shuffled his feet and shook his light-brown curly head like an irritated bull. "Will I get to be master o' the farm? It's my right."

"There you are!" The lawyer sat back. "Ye'll have enough monies to bring an application to the Privy Council." He smiled thinly. "I'll do it for ye when ye've been successful in this. Your uncles are paying me for this."

The brothers looked at each other in alarm. The Privy Council: their mother's wrath: it all began to be a bit frightening. Then Marie rose from the stool she had been sitting on. She stood, tall and slim, in the heavy linen skirt and close fitting velvet jacket that she wore to church. The rusty dead-leaf colour suited her pale complexion and bright orange-red hair which lay modestly snooded. For a moment she dominated the room.

"There is no doubt that we will win is there, Sir?"

The solicitor shook his head. "No doubt at all! The rights of the children are time-honoured, enshrined in law."

She turned then to her elder brother. "Have courage George. Explain things to Andrew and James. I will speak to my sisters." She turned back to the solicitor. "We'll go ahead. But will it be expensive?" Marie remembered her mother complaining when her father had invoked the Privy Council's protection.

"Dinna' worry, Marie, lass. We'll pay willingly. You want your young brother to go to the University do ye no'?" Her uncles were looking at her with kindness.

"It is my dearest wish and I thank you both from the bottom of my heart." Later when her mother learned of their action, she felt the weight of her rod upon her back and stood the pain, silent.

When the judgement came it was worse. Her mother retired to her room, only speaking when her brother came to visit.

George, delighted, was at last able to make decisions.

"It's glad we are to have ye at the helm, Master," William Watnoun had wasted no time in making his allegiance known. "All the men are with me. Your father would be proud o' ye."

Marie found herself sewing shirts and knitting socks for John to take to University right through harvest time. She drove her sisters hard but they sang as they worked and the girls' room seemed suddenly a place of light and happiness.

"This is the last time I shall be a farm labourer," John Hepburn swore as he worked his brother's harvest. Marie, looking at his excited face, smiled, but sadly. She knew that she would miss him and that he would never come back.

CHAPTER 4
St Andrews University

With his father's portion heavy in his pocket, and a heart light with excitement and apprehension in equal measure, John Hepburn set out for St Andrews University in late September of 1614.

"Dinna' fash yersel," old William Watnoun muttered as they saddled the horses in the half-light of dawn. "I've enough bannock to last us a week. I ken a big lad like you is aye hungered and mistress Marie saw to it."

"Marie, the best of my sisters, my little mother", she would be the only one he missed, thought Hepburn. As he was about to mount, she came into the stable yard and he hugged her close before swinging into the saddle and it was Marie and only Marie who waved them from the farm.

Ambling out of the yard on the big plough horses, John Hepburn could hear the reedy psalms of the few, poor and aged Franciscan monks left in the tiny monastery whose west wall was also one of the walls surrounding their farmyard. Hepburn hoped he would fare better.

"God be with you, John, now and always." Marie's blessing followed him down the road. It seemed more powerful than the monks' hymns. Almost at once the sun rose over the Bass Rock in a blaze of orange glory, brushing away the shadows of the night. Hepburn took a last long look at the fields in their autumnal colours spread out towards the sea.

"At last I'm away to make something of myself, Will!"

"Aye, and we've a good day for it, likely." Watnoun sounded satisfied. Riding against driving rain was something his old joints abhorred but he was never going to let any other man accompany his young master on his road to the University.

John Hepburn's heart lightened as the glory of the sunrise lifted his spirits. Across the Firth of Forth the Fife hills seemed but a stone's throw away. Scarlet rosehips in the tangled bushes by the road mingled their bright colour with ripening purple brambles, and the excitement of escape filled him. He was away. Life beckoned.

As the horses plodded on they saw the steam from the salt pans lie heavy and thick over Prestonpans. Salt panners handed down the secret of how much to boil the sea water and when exactly to pour the concentrated brine into pans to crystallise. He did not envy them.

Towards mid-day the stark grey tower of Craigmillar Castle began to dominate the sky-line.

"We'll be for the next road towards the sea now, John-lad." William Watnoun eased his aching back in the saddle and sighed in relief. "We'll soon be in Musselburgh and get you a passage on the ferry to Fife. I'd not like to be riding round by Stirling Bridge at my age."

They spent the night in a small inn, sharing a mattress and listening to the sound of the horses next door stamping and snorting. Next morning they were first at the ferry, the old man determined that his young master should not miss it. "Ye'll be a great man one day John-lad." The old man wrung his hand. "God send I'll be alive to see it."

"Never doubt it, Will." Hepburn clapped him on the back. "I'll be dressed fine and I'll no' be at any woman's beck and call and I'll never forget ye. Wait and see!" The old man just shook his head and turned sadly away.

The ferry made good time and Hepburn made nothing of the fifteen miles walk to St Andrews, carrying his meal sack and barrel of salt herring that were the usual term's payment, even for a bursar. He came over the headland following the old pilgrim road and saw, as they must have, the towers and spires of St Andrews etched against a setting sun as if they were floating on the sea. It was a magical sight but knowing he should be in by sunset he didn't linger and it wasn't until he heard the great St Leonards College gates close behind him that he realised he had entered a new life.

His meal sack and fish barrel were taken away and he was shown to a small room where another, older, boy sat working.

"This here is your senior man," said the Porter who had let him in. "He'll see ye right."

They stood looking at each other. Hepburn saw a slim dark-haired man, his clothes covered from neck to toe in a black gown, buttoned down the front and belted. With his black hair and lean face he had the look of a bird of prey. Hepburn decided to do what his Latin teacher had suggested and look humble.

"What are ye doing standing there like a great gowk. I'm just your senior man. We share this room and I'm to tell ye how to go on."

Hepburn looked up and grinned. "That's alright then. I was practising humility."

"Don't waste it on me. Are ye for a bursary like me? If your Latin is good they'll take ye. It's easier for the Regents to teach if ye understand what they are saying." He stood and offered his hand. "I'm Robert Monro frae Easter Ross, cousin to the Baron o' Foulis. My elder brother is Laird o' Obsdale."

It was Hepburn's first introduction to Highland pride and his gorge rose in fury.

"Is that right!" He turned away rudely.

"Nay, lad, what have I said?" Monro was bewildered.

"I dinna' hold with all that Lord this and Baron that. My brother is feuer to Sir Patrick o' Waughton Castle an' what do ye make o' that?"

Monro's dark face relaxed in a grin. "I'm aye given to the sin o' pride. Highlanders are. We tell each other about how grand we are. It's what we do."

"Well I dinna'. I'll be the man they want as a relation one day. Till then it sounds like cockerels on a muck heap."

"I'll not fight ye, you great monster!" Monro was openly laughing at him now. "Happen you'll need me to tell you how to go on. So what is your name, red-head? Ye'll have this bed and this desk to work at and if ye snore I warn ye I shall waken ye."

John Hepburn felt shame stain his cheeks. "I'm ow'er proud myself. I'll beg your pardon and shake your hand. I'm John Hepburn frae Athelstaneford, and aye, I'll need the bursary if I'm to stay here."

"We all do, nearly. It's St Salvator's College over the way that the rich bodies stay at. But ye'll ken the yins here that are paying when we go to dinner. They get better bread, and a richer stew if the cooks are short, and they always are."

"That doesna' worry me. I'm not used to grand food. Is the bursary awfy testing?"

"If you've the Latin, ye'll manage."

He was proved right the next day. All the would-be Bursars were lined up and the Regents saw them one by one. Occasion was meat and drink to John Hepburn and the Regents were impressed by his bright intelligent blue eyes that fairly blazed as he struggled to speak immaculate Latin.

The Head Regent congratulated him on doing his masters proud. "I'll be writing to Haddington to tell them we can offer ye a Bursary, Mr Hepburn. If ye return to your room, your senior man will show ye where to get a gown. Ye'll wear it at all times."

Besides his gown, John Hepburn was given a silver spoon to eat his dinner with.

"All bursars have one." Monro said. "We give it back when we leave. It's less worn than your gown but just as old, likely."

"Lingua Latina!" a passing Regent interrupted.

"Mea culpa, Magister." Monro bowed and whispered, "From now on we speak only Latin, Hepburn. Get used to it."

If anything John Hepburn was relieved by the dictum. His Latin was well founded and he had already begun to notice that Monro spoke a different Scots to him.

Once the Regent had been round to check that their candles were out at night, they could whisper in their mother tongue and Hepburn consciously started to mimic his senior man. With his ear for language it did not take him long to lose the broad Scots he had grown up with and in doing so he felt the equal of any man.

In all else he emerged the leader of the two, Monro's meticulous, pedantic nature overwhelmed by the fire within his room mate.

By the end of the year they were firm friends and when Monro mentioned that his father had permitted him to travel on to Poitiers University to study law for a year, John Hepburn was immediately interested. "Where about is Poitiers? I'll come too. I can't stand three more years of this torture. We're never allowed out but to learn archery and sword-play. Even football is frowned on and as for women the only one allowed in is the laundress and she's over fifty."

"It's a requisite of the job." Monro nodded. "It's to keep ye focused."

"The only good bits are Rhetoric and dinner."

Hepburn excelled at disputation. He enjoyed the verbal cut and thrust and his Latin seldom let him down, but Philosophy and Logic were a heartbreaking grind and the thought of a lifetime locked up in an office with quill and parchment horrified him. Poitiers sounded exciting, different anyway, and there would be a journey on a ship too. The idea made the rest of the year bearable; that and the food.

Dinner at noon was his best hour. The oatmeal or barley stew was rich in cabbage, kale and meat, not so varied as that served to the paying students, but still better than many a meal at home, spiced as it was with nutmeg, pepper and salt. On occasion rabbit or pigeon made a familiar taste. His silver spoon was busy at the communal plate, finishing up anything left by his smaller, more pernickety companions.

By the end of the year he had grown another four inches and his gown hung short with the sleeves only reaching half way down his arms. At his end of year assessment his Regent shook his head in amazement. "Ye're the size of a full grown man, John, and I can see ye've more to come. It'll be a new gown for you next year if we've any big enough!"

"I thought I'd go to Poitiers, Sir. My senior man goes to study Law there."

"Are ye for the Law, John?"

Hepburn blushed. "I doubt it. But I'm not for the church either so I thought I'd go with him."

His Regent sighed. "John Knox cam frae Haddington High School like you, John, but I never thought you'd follow his footsteps. Ye've been good to the other bejants though. I've seen ye often and often sitting with them in the quadrangle helping them with their Latin translations. There's something in you that makes them trust ye and follow what you say. Could you teach?"

Hepburn shook his head. "I need to be up and doing."

"So you lead your senior man into sin by rieving our apples by night, eh?" The older man laughed at Hepburn's confusion. "Fine I kenned who it was in the moon-light. Who else is so big? But your work never suffered so I turned a blind eye. I hope it gave you the colic."

His pupil grinned. "Not me! But Monro swore he'd never eat another so long as he lived."

"And him meant to show you the right way! It was a judgement, so it was."

"I'll be safe with him, Sir. He's very steady."

His Regent sighed and nodded. "God go with ye then, John Hepburn. Just don't forget to hand back your gown and spoon."

CHAPTER 5
Poitiers

Once their ship turned into the sea-roads towards Bordeaux, Hepburn's excitement escalated. Soon they were gliding along past ships of all sizes, some going their way, some with all sails set, tacking out determinedly against the west wind.

"That barque'll be heavy laden with wine barrels," one of the sailors pointed as a merchantman staggered on to another tack. "We'll be the same. Care to stick around and help load?"

Hepburn shook his head. They'd been at sea for over a month and much of the time he'd been petrified as the ship had pitched and rolled as if it had a death wish. The thought of enduring the lonely isolation of the Atlantic again, heavy laden with barrels of wine, made him shudder.

As they went, the sailors pointed out men-of war, bravely flagged and studded with gun ports, that mixed with merchantmen like themselves, forming a long trail running in to port.

At their last meal round the seamen's board, John Hepburn and Robert Monro tried to get some idea of what it was like in France. Recognising the sly grins around them Hepburn discounted half of what he was being told of strange mystical animals that waited at road ends in the dusk to devour travellers. However bands of dreadful, dangerous footpads struck a faint chord.

"May be that something we learned at St Andrews'll come in handy." Hepburn grinned. "We could try them with a bit o' Rhetoric and Logic."

"I'll aye keep my sword ready."

Hepburn turned back to the sailors. "Is it easy to learn to speak French? How did you all learn?"

Ribald stories were their only response. However after the meal one of the older sailors touched his shoulder as he passed.

"Dinna' try to learn the Bordeaux tongue. They speak their own way and likely as not where ye're ganging they'll speak different. Use your Latin. Most merchants have a bittie and all the priest-folk speak it. There's no shortage o' them in the streets." He looked at them sideways, unsure of their response.

"Dinna' make too much of where ye're from. Get yourselves in with a party of pilgrims that are going home to Paris. You'll know them from the shells they wear in their hats to show they've been to Compostella. Their road is to the North through Poitiers."

"We'll need to keep our religion to ourselves then, John." Monro muttered.

"That'll not be hard for me." Hepburn grinned. "It's you that have drunk the St Leonard College well water for three years. It's scarce infected me."

The Gironde sea-roads seemed to last for ever as the banks closed in. Then just when John Hepburn thought there was no room for them between the ships jockeying for the wind, they were docking and the call was out for men to man the anchor chain.

"God, it's hot!" The bosun beside Hepburn on the anchor winch wiped the sweat from his eyes. "Ye'd be better wi'oot the weskit. You feel the heat when the ship isna' moving and there's no breeze."

The two young men had put on what clothes they could to make their burdens lighter but now both tore off their buff leather waistcoats. Moisture still poured down their foreheads, stinging their eyes with its salt.

Below decks had become increasingly foul smelling as unwashed human stench mixed with rotting food and old vomit. But John Hepburn found the docks almost worse. Humidity pressed in on him with the heavy vinous miasma from claret casks that were piled everywhere awaiting loading. The sweet wind over the moving deck was gone.

"Water, Robert. We need water," he muttered through parched lips and the two young men staggered up through the town seeking shade but even more a cool drink.

"Aqua? Aqua?" He begged every man they passed and made drinking motions. Everyone just pointed up the hill so the young men stumbled on until suddenly they entered an open square whose main feature was a fountain.

"Thank God." Hepburn put his head under the water and let it play over his face and neck as he drank, then stood aside, as his friend staggered up for his turn.

They both sat, their backs against the fountain, legs splayed, letting any breeze present cool them. At length Hepburn staggered to his feet. "We'd best be on our way." He looked around to pinpoint the sun and as he did so noticed a group of grey cloaked figures issuing into the square to mill round as if waiting for something.

"Look, Bully Monro! They've shells in their hats, all of them."

His friend nodded. "Will you ask them or will I?"

But Hepburn was already approaching the nearest.

"Quo vadis, Magister?"

Relief lit his face when the man turned smiling.

"We go North. We go home to Paris."

"May we walk with you, Sir. We are students bound for Poitiers to study Law."

"A good School, I hear. But you are foreign?"

"We are Scots from St Andrews University."

"Many students come from there to Poitiers, I hear. When we stayed there on our way to Compostella there was a street, the Rue des Ecossais, that housed them all."

Hepburn's face brightened. This was good news.

The man looked at him in frowning question. "We were told that many of them were unbelievers, Reformists, Huguenots?"

"It is the same in Scotland," Hepburn muttered and said nothing more.

For a minute the man seemed to consider, then made his mind up.

"In Christian charity join us, then." He looked them over. "You had best procure a staff and bread and water such as I have or you will faint upon the way. The roads are hot, dusty and long."

The advice was good.

Hepburn and Monro made their way through the gates that the pilgrims had come out of and found a kindly friar who looked dubiously at the Scottish coin they offered, eventually took more than they expected but furnished each of them with an eight foot crook that had a full water bottle attached to it. He also put a loaf of bread into their hands and gave them his blessing.

"Dinna' be uneasy. A blessing won't hurt." Hepburn stilled his friend's mutterings. "They aye do that sort o' thing. It's just their way."

"It's awfy Papist!" Monro considered what he had said and laughed.

"I've been too long at St Leonards. That's what it is."

By the time they returned to the square they realised what their group had been waiting for. A group of women had joined them and they were setting off, led by a friar similarly clad to the one they had bought their staff from.

"He knows the road to our next stop." Their friend had come up beside them and seemed happy to converse.

Suiting their pace to the group, the three men brought up the rear of the party.

"It's tedious marching at this pace," confessed their new friend. "But the women go slowly. I'm glad of your company. Tell me about Scotland."

They did their best, but as Robert Monro described growing up in the Highlands and the importance of fealty to his clan chief and Hepburn, more taciturn, talked about harvests and work in the fields and the joy of leaping naked into the sea as the waves broke white and strong about you, he soon began to look bemused.

Without more than a glance at each other both knew not to mention the dread word, "religion," that lay at the core of their upbringing.

 "I find myself confused," their friend said at length. "It is just as well that everyone stops for the mid-day meal. We will sit in the shade of those trees for an hour until the worst heat is over and then we march, if you can call it that, until we arrive at our next destination."

A grace was said. Monro glanced sideways at his companion, frowning, but Hepburn just grinned. "Reminds you of St Leonards!" he teased. "Pretend it's a dominie in a black coat and it becomes the same."

Their friend did not miss the exchange and a grim smile played over his face for a moment but then he shrugged. "I'm on pilgrimage," he said to no one in particular. "They are only children. Perhaps they may see the light."

"If they are heading for Poitiers University it will be a candle in a forest. The place is still rotten with reformist nonsense." The friar passing by had caught his words.

Their French eluded the Scots who were still gazing round at the country. The fertility amazed Hepburn. The thick green flourish of the vineyards stretching to the horizon was something he had never seen before.

Orchards gave way to wheat fields so golden in the hot sun that John Hepburn found it easier to keep his eyes down on the dusty road than watch the peasants scything and bundling the hay.

Their inattention almost cost them their lives.

Mediaeval France was changing from small land holders living in villages. Rich merchants were buying their land, building chateaux and employing fewer workers. The sailor's stories of vagrant robbers were not imagination.

Four men materialised behind the pilgrims and came at them suddenly, sticks raised in one hand and daggers in the other.

Hepburn and Monro put their hands on their swords as they appreciated the threat. Neither had ever challenged another man to real combat and John Hepburn found himself equally repulsed and exhilarated.

"Don't draw!" It was an order and so forceful that both young men hesitated. Between them their friend had turned his staff into a pike.

"Use your staffs! Enough French blood has been shed by Frenchmen. Follow me!"

Automatically they responded. The three men faced the charge of the oncoming four.

"Thrust forward. Aim for the stomach. Now!"

As one, the staffs' sharp ends bit into three bellies and the men doubled up, their weapons falling on the ground.

"Left foot back, get ready." But the last man was already running down the road.

"They are hungry and we have bread." He picked his loaf up from where it had fallen and threw it to the men rolling on the ground.

"Come. We'll have no more trouble from them. They looked for easy pickings. You did well, lads. I could make soldiers out of you yet." He smiled at their shaken faces.

"I had my eye on that lot for ever. It's well to keep one eye to the rear. Do they teach you nothing useful in Scotland?"

"Tell us about being a soldier?" Hepburn had been amazed how easily they had won, how much he had enjoyed it.

For the rest of the day he listened avidly as he heard the story of the siege of La Rochelle and the bloody battle thereafter.

"I swore that if I didn't die I'd go on pilgrimage to seek absolution so that I can live the rest of my life at peace with myself and my God."

"He canna' escape the punishment for his actions by the word of a priest." Monro said later as they shared a palliasse. "His fate is already written by God."

"But comforting. It must be comforting to die believing in God's love and forgiveness."

"Pschaw! Priest talk! Don't be taken in by wickedness."

Hepburn chuckled. "You drank too deep at St Leonard's Well, I keep telling ye. You'd sleep easier without."

They trudged on through town after town until they saw at last a promontory of shimmering grey walls above creamy bluffs and their friend murmured, "Poitiers at last."

"Come on, Bully Monro. It's like approaching the promised land." Hepburn's heart lifted in delight. "It must have been about here where that English Black Prince hammered through a huge French force and got away to Bordeaux with all his booty."

"Frenchmen prefer to remember 732 when Charles Martel defeated the Moors here and drove them from France." Their soldier friend grinned at their excitement. "But look yonder at those cliffs beyond the city. That is where Coligny sited his cannon when he besieged the town not fifty years ago. It has never recovered. The University has not the numbers it had and no great names attend it."

"What a place for cannon!" Hepburn looked at it in wonder. "They had the whole town within their sights."

The stiff climb into the city left them all exhausted, so with a few words of thanks and farewell the two youths followed their companion's pointing finger to reach the Rue des Ecossais and hear, at last, their own tongue spoken around them.

Compared with the rest of the town with its walled houses set in gardens, the Scottish quarter was down at heel. Half timbered, one and two story houses clustered haphazardly together as if for support and turned the cobbled roads into narrow canyons with gutters where noisome waste flowed.

That night they lodged with men whom Monro had known as senior students at St Andrews and next day they followed them to the University quadrangle and applied to be Bursars.

Money was running low and both knew they could expect no more from home. Once term started the old feeling of boredom that had driven him from Scotland began to creep up on John Hepburn.

"It's worse than being in St Andrews. The Regents there treated us with kindness. They don't give a bannock crumb for the way we feel here."

Monro, who was struggling with Salic and Roman Law, merely nodded as he went on with his study. "I'm no lawyer that's for sure. A life of this would be insupportable. My father said it would give me a down-sitting but, oh God, the tedium! If we didn't get into the town I'd go mad."

They had made the town their own, wandering together whenever they were able to escape their studies. The town church with its painted interior scandalised Monro. " What Calvin would have said about this place would bring the roof down."

 "It's just trying to make you think heaven is a comfortable place. It's not trying to turn you to sin." Thereafter Hepburn explored the churches alone but of them all, the soaring pale grey walls of Notre Dame la Grande never failed to uplift his soul in happiness.

One afternoon a black robed priest came to stand beside him.

"I've seen you here before, my son."

"It lifts my spirit, Sir," Hepburn answered in Latin

The priest smiled a little. "This church works its magic on all our spirits and we are delighted to share. Your Reformation has allowed us to look into our souls and rid our church of abominations. God is not bought or sold. But our God offers pardon if we truly repent our sins."

"No Hell?"

"Hell awaits those who sin and do not repent but we believe it is in our hands to repent and be saved."

"What do you think?" He asked Monro later.

"All that mumbo jumbo and priestly power is not my way, John. I dinna' feel at home with images and suchlike."

"They're just pictures. They're not real. You don't have to believe in them having power in themselves."

"Many do though. They pray to them. It's not right, John. Better the truth than false comfort! But talking of comfort, I'll soon need to find work. I've scarce enough in my purse to get home"

"Aye it's been on my mind too. Remember what our pilgrim friend said about us being welcomed by the Scottish Guard in Paris? I'd rather try for a soldier than a lawyer any day."

Monro nodded. "My father would say that soldiering is a gentleman's profession. Let's go as soon as maybe."

Their friend had partly misled them. They were welcomed, but not by the Garde Ecossaise.

"He must have thought we had money, that one!" said Hepburn. "It's you looking so gentlemanly, Bully Munro."

"Huh! Likely he thought a muckle great giant like you would look fine in those striped breeks and white surcoats they wear. You need to be as rich as Croesus to join that lot." Munro shrugged. "I've been asking round. The French King's Guard is seeking soldiers. We'll try their barracks tomorrow."

CHAPTER 6
Recruited by Gray

Enlisted in the King's Regiment of the Guards, Hepburn and Monro found themselves part of a rot, numbering six men, officered by a rotmaster and under-rotmaster, sinewy dark little men whose main interest seemed to be the ritual humiliation of the miserable recruits under them.

"Rat one" and "Rat two" Hepburn whispered to Monro and gave thanks that his French had improved sufficiently to understand their orders. Punishments for even minor infringements were severe. Slow learners were clapped in irons, sweltering in the heat of the courtyard, at the rotmaster's pleasure.

"There is an executioner employed by the regiment," whispered the Frenchman who stood next to Hepburn in their rot. "He beheads those who rebel against their orders or those deemed to be cowards."

"They give you the choice of that or being shot by your own musketeers," muttered Monro on his other side.

"That'd be my choice. The way this lot shoot they'd probably miss!" Hepburn excelled in musket practice and his rotmaster had promised him an under-rotmastership if he chose to be a musketeer after his training.

"Fine hope," Hepburn had said to Monro later. "Give me a pike any time. Pikemen get more pay and who wants to carry all that gear."

"You're right there." Monro had nodded. "The pike is a gentleman's weapon and I tell you straight that in the charge I'd want a short pike and a rank of soldiers who know how to pousse and press forward."

Training was hard. The lice-filled palliasses that they lay on at night disgusted both of them and the long hours drilling in the hot sun followed by sentry duty were exhausting.

Aware that he had no fall back position, having spent his father's leavings, Hepburn set his mind grimly to achieve excellence. Monro might return to his father's house but there was no such welcome awaiting him.

Standing sentry at the gates of the Louvre allowed him to look at the great and the good of Paris. Counts strode past, their gold embroidered coats and elegant hats arousing lust in Hepburn's mind. Countesses swished through the gates, their wide brocade dresses brushing the sentry's boots. Even the King was no stranger and Hepburn's day was made when he thought he heard the monarch murmur something to his companion about "Smart soldiers, my regiment, eh?"

It was a heady life for a youth off a farm in East Lothian and John Hepburn relished the duty. Only the Garde Ecossaise, resplendent in emblazoned white silk surcoats and red and green striped trews, gave him grief. He envied those rich Scottish Catholic aristocrats who swaggered their life away in a Catholic King's court that welcomed their style and money.

"One day," he muttered to himself. "One day I shall strut into the Louvre in just such a way. It just takes time; time and a war where I can distinguish myself."

It was that difficulty that he and Monro discussed when they were alone. Monro had had a harder passage to becoming trained. Hepburn was heart sorry for his friend when their sergeant had caught him asleep on sentry duty at one of the gates of Paris. Lucky to escape the irons, he had stood on duty in full armour at the gates of the Louvre all one hot summer's day.

"My God, I'll check my sentry posts when I'm an officer," Monro had quaffed the huge tankard of weak porter Hepburn had ready for him when he staggered off duty that day.

"It's getting to be an officer that worries me." Hepburn rubbed the side of his face in thought. "From what I hear the trouble is all to the East of us in Bohemia. That's where the fighting is going to be."

"And France is not going to join in?"

"That's my feeling, Bully Monro. We're here, and fully trained, but we'll never be more than rotmasters if we stay. I wonder what we should do?"

Hepburn's question was answered a day or two later when Monro tossed a letter to him as they sat in their local hostelry relaxing.

"My brother Obsdale writes that Sir Hector Monro, who is Baron of Foulis and the head of our clan, is to marry the young daughter of Hugh Mackay of Farr, Mary she's called, and the wedding is to be in July this year. I'll have to go John. The Mackays and Monros are close kin, always have been."

"There's little welcome at home for me. I'll stay a kennan yet."

Monro left almost at once and hugged him on departure. "Who knows, we may find ourselves officers together yet."

John Hepburn missed him. Monro had been like a brother. Now he returned to wandering round cathedrals as he had in Poitiers. Notre Dame left him overwhelmed but unimpressed. Following the Scottish nobles he started attending St Germain l'Auxerrois, the square-towered parish church of the King that nestled beside the Louvre Palace. There of a Sunday he saw everyone of note. Cardinal Richelieu in his red robes came to sit across from the priest. King Louis XIII processed in, accompanied by his Queen and courtiers. As he stood, his eyes drinking in the scene of grandeur, colour and pageantry, a dark-cowled priest came to stand beside him.

"My name is Father Joseph. I have noticed you never take communion, my son. You are welcome at the Lord's table as is everyone here."

Hepburn blushed and stammered, "Thank you, Father, but I do not know how. I come from Scotland."

"Ah!" The priest gave him an understanding smile. "But perhaps you would like to join with us?"

It was like a sudden jolt. A wave of joy seemed to rush through his whole body. "If you permit?"

"Come with me." The priest led him to a small confessional by a side aisle. "Sit my son and I will sit here beside you but separate enough for you to feel you talk to yourself alone. Now tell me about yourself."

It seemed to take forever but John Hepburn learned more and more about himself as he talked and at the end he simply waited.

"This has been your first confession, my son, and God has heard it and in his mercy has absolved you of all the wrongs you know you have done and regret. Now come to his table with me and feel his goodness surround you."

Hepburn left to return to barracks, his head in a whirl but an enormous sense of relief and a growing conviction like a rock inside him, one he knew he would never lose. He had reached safe-harbour.

Another winter and Hepburn had enough money saved to see him home and enable him to live for a few months even if he found no work. He had begun to wonder how they were all faring at Athelstaneford. It suddenly seemed a long time since he'd been home.

Too long! When he got there, John Hepburn found his home bewilderingly foreign.

"My, ye've changed, man", his brother George's tone was less than complimentary. "Too fine to muck out the byre now! I dinna' ken what there is for ye to do, and that's a fact."

"Aye you're the spitting image o' your father," William Watnoun patted his back. "I kent ye'd be the one!"

They had all become so small and dirty. That was Hepburn's first impression, and when he looked at William Watnoun, old and bent as well.

Sorrow was his main emotion. He stood towering above them, his thigh length, leather boots polished to a spotless sheen. Above them his buff doublet, fine lawn shirt and workmanlike sword proclaimed the military man. As he looked at the mud stained hands and coarse clothes of his elder brother he wanted to turn tail and make for France again.

"Where is our mother?"

"Dead!"

It was all he got out of his brother except, "You'd dae best to stay with Marie. She's married now with Francis Lyall, the Surgeon Burgess in Haddington. Did well for herself did Marie."

The only man who seemed sad to see him go was William Watnoun. He came to hold his hand between his two ancient, cracked, scaly claws and there were tears in his eyes.

"I'll not see ye again John, lad. But I'll ask the good Lord to keep ye every Sunday, never fear."

That was his worst moment. Turning his back on the farm was a relief. Setting off to find Marie he felt like a child again, searching for her to bring comfort to whatever ill had caused him woe.

He was not disappointed. She lived in a comfortable house set back from the main road into Haddington and her face lit up with love and joy when he was shown in to her room by a serving girl. Throwing down her sewing she leapt up to embrace him.

"So big you've grown, John. I would never have known you. Oh my dearest brother, how good it is to see you and now you'll meet Francis, my husband. You'd never remember him. You were too young. He attended Father when he was dying and after Mother was away I met him again in Haddington at my Aunt's house."

"This is coming home." Hepburn settled himself on a stool beside her. "You've no idea how awful it was at Athelstaneford. What happened to Mother? George wouldn't say."

"He feels the guilt. Oh John so do I, but there was nothing else for us to do and one thing led to another."

"So tell me."

"Well, after you left for St Andrews, George was granted the feu and Mother retired to her room in a fury. We tholed it but then Sir Patrick at Waughton took ill and had to go abroad for his health."

"So?"

"So he needed money sent." She sighed. "His agent dunned George for the rent we owed. There was no way George could pay. He'd just got the farm. He hadn't even had a harvest. I told him to go back to our lawyer and it was he petitioned the Privy Council who said the debt belonged to our mother."

"Some hope!"

"She had been getting stranger and stranger, John, muttering to herself and only coming out of her room to scream at someone. We didn't know what to do. She refused to pay anything and the Waughton agent set the Privy Council on her and they put her to the horn. Sir Patrick would never have done that to his cousin but the agent didn't care. The next thing we knew, soldiers came to the house and took her away and all her things. They couldn't touch the house or the farm because they belonged to George but they took her bed and her wedding bowls and her clothes in her wedding chest and she screamed, John. She screamed as they took her away to the tollbooth in Edinburgh."

"Could you do nothing?"

"My portion didn't even look at what she owed and George wouldn't pay anything. But her brothers at Smeaton didn't help either and she was dead in a month."

John Hepburn's face was white. "I started this. It was my fault."

"No John. No! You have a future. God has a path for you and you must follow it. I would not have it otherwise."

"It was still my fault."

"Don't feel guilty. You lit the kindling but it was needed. It could have gone no other way. The farm is doing well now and George is in a fair way to becoming married himself. Young James helps him on the farm. Andrew moved into Haddington and is looking to be a Burgess. I see more of him than the others."

"There is no place here for me any more."

It was a fact his sister could not deny. She sighed.

"We'll talk to Francis about it at dinner. He always knows what to do."

Francis Lyall was the only man in his family that Hepburn found he had common ground with. Both had been to University and spoke Latin. They loved Marie as well so talk flowed easily.

The subject on everyone's lips was of the dreadful way their Princess Elizabeth and her husband the Elector Frederick had been treated in Prague by the encroaching Hapsburgs.

"Humbling a Scottish Princess! It's a scandal. No less! They say our King doesn't want to be seen to take sides but he's granting huge sums to recruit soldiers to fight for her."

Hepburn looked up with interest. "That sounds like something for me."

"Aye it could be." Francis Lyall nodded. "I'll surely keep my ears open."

"But soldiering is dangerous. You could get hurt, or killed." Marie was distressed. The men looked at each other above her head and shrugged.

"Marie, I am a soldier. I'm good too. I just need the chance to show it."

Her eyes filled with tears. "I'll miss you, John."

"You'll be proud of me when I come back rich."

She shook her head. "I'm proud of you now. You've no need to fight."

"Still, Francis, I'd be grateful if you would keep an ear open for word of a recruiter in the district. The money I've saved won't last for ever and I'll not live on you two. You've been kind enough already."

It was not many days after that when Lyall came home rubbing his hands against the late Spring chill, eager to tell them that he had seen recruiters setting up their tents on a field at Monks Rig farm by Haddington.

"I'll get over there tomorrow!" Hepburn's face lit with anticipation.

"Oh, John, must you!"

"What else can I do? Come on Marie. Be happy for me."

She shook her head. "However large you get, I still see that little boy guddling for baggy-minnows in the burn."

The next day, his boots polished to a fine sheen and his linen spotless, John Hepburn walked over to Monks Rig to find it gay with flags and tents set up on the stubble of a great field that had clearly grown barley the year before. The ground had been churned by feet and horses and he walked carefully to preserve the shine on his boots.

"Where's the recruiter?"

A soldier holding a horse that was sidling about, nodded towards a big tent.

"Sir Andra Gray's that way." He looked Hepburn up and down. "He'll be glad to see ye."

"Why?"

"Ye arena' in chains as far as I can see, and ye dinna' look like a vagrant, forbye."

A grin spread across Hepburn's face. "Having a hard time, are you?"

"Anything that isna' held down they thieve and once they get a smell o' money they grab it and go. Why do ye think I'm standing like a stookie stuck to this horse. It belongs to Captain Pentland and it's been taken twice already."

Behind a desk in the big tent sat a small dark-visaged man in full armour, accoutred as if expecting a siege. Hepburn saluted and stood to attention.

"You want to join? Any experience?"

"Three years with the King's Regiment of Guards in Paris."

"Trained?"

"Fully trained in the use of the pike and musket, Sir!"

"I suppose you can't pay for a captaincy, hey? What do you call yourself then?"

"John Hepburn, Sir, and no, I cannot pay to join."

"Damned indigent! We'll make you an ensign. You can train the men. You know what the duties are, hey?"

"Aye, Sir!"

"I'm Gray, Colonel Sir Andrew Gray to you, and this is Lieutenant Colonel Ramsay beside me. Captain Dunbar is about somewhere. He'll kit you out and give you your first week's pay but you'll sign for it and if you abscond you'll face the full rigor of the law. Hear me!"

"I came to join, Sir."

"We'll see! We'll see! Sign here and be off now. Captain Dunbar is the man to see. Be back here tomorrow, ready to march, hey!"

"The Captain's round the corner in the other big tent," a soldier muttered as Hepburn saluted and marched out. "He'll see ye right. Sir Andra just holds on to the money, like it was his own. Dinna' let it fash ye, Sir."

John Hepburn felt a bubble of laughter rise. This was going to be a great adventure. He could feel it in his bones. He just wished his friend Monro had been with him to share the joke of it all.

CHAPTER 7
Getting to Leith

"I'm an ensign, Marie," John Hepburn shouted as he came in the door that evening.

"Is that good, dearest?"

"It pays better than a pikeman. It makes me a gentleman!"

"Oh John! How clever you must be."

"Not clever." He shook his head. "They're desperate for anyone with experience. You should see the useless lot of vagrants that are pouring in."

Francis Lyall nodded and brought out a much folded paper.

"One of my patients gave me this. It's a part of the proclamation the Privy Council sent to the Middle Shires. It says, "All those incorrigible border dastards who are on the list to be transportit or hung, may chose to fight for the Princess Elizabeth instead.""

"Great. We'll have murderous rascals as well. No wonder I'm an officer and a gentleman. They're going to be in short supply."

"John, do you want to go back to those ruffians?"

"Marie, my little mother! This is my trade. I'll come back a rich man, you'll see."

"Let him go without tears, wife. He's a man now and we must respect his decisions." However, Lyall shook his hand warmly the next day and said, "You'll aye be welcome in my house, John. Ye ken that."

"Ye're a good man Francis. I'm happy for Marie."

He was gone on the word, his heart already bright with expectation and he did not look back to where his sister turned her weeping face into her husband's arms.

The chaos at Monk's Rig was if anything worse that morning. Already dressed in the leather jerkin and steel morion issued to him by Captain

Dunbar the previous day, he was besieged by groups of men dressed in rags and desperate to join. These he lined up and led to the main tent.

"Useful already, Ensign?" Dunbar's cynical tone brought him up short.

"They want to join up, Sir."

"The world and his wife want that this morning and how long do you think they'll last."

"They'll need training."

"Aye! Well once I've issued their equipment you can form them up in units, Ensign Hepburn. Teach them to march. We have to get them to Leith just as a beginning."

It was an almost impossible task but John Hepburn found that if he took small groups and taught them to walk in lines of two he could get them going forward. Halting to command ended in a pile up but at least they stopped. "Ye'd not pass muster with my Sergeant in Paris but ye'll do, just about!"

He had turned to train yet another group of ten who had struggled into their new uniform when trouble struck. A long line of men in chains passed, their legs shackled together and their wrists in irons. Grey with exhaustion, they staggered along. John Hepburn and his new recruits stopped to stare. One fell towards the end of the line and the whole group suddenly became chaotic. Hepburn saw two manacled hands raised with a knife in them and leapt towards the man, lifting him by his arms so he was helpless. He shook him till his knife dropped, then dumped him on the ground where he immediately fell upon the man shackled beside him and tried to strangle him.

"That winna do!" Hepburn picked him up again and shook him.

"Put me down you great red headed lump, you! He's a bloody Douglas and his lot are the reason I'm here."

"Haud yer wheesht, you murdering miscreant! Ye canna' just kill who ye please. He's on your side now." John Hepburn found his childhood tongue came back easily. "Now dinna' start anything or I'll put ye down."

The man shrugged. But the fight had gone out of him and he sagged to the ground where his victim kicked him.

"Touch him again, you, and I'll beat ye to pulp, my mannie!" Hepburn was having no further violence. "That goes for all you lot. Stand fast and I'll see what's to become of ye. Move and I'll do for ye, right?"

They stood stunned. Sir Andrew Gray and Colonel Ramsay who had come out of their tent to see what the row was about, stood similarly silent their mouths open in surprise. Only Dunbar, putting his head out of his tent laughed.

"That's another grand unit, Sir Andra. Were I you I'd give it to the redhead. He seems to have the measure o' them."

The senior officers looked at each other.

"He's got that right! Here you! Ensign Hepburn is it not?"

"Aye Sir!" Hepburn snapped to attention.

"How many men are there in that shoddy lot of criminals?"

Hepburn turned to do a rough count. As he did, another line in chains appeared beside them.

"In chains, Colonel? About a hundred."

"Right Hepburn! Let's see what that fancy French training did for you. You're their captain now. Get them to Leith and onto the troop ship and you'll keep your promotion."

"Even get the extra pay if you're lucky." Dunbar disappeared back into his tent but his voice continued. "Get them registered and I'll kit them out. You'd better set off at once. In those chains they'll take longer than the rest of us and I'd not set them free till they're on shipboard if I were ye."

For a moment Hepburn stood stunned looking at his new command. They were as nasty a set of villains as he had ever seen, ragged, with matted hair and beards and scarred faces that were so lean that he wondered if any of them had been fed for days.

"Gentlemen, follow me and I'll get you registered."

Almost to his surprise the line shuffled after him in complete silence. It was broken only by the sound of each man giving his name to Sir Andrew Gray and the clank of the shackles as the line shuffled through the tent.

For the rest of the day Hepburn found himself unlocking one man at a time, kitting him out and locking his shackles back on.

Dunbar merely heaved a mass of leather corselets and steel morions in his direction and went on issuing uniforms to the stream of indigent fellows who lined up in front of him.

"This'll take me all day and more." Hepburn was despairing.

"Think of your promotion and get on with it! Remember you're responsible for each man getting on the ship. You lose one, you forfeit his pay. Sir Andra is not soft when it comes to money. Being a captain isn't all a bed of roses. You didna' pay to be a captain, so ye'll need to keep them on the books to stay one."

It was no idle warning. As he went down the rows of manacled prisoners there were men who could scarcely stand. Their faces grey with tiredness and starvation they had all but given up. As he demanded their name they seemed unaware of his presence.

"This'll not do!"

Hepburn set off for the carts that had begun to roll into the field, piled high with loaves of coarse barley bread.

"I need one of you over here. My men are hungry."

"This is for your dinner, not for now."

Hepburn didn't hesitate he walked to the end of the line of carts, picked the driver off his seat and took his place. "Collect your cart frae over there. Just tell the man ye've off loaded."

From where he had fallen in the mud the driver mouthed imprecations but the very size of his assailant left him unwilling for a challenge.

"I'm paid already. Who cares who eats the bloody bannocks. I hope they choke ye, you big bully, you!"

Hepburn grinned. He then broke each bannock into four and shared them out, following it up with a pitcher of water that he passed down the line.

Some wolfed the bread. Some seemed scarcely able to chew it but they all looked the better for something in their stomachs he thought, and the job of accoutring them became that much quicker.

Dinner came and went and no one mentioned that Hepburn's lot had had their ration except a few vagrants. But no one listened to their whines except the men in manacles and they promised such retribution once they were free that the whining soon stopped.

It took Hepburn two days to get his men in uniform.

"Will we have pikes or muskets", he asked Dunbar on one of his sorties to get new corselets.

"Ye'll have nought till we reach Hamburg. Dinna' be daft. Give that lot weapons! Its wielding them has brought them to this pass."

"I thought to start their training on the way to Edinburgh."

"Get them all on board and you'll be lucky. Training! That lot! Don't make me laugh. They ken more about killing than you'll ever know, and you will find that out if you loose even one of the miscreants. "Incorrigible border dastards," they are cried and the Privy Council man that wrote it knew them well."

So, his company still in chains, Hepburn took his leave of Sir Andrew Gray and set off on the long road to Leith.

"Get them to the docks and lodge them in a locked warehouse. We'll be close behind ye, or one of us will, and he'll tell ye what to do next."

"What about food for the men?"

An evil grin played across his senior officer's face.

"Ye're their captain. You feed them. Your monies take that into account. They'll all get a week in advance and have to live on it. If any man dies or escapes his wage is forfeit and I'll be at ye for it."

Hepburn kept his anxieties to himself and nodded. "I'll be to the wage clerk then with your permission, Sir. I have yet to collect my pay and that of my men."

"He'll count them all and I'll recount them in Leith." Gray's shout followed him across the field.

"Sir Andra is a great one for the money." The clerk seated in the small wage tent had heard the exchange. "Just parade the men past me as ye leave and I'll give ye your due."

"I'll take a copy of your numbers too and signed."

"Aye ye're learning!"

They left next morning. None of his company had died in the night though the late April weather had not been kind and it had rained. He had slept alongside them, wrapped in his cloak.

The dawn brought a watery sun that strengthened as the men shuffled along. He could see steam rising off them in the way it rose from the saltpans over on their right. He made for Prestonpans, thinking that he would be able to get enough bread there to feed the hundred odd mouths he was now in charge of.

It was an awesome thought and he wished that he had someone to give him a bit of help but Gray had scouted that.

"Ye're a captain without having paid a groat. Work for it. Ye dinna' need an ensign. Your men are in chains."

"Use a whip if they falter. They'll soon do as ye say." One of the jailors who had marched the men up handed over the thonged whip he carried.

"Just dinna' let them free. They're a wicked lot o' bastards and were to be hung or transported, so dinna' waste pity on 'em."

It was years since he had been in Prestonpans but the place hadn't changed. He headed for the bake house where as a boy he had been slipped bannocks while his elder brother, George, negotiated terms for their barley.

"For heaven's sake it's never you, John lad." The baker had shrunk from the giant he remembered to a small fat man. "Ye're the image o' your dad. I used to enjoy a jar with him years ago. Now what are ye wanting and what on earth are ye doing with these criminals?"

Explanations brought him not only bread but the summoning of the inn keeper who offered stew for a price.

Hepburn looked round helpless. How was he to sort it?

"Take six men in a round and make one the leader. Give them a loaf or two and a bowl o' stew between them." An old prisoner at the end of the line nodded as he turned to the advice. "It's how the jail men did it. That is when they bothered to give us anything."

"They'll fight."

"The jailors whippet them if they so much as raised their heads. But put them in families and ye'll have no bother."

It was good advice and Hepburn took it.

"What's your name then?"

"I'm Andra Armstrong. The most of us are Armstrongs. They took our land and left us homeless and then they put us in jail for trying to get our cattle back."

As the days passed and Hepburn got to talking to the men it was a story that was repeated so often that he began to believe it.

Elliots, Douglases, Hepburns but mostly Armstrongs, just as he had been told. He linked them up again in their families and noticed that they seemed to be able to get over the ground faster. His grizzled adviser he attached to the end of the line where he walked so he could talk to him. By the end of the second day he offered to take his chains off.

"Na. Dinna' do that. They'll kill me. This way they listen to me for I led many of the Armstrongs here one way or another. Ye should never make favourites between soldiers. It winna' do."

"Aye". Hepburn remembered his own resentment when his King's Guard sergeant had preferred a fellow Frenchman for rotmaster when he knew that both Monro and himself were better trained. "Right enough! But tell me how you got this way?"

"When the King wants peace and the Wardens of the Marches want our land, there's naught for us. Armstrong land has aye been wild. We keep our own laws and our Lord keeps us right. When the English or the Douglases, God rot their black souls, want our cattle they make a raid and often times they know when no one is home. I came back to find my wife slaughtered and my children with their throats cut. When I took a rieving party to return the insult the King's men took us. We were tried, sentenced and our land forfeit within the week. I told my men to volunteer. Transportation is certain death. This way I thought we might live longer though those jailors didna' help by not giving us anything to eat on the road though they stopped at all the pubs, themselves."

"Well I'll see ye fed. Likely you're right about the chains."

It was one thing to promise but as they got further from Hepburn country it became both harder and more expensive to produce even one meal of stew and bread. On the last day Hepburn paid extra to have a cart follow them from Seton. He was learning about looking after men and relished the challenge. Being a captain gave him authority that he had never wielded before. Men who would previously have pushed him aside now listened.

But if Hepburn had hoped for some sort of organisation awaiting him in Leith he was to be disappointed.

"Where do we sail from?"

"There as likely as not," a seaman pointed out a pier where the waves were dashing against the rocks and splashing over the wall. "There isna' a ship ready if that's what ye seek. I've seen a bit paper frae the Privy Council to Alexander Downy, the skipper o' a merchantman. It said, "tae dress his ship wi' aw' convenient diligence and to have the same in readiness for the transport of some soldiers under the charge of Colonel Gray.'" He grinned as Hepburn's face fell. "Captain Downy is madder than a bull pulled off a heifer, so my friend says, and he's mate on Downy's ship. He's to take ye to Hamburg, for the service of the King of Boheme, See!" He thrust a leaflet signed by Lords Wyntoun, Wigtoun, Perth, Melrose and Lauderdale under Hepburn's nose. "My friend gave it me after his captain told him to stick it up Lauderdale's arse. Ye're not very popular, ye ken."

"So can we hire a shed?" He handed the sheet on to Andrew Armstrong. Armstrong could read. Hepburn had noticed that his men obeyed him quicker if Armstrong knew what was going on.

"For a price." The seaman grinned wickedly. "My master has one over there that's empty. Tell him I sent ye, It's Jamie Wilson, my name."

"Ah canna' leave my men, Jamie. Will ye ask your master to attend me?"

The man simply held his hand out.

"God what a set of thieves we've landed in."

"Fine one ye are to talk. Those men are not in chains for their health I don't doubt."

After a great deal of haggling Hepburn found he was the feuer of a huge ware-house. It was draughty, but once the doors were shut, much warmer and certainly dry. His men fell to the floor all but exhausted. Looking at them Hepburn wondered how many would actually live until they found a ship.

"I'll need to find ye food. I'll look for blankets too. But I'll need your word that ye'll no' try to escape or I'll not go and we'll all starve the night."

He was interested to see that the men came together in the groupings he had made for food. There was clearly discussion, low-voiced and fast. Then Andrew Armstrong spoke.

"We'll await ye, Sir".

Hepburn nodded and turned to go.

"But I wouldna' be too long."

Hepburn's laugh brought a grim smile to some of the faces round him. He hoped they'd stay smiling as he hurried off but he soon realised the enormity of his task. Bakers did not want to know and turned him away rudely. In the end a small inn advertised "A. Hepburn" as the proprietor and John Hepburn, desperate now for he knew he had been away too long, just walked in and poured his story out.

"Easy now, lad, easy. Tell me again. But first you say you're a Hepburn. You're not related to George Hepburn of Athelstaneford are ye by chance?"

"My father, Sir."

"Well, well and I'd not have asked but ye are the image of the man. He drank here often and often when I was a lad and my father used to serve him. He'd always a groat for me and a'. Fancy ye being his son."

After that things happened. John Hepburn did not haggle. He told the inn-keeper his needs, handed over the money and set off back to the warehouse.

He was just in time. A fight had broken out and the men were being involved willy-nilly as their shackles drew them into the line of punching fists.

"Stop." The order rang out sharp and loud and everyone froze. "Step back from each other. Do it!" The order was obeyed, almost as if the men could not resist.

"Now listen to what I have arranged, and one shove or fist and ye lose your bread ration."

Hepburn just hoped he had not misplaced his trust, or his money. It would have been easy enough for the inn keeper to forget the whole agreement and from the calibre of sailors and bakers he had encountered he would not have been surprised, but he had trusted Andrew Hepburn. The man had surely known and liked his father. He sat down to wait, his whip at the ready. His men gradually joined him on the floor and low conversations started.

Then the door opened and a cart was driven in. His clansman had done him proud. They ate better that day than they had done or would do on their voyage. Cross, hungry men were sated and when blankets were delivered they settled in their sets of six and slept.

"I'll always remember ye." Hepburn wrung his kinsman's hand.

"Aye you're like your father. He was a good man too. Good luck, son! See I kept one blanket for ye."

The next day Sir Andrew Gray rode in at the head of his marching recruits.

"Well done, Hepburn. You've got one decent sized go-down. We'll pack the men in there, lock and guard the doors and we should be fine. It'll save me paying for another place. Meeting of the officers the night at Jessie's pub! Ask the way frae someone."

"Bastard's gone without paying his share of the warehouse."

"Aye, that's our Sir Andra!" A slim man, much his own age turned towards him, his hand held out. "I'm Pentland, Captain John Pentland. I paid Sir Andrew to be Captain and he said he would find me a company from Edinburgh. He has my money but I'm still waiting."

"I'm Captain Hepburn."

"I ken. They've all been talking about ye, taking bets as to how many of the incorrigible border dastards ye've killed so far."

Hepburn chuckled. "None and they all made the journey. They're not so bad when ye ken them. Most are not criminals at all."

"Ye could have fooled me! They sold my horse twice in Haddington. In the end it seemed safer to sell it myself. I walked here. It's an awfy lot o' ruffians that Sir Andra has signed up."

Hepburn wished that they had chosen his kinsman's inn to meet in but when he eventually found his way up a vennel to Jessie's he could see that it was altogether bigger and the long low room he was shown into had a board that accommodated Sir Andrew and all his officers.

He found himself towards the bottom of the table, just the young ensigns below him.

"They dinna' look old enough to need a razor."

Pentland sitting beside him laughed. "If his money was good Sir Andra would take a lad in short coats. See what happened to my men." He thrust a pamphlet at Hepburn.

"17 May 1620 Privy Council Proclamation: it is the truth that a number of these persons being feeble and unworthy dastards, void of courage and of all honest and virtuous disposition, have withdrawn and absented themselves from their Captains and keep themselves hid within the burgh of Edinburgh, the Cannongate and Leith."

Hepburn gave a crack of laughter.

"It's no laughing matter. I've paid for my captaincy, paid a week's wages to those vagrant dastards and neither they nor my money are in evidence. We embark tomorrow. I wish I'd thought to put them in chains. At least you know where your lot are."

"What have the Privy Council done to help?"

"They've put out an edict for the runaways to return to us." He pushed another pamphlet over. See it says, "if they do not they will be sought out and hangit to the deade without mercy."

"It brings a whole new meaning to the quick and the dead", Hepburn chuckled. "That Council will be as pleased to see the back of Sir Andrew as he will be to get all his men on board."

"That is for certain." Another leaflet was passed up by an ensign. "But dinna' think that the ship masters are happy to take us. If they dinna' bring their ships the Privy Council will have their sails from them. Willing transport I think not!"

Another ensign leaned over. "I come frae Cramond. It's the same there. Besides they've ordered all incoming ships to give up their Dutch pilots to us on pain of confiscation of their sails and spars. We're not a bonny smell in seamen's noses just now."

"Aye, we officers are the only volunteers as far as I can see." Pentland nodded. "The Privy Council have surely cleaned the country's stable of criminals and we are transporting their scourings for them. Fight for the Queen of Bohemia? Be her white knights? That black hearted scum dinna' ken what loyalty is. I should have known it would be so."

"I joined to fight because I'm trained for it." Hepburn tried not to sound defensive but he needn't have bothered.

"Then you're better than most of us. I joined because I canna' live on my portion as a younger brother. My mother is hot for the "Princess Elizabeth", as she cries her. King Jamie left his daughter to Lady Livingstone to bring up so every one round about Edinburgh knew her and loved her. When she married the Elector Frederick of the Palatinate and he was asked to take the crown of Bohemia from the Catholic Hapsburg heir, Ferdinand, everyone in Scotland shouted hurray! Now the Spaniards and Hapsburgs have got together to throw her and her husband out, before they've even been crowned, there is a great outcry for men to go and fight to put her on the Bohemian throne. Sir Andra said I'd make a fortune frae booty and the like. It seemed fine when he said it but, God in heaven! It's a awfy mess the noo." Pentland shook his head in despair.

"I was the same," The ensign beside Hepburn nodded. "So are most of us one way or another. My brother's a lawyer but I hadna' the head for it so this seemed something like."

Hepburn, sitting between them, gave thanks for his training. He grinned as he realised it was the first time he'd had a kind thought for his sergeant in Paris.

CHAPTER 8
Journey to Prague

Bracing himself against the wallowing ship, John Hepburn hoped that their bad tempered and unwilling pilot would stop short of mass murder by running the ship on the rocks.

Captain Pentland had thought it a great joke that both captain and pilot were toiling under duress. John Hepburn was unable to laugh.

"I'd be damned cross if someone grabbed me just as I was going home and put me on a reeking troop ship."

His men were a packed mass of stinking misery below decks. They were free. He had stood by the blacksmith who hammered off their gyves, counting them on board. Exhausted from vomiting and fear, they scarcely seemed to notice the loss of their shackles. Hepburn had done his best. He brought them together by one of the gun ports and this he opened every day when he went below to inspect them. It was more to stop his own nausea at the foul stench and to allow the fitter men to sweep vomit and detritus out from their area that he did it, but while they shivered and swore at the cold blast, it seemed to energise them.

At first they just moaned and refused to eat but a sailor told him that dry food would cure sickness so he carried down a couple of loaves and ordered the men to chew some and swallow. It was a trial of wills. Andrew Armstrong simply forced the coarse barley loaf between the teeth of those who refused.

Gradually it became apparent to the Borderers that they were perhaps less affected than their neighbours, many of whom were now in a high fever and close to death. After that, his men appeared to accept his orders. There were deaths but not in his company. Soon there were mass funerals each morning. Hepburn shuddered as he descended the heaving ladder to the dark, fetid deck below and saw the sail-makers busy sewing bodies into coarse shrouds.

The other officers were uninterested.

"I'll lead whatever is left of my company when we dock," Captain Pentland said to Hepburn as they sat at dinner. "We've every thief and vagabond south of Perth. Scottish tollbooths house nought but women, and those bastards in the hold have brought jail fever with them. I'm not going near that lot. You're a fool to do it."

Grey had assembled 2500 men and crammed them, his cannon, muskets, pikes and armour into as few ships as possible to save expense.

As he sat at the foot of the officers' table, Hepburn began to realise that this was no romantic crusade on his leader's part but a strictly money-making venture.

"Our Colonel was paid by the Privy Council to recruit two thousand men. Any over and he gets extra for them." Dunbar looked down the board at Hepburn with a mocking smile. "They were counted as they walked on board and he got his payment before we sailed. Do you think he worries that there are fewer soldiers to fight for our Princess now?"

"He makes a fortune," Pentland muttered to John Hepburn. "If we all die or desert he keeps our pay so long as the Privy Council don't know."

"He won't make much from my men then", Hepburn whispered back. "I'm not going to lose anyone from my company to line his pocket."

It was a new sensation for John Hepburn and one he savoured, this sense of responsibility for men entrusted to him. He felt proud of their endurance.

As the burials at sea increased he said to Pentland, "I'd never recruit sweepings. My men may be jailbirds but they're as close kin as I'll find this side of Hell. My own folk have little time for me, even my sister Marie who raised me has her own husband to care for. I dinna' want to lose even one of those Border dastards. They're mine!"

As he watched the huge seas break over the prow and sluice through the scuppers, he found himself counting the days to landfall, anxious to keep his company intact and thankful to be above deck rather than below where vomiting and fever were raging.

Their entry to Hamburg in the pale light of dawn reminded him of the long roads into Bordeaux, where half timbered houses crowded up to the water, as they sailed past up the winding waterway to the docks. His excitement at arrival knew no bounds. All his men had survived, though as he watched them shamble over the gang plank, he could see that they looked, for the most part, like the corpses they had left behind, so pale and thin they had become.

"March your men out of town," ordered Lieutenant-Colonel Ramsay as he saw Hepburn at a loss. "Take that road there!" He pointed south. "Stay to the east of the Elbe River we've just sailed up. Once ye're out of town find a place to camp and wait for us. We'll issue weapons there so dinna' annoy the villagers until we arrive, eh?"

Saluting, Hepburn turned to Andrew Armstrong but that redoubtable man already had his fellow borderers in some sort of order and was keen to go.

"Get them out of town before they see the lassies, Sir. They may look right scrawny but a woman would have them going every which way. They arena' trained, ye ken."

Armstrong led and Hepburn followed up behind. He kept his whip in evidence but the men, once started, just plodded on, their heads down and wobbling from side to side as if they were about to collapse. There was no speech. Hepburn had time to look about him as the city gave way to flat strips of cultivation where wheat ripened, and then to scrubby trees growing on rough grass that was already dry and brown, the year much further advanced than it would be in Scotland.. As the sun rose, Hepburn found his mouth dry with the dust from the road churned up by the feet of the men in front, but as mid-day approached hunger became his main torment and when they reached a great flat piece of uncultivated moor-land that seemed to separate the fields of two villages he called a halt, led his men off the dusty track and set them to breaking down the scrub for firewood.

Andrew Armstrong approached him at length.

"They'll not last much longer without food, Sir."

"Aye I'm hungered myself", Hepburn looked at him straightly. "If I went to the nearest village to see what I could raise would ye be here when I returned?"

"Aye, maybe." Armstrong shook his head. "I'd do my best. But were I you, I'd divide the men into rots and put a man in charge of each. Threaten the rotmaster with getting less to eat if his men desert before ye return."

Hepburn nodded. "That's easily done. You'll be their sergeant then and the rotmasters'll be the men that were in charge of the groups of six men in chains on the way to Leith. See to it Sergeant Armstrong!"

Hepburn set off for the spire he could see in the distance as fast as he was able. The little village he entered certainly had a baker but there was no understanding him. He looked around wildly to where a crowd was gathering. It did not seem to be particularly friendly and the sweat on his brow was no longer only from the heat. Suddenly he had an idea and pushing through the gathered people he set off for the church and there thankfully his Latin was understood.

"I have money to pay for bread" he told the minister who met him at the church doors. "I would even pay for a small cask of stew or soup, and for a cart to bring it to us. I lead one hundred men to fight the Catholic horde who threaten those who follow Luther but my men are faint for lack of food."

He brought out his purse and offered it to the minister. This seemed to reassure him and opening it he took much of Hepburn's last pay.

"I will arrange it." He coughed. "You understand we've had experience of armies marching south. They also said they were fighting for us but they raped two of our young women and stole from our houses. I complained to their leader, Colonel Sir James Seaton, but got no redress."

Hepburn gaped. "No wonder the baker looked hostile! Sir, I promise that my men will not offend you, but Sir Andrew Gray brings a huge army to my camp and until we are gone I'd tell your folk to bar their doors and open to no man."

"Thank you, Sir, for your honesty." The man smiled at last, a genuine smile that transformed his thin mouth to kindness. "We do pray for your success. But we live quiet lives and suddenly simple farmers have to become warriors to protect their family and land against predators."

Hepburn shuddered as he thought of his family threatened similarly and was thankful when he returned and Armstrong reported no deserters. "They're o'er weak to go. It'll be worse later."

"My men will not thieve, rape or kill these villagers. Warn them Sergeant that they will hang for it. I'm sure the Colonel will be of like mind."

As he said it his heart sank. He was not at all sure of Gray's reaction.

The heat of late June was exhausting and after they had eaten Hepburn led them to the river and ordered them to bathe. This was a new and horrid concept. However he was glad to see that enough of them followed his example to force the rest to conform.

"Heaven send no women pass this way or we'll have a riot." Armstrong lay beside his captain allowing the sun to dry him. "I havna' done that since childhood and the Elbe is a mite bigger than the syke behind my father's house."

"They smelled too rank to suffer. They're not lavender now but it's better."

Armstrong chuckled. "Aye and it keeps them busy. You're learning fast Sir, so ye are."

By late afternoon a great dust cloud approached and the rest of Gray's army arrived, first the men, looking, Hepburn thought, even worse than his had done. Then came the baggage and food wagons and last of all the cannon on their wooden gun carriages, pulled by teams of six oxen. It was a formidable sight. Hepburn was amazed how bit by bit, tents were raised and the camp became ordered.

"Good camp site, Hepburn!" Gray, still in full armour despite the heat, paused beside him. "Well chosen. Well prepared."

John Hepburn grinned with pleasure.

Very soon the smell of cooking brought the men to crowd round where the cooks stirred huge pots.

Hepburn, whose men had eaten, went to see what they were doing and found them in a group with the others. He had been about to put in a request to have his outlay for food repaid.

"You've had your dinner, you lot!"

"Oh wheest Sir!" One of the rotmasters turned an agonised eye towards him. "Dinna' tell."

Hepburn found himself looking at a hundred pairs of imploring eyes. His order to leave the dinner line died on his lips.

 "I'll see ye after your dinner!"

He was rewarded by a hundred grinning faces and as he went off to join the other officers he heard the whispers,

"Aye he's a right wan!" and "Ah suppose he's no bad, for an officer!" and began to feel a warm content that these men were his. "I'll make them the best," he promised himself. "They'll not know themselves when I've finished with them."

The officers ate in their own tent, Gray and Ramsay at the table head and the rest spread round in order of rank. Now there was no talk of the rights of their Princess Elizabeth but much discussion of where booty could be culled. He had always known that the men were predators. Now he realised that most of the officers were of the same mind. They had joined to recoup their family wealth and had few scruples about how that might be achieved. The talk at dinner was about getting rich rather than tactics, and punishment rather than training. Gray led the conversation as he boasted of how he had looted from the Poles as an officer in James Spens's cavalry.

 "We were for Gustavus Adolphus," he said, as the wine loosened his tongue. "What we seized from those that wanted his cousin, Sigismund of Poland, as King of Sweden is nobody else's business, ye ken. I warrant you'll all be rich men once we've humbled these Hapsburg upstarts."

"I'd not like to be the town captured by our great leader," Pentland sitting beside him, muttered. "When he takes a dorp into contribution the burghers'll feel the bottom of their pockets alright."

"But the officers ken enough to train the men and keep order surely?"

Pentland grinned sourly. "They ken enough to line their pockets more like. You're about the best trained of any of us, John, you and that Captain John James Dunbar. He's a bonny fighter, that one, for all he's a thrawn bugger."

Dunbar had held himself aloof from the other young captains who rode together by day as their men toiled behind, and diced together of an evening once their few duties were done. Hepburn had been slightly in awe of his cold grey eye, but he was in need of advice so one dinner time he claimed the seat beside Dunbar.

"When will we set about training the men?"

Dunbar laughed. It was not an amused sound and Hepburn felt his ears redden.

"Train them! This lot! They couldna' train their grannies to sit up in bed."

"But I can. I want to train my company."

"Then ye'll do it in your own time and theirs and ye'll get no extra monies frae our leader for it."

"I don't want more. I can't bear to see them stravaig along like drunken pedlars."

Dunbar snorted again. This time, thought Hepburn, he sounded really amused.

"The days stay light well on now, and we're going at the speed of those damned oxen that pull the cannon. Ye've all evening after the men have eaten. In a while I'll be doing the same for my men, though they've been trained already. It doesn't do them any harm to be well drilled and keeps them frae mischief."

Hepburn nodded. "I'll do that then. We'll start tomorrow."

Dunbar clapped him on the back as he rose from the table later. "Get on with it, John. Once the men have their strength back they'll be at all sorts of devilment and God help the boores, which is what they call the peasants in the dorps round about." He gestured at the top of the table. "Our great leader will be organising the loupegarth so that sinners run between lines of men armed with sticks to beat them as they run. He's already chosen an executioner to deal with the worse offenders and believe me there will be some nasty deeds done by this lot."

Next morning, as he took his place at the head of his company and looked back at the huge unwieldy mass of men that was Gray's army, Hepburn remembered Dunbar's words and shuddered for the local boores.

"We'll be starting to train the men," he told Armstrong. "Pass the word to the rotmasters to get in the dinner line early. After they've eaten they are to bring my company to where I am. Any man who doesn't come gets put in irons for the night."

"Doubtless they'll be much uplifted, Sir." Armstrong grinned. "They thought being a rotmaster was a dawdle, so they did."

That evening was as much an education for him as for his men. His mental picture of his old French sergeant lost its devilish horns and almost acquired a halo. His tedious exhausting training was now a godsend. Sitting the men down on the dry scrubby grass at the edge of the camp he explained their duties.

"There's just over a hundred of you that are my company. We ought to have a hundred and twenty six in twenty one rots of six men of which one is rotmaster who leads and another, the under-rotmaster, who marches in the rear to make sure all's well. The six most experienced rotmasters will be called Corporal. We're to be a pike company, Colonel Gray says."

There was immediate argument. To Hepburn's anxious eye it appeared to be becoming heated but then Armstrong joined them and they started to listen.

"We've sorted it, Sir. The rotmasters are Tod Armstrong, and those two Douglas brothers, Tam and Grimkin. Aye," Armstrong grinned at John Hepburn's lifted eyebrow. "He's cried Grimkin for Archibald Douglas who was called Archibald the Grim. He was the bastard son o' a Douglas and a black faced battler just like our Archibald here. Then there's wee Jock Elliot, cack-handed Kerr and Tam Learmonth. The men call him Tam the Rhymer who the fairies stole".

"I'm not wanting anyone who's away wi' the fairies."

"Na' na' ye needna' fash. He's just a gloomy sort, but he's steady and the men heed him."

"I'll issue the pikes now. Get in groups of six and choose an under-rotmaster. I'll train the rotmasters and once trained they'll train the men in their rot. Sergeant Armstrong stay with me."

Tod Armstrong frowned. "Ye're going to be short five men, Sir."

Hepburn looked up

Sergeant Armstrong grinned. "Dinna' question Tod's numbers, Sir. It's like he has lists in his head."

"I'll be the one goes short then, I expect." Tam Learmonth turned a dour face towards his Captain.

"Na', Tam." Kerr patted his back. "I'll ask around for the cack-handers to make up numbers. They're mostly Kerrs and Maxwells out of the Edinburgh jails. They'll train different like me."

"But how will I get their pay?" Hepburn had little hope that Gray would give him much help.

"Dinna' worry, Sir." Armstrong muttered beside him. "The regimental registrar's an Armstrong from my auntie's family who went for a lawyer. He'll adjust the books. It doesna' hurt Colonel Gray's pocket and the other Captains have no idea who they're leading yet."

"Do you all agree to these arrangements, you lot?" Hepburn raised his voice over the beginnings of low voiced mutterings.

"Just so long as the Armstrongs dinna' rule the roost," said a voice.

Hepburn let his glance run over them all and the muttering subsided.

"Ye're a company now, my company! I'll see ye right and I'll train ye as soldiers but any who think to fight with old enemies will be punished and that right fiercely. Do ye understand?"

Silence met his outburst and then with a few sideways glances a universal nodding began.

"Right then. We'll start. I'll train corporals and rotmasters and then you'll train your under-rotmaster and the two of ye will train your rots. It'll take time but ye'll be the best when I've finished with ye."

That evening he issued them with pikes and with Armstrong beside him drilled the rotmasters first and then left his Sergeant to continue with them while he started to teach the under-rotmasters until their rotmasters were ready to work with them. What he thought would be a difficult job turned out amazingly easy. The men handled their weapons like old friends and he was slightly alarmed to see the delight with which they used them.

"We'll need a drummer boy, Sir." Sergeant Armstrong was hoarse with shouting after the first few days.

"Where on earth can we get that?"

"Aye, just leave it to me."

The next day at training a diminutive urchin in rags was tagging along behind Sergeant Armstrong. A drum hung from his shoulders by a rope and two sticks were stuck in a waist-belt.

"It's Wee Eck," Armstrong said prodding the boy forward. "Lift your hand in salute to the Captain, Eck!"

"But who does he belong to?"

"No one, Sir. He was part o' a travelling dance group who were put in the tollbooth for thieving. His mother is still there, he says, and his father died on the boat. If we took him, Sir, we could claim food and pay for him could we not?"

"Can he play?"

"Anything, Sir."

The boy snatched the drumsticks from his shirt front and his drum resounded with a country dance rhythm.

"I'll send him to the drummer of Captain Dunbar, Sir. He'll be very useful once we get to training the men."

Hepburn was laughing. "I'll get Sir Andra to put him on the list but if he sends us into battle jigging I'll be back to ye, Sergeant."

He was wrong. The boy had talent. Wee Eck was back within the week, all the drum rolls at his finger tips. A week later he was joined by a bigger version of himself, his drum at the ready.

"It's my brother, Wullie, Sir. I've been sharing my dinner with him but he's aye hungry. I've taught him the drum rolls, Sir." Two pairs of anxious eyes stared at him.

Hepburn had been talking with Armstrong's auntie's lawyer son to good effect.

"A company is aye allowed three drummers. You're both enrolled on the company strength. Ye'll attend training every evening with the men."

Frantic nods and broad grins confirmed the contract.

"He'll get his own dinner too?"

"I'll see to it."

CHAPTER 9
Captain of the Palace Guard

Flag-bedecked Hradcany Castle, perched on a hill with the low roofs of Prague spreading away from its walls, was a welcome sight. The rumbling cannon came to a halt and the drumbeat stilled. Men fell out and started talking. It was still early morning but the cloudless sky gave promise of another stifling, July day.

Hepburn watched his company form small groups round their rotmasters, his sergeant automatically moving down the line telling them to stay close. When Gray ordered a general parade he was proud of them. They stood out amongst the slouching troops, their stance upright, and their shining pikes at the present. He was confident that they would wheel to march in good order on the drum beat. His young drummers, sticks raised, watched him, ready.

"Nasty wee men," Sergeant Armstrong had said in an admiring tone, "they've terrorised the other drummers. Even Captain Dunbar's lot gives them space at the dinner line. What their father did for a living I know not, but when they threaten to cut your throat of a night I dinna' think they're funning."

John Hepburn looked startled. "Na na. They dinna' try it on me, ye ken. Ah got them their job so I'm a right one, but I'm thinking it's a good thing they're in our company, Sir."

As the sun came up, sweat poured off their necks. Beneath leather corselets their shirts were a sodden sweaty mess. Gray and Lieutenant Colonel Ramsay fretted on their horses and further down the line Hepburn could see James Dunbar astride a great bay mare. He envied him.

At last, the sound of braying trumpets heralded the arrival of the Elector Frederick to inspect these new adherents to his cause. With him, his wife the Scottish Princess Elizabeth and their courtiers made a colourful cavalcade. Colonel Gray, with Ramsay, went forward to dismount and kiss the royal hands.

But dirty men from the sewers of Scotland were not attractive to Elizabeth, daughter of King James VI and I. John Hepburn, looking up as she allowed her horse to walk down the line of men, was struck by the distaste on the plump face above the lavish blue and gold dress. It reminded him of his mother's when she was displeased.

"I'm right glad I'm risking my life to make my fortune and not for that proud hussie," he muttered to himself. "She doesn't care whether we live or die."

About to turn away, the King remembered that his personal bodyguard was small and with the Imperialists advancing, he might be safer with trained soldiers about the court. His suggestion was well received. Gray saw a chance to off-load the monthly salaries of a company and summoned Hepburn.

"You were a palace guard in Paris. You know the drill. Look to the King for your pay. We're away to Pilsen."

John Hepburn was delighted. It was vindication of all the dusty hours he had sweated at training.

"We'll get better food, better quarters, decent uniforms maybe," he told his company. Their bright acquisitive interest gave him pause and he turned to Sergeant Armstrong.

"Make sure they know that there will be no Border habits here! Thieving, rape, or murder will all be punished with death. When they come to grips with the enemy they can look for booty but not here. Not now! Remember Colonel Gray chose us because we were the best."

"The Auld Deil can pocket our pay, now, more like!" His sergeant seemed intent on rubbing it in. "There isna' another lot that kens how to present arms except Captain Dunbar's company and he pays his men himself."

Hepburn waved at Pentland as he led his troop after Dunbar. "The colonel could have chosen them."

"Those fly-by-nights, Sir! Just wandering vagrants, the lot of them! A dagger in the back up a dark wynd and someone else's money pouch in their pocket is their dead strength."

His captain was not to be put down. He relished his promotion, whether based on his colonel's greed or not. At twenty two to be captain of a King's bodyguard was an exciting prospect that he relished. Turning to the young drummer beside him he ordered "Beat the "Old Scotch March", Eck. We'll follow the King."

Settled to his duties in Hradcarny Castle, Hepburn enjoyed daily contact with the Elector Frederick. He even had moments of speech with Elizabeth Stuart. At last he was sauntering among the nobility, as the French King's Scottish Guard had. It wasn't long before the tall, kenspeckle redhead was on nodding acquaintance with most of the courtiers and with his flair for language, able to exchange greetings in German as well as the universally spoken Latin and courtly French.

That late summer of 1620 young, well born Scots crowded into Prague full of romantic fervour for Elizabeth Stuart. They might have little military experience but they were rich and had a lively desire to enjoy themselves away from the rigid, reformist life at home. Englishmen joined them and Prague partied. Musical evenings in palaces, balls at the Castle, drinking and dicing until the small hours, made night as noisy as day.

Excluded from that scene because both Scots and English turned away from a man with no lands, no fortune and no name, Hepburn stifled his resentment. He was well aware he had no money to lose on the turn of a dice. Instead he enjoyed the admiration Frederick's courtiers accorded him when he paraded his men in the castle courtyard. A word from the Princess and the Scots found themselves with silk surcoats with the arms of Bohemia and the Palatinate intertwined. His men loved it.

"It's aye better than being hung in Carlisle jail!" muttered Corporal Tam Learmonth.

But revelling in the attention though he was, John Hepburn sensed an approaching threat. John James Dunbar and several other captains appeared at court. Pentland had his left arm in a sling. A slim, dark

Scot, with him, limped from a leg wound. "You remember Jamie Douglas, John?" Pentland nodded at him. "Turns out he and I were the only captains that didna' drink and gamble so Gray gave us the sorties."

Hepburn swept them off to his favourite inn in the town below the castle. A low, thatched hostelry crouching beneath a great holm oak, it offered welcome shade after the burning heat of the day. They sat outside in the courtyard, beer tankards in hand, while Dunbar, his dark face showing a twisted smile, answered eager questions about what was happening to the regiment.

"Naught while Gray commands. He's never won a battle and by God he isn't going to break that record with what he's got."

Pentland nodded ruefully.

"If John James hadn't come to my rescue I was a dead man. We were sent to defend Nepomuk, a wee town built round a monastery started by this monk who was drowned by King Wenceslaus years ago for not telling what the Queen confessed. They think him right holy."

Dunbar took a pull from his tankard.

"Tilly, that crafty old General, was trying to move the Imperial army north through the passes thereabouts. Gray lined us up to defend the town, but some damned priest showed their lot a defaced painting of John of Nepomuk and shouted that we nasty protestants had done it. They attacked like Turks on heat." Jamie Douglas beside him nodded. "It was busy work but we stood no chance. Ours are from the stews of Scotland, untrained in ought but begging at street corners."

"My men ran." Pentland shook his head. "If Dunbar, here, hadn't charged, I was meat for the crows."

"I had the devil's own task leading my men through his yelling cowards. They probably did more damage to my company than the Imperialists. We retreated in good order. Gray got the guns away. He has his savings invested in those cannon."

"So this is where you hide after our fun at Nepomuk, Dumbarra!" A young man with dark hair curling to his shoulders and dark flashing eyes slapped Dunbar on the shoulder and pulled up a stool to sit beside him. "I have found friends at last. The court is full of foreigners."

"Duke Bernard of Saxe-Weimar," Dunbar introduced him. "May I present Captain John Hepburn of our army and I think you know Captain Pentland and Captain Douglas?"

Looking into those laughing eyes, John Hepburn saw a man he could like, though from his incipient moustache he thought him no older than his younger brother James.

"I see I missed a good party." Hepburn looked rueful.

"Fear not, there will be a repeat on a much grander scale, my friends." Saxe-Weimar took a pull at the tankard of ale that had been put in front of him by a bowing landlord. "Marradas and Buquoy have by-passed Mansfeld, who undertook to protect our southern borders, and are heading towards Prague. Our skirmish was just a taster. Tilly now has an army of 30,000 men."

Hepburn felt a tightening of his stomach. "My men are ready. We don't just polish our pikes. How many men can the King field?"

"Nothing like that!" The voice above him had a quality of command in it that brought Hepburn to his feet and turning to bow, he saw the others doing likewise.

"Count von Thurn," Bernard of Saxe-Weimar was saying. "Your Excellency, may I present my friends from Scotland, Captains Dunbar, Pentland, Douglas and Hepburn."

Thurn's rather stern face changed as he smiled at them. Hepburn warmed to this small fatherly man with his curly fairish hair that was turning white and tumbling into a full beard and moustaches. But he was awe-struck in equal measure. Thurn was a living legend. He had led an army to the gates of Vienna itself and though Hepburn had never spoken to him he had felt honoured when one day he had heard him murmur, "Well ordered men," when his company had been on watch.

"We welcome all the help we can get. This will be a deciding battle in my opinion." There was a sad look in his eyes and Hepburn looking at him beside the volatile Saxe-Weimar, realised that he was looking at the true heir to Protestant Bohemia.

"What have you been doing, you scamp." Thurn was obviously no stranger to the young German nobleman.

"Skirmishing, retreating! Mansfeld is better at raising money for an army than leading it to victory. He has taken Colonel Gray's regiment under his banner."

"And under his payment" muttered Dunbar under his breath.

"This is how I met my friends here." Saxe-Weimar went on. "We had no luck at Nepomuk. But there were thousands of them and just a skirmishing party of us."

"I fear most of ours are poorly trained too, Sir." Dunbar's words were explanation enough.

The older man sighed.

"Count Ernst von Mansfeld was with the Imperial army before he fell out with Archduke Leopold over some matter of not getting paid what he expected. Now he has become a General on our side but his heart is not in it, merely his treasure chest. If he should lose he is as happy to join the Hapsburgs again. Would that all of us could view the matter so easily."

He sat and the younger men sat and remained respectfully silent until he spoke again.

"When Ferdinand took power in Bohemia he brought back all the old scandalous Catholic ways. The folk on my estate were ordered to go to mass and pay for the monks and friars or be evicted. We follow the teachings of Luther and when I became a member of the Bohemian estate of nobles I knew I would never, could never, change.

I tried to advise the Emperor. He would not listen. He sent those fools Martinice and Slavata. I threw them out of the meeting hall window." He grinned suddenly like a little boy. "Pity they landed in the castle midden. The Catholics claim a miracle. I say that rubbish landed on rubbish!"

The young men sat silent, willing him to continue.

"We offered the crown to Elector Frederick. With his connection to England and Scotland and Denmark we thought we had power on our side." He sighed again. "But he lets that damned Calvinist, Abraham Scultetus, strip our cathedral of the carvings we love. We Lutherans love that cathedral as it is."

He turned to the Scots who were listening fascinated.

"His wife, your countrywoman, has as little tact."

"Aye Sir," Dunbar nodded. "The Stuarts are famous that way! Like her grandmother, she has lured thousands of young men from their safe homes to fight for her. God send they don't suffer the same fate."

John Hepburn nodded. "My father answered the call from our feudal superior, Lord Bothwell. My eldest sister told me that he'd been trying to build a doo-cot to give the family winter food stores and was thankful to return from Prestonpans un-blooded. But thereafter enemies of Queen Mary pursued him and Hepburn became a dirty word in East Lothian."

Count Thurn nodded sadly. "You know then how it goes."

Hepburn leaned forward. "Sir I'm not fighting for a woman. I'm fighting the Hapsburgs and the arrogance of Spain. They have gold from the Americas but we have right on our side, the right to live and worship as we wish, not as some inbred Emperor declares. My men will stand."

He grinned suddenly like a shy boy. "At least I hope they will. I've trained them long enough."

The others laughed. It defused the emotion of the moment. Thurn rose to go and the young men rose with him.

"God go with you gentlemen," he said. "I must return to the Elector," his lips twitched, "I hope he has not caused further offence in my absence or we'll not even muster 300 troops."

The five young men called for food and were soon spooning up a dish of stuffed cabbage accompanied by fresh baked bread.

Talk became more general.

"You knew that Mansfeld has taken our whole regiment into his Bohemian Army Corps?" Dunbar said presently as he mopped his bowl with the rough brown bread.

"Not until Saxe-Weimar mentioned it just now. Does that mean that he pays for us?" Hepburn looked interested. He had benefitted from being in the Elector Frederick's service. Gifts had come his way that had enabled him to buy a fine tooled breastplate and hire a servant to keep it shining. "Does he pay regularly?"

"So far! But you've hit the nail on the head. Our esteemed leader was right glad to lose the weekly payout. He wants to return home a rich man not a poor colonel." Dunbar shook his head. "I recruited and pay my men, veterans all, and though I joined Mansfeld's lot to guard the border I'm not under Gray's command."

"That's why he offered my company to the King, not yours?"

"Yours were the only men able to stand to their arms, John." Pentland patted his shoulder. "My lot would have thieved the palace bare. They're bad enough where they are. They know they risk hanging if they steal from a farmer so they cut the man's throat so he can't object when they slaughter his cow for their pot. I won't be sorry to see them in action. It will give them something to do."

CHAPTER 10
Battle of the White Mountain

Elector Frederick's coronation was lavish. John Hepburn led his company ahead of the soon-to-be Queen Elizabeth's carriage and having done so left them on guard outside while he promenaded inside the cathedral. The towering nave and plain stone walls looked coldly down on the dazzlingly dressed throng and he was pleased to be wearing his new tooled breastplate and embroidered surcoat. At the altar Hepburn could glimpse Scultetus, a wizened figure in unrelieved black.

"That damned crow is an uncivilised vandal," Bernhard of Saxe-Weimar paused beside Hepburn. "Thurn was right! The sculptures have gone."

Hepburn nodded. "I've never taken to Scultetus. He looks at me as if he wants to cut my hair."

Saxe-Weimar choked on a burst of laughter and touching his friend's shoulder, turned to leave. "See you at the Holm Oak tonight!"

The tavern was doing a roaring trade when Hepburn arrived. He found Saxe-Weimar seated at an outside table with John Pentland and Count Thurn, all of them laughing at something James Dunbar had been saying. He sat, grateful for the cool night air and when his ale pot arrived drank deep.

"At least the men were all there and no one was out of line."

"They were better than that, John." Captain Pentland was inclined to praise. "I almost felt proud to be in the same regiment. At least they didn't run like mine at Nepomuk."

"Aye! You never quite forget looking round after the charge and finding no one but yourself and five thousand enemy all interested in filleting you."

Dunbar had a sour tongue, thought Hepburn, but he knew how to fight and his advice was worth asking for. There was word of a pitched battle when the Imperialists converged on Prague. He found himself envying John Pentland, even his disastrous skirmish at Nepomuk. He had blooded his sword.

"I am thankful that this day is over." Thurn spoke suddenly. "Now the King can turn his mind from the design of his apparel. The treaty of Ulm last Spring bought time for the French and the Netherlands to ready their troops but it allowed Philip of Spain to reinforce his Hapsburg cousin. Tilly bear-leads Maximilian of Bavaria. General Marradas and Count Buquoy have joined them. My information is that they have by-passed Mansfeld and are heading for Prague."

"Pentland and I ride at dawn to join our men." Dunbar's face darkened. "I hope to God that Colonel Gray has got our cannon on the move. We'll need all the fire power we can raise. That is four regiments against us now."

Saxe-Weimar broke in. "That damned turncoat Wallenstein will be joining them no doubt."

Thurn nodded. "I'd rather fight Tilly. The "Monk in Armour", as they call him, is an honest Catholic. Wallenstein changes his religion to suit his own advancement it seems to me."

"Careful Sir," Dunbar's face was a picture of innocence. "Hepburn here is a changeling too."

They all turned to look at him with varying signs of horror.

Duke Bernhard of Saxe-Weimar made as if to refute the charge and then looking at John Hepburn's enhanced colour, he stopped. Thurn's look was mostly one of sorrow.

Cursing Dunbar in his heart, John Hepburn hesitated, unwilling to talk of something so personal, but he knew that unless he did he would lose their regard, even their friendship. It was hard to bare his soul but perhaps the words came unfettered because he was too weary to guard his tongue.

"I was brought up Protestant, right enough. My grandfather was Rector of Haugh but when the church reformed he could not change. He sold the living to his brother who gave it to my uncle, as bitter a Calvinist as Scultetus. My father was dead by the time I was three and my mother beat us into piety and poverty with her brother's full encouragement. He was never out of the house, never stopped making life hell on earth for us children. I escaped to university and then to Poitiers and Paris. There I met a gentler God, one who pardoned sins that were truly repented."

He looked round and saw they were intent on his words and smiled a somewhat unhappy smile.

"I have heard about pardons for sale and nuns and priests roistering in bed together. But in Paris the services were simple. The priests I met, chaste. I found the Lutheran services I attended on the way here very similar.

In Poitiers the Scottish reformed minister was as harsh as my uncle and the heaven he promised seemed like Hell. I couldn't stand him or his hell-fire sermons. But I met an old soldier who had reached peace of mind after a lifetime of killing. He was someone I wanted to be like and in Paris I learned to value what he called the cleansing power of confession and repentance."

He leaned forward and the words came fast now. "We may die. That is the risk we soldiers take. It is my trade, my choice, as is my choice of the side I fight for. My family motto is "Keep Tryst". I keep faith with those whose purpose is in the right and I chose the Reformed side, the side that protests against the wicked Imperialist push to take over the world. But when I die I don't want to go to any heaven where that black bitch, my mother, or her venomous brother, are waiting for me. I would confess my sins, hope for pardon and take the path I find."

Thurn leaned over the table, his hand held out. "I am honoured to count you one of us. Few young men I know have made such a considered decision. Know that I stand your friend. I can only hope our King lives up to his motto, "Diverti Nescio", "I know not retreat"."

"You make me proud, Sir". Hepburn stammered, shy now after his outburst. "You may be sure that I shall keep faith with you."

Saxe-Weimar leapt to his feet and slapped him on the back. "I knew you were a sound fellow, John. I'll fight beside you any day."

Only Dunbar sat silent, the malicious gleam in his eyes dulled for the time being.

That night was the last of their lazy joyous summer. Overnight the trees on the hills surrounding Prague began to show the yellow and red leaves of autumn and the evenings became sharper.

Dunbar led his company into quarters just outside the city.

"Ramsay and the rest are on the way. We had the devil's own job getting Gray to mobilise his cannon but by God we'll need them."

"How will it be, the battle?"

Dunbar's dark gaze pierced his apparent unconcern.

"Worried about how to lead, eh? Better learn how to retreat safely."

He grinned at Hepburn's frown.

"Nay, I'm no feardy, young John, but I'm not foolhardy. This lot know as much about fighting as my auld nannie," he paused, "Less. She was a hard woman."

"I've never seen a set piece battle, though I've read about the way it's done."

"Then ye've a fair idea of how it will be. We, being unimportant foreigners, will hold the left wing. The King's own troops will have the honour of the right, likely," he paused and with a quick look round to make sure no one else was listening, added, "and the King with his entourage will direct from as far back as he can manage to be."

A few evenings later Pentland joined Dunbar and Hepburn at their favourite tavern.

"Word is that Sir James Seaton is on the way. My ensign has a brother in his lot and he gets their news."

"If Seaton is here we are going to have to fight for Prague. You may put money on it." Dunbar's forehead wrinkled. "I hope to God that

Gray and Ramsay follow Seaton or it will be you and I, Hepburn, who will hold the left wing. Pentland's company are only good for picking Tilly's pockets."

October was a month of intermittent sharp frosts and conflicting news. By November it was clear that talk of Tilly's unwillingness to fight had been greatly exaggerated. By-passing Mansfeld entirely, he swung his huge army North and crossed the Vitava.

"Thirty thousand men at least, Bucquoy and Marradas at their head and Tilly masterminding the whole," said Dunbar, a battle-light in his dark eyes. "Now we'll see work,"

Frederick's supporters flocked to Prague, flags flying. Commanders in full armour, their helmets plumed in rainbow colours, led marching companies of musketeers and pikemen and having reached the city demanded billets and food for their men. John Hepburn was kept busy directing them to the various quarters allotted to them. He was on sentry duty when Prince Christian of Anhalt clattered in to Hradcarny Castle courtyard with his troop of cavalry, smartly mounted, well armoured and in good order.

Lean-faced with dark curls rolling down his neck and neat beard and moustache he looked much younger than the fifty years he had to be, but Count Thurn had told Hepburn to watch for him. "He and I were young soldiers together," he had said, his voice sad. "We'd thought to manage our estates and raise our children, not fight again together for our very existence. Let me know when he arrives. We have much to say to each other."

Less spectacular was the arrival of Lieutenant Colonel Ramsay leading Gray's regiment. Their unpolished half armour and less than military order showed all too clearly their lack of training.

"Put them somewhere that they won't be tempted to disappear from, John" he ordered, "and then I want to see all my officers at first light tomorrow."

They gathered in a cold guard room in the castle. It was small but there was standing room. Hepburn knew them all from their long march South but he had not been close to any of them. He thought they looked tired and miserable. Some sported bandages from recent skirmishes. Jamie Douglas winked at him across the room and got a grin in return.

Ramsay looked harassed

"We have been placed under Count Thurn to defend the left wing. Tilly will fight."

"Where are our cannon?" Dunbar's voice was sharp.

"On the way with the Colonel." Ramsay turned away at his junior's expletive.

"On his bloody way! Good God, James! They will never arrive in time." Dunbar's tone was sharp. "We need those cannon or we are defenceless. Have you seen what Bucquoy has? King Frederick has nothing to compare."

"They don't listen to me, John. You know how it is with those two. They are too busy counting the cost of transport and estimating the risk of losing precious stores of ball. Recruiters have two hats."

"Well after this, mine is lifted in good-bye." Dunbar stamped out leaving the rest of them looking uneasily at each other.

That day saw them filing out, part of a never-ending stream pouring through the gates of Prague. Drums beating, colours flying, occasional cavalry troops trotting past, Gray's officers led their men towards the left of the line that they could see forming on the hillside beside Prague known as the White Mountain. Slow cannon were being hauled from the castle by teams of oxen and the rumble of the cart wheels, the beat of drums and shouted orders made a cacophony on the quiet slopes.

Hepburn lined his men up where he was ordered and took his position in front. Beside him stood Wee Eck his drum at the ready. He noticed the boy shivering and knew it was not just the frosty air that was responsible. He felt the same frisson of excitement tinged with alarm. Behind him stood Sergeant Armstrong holding their colours, handling the weight as if it were a plaything.

"Ye should have an ensign officer body to hold the colours." Armstrong had explained earlier. "I'm meant to pick them up when he gets himself shot but we've never been given one by Colonel Gray so if I go, the senior corporal of pikes kens to lift them."

Hepburn was not worried by the omission. He had been closer to his men this way. Looking round he saw that pike companies alternated with musketeer companies down the line. He glimpsed Pentland and Jamie Douglas standing before their pikemen in the distance and waved. Both raised an arm in return but he thought Pentland looked flustered. Further over he could see Dunbar, and beyond him he glimpsed Sir James Seaton on horseback, his musketeers and pikemen behind him. He was having a word with Lieutenant Colonel James Ramsay who was also mounted and now moved to take his place ahead of Gray's troops.

"My men have behaved amazingly so far", thought Hepburn as he looked behind him. There was something a little grim about their expressions and they were not talking to each other as they usually did. He had the feeling that they knew more about what was going to happen than he did and sent up a prayer that at least he would not let them down.

At the foot of the hill a small stream meandered. Usually it was the only feature in view. Today, to John Hepburn's astonished gaze, a forest of men had grown in great squares, row on row, their rear marked by a row of cannon. Behind them cavalry fretted and fidgeted. He had never seen so many men assembled, so many disciplined men. He began to worry.

A man on a grey horse appeared and moved down the line towards him. He recognised Count Thurn in full armour. His standard bearer trotted behind him.

"Captain Hepburn. Your men are well ordered I see."

Hepburn saluted. "I am honoured to be under your command, Sir. My men are ready." Or as ready as they ever will be, he added to himself.

"Just stand firm until I give the order to advance."

"Sir!" Hepburn saluted again and his commander trotted on.

Then suddenly the cannon started. Not his cannon, theirs. Bucquoy had opened hostilities. He could see a few puffs of smoke from the centre of Frederick's line which must mean that his side were responding. The flash and roar of the cannon opposite was terrifying. He felt, more than heard, his men begin to shuffle uneasily.

"Stand firm men. It's just noise."

Then there was a roar and whine and a whole file of musketeers beside them disappeared in a spatter of blood and the screaming started. Another roaring whine and a ball ploughed past him into his men, splintering pikes and arms and bodies as if they were matchwood.

"Andy Douglas has lost his heid." The rising hysterical scream came from behind him.

Sergeant Armstrong turned and his bellow drowned the screams for a minute. "It'll no happen to you if you stand firm, Jock Kerr. It disna' happen twice the same place."

For some reason this seemed to quell what was clearly about to be a stampede, but looking back, Hepburn caught his breath at the bloody sight where Douglas's headless body lay askew. Great blood vessels had pumped blood in every direction as he fell and the front rank looked as if they had been at a pig killing.

"Beat, "Stand Fast" drummer!" Hepburn, thankful his white face was hidden in his casque, stood frozen to the spot, only just able to get the words out.

"Good idea Sir!" The growl from behind was welcome insubordination.

The squares ahead of them started to move forward. Tilly was testing the left wing.

Musket balls rattled against armour as they came. Most were too spent to do other than cause flesh wounds but the screaming of men increased. Officers started shouting. Other drums started their insistent beating. Tilly's men were roaring defiance as they came on. "Sacrilegious murderers! Church despoilers! Go to Hell where you belong!"

"Pikes hold your ground!" Terrified though he was, John Hepburn felt a pulse of delight that his voice remained steady. To his right he heard the voice of the captain of musketeers.

"Fire!"

Out of the corner of his eye he saw the front rank moving back to reload as the second rank prepared to fire.

Hepburn, still awaiting word to advance, assessed the scene of chaos. If he did not do something the front ranks of the opposing squares would be upon them. He lifted his pike.

"We will move forward in good order, Sergeant! Beat it, Drummer!"

Thankful for action his men responded. The front rank lowered its pikes and they advanced into the melee. To his left he sensed the musketeers joining the charge wielding their muskets like clubs. Then John Hepburn found himself fighting for his life. He was amazed how easily the cut and thrust of battle came to him. In half armour with his helm down pikes glanced off his breast plate. His long training in France stood him well. Arm and leg moved together and his pike slammed forward getting a musketeer in the throat. Blood spurted and the man dropped. Back came his pike and pushed again. Another man fell, screaming, his belly opened by the pousse. Behind him his men fought in silence with an occasional grunt. He seemed to live in a great silence where only he and the man opposite existed. Another screaming face and his pike bit deep but he was slow in clearing the point where it caught on his opponent's half armour. He half saw a musket rise above his head. It was too late to drop the pike and free his sword and he knew a sense of regret that it would be all over for him. But his assailant suddenly folded. A pike had almost cut him in half.

"I gave the colours to a rotmaster. Ye wouldna' have me miss this, Sir." His Sergeant paused to deal with another musketeer and Hepburn laughed.

"No fear, Sergeant," his childhood speech came easily. "We'll sort this lot together, an' it please you."

Then Pentland's company ran. The musketeers beside him followed them, blundering into his pikemen and breaking their wedge formation. In a moment no one knew who was friend and who was foe. But Christian of Anhalt, seeing the chaos, led his men at full gallop into Tilly's flank. They broke and ran before the flashing sabres. It gave Hepburn time to regroup. But now their flanks were undefended and Tilly seemed to have unending supplies of men. The great squares moved on.

"Time for us to leave, Sir. That is if ye're not wanting to be killed."

Hepburn raised his head and looked around. "Our regiment has gone!"

"Long since!" Armstrong chuckled. "But it was sic a grand rammy I hadna' the heart to tell ye."

Hepburn raised his voice, "Prepare to retreat in good order. We will not lose more men." He heard his drummers start the beat and knew a momentary pleasure that the boys had survived. His men responded, the front rank passing through to the rear while the second rank held their pikes at the ready, then they in turn retreated. On it went, his pike men falling back in good order until the company were in the shelter of the trees and the opposing forces had lost interest in them as they scoured the battlefield looking for booty. Once they were clear he tore off his casque. The sweat beneath poured off his face and his hair was a sodden mass. The air was a benison, however hot, but looking at the metal helmet he was thankful for its protection. There were scars of shot tracks and dents that could have been fatal blows that he simply did not remember receiving. He breathed in deeply, and grinned at the bloodthirsty faces round him.

"Let's get the Hell out of here, sergeant. Which way did our lot go?"

Only some men shambled to their feet and he realised that many were not as unscathed as he.

"Leave your wounded." He remembered Gray's words. "They're

useless drains on our purse. There's more where they came from."

He knew what his men expected. The wounded didn't meet his eye. Some tried to rise. An extraordinary feeling of responsibility took hold of him. These were his men. They might be gallows meat but they had fought beside him and had not wavered. He was damned if he was going to leave any one of them.

"Sergeant, set two fit men to each of the wounded and another to hoist their weapons. Tilly's men will be all over Hradcarny Castle and Prague by now. We'll go West by the sun and keep to the forest. They'll be watching the roads."

The zest with which the men complied made him realise that he had made the right decision. He found he cared little about Gray's strictures. These were his men. It gave him a warm feeling of comradeship, something he had not felt since he and Monro had set off for France together. He found he was smiling as he led the way deeper through the stands of oak and beech.

They heard men blundering around in the forest rather than saw them but coming into a clearing they found John Pentland sitting contemplating about ten hangdog looking men.

"You took losses, then?"

"Not dead," Pentland shook his head. "A cannon ball tore through the middle of our company and they ran. I doubt we'll see them again. God, John. It was frightening standing before that bombardment."

"But exciting too!" The wild light of battle still lingered in Hepburn's gaze. "Where is Dunbar?"

"He went with the remains of Sir James Seaton's men. Just as well. He would have done Gray an injury for not bringing up our cannon. Without them we had no chance."

"What will you do?"

"Find Gray I suppose, and you?"

"Same thing. I'm promised to him and when you think about it he pays both me and my men and we want our pay. Today we earned it, by God! Will you come with us?"

"Aye, John, but I've had enough. I'm stuck with Gray till I can bid him farewell, take the pay I'm owed and make for home. Ramsay's taken, and half the other officers. They were caught in the thick of it. Happen I'll join my brother at the law after all."

"What happened to the King?"

"He left after their first salvo. He's fleeing north, so Dunbar said, most of my men with him, I should think."

"My guess is Tilly's troops will head that way too. If we slip away West to Pilsen we'll not be taken."

CHAPTER 11
Frankenthal to Alsace

His quarters in Pilsen were a step down from those in Prague. Billeted in the small upper room of the local tavern, he shared a hay-stuffed mattress with Pentland. Later, Harry Taylor and Andrew Falkes, English captains recruited by Gray on his way north from London, were crammed in to sleep on a palliasse beside them.

"Gray had to pay their ransom," Pentland told his friend. "I'll wager he raked them down for being captured."

The town was full to bursting with armed men who could barely communicate with each other. In some way, known only to himself, Sergeant Armstrong managed to billet his men within two roads of each other, "So's I can lay my hand upon them if the need arises, Sir," he explained to Hepburn. "Good work, Sergeant," Hepburn encouraged him, "but remind them there is to be no forcing of wenches and no stealing. They risk the rope if they're caught."

Whether it was his words or his sergeant's threats he was never sure, but it was not his men that Gray received complaints about. However before his soldiers had time to become bored a villager limped in having escaped from Loket, a nearby town built round a castle, to report that Imperialists were besieging them.

"Just the thing for you, Hepburn," Gray nodded in his direction. "Time you learned to skirmish."

Leading his company, with the messenger acting as their guide, John Hepburn came in sight of Loket's towering castle with its Romanesque rotunda, nestling in the bend of the river Ohre.

"See, Lord, how the river protects us except from the east," his guide pointed. "I swam it by night to find help. The Imperialists are drawn up on the other side."

Hepburn nodded thoughtfully. "What is their strength?"

"Two enemy companies and a cannon, Lord. Their foot soldiers wait for the cannon to splinter the gate. Then they'll kill us all."

"Two companies against one are poor odds, Captain." Armstrong looked doubtful.

But Hepburn's eyes shone with sudden excitement. "I have an idea, Sergeant."

He led the way deeper into the woods. The spreading leafless branches of great beech and oak trees were poor cover but eventually he found a stand of white pine. There his men dug themselves small shelters, breaking branches to make walls and roofs and piling moss on top. Even so it seemed a long cold night to Hepburn. He forbade fires so they ate what bread and cold meat they carried.

Just before dawn when the sky had lightened enough to let them see where they were going, he called them to order. Travelling as fast as he could they crossed the river to come back towards the castle from the East. There in the half dark, they stumbled on the cannon-pulling muleteers asleep in a sheltered dell with their mules.

Armstrong gestured and a rot slipped forward. The muleteers knew nothing, so silent was their approach. They lay, their throats cut, as the rest of the men came up on them.

"I'm glad you lot are with me!" Hepburn moved on where he could see the town walls with the Imperialists' cannon lined up on the great door-way. The heavy nail-studded wood was already splintered. It would not hold much longer. He whispered to Armstrong and the man nodded, to disappear for a moment.

"We're ready, Sir."

As he spoke the sun burst above the skyline behind Hepburn, flooding the area ahead as if it were a stage.

"Follow me!" Hepburn was up and away, his pike at the ready. The lethargic cannoneers, sleepily priming their cannon, died on Scots pikes. As they dropped, two men hammered out the prop that raised the cannon mouth and another lit the fuse. There was a roar and a cannon ball roared down the path into the main body of men waiting to burst through the gate. Chaos resulted. Men lay dying, blown to pieces, armless, legless, flailing around.

Into this poured Hepburn's men, well drilled, well organised and lethal. Push with the pike, step back and clear the point, push again, arm and leg together then retire. On and on they went, grunting with effort. Ahead of them a wild red haired giant led them, shouting encouragement.

With the sun in their eyes and unready to fight the Imperialists stood no chance. Their musketeers had not even loaded their muskets. They used them to beat their way to the river and swim across if they could. Many drowned. The river, Hepburn noticed, was running red and he realised that the deep colour was only partly due to the reflection of the rising sun.

The battle was over in half an hour and the great door of the town opened as townspeople poured out, to loot the bodies, toss them in a heap and escort Hepburn and his men in, in triumph.

"Nicely done, Sir," said Armstrong as he ordered his men and started to count the wounded.

"We'll leave those men who can't walk to be treated by the townsfolk. They are well grateful for this relief. Colonel Gray will send local soldiers to garrison the place. Our wounded can rejoin us when they are fit. My orders were to get back to Pilsen."

"The only thing he was pleased about was getting a cannon and the mules to pull it," he said later when he and Pentland were at dinner together.

"That's our Commander! Still you've fairly blooded your pike now. What did you think of it?"

"It was like I was born to it. All my training in France seemed suddenly worthwhile. I tell you, John, this is what I was raised for and no mistake. I can't wait for the next time."

However a couple of weeks later at the end of January 1621 Gray decided to withdraw. "We'll get out while the roads are still hard with frost. Then the cannon won't founder."

As they moved north, Hepburn recognised some of the villages they had marched through on the way to Pilsen. They were waste-lands now. Houses were blackened shells. Villagers had returned to live in lean-to huts but they were in rags and clearly suffering from the cold. No longer could Gray demand food for his troops. The villagers had none to give and looked at Hepburn's men with angry hopeless faces.

It took them almost a month to reach the Palatinate, Frederick's original Electorate. More men had died on the march. They seemed to take a virulent fever that made their breath rattle in their chests. Few recovered but Hepburn wondered how much of that was being compounded by lack of food. His company was down to half strength. Tod Armstrong had just two men under him now. Tam Learmonth the Rhymer was limping from a leg wound that had never healed properly.

"Ye'll be leaving me behind soon, Sir. I can see it." he muttered as John Hepburn inspected his depleted Company.

"We'll leave no man o' mine." Hepburn's voice was sharp. "The boores'd cut your throat soon as look at ye. You'll ride strapped to a cannon if ye canna' walk. Try for seeing the gates o' Frankenthal and a warm fireside and dinna' upset the rest o' the men with your silly visions."

It raised a chuckle but he could see they were all toiling and it was like an answer to prayer when the distant towers of Frankenthal appeared, shimmering in the morning mists.

"We'll be safe here at least," Gray said as they marched on with suddenly quickened pace. "Lord Essex has garrisoned the town. He'll be our paymaster. All officers will attend me when you have billeted your troops and I shall introduce you to him."

"More bloody English men," muttered Sergeant Armstrong, his arm still in a sling but determined to remain in charge. "The men are more used to rieving from them than sharing. It's what brought them here, think you!"

"Just add, "No fighting with the English," to the usual "No forcing of wenches and no thieving," and we'll do. With luck, we'll not be here long." Hepburn himself was thankful not to be on the move for even a short time.

They were in for a shock, however. Tilly had got there before them and was besieging the town.

Frankenthal, with it's high walls formed one of the main bastions of resistance to the subjugation of the Palatinate.

Tilly had invested the city with a small unit and pushed on towards the Upper Palatinate with his main force. As they came in view, Hepburn could see the cannon ranged against the walls and the puff of smoke and flame from the muzzles that came before the thunder of the shot reached their ears.

Hepburn rode up beside Gray. "If you send in our cavalry before those damned cannon can turn on us, Sir, my pikes will clear the rest out."

For once he and Gray were in agreement. Hepburn, returning to his company with a light in his eye shouted for his drummer to beat to arms and hurling their packs to the side his men readied themselves. Tired they might be from the long march, and hungry, but the prospect of battle invigorated the Borderers as it did their leader. Swinging off his horse and hurrying into his armoured helm with its green plumes he took his place at the head of his men. He found Pentland there before him, their colours in his hand. "I thought I might as well act as your ensign as my few pikes are joined with yours, John."

"We are honoured. I'll try not to make your day a hard one. Beat "Forward March" drummer!"

Then they were off. Mansfeld's cavalry passed them in a howling thunderous roar of sound and the clash of arms told them that they had reached the besiegers' cannon and were massacring the gun crews. The thunder of the guns stopped so suddenly that the silence was palpable. The screaming of wounded and dying men rose like a descant. The sound spurred the Scots like a wounded bird excites a cat. Hepburn had no need to shout for the charge. The drummer was already beating it but with a growl that seemed to come from a giant animal behind him he felt a surge impelling him forward. Their excitement was contagious: a minute more and they met their prey in a crash of arms that brought cheering men to Frankenthal's parapets. Then the killing began. But always ahead, his pike moving to and fro in deadly action was Hepburn's huge figure, his green plumes a rallying point for his men.

Dug in to await a long siege their opponents were in disarray. Their sconces were high on the castle side to protect them from bullets fired from the parapets. Now these earth walls trapped them and as his men poured into the ditches, Hepburn's pikes took deadly advantage.

"That was a nice wee action." Sergeant Armstrong paused beside his captain as the last of the besiegers were being led off the field, having thrown down their arms. "The men are making good their weapons and armour. Tilly has right good armourers. There'll be booty too I make no doubt."

"I'll not stop them. Form the men up in a bit and we'll march in. We'll get better billets if we're first."

There was little enough room for yet another army to squeeze behind those walls but somehow they carved out a small area for themselves where Gray's diminished regiment filled the houses, crowding the families in them but settling remarkably well.

"They're friendly folk," was Sergeant Armstrong's comment when his captain asked him how the men were. "We're better away frae the rest. The locals dinna' speak Scots and Borderers have little love for the English."

"The Earl of Essex and his men were here before us and they are off limits. Besides he's paying for our rations."

"That wee manikin! Robin they ca' him? His men love him like a brother for he shares everything with his men. He was yin o' King Jamie's favourites when he was young. Then when he had had enough, King Jamie married him off to a rich wifie who didna' take to him at all. So he went to the wars. They say he's happier with men."

Armstrong went off with a leer and Hepburn stood amazed that his sergeant should be so knowledgeable. He didn't doubt any of it and at dinner, later, sitting beside Pentland and Jamie Douglas, he found that their information was no different.

"Aye he's one of King Jamie's cast offs and no soldier. Like our revered leader he's never won a battle." Jamie Douglas chuckled but Pentland broke in, "At least Essex pays his men. If we join with him perhaps we'll see some money."

"Fine hope!" Hepburn's tone was cynical. "Gray says he is giving it to us in kind, but my men haven't got fat."

They were at dinner, Gray and Mansfeld at the top of the board on either side of the grig-like Essex. Lieutenant Colonel Ramsay drooped at Gray's side, their heads together and meat-rich bowls of cabbage and meat stew between them. In the middle sat the captains; the Scots, Hume, Douglas, Pentland and Hepburn sat opposite each other so they could talk.

Beside them the English officers swapped stories from home and beyond them the ensigns scrabbled for food like a litter of puppies.

But Hepburn felt caged behind those high stone walls. Waiting to be besieged again made him restive. "We should get out and away before Tilly returns. He'll do it properly next time."

His anxiety was catching. Mansfeld was also keen to move on. "I can't call on my supporters to raise funds or recruit more soldiers if we stay holed up here," he was saying to Gray and Essex at the top of the table. "We should go while we can, make for Alsace and winter there in their rich countryside while I recruit."

His financial argument overturned Gray's desire to stay at Essex's expense and once more the rag tag of an army marched out of Frankenthal into the bitter wind from the west.

Day after day they plodded on. Food was scarce and more men fell out and were left to die or be slaughtered by local villagers. John Hepburn piled his sick and wounded on ammunition carts.

"I trained them. They trust me. I'll not leave them! Sir," he told Gray when he remonstrated. "They'll soon be well enough to fight again, you'll see!"

At last they met the "Spanish Road" that carried troops to and from Spain to the Spanish Netherlands. Crossing it at dawn when no enemy forces were on the move, they soon reached the warm plains of Alsace.

Now they set up a more permanent camp and Mansfeld disappeared into Switzerland from where Protestant recruits swarmed to his standard and the officers were kept busy organising and training their newly full companies.

By offering to take the survivors that Gray had recruited in Scotland, John Hepburn kept his company mostly Scots.

April turned into May and training went on undiminished. News came in of a great battle at Wimpfen. "Tilly beat George Frederick of Baden-Durlach." Pentland shook his head. "He must have been trying to reach us, maybe hoped we would join him if he did."

In June, Christian, Duke of Brunswick-Wolfenbuttel, the Bishop of Halberstadt rode into camp ahead of his tattered cavalry regiment. In armour, stained and dented though it was, he was a great bull of a man with a voice that effortlessly reached everyone.

"Tilly took us at Hochst. God that man can fight! He had Cordoba with him, of course, or we'd have won. We'll need some recruits, hey Mansfeld. Any spare? And don't eat all those horses I see grazing. We'll need them to fight."

They took him to their hearts, men and officers alike.

"You wonder what sort of sermon he preaches," Pentland muttered to Hepburn one evening.

"Up and at them and the de'il take the hindmost!" Hepburn laughed. "I'd serve with him any day."

Isolated as they were they had little news of how Frederick's claim to his throne was progressing and it came as a nasty shock when in July that year of 1622 a royal messenger from Brussels brought Mansfeld and Brunswick the news that King Frederick no longer required their services.

The noise from the commanders' tent could be heard all over the camp, as the Bishop of Halberstadt's great roar echoed round the camp.

"That weak-kneed King! So Tilly got me at Hochst and wasted poor bloody Baden-Durlach at Wimpfen and all for nothing. He's wrong if he thinks the Hapsburgs will negotiate."

"Our King Jamie has been telling him that he will arrange all if Frederick stops fighting and agrees to parley." Jamie Douglas always seemed to be ahead with the news. "Mansfeld will feel the loss of Frederick's money. He gets a pittance from the Grey League, those Protestant rulers of South Eastern Switzerland, to keep the Valteline mountain passes between Spanish Lombardy and Hapsburg Tyrol safe from the Spanish. But that wee income'll scarce feed us all. He's a broken reed."

He underestimated his leader. A week later, Mansfeld called his officers together.

"We are employed by the Dutch Republic. They realise our worth. Mobilise your men. We'll do any further training on the march north"

CHAPTER 12
Fleurus and Bergen op Zoom

They looked very different from the odds and ends that had slipped out of Frankenthal six months previously. It took hours for the huge regiment to wind its way out of camp led by Colonel Gray, as usual in half armour and seated on a fine chestnut. Beside him rode Lieutenant Colonel Ramsay ahead of an ensign holding the regimental colours. Following them marched company after company of infantry, their captains on horseback leading them with an ensign also on horseback beside him. Standing in his stirrups to look both ways, Hepburn felt his heart swell with pride at the impressive sight.

He wore the same leather corselet over his shirt that his men did and his trews were stuffed into long, shining, brown thigh boots. His morion sported green plumes that made a dramatic contrast to his fiery hair. As the sun rose and the army sweated, he was thankful to be dressed light and marvelled at the discomfiture that his Colonel must endure to remain fully accoutred at all times.

Behind them Mansfeld accompanied the Bishop of Halberstadt who was riding a great war horse ahead of his fully recruited and remounted squadrons of cavalry. They were followed by teams of oxen pulling the heavy cannon. Trailing away into the distance shambled a vast assemblage of women, children, servants and other hangers-on that they had gradually acquired during the long camp and recruitment process.

Looking back at the huge cloud of dust behind them, John Hepburn was reminded of the miserable days when he had marched at the tail of Gray's regiment on its way to Prague. Now his men were smart and they looked well after living off the fertile lands of Alsace. He was eager to see the Low Countries.

Gonzalo Fernandez de Cordoba, the Spanish General, was equally eager that he did not. The Marquis de Spinola had sent him an urgent demand for help in the Netherlands. His orders had reached General Cordoba in the Upper Palatinate where he and General Tilly were subduing the last flickers of revolt. Well satisfied with the defeat of Count Durlach-Baden at Wimpfen he had been about to besiege Frankenthal, now the last major town still in Protestant hands. Mannheim and Heidelberg had fallen, Julich, that key position for any northerner trying to relieve Bohemia, had surrendered. Frederick in exile had dismissed his armies and was hopelessly dickering with the Hapsburg Emperor for a truce while desperately calling on his Royal relations in Denmark and Britain for help. Cordoba had hoped for a quiet winter.

It was not to be. Spinola's messengers were forceful. Mansfeld had been hired by the Dutch Republic to relieve his siege of Bergen op Zoom and needed to be stopped. The Dutch were massing to the east of Bergen. He had his full army investing the town and he did not wish to be caught between two Protestant forces.

Cordoba set his men to forced marches across the hilly country of the Ardennes. They were exhausted but they were well trained and they covered the ground fast enough to be able to face Mansfeld at Fleurus, a small town on the borders of the Netherlands, by August.

The Protestant commanders surveyed the field.

"Those bloody Tercio from Naples hold the right wing and block our road." The Bishop of Halberstadt looked grim. "They made short work of Durlach-Baden at Wimpfen so I heard."

"Perhaps we should wait for our cannon and pound them to pieces?" Mansfeld bit his thumb and looked thoughtful. Gray nodded. "Good idea. I'll get my men drawn up in companies ready to advance when the guns have done their work."

"For God's sake, man, do you want to stay till your beard grows white!" Halberstadt's nervous energy seemed to communicate itself to his horse which reared and whinnied. "Up and at them is what I say!"

He turned and raised his arm. As if impelled by a mighty wind his cavalry responded. Mansfeld and Gray just escaped to the side as the surge of horses and screaming men poured past, lances raised and then lowered.

"My God they've started the battle. What should we do?" Gray turned in alarm. The rest of the men stood as they had at the White Mountain, company by company awaiting orders.

"Move up slowly. We'll see how Halberstadt manages."

John Hepburn, ahead of his company stood like the rest.

"That mad Halberstadter is a bonny fighter." Armstrong stood beside him, his pike at the trail. "But see you, Sir, they've got musketeers in those trees over there and here too." He pointed and Hepburn saw the muzzle flashes directed into the flanks of the charging cavalry.

"The cavalry'll no' stand a chance if the musketeers are left to commit mayhem, Sir."

"You're right Sergeant." Hepburn rode forward to Gray.

"Permission to take my company to clear the woods on the right, Sir? Their muskets are wrecking havoc with the cavalry."

Gray looked doubtful but then nodded. "Off ye gang then. I'll send Hume to clear the west flank if ye're having success."

John Hepburn, already in half armour, was off his horse and fitting his casque as Gray finished speaking. This was a job for Scots if ever there was one. They flitted through the trees, silent death at the point of their half-pikes and on their daggers. Cordoba's musketeers found their long guns blocked by trees when they tried to face this new menace and using them as clubs was no defence against reivers armed with pike and dagger. They died and the firing stopped. Within the trees opposite, Hepburn saw Hume's white plumes and grinned.

"That gives the Bishop a free run at them, eh Sergeant?"

Halberstadt's first charge had been repulsed. The Tercio were crack troops and well dug in. Men and horses littered the field.

"We go again, men. I've scores to settle with these damned Catholic hordes!"

Five charges he led that day and at the last the Tercio gave way.

"The Bishop has broken through!"

Mansfeld rose in his saddle and waved. "Forward! March forward! We're through!"

The great army shepherded the Bishop of Halberstadt's cavalry through as Cordoba retired. They had taken serious losses and the ground they marched over was strewn with dying horses and men thrashing about and screaming.

"Leave them to the women!" Gray shouted. "They'll try to save ours and finish off theirs. We'll get the weapons off them at our next camp."

They moved on but it was clear that Halberstadt was seriously wounded. He swayed in his saddle and had to be supported by one of his men riding close.

As they reached flat land away from the battlefield, Mansfeld called a halt. The foot troops formed a square to protect the remnant of the cavalry and at its centre sat Halberstadt. His men had helped him off his horse and removed his armour. Hepburn could see that his arm was pouring blood and his face was ashen as the surgeons attended him.

"I cannot save your arm, Sir."

"Then take it off, man. I have to ride for Bergen tomorrow."

As the army looked on Christian, Duke of Brunswick-Wolfenbuttel, Bishop of Halberstadt, lay back and endured the amputation without a word. His men watched it, stony faced. The rest of the army marvelled.

"They cry him "The Mad Halberstadter," Sir" muttered Armstrong. "But he's a man to follow, right enough."

They rode north the next day.

Cordoba harried their rear but only managed to massacre the army of women and followers and capture the slower cannon.

Gray was for turning to retrieve them.

"Ye'll not get the men to turn now, Sir." Ramsay riding quietly beside him shook his head. "Just look at Hepburn, Hume and Douglas go! They're racing each other to be the first to attack Spinola."

"But the money I spent!"

Ramsay's tone was dry. "Better tell Hepburn and Hume to capture Spinola's armament then! They'll not turn back."

Gray's Regiment was making forced marches, their blood lust strong. Once Bergen op Zoom came in sight Hepburn could see it was strongly beseiged by Spinola's army who had dug trenches and thrown up sconces in great circles around the land side of the city while Spanish men-of-war blockaded it from the sea.

"Bergen is at its last prayers." John Hepburn, riding beside Gray as they came up upon the scene, turned urgently to his Colonel. "This is no job for the cavalry, Sir. We'll take them in a charge, will we not? My men are eager. We all are. There'll be no stopping them now."

He took Gray's nod as approval, swung off his horse, gripped his pike and shouted to his drummer to beat the charge. Other drums took up the refrain and the infantry moved forward to face the sconces and Spinola's trained forces.

"Capture their cannon for me!" Gray's shout followed him as he charged and a laugh caught in his throat.

"See that mad, red haired bugger go!" Hume, ordering his musketeers, turned. "Beat the charge drummer. We'll not let those Border reivers get ahead of us. Give them a volley of shot Sergeant, and charge you Swiss varmints! We'll be through before them."

Spinola was well dug in and his men veterans. They fought with dogged persistence, sconce by sconce. The dust rose as the sun heated up and the smell of blood and faeces and screaming death rose in a hot miasma.

"Think you that hell is like this, Andra?" Shoulder to shoulder Hepburn and Armstrong moved forward their pikes shortened to killing machines.

"Left foot forward and pousse wi' the pike. Back on the right and free it and step forward to do it again." Hepburn could hear his French sergeant's voice echoing in his ear and he obeyed it. Men reached for his bowel with their swords but the longer pike got them first and they died screaming. Hepburn no longer heard them. As ever he reached a quiet world of his own where there was just him, his pike, his sergeant at his side, and somewhere his men toiling and grunting as their weapons struck home.

They followed his green plumes, a great battering ram of pikes. Beyond him he saw Hume's white plumes as he wrought havoc and on the other side Douglas came up on a sconce and waved before he plunged into the melee once more.

Suddenly they were through. The opposition melted. Men were running. There was no more musket fire.

Hepburn turned. Hume and Douglas joined him, sweating and blood stained and when he looked down he saw he was in a similar state.

"Pentland is coming through in a more lady like fashion, I see." Douglas grinned. "He has Gray beside him and Ramsay. I think they are desperate to capture a cannon or two."

"Aye. The Colonel did say summat about that!" Hepburn grinned. "Reckon I forgot."

"Tell him ye were desperate to reach your new paymasters. He'll understand that." Douglas's dark smile was echoed by chuckles. Gray's priorities were well known.

As the army came together they took stock.

They had broken Spinola's hold on Bergen op Zoom and could see Spinola's officers organising the retreat of siege engines, cannon and equipment.

"Let them go." Mansfeld was clear. "We will not relieve the city. The Dutch are waiting to go in. We've done enough. We should move on and establish ourselves as part of the Dutch Republic's Army; get on their pay roll and receive the money they already owe."

Hepburn called for Sergeant Armstrong to gather his men. His company had taken losses. It appeared that almost a whole rot had been killed and there were many wounded. However once his men had been persuaded to stop looting the dead in the trenches he was surprised at how many were left. Hume and Douglas looked to have taken greater losses.

"It's the training makes the difference," Andrew Armstrong seemed to read his mind. "Ours are better able to use their weapons."

CHAPTER 13
To King Gustavus Adolphus

Hopes of a halcyon winter in Brussels partying amongst the great and the good at the Court in Exile were immediately dashed.

"King Frederick and his Queen have better use for their monies than our enjoyment." Douglas settled beside the other Scottish captains at their dinner. "We're for winter quarters in East Friesland. A long windy march East to a flat peasant-filled waste! It seems that their Lordling favours the Hapsburgs and needs to be brought to his senses."

"We have to charm him?" Pentland was incredulous.

"We have to make life so bloody awful for him that he never steps out of line again!"

Hepburn chuckled. "My men are good at that. They'll rieve him blind. If the Lordling has a single cattle-beast that is uneaten by the end of winter I shall be surprised. They'll be so delighted to co-operate with their orders, for once."

Friesland was as wet, windswept and miserable as Douglas had predicted. Hepburn's men were undaunted.

"Reminds me of home," Armstrong merely put more shirts on under his leather corselet and acquired a heavy cloak.

"Its aye easier to liberate a farmer frae his cows when there's a thick haar." Tod, his cousin, was proving adept at keeping the cooks able to supply the army with meaty stews. "This country is a challenge, Sir. There's few hills and trees so rieving is best done at night or when there's a right haar like today."

Hepburn hated the heavy sea mist. "It makes me uneasy to be hedged around with white nothingness," he confessed to Pentland one evening.

"There's no one to attack us, John. Spinola has his own problems. They say Louis of France has taken arms against him to clear the Valteline at last."

Winter gave way to spring but the better weather brought Sir Andrew Gray with bad news.

"Things are not going well. I'll not disguise it. When the Valteline became safe, the Grey League stopped Mansfeld's allowance and the Dutch no longer need us. I'm away home to recruit again. You lot are on your own."

"I'll not stay to starve." Hume was quick to react. "I'll away to the Dutch Republic Army. There's a commander there that said he'd take us any day."

"I'm for home with Pentland here." Douglas smiled across at his friend. "My men are all Swiss or French and they'll likely want home."

Pentland turned sadly to John Hepburn. "I'll miss you, John. We've seen much together but I'm for a warm law office and a wife and family. I came to make a fortune but it hasn't happened. Our Princess Elizabeth is further frae her Bohemian throne than ever. What will you do?"

Hepburn hesitated, frowning. "I don't know, John Pentland, and that's a fact. I've no doubt the Dutch Army would have me. Hume, Ramsay and I were all mentioned in despatches after Bergen so they ken my name. But they're a straight laced, Calvinistic lot and I don't want to find myself with another Uncle Edward as my Colonel. Besides, there's my men. They've fought for me, thieved for me and followed me. I'll not leave them leaderless."

Overhearing him, Gray paused on his way out of the room. " Gustavus Adolphus is still recruiting. Try Sweden. I made money there!"

A month later as he stood to attention before the huge Swedish King, John Hepburn hoped that Gray had offered good advice for once.

King Gustavus Adolphus, "Lion of the North", stood as tall as the young Scot but had clipped blonde hair above owlish eyes and the tendency to bulk that his thirty odd years had brought. He faced the slim young giant whose bright red hair luxuriated wildly down to his shoulders and a frown gathered.

Realising the challenge he could not avoid, Hepburn fell on one knee.

"Sire, I desire to serve you."

"Get your hair cut." The King's response was sharp. "I'll have no one in my army with hair longer than mine."

"At once Sire." Hepburn tried to sound keen.

"Humph!" Gustavus Adolphus turned away to talk to his fawning courtiers.

But Hepburn was back next day, his hair short under his steel morion and his men in the same order. It had taken most of the previous night.

"We've enough hair for mattresses for the whole damn court, Sir" Armstrong had two pike-men sweeping hair into sacks. "Will I sell it?"

"The lice would carry them away. But give it a try." Hepburn kicked a stray curl into the pile. Then as a thought came to him, "Exchange it for green sashes. The Swedes wear yellow. We'll wear green."

"Good men. Good order." Gustavus was impressed when they drilled for him next day. "But my men can shoot and use the pike. Can yours Captain?"

"A week, Sire! And we'll show you!"

"More long nights, Andra?" Tod Armstrong groaned.

"If ye want to eat regular, Corporal!" His sergeant's tone was crisp. "It's as well it's light late on, or ye'd be doing it by touch!"

John Hepburn would have seconded that remark. He was gambling his future and had no mercy. "Corporal Jock Elliot here has met a cousin who is Sergeant of Musketeers. He's joining our company to train ye as we did before and I'll be with you too."

"And that's all we need."

Hepburn's lips twitched but he ignored the whisper. "Get to it!"

They had marched north through Denmark, then taken ferries across to the Swedish mainland and marched again, Hepburn driving his men on despite their growling discomfort. His tooled armour had been sold for food as had his men's breastplates. They were down to buff jackets and pikes and badly in need of a decent meal. He knew there was no going back.

A week later when a very tired company paraded to demonstrate their ability to use musket or pike Gustavus realised he had found a kindred spirit and an answer to the growing mass of chaotic recruits.

"Train my Scottish soldiers and you can lead them!"

"I'll need your authority, Sire."

The King nodded. "You have it Lieutenant Colonel Hepburn! But mind, your promotion is temporary depending on your success!"

His new status was necessary. John Hepburn met downright hostility from the pampered younger sons of Scottish nobility who had arrived exhausted in Stockholm at the head of what turned out to be mostly their family's labourers. They'd survived the sea crossing to march across Sweden, their eyes bright with greed and an inflated opinion of their own ability to use a sword.

"Cannon fodder. Just cannon fodder!" was Sergeant Armstrong's pithy comment.

"We make them soldiers, Andra, or we die with them!"

The grizzled sergeant's face split with a wry grin. "Then I'll be away to alert Sergeant Elliot and we'll get our rot-masters amongst the men, whilst ye redd up those drooping lilies they cry officers, Sir."

"And that's insubordination, Sergeant!" Hepburn's shout followed him as he went but his heart sank as he sent messages for a general meeting of officers.

Titled sprigs of nobility were not inclined to obey a man off a farm in East Lothian. John Hepburn eyed their insolent disinterest and lost his temper. "Your useless men will run as soon as the first cannon ball rips a head off and the blood spurts. If you stand you'll die, for all your pretty sword work. You are indolent, greedy, children with about as much prospect in battle as a barnyard chicken under the knife!"

"Hear, hear!" The unexpected support came from an older man at the side of the room. Hepburn turned and he came forward. "Hector Menteith from Edinburgh! I led a company of musketeers in the Netherlands 'til my men died of plague and I brought the remnant East like you, Sir." He turned to face the room and his quiet voice carried. "Untrained we'll die! You may be sure of it."

They stood shoulder to shoulder as the room gradually became silent. Then Hepburn spoke. "The King wants a Scottish regiment. Believe me we'll do best together. The Swedes offer no respect to foreign troops they cannot understand. I shall expect you on parade tomorrow morning, a captain to each company of a hundred and twenty men with an ensign beside him. Those who do not take part will leave these barracks. I have the King's authority! Go now!"

He turned to his new ally as the other men shuffled out already grumbling to each other. "Thank you for your support. I'm in need of a lieutenant colonel of musketeers, Mr Menteith. Will you serve with me?"

The older man's grizzled moustache lifted in a grin. "Gladly, Sir! But I've few men left."

"My sergeants are sorting out likely musketeers and pikemen. You'll have a command by morning."

Monteith gave him a long quiet look. "I'll not bet against that, Sir."

That winter John Hepburn drilled and taught, marched and paraded. He forbade officers to drink and dice and the first captain to stroll late to parade was summarily discharged and put on a boat back to Scotland. The huge man with red hair was awesome in anger.

"I've found my trade," he said once to Andrew Armstrong and got a wry grin in return. Aware that time was limited his sergeant had not spared the men. Hepburn had seen Scots soldiers running the loupgarth with their fellows laying on whips as the offender ran between their lines. A soldier who turned up too drunk to march was sat on the wooden horse in the middle of the parade ground all one December day, his legs tethered beneath the sharp cornered block and tears of agony freezing on his cheeks. Some few took ship back home. Most knew they'd no welcome waiting and drilled. By Spring they were all trained fighting men. Hepburn, now in his mid twenties, was as strong as he had ever been, his lean weather-beaten face old for his years but his confident leadership a beacon for his men.

Gustavus Adolphus, unversed in the tactics of war, had invited Dutch army trainers into his camp. They were not popular with the Swedes but, encouraged by Sergeant Elliot, John Hepburn sought their advice and used their drills. By late spring all his men were equally adept with pike or musket. The musketeers could advance or retreat still firing with lines only six men deep in the Dutch fashion.

"Our thin lines are more mobile and less exposed to cannon ball. Sire." he said to the King on one inspection. "Your idea, I believe, as are our mixed companies of musketeers and pikemen."

"I did say that?" Gustavus Adolphus sounded dubious.

"The Dutch instructors assured me of it. Everyone admires your sagacity."

"A modern army, Hepburn!"

"Aye, Sire! Your Scots soldiers are ready for you to lead."

"Good work!" The King looked at the massed men with green sashes across their chests lined up company by company. Pikemen stood to attention on the right, musketeers on the left, captains to the fore with their ensigns behind them proudly displaying their colours.

"Twelve companies, Sire with all ancillary men and drummers."

"A complete Brigade of Scots!" Turning to the red haired giant at attention by his saddle-bow the King beamed. "You trained them. You'll have to lead them, Colonel Hepburn. I'll have your promotion posted today!"

"Aye, they're all saying thon yeller haired King canna' do anything without ye," Armstrong said as the men dispersed after their nightly training. "I'd keep an eye behind when ye walk the Swedish lines Sir!"

"Na. I'm not about to take other men's honours, Sergeant. I'm after leading my Green Brigade."

"They're simple folk, Highness," he had told Gustavus Adolphus in rapidly improving German. "They can't understand Swedish so they get into fights. Now they'll know to talk to men with green fairings."

"This also was my idea." The King nodded. "Of course, I will order your position in battle as I wish. My Yellow Brigade will hold the right wing, naturally."

"Those Swedes show us the way in battle? Aye right!" Tod Armstrong's tone was scathing.

"Dinna' worry. We'll win the battles when they run!" His bigger cousin grinned. "Just learn the Swedish for "step aside!" and ye'll do fine."

Hepburn, now the proud owner of a Colonel's coach as well as 380 thaler a year, was too busy looking for a second officer for his pikes to heed the bickering. None of his captains had enough experience for the promotion and he was loath to ask the King for a Swede. However one evening as he sat working a shadow fell over the reports for food stocks and sickness.

"John you great galumph. This is where you've got to. Any grander and you'll be bucking for King!"

Hepburn looked up, a grin splitting his face. "Jamie Douglas, old friend! As dapper as ever! I thought you'd gone home with Pentland."

"Aye I did and found cauld kale waiting. My mother had died, my affianced heiress had wed my brother and my father has turned old and sits by their fire. They were all so," he searched for the right word, "so self-satisfied. There was no place for me. I was desperate enough that when that rogue Gray turned up recruiting I rejoined and we took a thousand vagrants back to the Netherlands where he found no sponsor and left the whole lot to die in hovels set up on the beach. Luckily my father knows Lady Livingstone who fostered our Princess Elizabeth and I had letters from her to the Queen in exile so I put my best jacket on and did the pretty and she made me equerry to King Frederick."

"You landed lucky!"

"I landed unpaid! So when he sent messages to the King of Sweden I said I knew the quickest way and he believed me."

John Hepburn was laughing by then. "It's your air of superiority Jamie. It used to annoy me so much till I realised the ignorance it covered!"

"Well, I've been hearing of this great red haired Scottish lout that only King Gustavus Adolphus can control and suddenly I remembered seeing you at work at Bergen and all became clear. For God's sake, John, employ me. I'll take a company, I'll take a rot, I'll sweep the bloody floor but unless someone pays me I am going to die of hunger dressed in court clothes."

Hepburn heard the desperation under his old friend's light tone. He noticed the lined cheeks and overlarge finery. He held out his hand. "Welcome to the Green Brigade, Jamie. You'll be on the payroll this night."

"I'll need to retrain, Colonel. I'd not want to seem favoured."

"You'll start tomorrow. The King orders every officer to be able to lead musketeers or pikes or cavalry. It'll be hard work. I canna' spare ye!"

"I'd not want it, Colonel." He turned back at the door. "Is that old cattle thief Armstrong still with ye?"

A delighted grin lifted Hepburn's moustaches. "Aye and we've a Sergeant Elliot of the muskets who's a cousin of Wee Jock! You'll maybe even find a few more that you know. Tell them I sent you to learn the new way and they'll see you right."

Through the next weeks he was amused to watch his old comrade gain ascendancy over his officers.

"He charms us all," Menteith murmured one evening as they sat together. "He doesn't brag or bully. He just makes people look to him. It's as well he reveres you, Sir."

"Douglas! Reveres me? You jest!" But the older man shook his head. "See the way he leaps to your order. There's none quicker and the others follow his lead. You'll need another lieutenant colonel for your pikes, Sir. I'd grab him before some Swede offers him promotion. He's popular about the court, I hear."

Hepburn found Sergeant Armstrong of much the same opinion. "He's more experience than those well trained puppies, Sir. Besides he'll tell ye the court gossip right enough and that's no' bad thing."

So when Gustavus Adolphus appeared like a bear with a sore head, found fault with the meticulous Green Brigade line up and drank deeply with his Swedish commanders afterwards Hepburn, bewildered, turned to his new lieutenant colonel.

"What's up with the King then? He's no drinker!"

"You haven't heard?" Douglas shook his head. "Queen Eleanore had a stillborn son. She insisted on reviewing the Navy in a squall and fell. Those German princesses are aye poor breeding stock."

"What for did he marry her, for God's sake?"

Douglas grinned. "She was right sonsy and all over him. Now she's fat with sweetmeats and favours queer dwarfie men at court."

"No wonder he's crotchety." Hepburn shook his head. "I'd better give his thoughts a new turn."

He found Gustavus Adolphus sitting alone at the head of the table where his officers had dined with him, a half empty wine glass by his hand.

"I did not ask you in to my presence, Colonel Hepburn." His tone was cold.

Hepburn's momentary fury subsided as he saw the misery in the King's face. He kept his tone up-beat. "Your pardon, Sire, but if you wish to give your encroaching Polish cousin Sigismund a bloody nose my

Green Brigade is ready."

"My encroaching cousin, Sigismund! By God that was well put! You were right to remind me." Gustavus Adolphus rose to his feet, if unsteadily, and leaned on the table. "Call my commanders, Colonel Hepburn. The ships are ready. Why waste the summer weather. We'll sail for Poland as soon as the wind sets fair!"

Sail they did, dozens of little boats, clattering along through the spray driven by the prevailing west wind.

"Aye it's a bonny sight!" Sergeant Armstrong was leaning over the rails peering ahead where already he could see a break between sea and sky that promised land.

"All the better for being above decks?" Hepburn teased.

"You're not wrong there, Sir!" Tod Armstrong joined them. "I've got the men coming up in relays. They'll arrive ready to fight that way."

He was right, and Hepburn felt a fierce pride as his Brigade disembarked in good order and marched past.

Towering above them mounted on his great grey, Gustavus Adolphus felt a surge of pleasure to have escaped the tears and hysterics of his women folk. His saving grace had been escape to Ebba Brahe's house. She had been his childhood love, the Swedish gentlewoman he would have married if his mother had allowed it.

He came back to the present with a shock, realising that John Hepburn had been talking for some time.

"Good men! Good order! We'll make camp and plan the campaign tonight. Make sure all my officers are in attendance." Wheeling his horse he rode off to meet the Swedish soldiers then disembarking.

Hepburn looked round to where Lieutenant Colonel Douglas stood.

"Do you think he heard a word I said about pay and conditions for the men?"

Douglas laughed. "From the far-away look in his eye I guess he was running his goodbyes through his mind."

"Not with the Queen, then. She's still prostrate."

"Exactly so!" Douglas grinned. "Kings have opportunities we only aspire to."

CHAPTER 14
War in Poland

"Your Brigade's mustered, Sir!" Sergeant Armstrong came to attention where Hepburn, mounted on a heavy shouldered chestnut, was letting the sun make a glory of his shining breastplate under the golden chain denoting senior rank that he delighted to wear. "It's right bonny country with all those pine trees and no hills."

Jamie Douglas rode up beside them. "At least we're not trailing those monster cannon Gray had. Have you seen Colonel Sandy Hamilton's wee leather cannon, as he calls them?"

Hepburn smiled. "Dear Sandy! Aye. I visited his workshops in Sweden. He gave me several to try. One man can carry them but put three together and we'll have a salvo that will surprise the King's cousin Sigismund."

"They're not just leather are they?"

Hepburn grinned. "My very question! No they're iron right enough, but thin tube bound with copper wire and the leather cover shrunk on the top. I've seen them in action, James, and they'll not burst. "Dear Sandy" gave me his word."

"He would though, wouldn't he!" Douglas laughed shortly. "I'll be well ahint ye when you set them off."

Nidorp, a small castle within a walled city, offered the first resistance. But once their cannon had breached the walls the Swedes were through like ravening wolves led by a whooping Gustavus Adolphus on his great grey. John Hepburn moved his men in behind to support the mad advance so that the King could safely wave his sword in triumph as his soldiers ransacked the town.

"Spare the burghers Sire." Hepburn had his Scots under tight control. "They'll be better disposed towards us."

"They did not capitulate! Now they pay the price. Dorpat will treat, you'll see! Oh! My Swedish troops are magnificent."

But Dorpat did not treat. All morning the Swedish cannon roared. John Hepburn, seeing a side gate splinter, headed a killing formation that powered through the breach, his half pike in his hands. His ensign, Alexander Hay, a stocky Aberdonian, strode firm behind him, their colours high as the men followed the path their colonel was cutting. Jamie Douglas, breathless and blood-spattered, kept up, his men screaming defiance behind him. Hepburn's half-pike struck again and again. Beside him he could hear his sergeant grunting as he wrenched his weapon free. They fought their way to the main gate, taking the soldiers there in the rear.

"Get the gates open Sergeant Armstrong. It's time to let the rest in! We've done the work!"

Gustavus Adolphus astride his war horse and in half armour galloped in ahead of his running infantry, their yellow sashes mingling with the green already there.

It was enough. The castle commander lowered his flag and capitulated. The king, himself, received his sword.

"He'll get a grand lot of ransom for those fancy officers," Tod Armstrong muttered to his cousin. "It should be ours. We did the work."

"The colonel will see that we get our share, Tod. You'll see. He's aye fair that way. Not like some of the other commanders."

But John Hepburn was in no mood for being approached. In his fury he had barely contained himself from attacking the Swedish colonels clustered around their King, bottles of wine in their hands, drinking toast after toast to each other. He burst through their ranks, half pike still dripping blood in his hand and his sweat stained face twisted in anger.

"Your bloody Swedes slaughtered everyone in that seminary in the town, Sire! How could you let them! I've just dug three huge graves and we shovelled in young children and priests with not one weapon between them. They ran this way and that and your men laughed and speared them and clubbed them to death. Little children still held their bigger brother's hands as they lay, their throats cut. My men wept as they buried them. God wept with them, Your God and mine, Sire! How could He not?"

"Damned Catholics! They were damned Catholics!"

"They were unarmed children, Sire!"

"Well go and get pardoned by some priest we've let escape then!" Gustavus Adolphus shrugged. "I'd forgotten you were one of that accursed lot."

"I am a loyal soldier of Your Highness as I have proved today. I kill your enemies, Sire, and I do not enquire their religion before I dispatch them, but I do not kill children, be they Catholic or Protestant. It is an abomination!"

"I had no hand in it. You have no right to address your commander thus!"

Too late Hepburn started to stammer an apology. The King turned his shoulder and rode off.

Later that evening after Gustavus Adolphus had basked in the wine-flown admiration of his senior officers at their celebration dinner, he turned to his Green Brigade colonel, the one man still upright.

"You do not drink with us, Colonel Hepburn?"

"My admiration for your Majesty needs no wine." Hepburn's gold–red moustache rose in a lopsided grin as honesty broke through. "Tell the truth, Sire, I prefer a long Leipzig beer after a hard day."

"Still against me?"

"Never, Sire!" John Hepburn's quiet tone carried conviction. "I would follow you to Hell and beyond and fight for you all the way."

Gustavus Adolphus was mollified. "I'll forgive the way you spoke. You were battle-weary but right to bring it to my attention. I'll make them love me by endowing a University with their ransom monies. Now I can sleep easy? Eh?"

John Hepburn bowed his head. "They'll revere the "Lion of the North", for ever, Sire."

"Then let's to bed." The King rose stiffly. "It was work, hard work, eh? But in future keep the rowel of your Catholic conscience for yourself, Colonel!"

"For Christ's sake, John, you don't bring kings to book!" Jamie Douglas, beside him at table, almost wrung his hands. "First thing they tell you as a diplomat is crawl to the buggers. He'll hate you now. You'll see!"

"I fair lost it!" John Hepburn blushed. "It was my red hair talking. My sister Marie said it would be my ruin. But the man's a berserker Viking and his Swedes just savages! I worry for Selburg!"

But Selburg capitulated.

"Wise men!" Gustavus Adolphus was in a good humour, riding amongst his Swedish officers. "I'll leave some of you here and move straight on to Duneberg before the snow comes."

"What did I tell you," Douglas muttered when the Scots were ordered to attack. "He'd like to see you fail, Colonel, that or dead. Duneberg Castle was built to last by damned Livonian knights four hundred years ago!"

But the old walls did not withstand the Scottish Brigade. The green sashed warriors poured through a breach to engage massed Polish pikemen. Foot by foot, inch by inch, the Scots pikes pushed on, following John Hepburn, his green plumes high above the fray and his drummers behind him beating the charge. Jamie Douglas followed those plumes, his pikemen thrusting forward as if at drill and Lieutenant Colonel Menteith, left to command the musketeers, pushed hard behind to clear the battlements and shoot down on the remaining resistance.

Gustavus Adolphus received the Polish commander's sword from a blood covered, kneeling John Hepburn and waving it above his head led his rapacious Swedish troops in to the castle.

But the King, unwilling to admit it, had learned.

"Any man found looting will be hung! See to it Colonel Hepburn!"

"Right, Sire!" Passing the order to frowning Swedish colonels, he returned to where Douglas and Menteith sat their horses looking for orders. "For God's sake keep the men in tight formation. The King means to winter here and we don't want to foul our own nest."

"No more booty, Sir?" Sergeant Armstrong sounded fed up.

"None, Sergeant! For God's sake you've already looted the Castle blind and I didn't stop you! Leave the townsfolk be."

"Aye, Sir. I hear ye!" Armstrong sighed and turned to his men. "Ye'll obey the Colonel or I'll shoot ye myself."

"The King might have said thank ye!" Tod Armstrong nursed a pike wound to his upper arm.

"Get that arm seen to." His big cousin pushed him towards the rear. "The surgeons are that way. The Colonel will get us the best billets and the Swedes'll have to bury that lot in the castle while we are getting a good dinner."

They wintered comfortably in a corner of the town where there had been little fighting and the houses were comfortable and windproof. His men had amassed an amazing amount of loot from the bodies littering the castle forecourt where most of the fighting had occurred, armour, shirts, leather corselets to say nothing of silver gilt helmets, pikes, halberds and muskets. Through the winter they bartered these.

"It keeps them happy and out of trouble, Sir." The two Sergeants, Elliot and Armstrong, drilled them every day. "They'd be bored otherwise and they'd forget how to load and fire as quick as they do now. It gives them less time to get into trouble wi' the lassies too"

"Aye keep them at it." Hepburn had troubles of his own. Gustavus Adolphus was crotchety.

"He aye has to be at something, the King." Douglas and he had gone hunting. The ground was hard but there were deer if you could get near them and Jamie Douglas had acquired two deer-hounds, from where Hepburn did not seek to inquire.

"For once I wish the Queen was with him. She kept him off our backs."

"You mean while she lies on hers?" Douglas suggested crudely.

Hepburn chuckled. "You put it well. But you're right. She must be over that last miscarriage. I'll suggest he sends for her."

"And her ladies in waiting!" Douglas rubbed his hands. "I've a fine new coat with fur about the collar. Who knows, I may meet an only daughter whose father owns a Barony."

"War's no place for wives, Jamie. One day I'll make my own fortune."

The King was delighted. "Fine idea, Colonel Hepburn. See to it!"

From the moment Queen Eleanor arrived in a state coach with so much luggage that Hepburn wondered how they would fit it into the castle, the town partied.

"I hope this isn't Prague before the White Mountain disaster!" Hepburn avoided most festivities by overseeing the refortification of the castle and mending the town wall. But even he commissioned a dark green velvet coat with gold facings.

By spring the Queen was again with child and Gustavus Adolphus was beside himself with delight.

"She must go back to Sweden, Hepburn. This time there will be no mistakes."

"I'll approach your Swedish Commander at once, Sire. The Queen shall have the best of care."

"God, I don't envy them." he muttered to Jamie Douglas as he courteously waved his hat in farewell to the soldiers accompanying coaches of complaining dwarfs and ladies in waiting. "The Balls were bad enough! All those little nightingales hopping about just made me nervous."

"Aye, right!" Douglas hesitated. "Don't take it amiss if I say you've more assurance than any here except the King who knows he is always right."

"Oh wheesht!" Hepburn laughed.

"He can do little without ye John and that's a fact."

"Long may it continue."

"I'd rather be a Baron in Sweden!"

"Not me! Marry a woman who holds the purse strings like my mother!" He shuddered.

Only Sergeant Armstrong was aware that his colonel was well content because he had engineered it.

"Cathy's a widow woman, Sir," Armstrong had pushed her into John Hepburn's billet one freezing day soon after they had arrived in Duneberg. "She's by way of being an Armstrong through her mother and I found her in a bad way, Sir, for she hasna' eaten since her man died at Dorpat."

Hepburn looked at the skeletal figure in a black shawl that cowered rather than stood before him and shook his head.

"What do ye expect me to do for her, Andy? I'll gladly give her some money for food."

"Na. She's not wanting charity. I thought ye could use a lass to cook and clean and keep your armour bright. All the other colonels have servants. Ye've only got that useless pikeman frae Haddington, Tam Watnoun."

John Hepburn felt a grin forming. Tam was a relative of his old farm hand but Armstrong was right. He was no servant for an officer. He wasn't much of a soldier either.

"Tam might well use some help."

"My very thought, Sir."

At first too shy to even speak to him, she blossomed with the food he insisted she ate. Now he returned to a warm room and a pint of Leipzig beer and in the morning he could hear her singing as she set the fires and made his breakfast. It took a month for him to charm her into falling in love and when she did, his happiness seemed complete.

Once the Queen and her ladies had gone, Gustavus Adolphus was full of vigour and plans for attack so Hepburn produced his charts. "See, over to the west of Courland is that great flat plain they call Semigalicia, Sire. I am told that the East side is marsh land with few roads." His finger moved. "I thought you might wish us to move right through and cross the river Vistula to the good farm land beyond, cut our trenches and wait on your cousin, King Sigismund. It is a long march but we'd be there by midsummer and ready for him."

The King rubbed his hands. "My very thoughts, Hepburn! I'll see my Commanders one by one and tell them. Make them understand, hey? Then we'll set off."

They were not a moment too soon.

CHAPTER 15
Pitched Battle with Sigismund

"They're hard men!" Sergeant Armstrong was as usual at Hepburn's right hand as he rode out to reconnoitre the huge Polish army that was gathering against them.

"Bigger the squares, greater the damage one cannon ball will wreak." Hepburn was concentrating on their fortifications. "Look yonder on the right? We'll need to extend that ditch and sconce. I want to hide musketeers on their flank and have our old friend Count Thurn's cavalry lurking behind them where the Poles can't see them." He turned away satisfied. "We're as ready as we'll ever be. Hurry up Armstrong, lad. Don't lay your lugs in your dish the day. You'll not want to be caught short tomorrow."

The great square blocks of men moved into place against them the next day, just as they had done at White Mountain. Russian Cossacks, their chain mail and steel caps shimmering in the morning sun, moved into position on the flanks supported by horsemen sporting Turkish style helmets with tail-jointing. John Hepburn could hear the jingle of their harness as they trotted.

"What a sight!" Gustavus Adolphus surveying his military placements, shook his head.

"Pity they'll none of them be writing home, Sire!" Excitement shone from Hepburn like sunlight through a cloud. "We're going to murder them, today."

The King's face broke into a smile. "Our new tactics will work? I shall win?"

"Indeed you shall, Sire, and win so well that I warrant men will sing about you for ever as the Lion of the North."

The Swede seemed to warm himself at the fire of his companion. "We go then. Give the word, Colonel Hepburn! Cannons to fire at will."

Hepburn turned and galloped down the line. As he went he heard the roar as the great Polish cannon belched fire and the "swoosh" as a ball passed behind him.

"Our cannon are lighter. They will not bear yet, Colonel!" Tortennson, Gustavus Adolphus's chief cannoneer, shook his head at the order. Hepburn rose in his stirrups to look. "They will soon. See they advance already. I must get back. Fire at will, then. You know better than I when that is." He was away on the word and the Swedish colonel, smiling grimly, turned to watch the advancing hordes with narrowed eyes. His guns were loaded and primed, their angle set to their furthest trajectory. He had marked the ground himself. As the huge squares of marching men reached his marker he lifted his arm. As one, matches were lowered to the touch-holes and the roar shook everyone to momentary immobility. Then the gunners were at it, reaming, priming and loading to fire again. The noise was devastating but the carnage Gustavus Adolphus's guns was exacting was a complete riposte to those who had advocated heavy cannon.

The tattered Polish squares marched on. Pikemen kept their pikes at the ready. Musketeers paused to fire then stood aside to let the next rank move forward into the firing line. Men began to fall in the Swedish thin lines but the gaps were always filled.

The Swedish lines looked fragile. Each company of a hundred and twenty six men was now made up of seventy two pikemen with their corporals and rotmasters drawn up only six men deep and beside them fifty four musketeers, massed similarly, as advocated by the Dutch military experts. In front of each company their ensign held their colours high and before him stood their captain, both standing before their pikemen to allow their musketeers a free field of fire. On their wings lurked cavalry.

"God, I hope they stand the assault of those huge squares!" John Hepburn muttered as he rode back to his brigade.

"They can have no strength!" Sigismund, on horse-back with his general staff around him, turned in delight to his second-in command. "First we'll slaughter their centre section then the wings will be easy meat. We'll show that damn Swede who should be King."

Once behind his lines, Hepburn leapt from his horse, threw the reins to young Watnoun and grabbing the half pike the young man held out, marched forward to the head of his men.

Ensign Hay had his colours well on display. If he looked pale his colonel could forgive him. It was his first real action. Behind him Sergeant Armstrong nodded dourly.

"We're ready, Sir!"

There was a mailed hand raised in answer that gave his men a lift of heart. A frisson of the wild excitement their leader felt coursed through their veins.

"Aye he's a mad bugger." Tod Armstrong muttered as he shifted his grip on his pike ready for the order to move. Along the lines Hepburn could see his captains and lieutenant colonels standing firm ahead of their companies, swords in the hands of the musketeer officers, pikes at the ready in the rest. Over to the left he got a wave from an armoured man on horseback and knew that Count Thurn, now landless but still fighting for the Protestants, was also ready. Far on the right he could see Gustavus Adolphus, riding into position in front of his Swedes.

Lieutenant-Colonel Menteith raised his sword and the whole line seemed to sigh with the sibilance of a striking snake. The Polish squares were in range. Front rank musketeers sank to one knee, the second rank bent and the third stood high.

"They surrender. Look they kneel." Sigismund turned to his staff a smile dawning. Their transfixed gaze made him turn back.

"Fire!" Hepburn's bellow was echoed down the line. A huge volley, three lines deep shattered the approaching squares, already shredded by the cannon. The next three rows of musketeers were already moving forward into position.

"Fire!" and another shattering blast hit the Poles. Then the Scots were off racing across the empty field to hurl themselves on the tattered ranks ahead. Pikes bit deep, turned and withdrew to bite again.

141

In half armour and great leather thigh-boots, his green helmet-plumes as much a marker for his men as their flag, Hepburn led his yelling men into the Polish squares, "Forward pousse! Turn and retire the weapon! Pousse again!" His voice bellowed his old French King's Guard Sergeant's orders and his arms obeyed while his mind assessed the battle progress unaffected by the screams and bloody carnage around him. .

Sigismund unleashed his cavalry. Now the pikes faced mounted men. Horses went down, their hooves thrashing. Pistols exploded in his ear. None touched him. Along the line he could see his musketeers, some using their guns as clubs some with their swords out doing killing work. Behind him the Scottish pikes bit deep.

"Now, Thurn, now!" His yell rang out.

As if he had heard the order, the Swedish cavalry moved forward, circled the wild melee and gathering speed took them in the side, slicing through the last of the squares and hurling themselves on Sigismund's reserves.

The Poles broke and ran. It was the end of the battle. Prisoners were taken and jealously guarded for their ransom money. Soldiers strayed about picking up pistols, swords, anything of value, and joining them, the rag-tag baggage train of women who followed their men stripped the dead.

"Naked we come into this world and naked we leave it." Gustavus Adolphus's minister looked up at Hepburn from where he knelt to close the staring eyes of a man who had stood not an hour ago to receive a blessing. Further over, Hepburn could see the purple bands of a priest performing the same duty.

"Be quick, Sir," Hepburn murmured as he passed him. "We shall be putting them underground as soon as I can raise a burial party." He turned to find Armstrong at his elbow. "I've got ye a dozen or so Hollanders, Sir. They dug our sconces in no time. Ye'll need to give them extra wages like, but a few pistols to sell would do it, I reckon."

"It's a start, Sergeant. Get Lieutenant-Colonel Douglas to go round the rest of the officers and ask them for help. We'll not wait till they smell. It's a knacker's yard enough as it is,"

"Winning aye has its down side, Sir, though the booty is better." Armstrong seemed as unhurt as he was.

At dinner that evening Hepburn spoke across the carousing Swedish colonels.

"All your ideas worked, Sire. The lighter cannon, the thin lines, and then the shattering volley before the charge were magnificent."

"I am not sure you did not suggest that Colonel Hepburn."

"If I did it was because Your Highness put the idea into my mind."

"Quite right, I expect I did." The King sat back, well satisfied. "You have been most useful, Colonel Hepburn. Get your men into barracks for the winter. Remember no slacking! Keep them in training. I shall return to Stockholm where the Queen must be close to her time, but when I return we'll have a Prince to fight for, you'll see."

Hepburn bowed. "We'll look for your return, Sire."

CHAPTER 16
Dirschau

Through the winter Hepburn kept his veterans and the new recruits that poured in from Scotland hard at it, training. Pikemen learned to cast ball, fire muskets and even ride. Musketeers were taught to ride and wield pikes. Already they could load and fire faster even than the Dutch who were reckoned the best in the world.

"The men's not a problem," Armstrong muttered at the end of a long day when things had not gone well. "It's those officer-bodies, Sir. They're unco' full o' themselves and they dinna' like each other much."

Jamie Douglas, overhearing, agreed. "If I have another bloody ensign or captain tells me he should stand above someone else for his father owns more land, I'll do him an injury, John. So I will."

"Scottish pride is an awful thing!" Hepburn grinned at them. "Why for are you not trying it on with me, Jamie?"

"Aye right! And get my teeth to play with!"

Armstrong chuckled. "Maybe we should send them out on skirmish, Sir. There's nothing like real action to weld men."

At first Douglas, Hepburn or Menteith led. But once blooded, Hepburn sent two captains, each leading a half company, on sortie. Bivouacking on icy ground, keeping their men fed and defending each other under attack proved highly successful. Captains who could hardly speak to each other came back good friends.

"They're bringing in useful news as well. Sigismund is garrisoning the towns all the way to Danzig. The longer we wait the harder we'll have to fight."

Then fever broke out amongst the men.

"It goes like this, Sir," Armstrong reported. "If the fever disna' break they die, otherwise they just get better, though they've lost a lot o' flesh and they're no able for marching far."

The Brigade surgeons purged the men and prescribed herbs without effect. Each day there were burials.

"We'll lose half the men unless the King gets back. What does he think he's doing? He's got his heir now!"

Word had come that Gustavus Adolphus had a son. The Swedish troops were drunk for a week. As they nursed their aching heads a second message arrived announcing a daughter.

"No one knew for a week, not even the King, apparently." Douglas as usual had all the news. "They say she's a dark funny little thing but the King is delighted and is making the Riksdag name her his heir. He's called her Christina after his mother."

Gustavus Adolphus was in high spirits when he eventually returned.

"We'll drive my encroaching cousin out of Poland, Eh Colonel Hepburn? My Swedish commanders report full readiness. I hope your Scots are as prepared."

"We have trained all winter, Sire, doing just what you ordered. Every man can take any part on a battlefield."

"Good thing! I'm glad you haven't been spending your time at confession or whatever!" The Swedish colonels round about the King sniggered. John Hepburn merely smiled. He was getting used to his King's humour.

"Been getting new armour from Padua, I see. He'll out shine us all if we're not careful, eh?"

"No one can equal your Highness in battle. I can only follow your lead, Sire."

"How do you put up with it, John?" Douglas, beside him ground his teeth.

"You told me not to bite the hand that feeds me!" Hepburn went off chuckling. "I'm just thankful to be mobilising."

Men and cannon set off over the plain. The wind by the end of March was still keen but the snow had melted and the army turned the fields to black mud.

"They'll not be growing much where we've been without a right ploughing and harrowing." Armstrong was looking back at the devastation their track had left.

"At least there'll be men in the villages to do it." Hepburn had been rigorous in enforcing his rule of no interference with the local people. "They'll welcome us and not the opposition. Sigismund's lot don't care who they slaughter."

They followed the Vistula east towards Dirschau, a small fortified town.

"Good place to bivouack, Colonel Hepburn. Strong Teutonic castle but once we're in the town I don't doubt they'll treat." Gustavus Adolphus was in high spirits as he jingled along on his great war-horse. The fashion was for long spurs with huge rowels that contained metal beads that tinkled. Hepburn had them too and loved the music that attended his every stride.

However something of those Teutonic Knights persisted in Dirschau. They wasted three months besieging the town and it took a brisk battle at the end to take the citadel.

Afterwards, Hepburn was appalled to find his King being treated by the surgeons.

"Ach, I expected my Swedes to be fleeter of foot in the charge, Hepburn. When I turned they were nowhere and some wretched Pole shot me in the back."

"The ball passed behind his scapula, Colonel and is lodged by his spine." The surgeon was sweating. "I dare not probe for it there. I might paralyse him."

"Because he is the King or because it is in an impossible position?"

"The second. We will have to hope his body discharges it in time."

"He should have had us behind him," John Hepburn said to Douglas later that day. "It was a bonny fight and our men keep up with me!"

"Scotsmen after booty! If you were not so large, John, they'd trample you under in the rush."

Hepburn went off laughing but his mind was troubled. They could not afford to lose Gustavus Adolphus.

"He has the good will of all the Protestant crowned heads. We'd be poorly placed without him," he confessed to his two lieutenant colonels later. "We'll need to be watchful. The Swedes are awful prone to run home if things turn sour. They've not far to go either. I've got five countries and nowhere to rest when I get there." He twirled his luxuriant golden-red moustache into place as he often did when thinking. "Nor was he best pleased to see me scatheless either."

"Better limp then next time you get an audience." Douglas's eyes twinkled in mischief.

"Aye or your arm in a sling." Menteith was openly chuckling.

Two days later they were less amused.

"The King wants me to relieve Mewe. He's offered me three thousand infantry and Count Thurn with five hundred horse."

"But word is that Sigismund has thirty thousand troops besieging it!" Menteith was horrified. "You have offended His Majesty, Colonel. He does want you dead!"

"He's right though. We need to relieve Mewe to unlock the path to Danzig. While Sigismund besieges the town unchallenged he can turn his guns on us as we pass and harry our flanks. We'd better reconnoitre tomorrow. I'm not going to throw away men I've spent sweat on."

The three men rode out together, reaching high ground screened by trees, with the morning sun pouring onto the siege works around Mewe. From where they sat their horses Hepburn could see the distant towers of the castle. The local guide he had taken with them pointed. "The town is held in the embrace of two rivers, Lord, our own Vistula on the right is joined by the Versa. It is said that King Sigismund has trenches beyond the rivers preventing access to the rear of the town."

"And his main force sits right in front of us, plugging the easy approach!"

Hepburn's eyes travelled over the foreground. "Batteries of cannon on either side of the main approach, masses of infantry bivouacking in the fields and look Jamie," he pointed, "cavalry lines as far as you can see. Prince Udislaus has his whole regiment."

"You'll founder on a direct charge."

"I agree." Hepburn looked around him thoughtfully. "One thing is certain. With the two rivers where they are they can only deploy a certain number of troops at any one time or they'll fall off that triangle of land into the water."

"Aye, but they can field one unit at a time for long enough to kill every one of the men you lead against them!" Menteith shook his head.

Again Hepburn looked up at the sky. "Looks like a cloudy night, maybe even rain and now that September is in, the nights are lengthening. I may have an idea."

"Will we be dead too, John?" Douglas was only half joking.

"No, Jamie! Unless you trip over your pike and spit yourself. Trust me."

"The devil of it is that I do trust him," Douglas said to his fellow lieutenant colonel that night. "He's a daft chiel but he never wastes a man."

CHAPTER 17
Relief of Mewe

Two weeks later Gustavus Adolphus summoned Hepburn.

"I ordered you to relieve Mewe, Colonel Hepburn! Are you afraid or were you too busy polishing that gold tooled armour of yours?"

The Swedish colonels around him sniggered sycophantically as usual. Hepburn merely smiled.

"We are just about ready, Sire. I needed to make preparations."

"Confession was it? Couldn't find a priest?" Gustavus Adolphus winced and moved uncomfortably and John Hepburn felt his rising temper melt. The King was still in pain.

"If Your Majesty is well enough, I estimate the main army should be mobilised in the next two weeks and ready to move."

"I'll see some action first, please."

"As you wish, Sire!" Hepburn bowed and withdrew.

"I think my very presence has begun to irritate His Majesty." He said to Douglas later. "I can't think why. I'm always so subservient."

"Aye but even with your hair cut you look magnificent, John. Ten years younger than the King and such a flaming moustache and beard and now that the poor man stoops with pain you tower above him."

"Pish." But Hepburn couldn't help a small sense of satisfaction. He was putting up with unmerciful ribbing from the King and while his upbringing had given him endurance it riled him when his fellow colonels laughed.

"Why don't you tell him your plan?" Menteith was a peace maker.

"And have Sigismund ready? For God's sake Hector! They'll have their spies in our camp as we have in theirs. Do you think the King could keep it from his Swedish commanders? They chatter like bloody gannets on the Bass Rock. I'll not hazard my life on their silence!"

"Right enough!" Douglas nodded. "When do we go?"

"Tonight, if the weather is foul enough to bring sunset on early. Armstrong has all ready for my sortie and you two know your part. I've talked to Thurn. I trust him. He's a good man. He'll be with you, Jamie, and you'll need to move as fast as you can. He's on horseback!"

"We'll not fail, ye John." Douglas smiled; the bond between the Borderers strong. "Ye'll ken when we're in for the cannon will start again!"

As the clouds gathered that evening, so did Hepburn's men. Douglas had put together two companies of pike-men, choosing mainly Borderers, though Ensign Hay had insisted on being included.

"You look like tinkers, not soldiers!"

Hepburn laughed as he inspected them.

"Aye we're carrying everything but the missus." Armstrong growled.

"You'll need it. Make sure it's tight to your backs. You'll need your arms where I lead, and, remember, go silently. Think the Carlisle jailors are after ye."

They set off as the sunset was obscured by threatening black cloud. "It'll rain soon." Tod Armstrong muttered. "I'm no' one for the wet."

"Hud yer wheest, Tod." His cousin's voice was sharp. "Our lives depend on it."

After that the men moved quietly, reivers' skills remembered as they went. Except for an occasional muttered curse when their burdens shifted with a clank, they seemed to melt into the darkness.

"I'd forgotten how deadly it is to ignore silence in the Borders." Douglas had seen them off and now he set Menteith on his way with the musketeers left over from the other two companies to invest the tree line from which they had reconnoitred. Count Thurn was ready when he entered his tent. His officers disappeared and as if by magic he heard the sound of men mounting and moving out.

"Have you told the King, Colonel Douglas?" Thurn was already buckling on his sword belt.

James Douglas grinned. "I've left Colonel Hepburn's letter explaining his plan with my orderly. He will deliver it to the King first thing tomorrow."

A wry smile lit the older man's face. "He'll not be pleased perhaps."

"He likes success, Sir. If we are in to Mewe he will treat it as a good joke."

"And if we are not?"

"I'll likely be dead and so will John so we'll not be worried!"

With that they were off, the cavalry hampered by the dark, almost as slow-moving as Douglas's infantry. Behind them rumbled carts full of cannon ball, ammunition and food. Their task was to fall upon the besiegers encamped round the confluence of the rivers to prevent supplies reaching the city. As they trudged on James Douglas voiced a prayer for his big friend in his mind. His was the forlorn hope.

Hepburn, had he known it, was beginning to enjoy himself. With one of Sandy Hamilton's leather cannon strapped to his back he was leading the way towards the Vistula. They crossed the river by a small footbridge, half hidden by trees and turned south where they could just make out the spires and castle towers of Mewe. Now they hugged the river. As they went the banks got steeper and more tree-lined. Alders and willows clung to the grassy slopes creating a huge canopy of green above them. "Lucky the trees haven't shed their leaves yet," he muttered to himself. "We'd be bannocks on a Polish griddle else."

Soon they heard the rattle and voices of the great Polish army camped above them in the cramped triangle that led from the forest in the east towards the city. The Borderers slowed, choosing their steps with care. The rush and chuckle of the Vistula pouring past them drowned their footsteps even to their own ears. Their eyes were used to the dark by now and this was something they were good at. Hepburn allowed Armstrong to lead on. He seemed to know exactly where to put his feet and his commander followed. Eventually he touched his shoulder.

"I think we're past the camp now, Andra."

The man in the lead nodded and turned upwards. Now they were using their arms to pull themselves up the steep slope. Tree roots, twisted branches and rocky outcrops gave them purchase. Rain added to their misery making the grassy slope slippery. Occasionally Hepburn heard a foot slip and a muttered curse but the noise of the water was strong. The Vistula was in spate after the autumn rains. At no time did they meet a challenge or hear an alarm. No one in the Polish army had thought to place sentries above the bluff running to the river. Hepburn had counted on them thinking the tree grown cliff impassable.

They came up behind a great outcrop of rock close under the city wall.

"No man's land! Just where I want to be! Well done Andra-lad. It's as well the English didna' hang ye!"

A grim smile crossed the older man's face. "It's following ye Sir that might be fatal!"

He got a grin for that and then they were busy.

When the sun rose the appalled Prince Udislaus was brought the news that an opposing force had suddenly grown out of the ground between him and the walls of Mewe.

"We'll soon get rid of them!" Left in charge by his father, who had started to move his heavy artillery and infantry towards Danzig where Alexander Leslie's regiment was deployed, he was eager to prove himself.

"Will I send for the cannon to return, Sir?"

"To kill that puny lot! Never! Order my cavalry to mount. We'll wipe them off the face of the earth."

"Aye they're a bonny sight." Armstrong stood beside Hepburn, his pike at the ready. With the morning sun glinting off their chain mail and their tooled helmets shining, the Polish cavalry were indeed terrifying.

"Ready, men! Ye ken the drill. We've done it since Bannockburn." Hepburn sounded so confident that a few grim smiles started where anxious faces had been. As he looked round he saw that his Green Brigade colours flew from a pike stuck into the ground.

"Who the hell brought that?"

Behind him Ensign Hay, looked nervous.

"I wrapped my cannon in it to stop it clanking, Sir. I thought we should use it."

"Good man. Shows we're the people has everything!"

As he turned back to face the enemy his face lit in anticipation.

"Here they come, now!"

Screaming defiance, the Polish horsemen gained speed to hit them at the gallop, their lances ready to stab. But just before they met, the front rank seemed to stumble and fall. The next rank ploughed into them and a mess of horses and men rolled about in a horrid yelling barrier that prevented the attack.

Hepburn had brought rolls of iron chevaux-de-frise, the time-honoured Scottish defence against mounted men. Rows of sharp metal spines connected by chain links had tripped the horses and the weight of the charge had done the rest.

"Cannoneers! Fire!"

There was a roar, and grapeshot from the six leather cannon they had carried with such effort tore into the next two rows, hurling men out of the saddle and tearing flesh from bone. Blood spurted everywhere and the screaming of horses and men escalated as the force of the charge catapulted the rear ranks into the fallen.

"Reload the cannon." Hepburn's voice was quiet and steady but it carried down the ranks. "Stand to your weapons."

"They'll regroup."

"Aye, Andra they will, but they'll have to pick their way and that'll slow them down a bit."

Mortified, Udislaus brushed off another offer to send for the infantry. His men were eager to avenge their friends. Again and again they charged but the Scots pikemen stood firm. Like a series of porcupines their long pikes, one end braced in the ground, spitted horse or man that charged them. Chain mail was no barrier. Lances were useless. Wielding their swords they often got closer but there was always a man to step forward and a dagger ready to stab upwards into the heart.

Again and again the spreading blast from the leather cannon saved them from annihilation. But they had only so much ammunition and all too soon the cannon stilled.

"We can aye throw the things at them if the worst comes, Sir," Armstrong's words raised a smile but it was a grim one.

All day John Hepburn and his men sweated and killed. It was not dashing. It was not exciting. Exhilaration was what the Polish cavalry felt as time after time they regrouped and charged. The Scots stood dour and expectant. If a pike unit was breached another moved across to take its place and the men that were left reformed to fill the line. Like giant fans with the spikes forward, the pikemen repelled charge after charge.

Sunset brought the fighting to a messy close. It was only when the noise of battle ceased that they realised that the defenders of Mewe had been cheering them on from the ragged battlements.

"Heaven send Douglas has done his bit," Hepburn thought as he clapped his men on the backs and ordered them to eat and rest in relays. "We'll not hold out many more days."

"Its yon Polish Prince wi' his foolish pride that has given us the day, Sir." Armstrong looked as tired as Hepburn felt.

"Long may it last. We'd have had more trouble dodging a row of musketeers or even some low cannon ball." He looked around the small area they were in and shook his head. "When the men are fed we'll shift to stand against that great rock we came round. They'll not be able to outflank us then. We'll need to last another day, I'm thinking."

"Aye, Sir." Armstrong shrugged. "I'll be lucky to see it then."

"It's not a month, Andra!"

The older man started to laugh. "Ye make it sound so easy, Sir. We're all taken in. I'll just get some bread and meat inside me, however, in case it has to see me all the way to heaven."

"Or wherever Carlisle jail birds go!"

When Prince Udislaus surveyed the killing field next day he was delighted.

"See they cannot abide our Polish steel. They have retired for their last stand."

However the news reaching him was not all good.

"Strong forces attack the sconces to the West of Mewe, Sire. Their cavalry have already taken our cannon and the infantry are pouring into the back of our defences."

"Send our musketeers and pikemen round to outflank them. My cavalry will finish off these few upstarts. They are nothing but a minor diversion."

Hepburn's Scots were delighted.

"The infantry is marching off round to the river, Sir!" Tod Armstrong had eyes like a hawk.

"Good! Menteith will be waiting." Even as Hepburn spoke he heard the rattle of musketry and saw flashes from the trees on the skyline. "He'll harry them all the way to the river and they'll never know how many men he has lurking in those trees so I'm hoping they won't launch a counter-attack."

"Could be they'll think it's the whole of the King's army." Sergeant Armstrong grinned. "Ye'd make a grand magician, Sir. It's all done with smoke and mirrors like."

Then they were in action again.

This time Udislaus sent in his heavy cavalry, their steel breastplates and targes a real problem for the pikes to pierce and their swords began to wreck havoc with the small force against them. Hepburn had his sword in one hand and his dagger in the other as did many of the other Borderers. They stabbed upwards under the armour as the horses descended on them. It was desperate in-fighting. The Borderers were soon covered in blood and unaware whether it was theirs or another's.

"Perhaps I bit off a bit more than I can chew, this time," Hepburn thought as he hacked at yet another rider and saw him topple. Then suddenly the wall of men and horses eased. There was the crackle of gunfire. Was it the end? John Hepburn looked wildly round and a huge grin split his face.

"Colonel Mostyn, at your service!" A stranger in battered half armour, an officer's gold chain round his neck, stood shoulder to shoulder with him, his sword doing killing work.

"Count Brahe has fielded his arquebusiers now that your friend Douglas has brought us ammunition. We were casting ball all night." He paused to parry a Polish sword and thrust deeply below his opponent's breastplate. The horse reared away but his rider was dead in the saddle.

"Brahe is Swedish, you see," He went on conversationally as he hacked yet another cavalryman from his saddle. "They have scores to settle."

Mostyn and Hepburn fought together all that day as the Poles mounted charge after charge but the guns made each charge less effective until by evening they stopped regrouping and as night fell it was clear that the Poles were pulling out and heading south to join the rest of their army.

Their retreat was encouraged by the cannon from the battlements that suddenly started to roar.

"Douglas must have brought cannon ball too. Very thoughtful!" Mostyn seemed to take it all personally. "It's been rather boring for the last week or two, you know. Once we'd melted down the cathedral organ pipes for musket ball we ran out of ammunition and music. "

"We had to wait till the light and the weather were on our side." Hepburn found himself apologising.

"Not at all, old man! Quite understood! When we saw you appear like a genie from a bottle right in front of the walls, Count Brahe laughed so much I thought he might have an apoplexy. We've been cheering you on ever since."

That night they feasted as best they could on the provisions that Douglas and Count Thurn had brought. If it was ordinary for the Scots it was relished by the besieged men who had been on quarter rations for months.

"I guess the king will be glad to see you, John." Douglas hugged him in a huge embrace. "I certainly am. I never thought we'd pull it off. But it went just as you said. We cleared the sconces at dawn before they were ready for us and started ferrying the ammunition and food across. Then suddenly an army of pikemen and musketeers appeared but they were as surprised as we were and Thurn made short work of them. Our scouts said there were cannon behind them but they all moved off to Danzig."

"Probably thought Udislaus would do the business! By God, Jamie, there were moments when I was in two minds whether we'd make it or not." Hepburn was in high spirits. "But, as Sergeant Armstrong says, it was a great wee action and though we've wounded, we lost scarce a man."

CHAPTER 18
Knighted by Gustavus Adolphus

They took Marienburg by siege. There was no other way into that huge fortress. The Governor marched out with drums beating and flags flying.

"It riles me to see them go so jaunty." Tod Armstrong stood watching them pass.

"Dinna' look at their colours, lad. See their faces. They're thin as rats in the sewers, and as hungry." His big cousin clapped him on the back. "It'll be months before that lot are fit to fight again."

Leaving a Swedish colonel as Governor the main army pushed on to take Elbing, seaport of the Teutonic Knights.

"We'll winter here, Colonel Hepburn. See to billeting the troops." The King was clearly still in pain from his wound and had taken no part in the attacks.

"He's not a well man, the King." Hepburn said later to Jamie Douglas who had taken to dropping in to his rooms for a glass of an evening. "He can scarce turn his head and he can't bear the weight of his breastplate."

"He was well enough to fly into a rage, when that useless Ambassador Roe from our King Charles went first to treat with Sigismund!" Jamie Douglas as usual had all the court gossip.

But for once Sir John Hepburn was before him. "Don't remind me! Count Oxenstierna asked me to sort it. He had told Roe he must make his bow to "The Lion of the North" first. I had the devil's own job convincing his tetchy Highness that in Britain they go first to the less important person. That wee Frenchman, Hercule de Charnace, helped by saying that it made it easier for France to offer Sweden all their financial aid if Roe had finished with Sigismund. I've sat in the talks beside the Rex-Chancellor since and, oh Jamie, that is such a wise man!"

"We're going to need someone with a bit o' wisdom. The "Lion of the North" is more Viking than statesman." Douglas rose to go but turned at the door, "Until then we'll make merry. I hear our King Charles has sent a delegation of grandees to honour King Gustavus Adolphus with the Order of the Garter. You'll need a new suit, John! Stand still enough in that sombre green and the Queen's ladies will mistake ye for the wall drapes!"

But that evening as they all crowded into the great hall of the castle where rush candles burned in wall sconces and threatened to drop wax on the finely dressed assembly below, Hepburn felt content in his dark green coat.

"Someone has to maintain the dignity of the Green Brigade," he chuckled as his lieutenant colonel of pikes came to stand beside him. "There's you in pale blue velvet and silver mincing about, and have you seen Hector Menteith? The man's in pink!"

"We'll get partners for the dancing afterwards, you'll see."

"I'm too big for jigging. Besides, the ladies smell worse than the barracks." He thought longingly of getting back to where Cathy would have a long tankard of cool beer and a warm bed ready. "Cathy doesn't smell as rank as these well born lassies."

"Spends her time up to the elbows washing and scrubbing for you, no doubt!" Douglas grinned. "These ones haven't got the bathing they're used to, and their clothes winna' wash. But they're well endowed just the same, in dowry, if nothing else. You should think of that sometimes, John."

"I'll make my own fortune, John. Who knows? The King may give me a barony. They say he's thinking of giving James Spens one."

"Spens is gey near sixty. It's a long time to wait."

They watched as Sir Peter Young, Sir Andrew Keith, Sir Robert Primrose led by Sir Henry St George, Garter King-at-arms of England, processed up to where Gustavus Adolphus sat on a throne raised on a small dais at the end of the hall. His Queen sat beside him, overflowing her slightly smaller seat.

The ceremony conferring the Order on the King was greeted with rapturous applause. Then Gustavus Adolphus got painfully to his feet and drew his sword. His lord-in-waiting lifted his hand to still the chatter.

"In honour of this occasion His Majesty will now knight those he considers worthy of the honour."

Hepburn watched as Henry St George knelt stiffly to receive the accolade followed by Sir Peter Young.

"Colonel John Hepburn!" The lord-in-waiting announced.

John Hepburn stood transfixed.

"Go on John!" James Douglas gave him a sharp push. "And remember to kneel!"

"Thought I hadn't thanked you for Mewe, eh Colonel?" Gustavus Adolphus was enjoying the wild surprise in Hepburn's face.

Looking round at his immediate circle he chuckled. "This is the only way I can get this stiff necked Scot to kneel, eh!"

"Sire you know I am your man and I thank you." Hepburn felt the sword touch his shoulder and rose, bowing deeply. "This honour only binds me closer in your service."

"Nicely said, Sir John!" Douglas and Mentieth crowded round him patting him on the back as other colonels were knighted.

Then the celebrations started. Feasting and dancing went on into the small hours. For once John Hepburn took his part. He knew that the King would wish to see him delighted with this unexpected honour.

Christmas came and went with no let up in festivities. "I'll be leading a bloody quadrille into battle if this goes on." Hepburn was becoming seriously worried as his men partied. The Scots were drunk for a week at New Year.

"Just let them sober up in their own time, Sir." Sergeant Armstrong appeared to have the hardest head of any. "We'll be ready when ye've need o' us."

"Enjoy yourself John. You're only young once." Douglas was seldom in bed before dawn.

Once spring came they took Danzig. The Green Brigade was under orders to kill only soldiers. Hepburn knew the town was full of Scottish merchants.

"An ancestor of mine saved them a couple of hundred years ago." Douglas had been leading his pikemen. "One o' the gates is named for him. When I say who I am they offer me a drink. I'd be incapable if I'd accepted them all."

But Hepburn did not smile. "Word is that Gustavus Adolphus is short of money again. Our Parliament won't grant King Charles money to send to the Swedes so I've not got the full amount for the Green Brigade this month."

"That's bad news."

"Gray and Mansfeld all over again! I've been to see Count Oxenstierna. He said, "Don't worry". But I do."

A few days later Douglas announced "Your friend Oxenstierna has sorted it, Colonel. We'll be fine now. He's demanded a huge loan from the English Eastland Company in Elbing. They couldn't refuse."

"So?"

Douglas chuckled with delight. "So the English Privy Council have to pay them back. They've powerful lobbies in London."

"Thank God!" Hepburn sighed in relief. "I hate short changing the men."

"Word is that Christian of Denmark is beaten and negotiating with Tilly. That leaves our King Gustavus Adolphus the last defence against Hapsburg domination."

"We'll get Christian's Scottish soldiers, then. I've a friend, trained with me in France, called Monro, Robert Monro. I heard he was with a regiment there. It would be great if he came this way."

"What happens to us?"

Hepburn looked happy. "The King has put the Green Brigade under Count Oxenstierna. We'll do now." He did not enlarge on this statement. He was not about to tell any one that his efforts during the negotiations with Poland had so impressed Oxenstierna that the Rex Chancellor had asked him to become one of his chosen few informants.

"Write to me personally, Sir John. Keep me aware of any problems you or the King have. He is a great man but prone to rash decisions. Guide him with tact. Win his battles for him. We cannot do without his charisma if we wish to stand against the great Hapsburg menace. He is the Lion of the North!"

Hepburn looking into the calm wise eyes of the older statesman with his slightly receding dark hair and greying beard saw a fatherly interest and caring that he had not known before.

"I am your man, Sir. Now and always! You may depend on it."

Oxenstierna nodded. "I knew I had judged you right, Sir John. You ask nothing in return. But you will find an addition to your colonel's pay. All my trusted men accept it. Just don't tell the King!" He laughed. "He might want one too!"

CHAPTER 19
In Action with Monro

"It's good to see you, John." The dark haired highlander's grin was affectionate, "but I don't need you. Rugenwalde is ours."

"I'm not staying, Bully Monro!" Hepburn held his hands up in a gesture of surrender. "Oxenstierna sent me to relieve you. But you've got the Imperialists on the run so I'll follow them up. My men need action. We've had a year of hanging about Danzig where they hate us because the Rex-Chancellor has taxed them sorely." He grinned. "I guess they hate me most of all for I got them to agree to the taxation. The King sent me as his ambassador, Oxenstierna told him to. Said I was better than any Swede! If he's to take on the Hapsburgs we'll need money."

They sat comfortably together in one of the few undamaged rooms in Rugenwalde Castle that August of 1630. An evening breeze from the sea cooled the room and made shadows dance against the walls as the candle flames flickered.

"So now you're an ambassador as well!"

"Needs must when the Devil drives! I learned that the Poles were in a bad state from a trumpeter of theirs that my sergeant got well drunk on whisky, so I was able to give Oxenstierna bargaining power at the negotiations with Sigismund. We forced them into a five year truce. Now with Christian of Denmark a whipped dog and Sigismund unable to stab us in the back, Gustavus Adolphus is Lion of the North and all the allies' monies come his way. Just as well too. The Hapsburg eagle hovers over us, hungry for prey."

"He's a great man, your Swedish King, John. My colonel and I met him in Stockholm and he was all kindness, said he valued his "Green Brigade". We looked in at Verbowe as well, to see what Colonel Hamilton is about."

"Dear Sandy! That man'll blow himself up one day! The King has given him a foundry and he makes all our cannon. I'd not be here if it were not for his newest wee leather cannon, as he calls them. They held the Poles at Mewe when we were in sore need!"

"Aye, a very experimental man right enough!"

Hepburn was laughing

"You're one to talk about safety, Robert. Your sergeant told me how you belaboured the sailors and troops on your ship when it ran aground and had them cut down the masts for a raft and got them all off safe after they were down on their knees awaiting the next world."

"I'm not one for the swimming. We had a piper try it and he was swept away. I'm glad to be back fighting Tilly once more! He made a right mess of us in Denmark."

"I think you just started our war against the Hapsburgs when you borrowed the Governor's muskets and beat the Imperialists out of Rugenwalde."

"Our muskets were wet frae the sea and the ammunition was in another boat. What else?"

"Aye, you make it sound so reasonable. You always did when you'd done something outrageous." Hepburn was laughing again. "Man, its good to see you. Once I've made sure Tilly's men are not coming back I'll return and go with you to meet Major General Kniphausen. Oxiensterna ordered me to place our men under his command." He thought for a moment. "He's no great shakes as a leader but he pays regularly, for all he hates the Scots with a passion."

"What for does he do that?"

"I don't know. It's naught I've done." He hesitated. "Tell the truth, I'm happier when the King is in command, for all his favourites and fikey ways. However tonight I'll enjoy your billet here, Robert. Do you think our French sergeant would be proud of us?"

"Dumbstruck more like! It's a long time since we shared a room, John. I'm married now. I wish to heaven I wasn't. War is no place for women. Remember I went home to Reay's wedding?"

John Hepburn nodded.

"Well, with all the partying and marrying I became betrothed and married soon after. I've two children. I'll need to find them a place to live somewhere close-by. What else? I had to follow my Chief, Forbes Monro. He raised a regiment for hire as he was skint from too much jollification upon his Grand Tour on the Continent." He thought for a bit. "He's fine now with enough money to pay for all his family and dinner every day. It's the rest of us that struggle to make ends meet."

"Perhaps we'll pick up some booty soon. I could be doing with it too."

They went together to report to Kniphausen who put them to work at once, ordering Hepburn out with a troop of cavalry to reconnoitre the defences around Kolberg, an Imperialist-held town on the coast nearby, while Monro was told to keep his men on standby.

"Tilly's forces are on the march from Gartz to relieve Kolberg, Major General Kniphausen. We'll need time to get a sufficient force in position to attack them." Hepburn, back from reconnaissance, pointed with his finger at the map on the table before them. "But this town, Shevelbean, with its castle full of their soldiers, could hold us up. If we sent a small force to attack the town until we can get our main troops between Kolberg and Gartz, we can annihilate the relieving army. Kolberg will then surrender."

Kniphausen gnawed a lip thoughtfully as he digested the strategy.

"This was my idea exactly Colonel Hepburn." He turned to Monro, who stood beside his friend. "Lieutenant Colonel Monro, lead your Scotsmen into Shevelbean. Take it and defend it to the last man. The last man, I say! You will not surrender!"

"I'm sorry, Robert." Hepburn put a hand on Monro's shoulder as they left Kniphausen's tent. "That was not my suggestion. All you needed to do was keep the Imperialist troops in Shevelbean busy for a day or two and then get out. You've earned a rest, especially as I hear it's a plague ridden hell-hole."

Monro shrugged. "Might as well keep the men active."

His friend nodded. "Right! But we'll not be far away and if you're in real trouble I'll come for ye some way, Robert."

They clasped hands. Then Monro was gone, shouting for his captains to attend him.

Hepburn, ordered to lead the infantry party to cut the path to Kolberg, found his Scots were to be reinforced by a well ordered regiment led by an unassuming colonel called Teuffell.

"Glad to have you along, Sir." Hepburn bowed briefly.

"My men are fit and well armed. Where you lead we will go."

"I can't ask more, Sir." He hesitated, wondering if he was going to cause offence. "We are reinforced by Colonel Bauditz with his cavalry."

"Oh my God! Not those butterflies! They ride where the wind blows and their colonel is deaf to advice. I know it from hard experience. We should keep them in reserve," he paused and then continued, "for ever!"

Hepburn went off laughing to rouse Douglas and Menteith.

They set off two days after Monro and by the time they came towards Shevelbean they could hear the sounds of battle. Going forward to reconnoitre John Hepburn could see that Monro was now besieged in the Castle but as he watched he saw the houses round the castle walls spring into flames and men pour out of them followed by brisk firing from the castle walls.

"Well done, Robert man," he shouted and turning, rode back to where his soldiers stood at ease. "I'll lead the main group on to trap Tilly on his way to Kolberg. Colonel Bauditz would you, of a kindness, let your men sweep past Shevelbean where the enemy can see you coming. No need to engage. I believe they will think you are reinforcements and pull out. We'll see you tonight at our rendezvous!"

"Not engage!" Bauditz was affronted. "My men will fight!"

Hepburn sighed. "We'll need your excellent cavalry to protect us,

Colonel. Just the sight of you will be enough to panic these wretches." Teuffell chuckled beside him. "They surely cause me to sweat already!"

"Heaven send he obeys. Kniphausen will have me shot if we disobey his orders." Hepburn shook his head sadly as he rode on.

But at the end of the day as they settled into their position on a hill guarding the one pass into Kolberg, Bauditz clattered in with his company and a broad smile on his face. "It was just as you said, Colonel. We swept down and they ran so we just galloped past and here we are!"

"That'll give Robert Monro his victory." Hepburn muttered. "Maybe some good booty too! He'll like that."

As he spoke, enemy troops appeared in the pass below. Unsuspecting, they marched stolidly on, pikes at the trail and muskets slung over an arm. The weather favoured Hepburn's men with a heavy mist that cloaked the soldiers that Hepburn and Teuffell had massed on the slopes above and now the two colonels came off their horses and went to the head of their infantry. "Take your stand, load and prime!"

Hepburn had his sword raised. When he dropped it the front two musketeer ranks fired, turned to march through to the back and reload as the next ranks came forward. Teuffell's men went with them. Moving downhill all the time, their pikemen beside them, musketeers from each company poured shot upon the infantry below causing havoc. The Imperialist cavalry, summoned to charge the musketeers, were met by pikes and as they piled up hacking and being brought down, the musketeers continued their deadly toll. The Imperialist cavalry turned and fled.

It was too much for Colonel Bauditz. "Forward, men! Charge!" and he was off after them, far in advance of his infantry.

"Stop! Wait! We go together!" Hepburn's shout was useless. Colonel Bauditz was in search of glory.

"And Colonel Bauditz met the enemy's cavalry men in such a way that they began to flee and withdrew behind their infantry," Hepburn wrote to Rex Chancellor Oxenstierna later. "Since Colonel Bauditz did not realise this they fired two salvos against him on the flank, from which he suffered great damage. Hereupon the enemy attacked again screaming, so that in the foggy weather his cavalry men not only attacked each other, but were put to flight and came back into our musketeers who received both our cavalry and their infantry."

Chaos had resulted with the mist thickening so that they could scarcely see who they were fighting.

"Christ! Bauditz's men are falling back on us!" Hepburn shouted. "Pikes keep them off. Go for the horses and yell at the men." Hepburn hit a cavalryman with the flat of his sword. "Get your men off us you bloody want-wits!"

In the melee the enemy retreated fast so that when the mist lifted both Bauditz and they had gone. Kolberg capitulated but Hepburn fretted.

"It was a battle we could have won," he said to Monro later when they met up at Gustavus Adolphus's headquarters at Greifswald. "Heaven protect me from glory-seeking colonels and generals who never win."

"We had a nice little rammy ourselves." Monro was inclined to self-satisfaction. "Once we took the castle they came back at us in force and occupied the houses beside the castle wall. My cack-handed lot tried to hurl burning torches at them but they fell short so I hung over the battlements with a fire-ball on a pike and set the nearby roofs alight."

Hepburn was laughing. "You make it sound so reasonable, Robert!"

"What else? Bullets were flying about my head and they were bringing up their artillery, so something had to be done. This way the flames soon warmed their breeks and they ran. I went back after to make sure the boores had put the flames out and just as well too for the first thing the King said to me was, "I hope you did not upset the people of the town!"

"Aye he's great on that. Good thing too. When you see the poor folk hanging from the trees in the towns that Tilly has sacked, and women and children lying scattered in the streets like dolls left by children after play, it sickens you. Doesn't make the ones left alive keen to help, either!"

"I'll remember. But the only folk we did ill to were a couple o' Bauditz's Cavalry who galloped up shouting, "All is lost. Flee!""

"So?" Hepburn lifted a red-gold eyebrow.

"I didn't like the look of them, so I clapped them in irons and went on sorting out the cannon that the Imperialists had abandoned. My men were too busy collecting booty to listen." John Hepburn started to laugh again but his friend shook his head at him.

"Na, na, There was no one coming back to that hell-hole. It was an awful place, full of dead men rotting in the streets before we arrived and even fuller when we left. We buried our own, of course, but I've told the local boores that the rest is up to them. My men are not grave diggers: they're highland gentlemen."

CHAPTER 20
Taking Gartz

At Greifswald, Gustavus Adolphus had amassed a huge army. Looking at the extent of the camp, Hepburn was impressed. "Time I was back at the King's side or he'll not know me any more! However irritating he is I'd rather attend His Majesty than obey Kniphausen."

"Then come with me, John." Robert Monro pushed into the group of Scottish officers round him. "The King sent me a Swedish captain called Dumaine to take the place of one of mine that died. But it's my right to choose my captains and I've given the company to my kinsman who is next in line for promotion. Folk say you can make the King do anything."

Hepburn shrugged and lowered his voice. "I'll come but when do Kings see sense?"

The Lion of the North beamed upon them. "My Scottish officers back from skirmish! I hear you did well, Lieutenant Colonel Monro. Your Colonel goes to Scotland for more recruits so you must take charge. Take your men and march for Stettin where Colonel Leslie commands. You'll find the rest of your regiment there."

"But Sire I don't need Captain Dumaine. His men can't understand him."

"He'll learn the commands." The King turned away.

"But I choose my captains!"

"You dare gainsay my orders!" Gustavus Adolphus's face darkened alarmingly and John Hepburn moved quickly to stand between the two men. "Lieutenant Colonel Monro is worried because his men speak Gaelic, especially in the heat of battle. He only needs your assurance that he can ask Captain Dumaine to learn it as well as English."

"He has it. He is my choice!"

Hepburn bowed and fairly pushed his friend out of the tent muttering,

"I told you, Robert. Kings have favourites. Get used to it!"

"Sire," he continued as he returned. "I am yours to command."

Gustavus Adolphus turned towards him. "You think I can do naught without you, Scotsman, but you are wrong. I have put it about that we go into winter quarters here, so old Tilly will rest his weary bones."

"I heard it from the boores along the way, Sire. Do you want me to give my men leave for Christmas? There is only one week to go."

The King laughed delightedly and the men round him joined in. Hepburn looked round. Colonel Teuffell was grinning. Big bluff Colonel James Ramsay, a glass of red wine already in his hand, guffawed till his jowls shook and even the narrow intelligent face of James Ruthven sported a slight smile.

"We march on Christmas eve, Colonel. We'll have Gartz before they sober up enough to notice."

Hepburn's laugh was joyous. "We'll be ready Sire. Ready and willing! I'll tell my lieutenant colonels. Christmas was never a day for lethargy at home and this will mean my men are too busy to drink themselves to a standstill at New Year."

A sly smile slipped onto the King's face. "But are you not required to confess at Christmas Mass, John?"

The Swedish colonels round him sniggered. The Scots looked anywhere but at him. Hepburn sighed. "As you well know, Sire, I have never put the state of my immortal soul before Your Majesty's orders. There is no conflict. My duty is to you."

Gustavus Adolphus was touched. Stepping forward he buffeted Hepburn's shoulder and turned to his now silent court. "I missed you, Sir John. My war cabinet is complete now you are here. What would we do without your Green Brigade?"

On Christmas Eve they marched towards Dam, a little village outside Stettin. Regiment after regiment of infantry moved out, colours flying, and in the case of the Scots, their drums beating out the "Old Scotch March", that rhythm that already terrified the Hapsburg forces. Behind them jingled a full complement of cavalry,

"Laager in the villages round here, Sire. I hear from my friend Monro that Stettin is plague-ridden. He has bivouacked his men in the fields so they will not catch the contagion." Hepburn's advance scouts had already made contact with Colonel Alexander Leslie's forces.

"Good idea, Colonel. There is sweet water here and the men will not have the women of the town to contend with." Gustavus Adolphus was in high spirits and Hepburn rejoiced to see him recovered from his wounds.

"I have yet to see him in armour," he said to Jamie Douglas that evening "but it's clear he is spoiling for a fight."

"You'll not see him that way, John. He's not able to tolerate the weight on where the ball lies. The surgeons couldn't remove it."

"It's close to his spine. I knew that." Hepburn shook his head. "This makes my job the harder. I need to persuade him to be in overall charge somewhere out of the battle line."

They attacked Gartz on Christmas day.

"I'll stuff their mouths with Christmas puddings," The Swedish King was in rollicking form. "Cannons fire!"

"Musketeers forward. We attack their trenches outside the walls."

Off his horse and in half armour, his officer's golden necklet bright against the tooled breastplate from Padua that was his greatest joy, Hepburn's huge frame led the way. Jamie Douglas was at his right hand and he knew his men would be close behind, their green sashes already well feared and their drum-beat enough to raise the hairs on any defender's neck.

"My Swedes must enter the town first!" Gustavus Adolphus's shout followed him as he went.

The musketeers against them fell against the accurate continuous hail of bullets his men poured into their ranks. Then they were into the trenches swinging their guns like clubs. Always ahead, John Hepburn's sword was a killing machine. He turned, sweating, "Occupy the trenches, Green Brigade. Let the Yellows through the gate."

There was muttering but Armstrong had his men well in hand. The repeated orders down the chain of command stilled them as the men stood fast and let the Swedes break through the city gate. There was little resistance. Seeing what looked like the main army in attack the troops in the town were fleeing out by the opposite gate.

There however they met Leslie's army, who had moved South from Stettin in support.

Thinking that they could break through this smaller host the General in charge of Gartz massed his musketeers and cavalry and attacked.

Colonel Leslie was ready. His cannon loaded with chain shot spat flame and the charging men were cut in half. Rank after rank exploded in a bloody fountain that stopped their charge and turned it into a rout.

The Gartz garrison ran. The troops still in the town, appalled by what they had seen, were caught between forces. They surrendered.

"Leslie reports that he has captured Don Ferdinand de Capua, who is said to be a Major General, Major Anthony, a young Count of Thurn they were using as an ensign, many more officers and at least two hundred men who no doubt will join with Your Majesty's troops." Hepburn grinned. "They're fair impressed with Colonel Leslie's Scots and of course your own Swedes, Sire."

Gustavus Adolphus was radiant. "My men did well! You saw them, Sir John!"

"Indeed Sire. They made the breach and we followed."

Later he was congratulated by Armstrong. "Aye that was right clever o' ye, Sir. The men were unhappy about letting the Yellows go first but when ye led us in after and ordered us to leave them to it an' see what booty was about they thought the world o' ye!"

"What a deadly fellow Leslie is," Hepburn said later to Jamie Douglas as they celebrated in Gartz.

"A killing machine, no doubt about it!" Douglas raised his glass. "Good booty though, John, and the King is in a right good humour, thank the Lord!"

There was little doubt that Gustavus Adolphus was on a high. The next day when his army stood in order for prayers he thanked God for their victory. Afterwards he made it clear to his officers that he was about to push on.

"We'll leave half the army to blockade Landsberg. That'll stop Tilly pouring back into Pomerania behind us. You, my friend," and he turned to Field Marshal Horne standing morosely beside him, "I'll give you Colonel Hepburn here and his Brigade to do it with. They'll keep all safe."

Hepburn nodded, smiling. He liked Gustav Horne.

"Horne's a good sort of man, for all he looks sad," he muttered to Monro. "He's grieving still. His wife, who was Count Oxenstierna's daughter, took the plague and died. It's said he held her in his arms all the days she lingered but nothing was of any avail. He made her a silver coffin. Since then he has fought as if he doesn't care whether he lives or dies."

"Poor man!" Monro shook his head. "It's what we all fear."

But his big friend was not listening. He was standing forward to salute Gustavus Adolphus. "I'll tell my men, Sire. We'll be ready to march when the Field Marshal orders."

As they came out of the tent together, Monro turned to grasp his hand. "I'll see ye, John, God willing. It's as well my men have their plaids and are used to trudging through snow, I'm thinking."

His heart lit with excitement as Sir John Hepburn sat his horse watching the army mass in their companies and brigades, the brighter tartan plaids over the usual steel breastplates and the watery sun twinkling on their steel morions. Pikemen trailed their weapons, musketeers held their guns on their shoulders to keep them dry, cavalry ploughed on through the snowy roads ahead of them and slow oxen teams pulling the cannon carriages rattled behind.

"It's a bonny sight, right enough." He turned to Jamie Douglas beside him. "But we've less armour and clothes than that lot. Time we kept the booty we take. Our pay doesn't keep us as smart."

They marched south the next day. Horne's army laagered in the small villages around Landsberg and once settled, the officers led raiding parties towards the walled city. A few sporadic shots greeted them if they approached too close but there was little interest taken.

"We'll leave a Swedish unit to besiege the town," Horne said. "They only have to keep the Imperialists walled up so they can't reinforce Tilly. My King will need his Green Brigade for Frankfurt on Oder. It's the gate to the Hapsburg heart-land."

"Landsberg's heavily fortified with experienced troops, Sir." Hepburn looked dubious.

"You doubt us, Sir John?" The Swedish Field Marshal snorted and tossed his head.

"Your courage, Sir? Never!" Sir John Hepburn let his glinting smile, warm the restive Swede. "Their guile is my concern."

"I'm sure they'll manage." Horne's tone was final and Hepburn bowed to it.

CHAPTER 21
Destruction of Frankfurt on Oder

They filled the villages round Frankfurt on Oder to saturation and then Gustavus Adolphus clattered in from skirmishing, Monro at his side, and everyone had to move to accommodate the extra troops.

"I've left my men to laager with your Scots, John." Monro chuckled as he dumped his kit in Hepburn's room and looked around to see if there was anything to eat. "Your Sergeant Armstrong is a right one. He just said, "Aye Sir" and got on with it. Didn't look too happy though!"

Hepburn sighed. "We're short of everything. I wrote not three days ago to the Rex Chancellor. He's our only hope. The King thinks his army lives on love of him and air. His favourites grab all the booty and for all we're the best drilled of any of his army the Scots get the least."

Monro opened his mouth to remonstrate but his friend held up his hand. "He sweet-talks you and you think him magnificent, Robert, but you'll soon see that his praise is just that, words. Oh, aye, he gives baronies in Sweden to his favourite Scots. There's Ramsay, that wine tub, as has one for getting a wounded arm and suchlike but have you seen hint or hair of the booty you took on that last sortie? I'll warrant not and what about Dumaine?"

Monro sighed. "Aye well, but having Dumaine brings the King to skirmish with us so it's not all bad and he told me personally that he would see me right for all the good things I've done!"

"And have you anything to show for it?"

"Not yet! But it's early days."

"You'll wait till Hell freezes! In the meantime we have just enough to eat but the men are poorly clad and this is no weather to be without clothes. We're losing men from sickness all the time. I've told Armstrong that after the next battle he's to forget the order that booty has to be handed in and every man is to find a body with better kit than his own and strip it."

Monro started laughing. "They'll be warm soon, then! The King means to attack Tilly as soon as maybe. 'Tis said Tilly is well dissatisfied with his men."

"Aye word is that he muttered, "With these troops I cannot risk my reputation." We heard that too."

They settled down in Hepburn's small room at the top of the burgomaster's house. It was the only two storey building in the village and he had insisted on a fire. As they sat after their meal, Monro with a wooden mug of wine and Hepburn with his accustomed beer tankard, time slipped by and they were students again, sharing thoughts.

"The King pushed us hard, ye ken," Monro started. "We were wading through snow part of the time and if the roads hadn't been frozen solid we'd have been mired beyond moving, especially the cannon. One time the King was walking, his speeing-glass to his eye, and he fell through the ice into a burn. That Captain Dumaine ran for him but the King waved him away, told him not to make a stushie lest the town he was reconnoitring noticed. But it was too late and the bullets started whizzing about them. Nothing daunted, the King just stomped out of the water, called for a glass of red wine and a bowl of stew and went off to change with Dumaine pattering on beside upbraiding him for hazarding himself in a way I wouldn't dare! Ye're right there, John. He's soft on his favourites. But he's brave."

"I never doubted his courage." Hepburn shook his head. "But he's not even handed."

His friend nodded thoughtfully. "Aye maybe so, but we did right well. Tilly's lot ran leaving the towns begging for mercy. Even Brandenburg only waited till the first salvoes from our cannon fell about their ears."

"Now there's a case that bears me out." Hepburn tapped the table with a finger. "What does the King do then? He leaves that bloody useless Kniphausen, whom he loves dearly, in charge; and when Tilly counter attacks in strength, does Kniphausen go for an accord like a sensible body? No! He shilly-shallies till they've burst the gates and then, when it's too late, he sends Colonel Lindsay to hold them while he gets out the back door."

"Aye," Monro shook his head. "That was badly done. Lindsay had six companies of Lord Reay's with him, and they fought to the last man. It was a massacre. My men are itching to get back at him."

"They'll get their chance." A grim smile crossed his friend's face. "I'm making a reconnaissance with the King tomorrow."

But the next day scouts brought news that the garrison of Landsberg had broken through the besieging Swedes to swell Tilly's forces already in Frankfurt on Oder. Gustavus Adolphus sent men to harry them but it was too late. They had even manhandled their cannon across the river. Landsberg lay empty.

"Those Swedes couldn't keep pigs in a sty!" Hepburn was disgusted but his scout hadn't finished.

"It seems a party of the besiegers were out hunting deer and met Colonel Wallenstein in the forest but the idiots didn't realise who it was till he'd long gone. They did capture a fellow on foot who came from Landsberg who told them Donaw's "Old Saxons" and Colonel Wallenstein's musketeers were quartered there."

"They'll bring a light to Tilly's eye and no mistake." He remarked to the King when he reported for duty.

Gustavus Adolphus was uncaring. "We will have them, Colonel Hepburn, you'll see. Forget reconnaissance. Get your men ready. We march on Frankfurt tomorrow."

"At least its warmer now that April is here," was Monro's response to Hepburn's instructions. "It was hell slogging through that snow in the New Year."

They moved out, company by company, captains leading on horseback, their colours behind them and drums beating, as pikes and musketeers followed. Hepburn, standing in his stirrups to look back, could not deny it was a stirring sight. Cavalry jingled past them as they marched, and behind they could hear the grinding rattle of gun carriages and the swearing of the soldiers as they urged their teams of oxen on.

"Aye, it'll bring a tear to Tilly's eye when he sees this lot." Jamie Douglas rode beside Hepburn. "It's time we saw action. The men are restive."

"They're cold, badly armoured, hungry and unpaid." Hepburn's temper was on a short rein after a night sharing his bed with Monro instead of Cathy. "For all the booty Gustavus Adolphus amassed this last sortie, I've seen none of it and I feel responsible for the men. Prayers every morning brings no rewards and my men have done all I asked of them."

"Aye well," Douglas sounded grimly satisfied, "Frankfurt will show rich pickings and the word is that the men will not be stopped from looting in return for what Tilly ordered at Brandenburg. Monro's highlanders have a long memory for ills done them and our Green Brigade will not be far behind when it comes to sacking a city."

They had laagered in the fields to the north of Frankfurt by three that afternoon. Tents were put up and all the business of victualling an army started as cooks set up their cook-tents and men brought wood for the fires. Sentries were set, chains of command in case of alarm made known, and at last the whole army came together for prayers before eating.

"There'll be some tight stomachs the night, with some wondering if it is their last supper." Monro entered Hepburn's tent to find the Scottish officers assembled.

"Aye. The Yellow and Blue Brigades lodge on the Castrene side o' the town in the vineyards, here." Sir John Hepburn pointed to a rough map on a table before him. "Damitz's Whites lie close to the walls to the North in case they break out to swamp the artillery beyond them." He had been at Gustavus Adolphus's briefing and was bringing his officers up to date. "We Scots have the right wing where the water runs close beside the wall. I've had a Sergeant swim the stream and he reports that the outer wall is scarce manned. If we break through we'll find another lower wall and they're all lodged behind it. Tonight the Green Brigade will cross the stream to lie close to the outer wall."

"Their sentries will never see us move in the dark!" Jamie Douglas's eyes were bright with excitement.

Hepburn's moustache twitched in a half grin. He was excited himself.

"Our cannon will breach the first wall and in the smoke we'll slide close in on the second wall, wait till it is breached, and in we go. Then the rest of the Scots pile in after us and we blast our way though to open the main gates. Meanwhile, the other brigades are keeping Tilly busy by making mock attacks."

Their plan worked. Looking across, they could see Gustavus Adolphus's main forces lined up in front of the city, the Forlorn Hope to the front. Then their cannon started its deadly roar. Cannon from the walls responded. Men of the White Brigade fell and the screaming started. The Forlorn Hope moved forward through a hail of bullets and the noise seemed to envelope town and attackers in a dreadful paean of death.

The cannon behind the Scots spoke and the gate on their side splintered. Sir John Hepburn moved forward under the drifting smoke. On foot, a half-pike in his hand he led his men, through the gap, tearing aside the shattered wood. They fell on the few startled defenders between the walls and slid inside close to the second wall where they were protected from bullets while their cannon roared again. Smoke covered the scene but they could see the breach appear and as they went they heard the rest of their brigade splash through the river behind them to be followed by the growl of angry highlanders eager for vengeance. Battering rams made short work of gates and the Scots were in Frankfurt and in a killing mood.

They followed their colonel's green plumes like a huge ravening beast fanning out to tear the town apart. But Hepburn pushed on towards the main gates, his half pike taking terrible toll. As he glimpsed the great nailed wood doors ahead and thought the job almost over his leg buckled under him and he went down. A strong arm pulled him up and he saw through a dizzying haze a great fountain of blood pouring from his thigh.

"They've shot ye, Sir." Armstrong's face seemed to recede as a darkness hovered. Monro's face appeared. "I've taken a ball, Bully Monro."

"I'm right sorry John. See him to the surgeon, Sergeant. Ye've made the path, good friend. We'll tread it!"

He was gone, taking Hepburn's place, shoulder to shoulder with Colonel Lumsden. The highlanders' half pikes took terrible revenge for Brandenburg. The garrison had set small cannon to fire a broadside and Monro saw men fall. But there was no hesitation. The Scots pressed on, unstoppable. From then on there was carnage. On the vineyard side the gates fell and Gustavus Adolphus's own Yellow and the Dutch Blue Brigades flooded into the town. They met furious opposition and for a moment they hesitated but the brigade of Irish attached to the Blues stood firm. Wielding their muskets like clubs, and their pikes a wall of death, they rode the counter-attack. As each front man dropped another took his place. Donaw's "Old Saxons" had met their match. Behind them the Yellows and Blues rallied and thrust on again and the east of the town was swamped with Gustavus Adolphus's men, their killing humour un-assuaged while anyone lived.

Tilly had raised a dragon when he massacred the men of Brandenburg. His troops but also the townspeople of Frankfurt on Oder, men, women and children, paid the price. There was booty. Carriages and wagons, loaded with silver and gold lay about the streets. The Swedish army went wild.

"I give orders and nothing happens!" Monro met Colonel Lumsden who was organising the removal of a coach full of food and gold chains.

"You're not giving the right orders then." He laughed. "I'm not having any difficulty here!" He patted Monro on the back. "That was a bonny fight and no mistake. Just give your men the evening off. They've earned it."

Monro sighed. "We've lost our colours, our colour bearer, the lot."

"Dinna' worry. They'll return some time with more colours than you could believe. There's four colonels of their's dead, one of the Wallenstein clan, Heydo, Herbenstine and Loure to say nothing about three thousand of their men. Cheer up, man. We've given Tilly a right bloody nose this time."

By evening nothing remained but thousands of dead, stripped naked and left lying, their wounds ghastly and the agony of dying still on their faces.

Sir John Hepburn, bandaged and pale from loss of blood, limped back to take command. His men cheered as he staggered in amongst them and his heart warmed.

"We've got enough equipment to see us though a year or more," Armstrong reported. "And clothes as well."

"Well now you'd all better find some digging tools and we'll bury our own in the cemetery and the rest of them you can let the Dutch dig holes for." He grinned. "It's what they are best at." That raised a laugh and his tired men turned in good humour to follow his orders. His voice followed them as they moved. "First clear out the part of the town that you wish to laager in and you'll be warm and well fed for once. There's hundreds of horses slain even though Tilly's cavalry ran, and if you can't lay hands on some bread and food you're no soldiers of mine."

He turned to Monro who materialised beside him to take his hand and wring it. "I'm right glad to see ye, John!"

"Aye I missed the best of it! The King has trusted me with clearing up the mess and stopping looting. Fine hope! But if you've any men that'll take an order, I'd be grateful if you'd make them man the gates and battlements to make sure Tilly is not coming back. I'll get the Yellows to put up a guard for His Majesty in the town." He limped off as Monro turned to take hold on some passing plaid-clad pikemen and demand where their sergeant was.

That night Hepburn's men celebrated and slept warm. The next day Gustavus Adolphus ordered his army to assemble to choose weapons and armour from the stripped bodies of their enemy.

"We'll no be behind in coming forward, Sir." Armstrong looked smug. "But fine ye ken Sir we've got the best already."

Hepburn limped off laughing. He had managed to secure the town and, well content, ate the evening meal with his own officers and any other Scots officers who wished to join them.

"We lost eight hundred men," he told them, "Five hundred from the Yellow and Blue Brigades and more from the Whites. The Irish took the worst losses."

"I reckon we lost upward of a hundred or so." Douglas had been doing the muster rounds for his colonel.

"It was taking the gates did it." Monro nodded. "After that they ran. Pity you missed it, John. My pike was hot with blood by the end."

CHAPTER 22
Landsberg to Berlin

Five days later the Blue Brigade were still digging huge pits outside the town for the last wagon-loads of rotting bodies.

"April is o'er clement for such a victory." Sergeant Armstrong sniffed loudly. "It is just as well we cleared our own laager. The West wind's a help too with us living on the West side of town. It gives the Blues some incentive to keep going. They're by the East wall."

Gustavus seemed to feel the same. "Get your Scots ready, Sir John Hepburn. We'll besiege Landsberg. You'll need at least 2000 musketeers so take Monro as your lieutenant colonel with his men. Horne will lead eight hundred horse and I've sent twelve cannon already on the way."

"The King's wearying," Hepburn told Monro as he ordered readiness. "He aye needs action. The Duke of Brandenburg not swearing fealty is like a thorn in his shoe. The man's his brother-in-law after all! I just wish he'd let my knee heal before he demands action, but needs must when the devil drives and if I wrap it tight inside my boot it should do."

"I hear Donaw's Old Saxons that escaped us at Frankfurt holed up there. It won't be easy, John."

"Taking Landsberg makes Pomerania safe behind us and opens the door to Brandenburg and Silesia. We'd have to do it sometime, Robert, and when is it ever easy if we're asked to do it?"

They marched out on the fifth of April 1631, Spring warmth already budding the trees and lightening the men's spirits. But they found Landsberg well defended with cannon-infested sconces whose earth walls their own cannon could not penetrate.

"Attack them, Colonel Hepburn!"

"I'll make reconnaissance first, Sire." Hepburn turned away from his leader's frown.

"We'll lose men needlessly in a frontal attack, Robert," he said to his lieutenant colonel. "I won't do it."

"But if the King commands?" Monro seemed unhappy.

"The blacksmith who shoes Field Marshal Horne's horses drinks wi' my cousin Tod." Armstrong, as ever at Hepburn's side, broke in without respect. "He said he kent a way in."

Both officers turned. "Get him!" Hepburn ordered.

The huge dark haired smith propelled forward by the Armstrongs shuffled his feet but appeared confident. "Make a flatboat bridge over yonder canal, Lord, and I'll lead you through the shallows around the sconce then one force can attack the walls and one the sconce at the same time."

Hepburn looked where he pointed. "Sounds good! We'll go before dawn tomorrow, sergeant. Don't lose this man or let him drink tonight!"

As the mist rolled off the canal in the paling darkness before dawn, the musketeers moved out of camp and spread like a silent deadly miasma across the water of the protecting canal.

Hepburn, sword in hand, Menteith beside him, led his musketeers to overrun the half awake sconce taking most of the defenders prisoner and silencing the cannon. Monro had a harder fight on his hands. He fell back at last only able to pin the defenders down with musket fire. But with the sconce taken, Horne's soldiers were able to breach the undefended East gates and a white flag appeared on the ramparts.

Gustavus Adolphus was jubilant. "My magnificent Swedes!" he kept repeating.

"Bauditz and Bannier got well drunk after doing naught. The King made that blacksmith rich and have you noticed any greatness falling on us? We did the work!" Hepburn's tone, as he rode beside Monro, was acid. "It's always so."

"Hush, John, he is the King!"

"At least Brandenburg and Silesia now lie open to us. That should keep him in good spirits. When he's sour it's even harder to bear his ingratitude. You're an awful souk sometimes Robert!"

But a delighted Gustavus Adolphus returned to Frankfurt on Oder saying with relief, "At least the wind smells sweeter than when we left. Find out if Brandenburg has come to parley, Colonel."

Sir John Hepburn had no good news on that front. Leslie, left as Governor, had shaken his head. "The local Princes have come in with gifts and sworn fealty to your Highness but Saxony and Brandenburg are silent still."

"The Duke of Brandenburg is my brother-in-law, God rot him! Why does he thwart me so? He's no bloody Catholic. "

Hepburn kept his face neutral. "He is afraid of the long Hapsburg arm when you have returned to Sweden, Sire, and Saxony is a two-faced viper with a venomous bite. Whether he joins us or not he's unreliable."

"He'll join us if Brandenburg does. What would you do, Colonel Hepburn?"

"March in battle order to Berlin. You tried a friendly approach and the Duke gave us Spandau and asked for it back the next month. Colonel Axeltilly, whom you named as governor, had scarce unpacked his gear when he had orders to quit. The man trifles with you, Sire!"

The King took a turn or two round the room. The other colonels avoided his gaze.

"The bastards had no wish to be tainted with my advice if it exploded in my face!" Hepburn said later to Douglas as he gave the order to get the men in marching order. "But the King made a sort of "Hurrumph" like he does when something pleases him and we're off to Berlin, drums beating, colours flying and muskets and pikes well in evidence."

They camped in the fields round the Berlin city walls.

"Set your cannon well to the fore, Sire." Hepburn suggested.

Gustavus Adolphus laughed. "My idea exactly, Colonel! Now we'll see what's in his mind."

Sir John Hepburn's persuasive plan brought the Dowager Duchess out to visit the King, accompanied by all her daughters and behind them, men carrying enough food to victual the whole army for two days.

Gustavus Adolphus's dinner for the ladies was magnificent. The Dowager promised compliance and her daughters made eyes at the younger colonels.

The King, in rollicking humour, kissed his mother-in-law farewell murmuring, "Just tell your son that I'll send you all in chains to Stockholm unless he rapidly convinces me that he is with me."

Two days later the Duke swore fealty.

"Now for that weasel Saxony."

"Aye, Sire!" Hepburn's tone was disenchanted. "He hung back while Tilly razed Magdeburg. They hoped he would relieve them. They did not surrender. How a Lutheran Duke could see his own people massacred like that is beyond my reckoning."

"And you a good Catholic too, Colonel!" The King looked at him quizzically.

"I'm not a murderer. I'm a soldier and your man, Sire, as I have proved beyond doubting!"

Gustavus Adolphus stilled the sychophantic sniggers round him with a glance.

"I may tease my officers, but know that I rely on this man. My Green Brigade is led by my right hand." He turned back to a frowning Hepburn. "There! Would you have your King apologise?"

Hepburn, his face clearing, knelt to kiss the King's outstretched hand. "No, Sire! I can bear your jokes against me, while I know you trust me."

"My hand on it!" Gustavus Adolphus pulled a ring from his finger and held it out. "See my pledge."

Hepburn bowed. "I shall wear it unto death, Sire"

"He's not a bad old stick," he said later to Monro when they sat together one evening. "I suppose it's his Swedish sense of humour. He means well mostly." He paused, thinking. "I'd really like him a great deal more if he had fewer God-awful favourites and arranged to pay us what he owes instead of promising riches that never materialise. I write weekly to the Rex Chancellor begging for money to pay the men."

"Aye." His friend looked down at his well worn plaid. "My men exist on booty and anything they can steal from boores along the road. I've forbidden them strictly from looting the villages but a hungry highlander will take where he finds it."

His forebodings were borne out a few days later. Gustavus Adolphus mobilised his army and marched south. They laagered in villages when they could, though now that the summer heat had arrived tents in the open were almost as pleasant. The senior officers lived and slept in their coaches though Hepburn found his so cramped that he just used it to carry his gear.

"I'd rather ride in the day and once this leg of mine has healed I'll march with my men. They like that."

He was on horseback, ordering his troops for the day's march, when he saw a small group of men approaching, clearly highlanders from the tattered plaids that hung about them.

"Summon Lieutenant-Colonel Monro," he ordered Sergeant Armstrong.

There were horrified murmurs as the highlanders tottered into the camp. The men formed a ring about them but were loathe to approach and Hepburn, swinging down from his horse, could see why. They had been savaged as if by wild animals. Their noses had been cut off and their ears and hands. Putrefaction had set in with blackened livid bloating. Only one of them had eyes. He had led them home. Empty running sockets bore witness to the atrocities they had suffered.

"The boores did it, Sir" The leader's voice was just a croak.

"You were looting?"

"We were that hungry, Sir. There's never enough and our plaids are just rags."

"What now?" Hepburn turned to Monro who had arrived to take a horrified breath when he saw his men.

"Which village was it?" Monro had gone close without hesitation.

"They call it Warts or some such. It's got a church wi' a square spire."

Monro raised his voice so all the men watching could hear him. "Ye have been looting and the punishment for that is death. But know that that village will no longer rise from the earth tomorrow. Do ye understand?"

As one the men fell to their knees. "Say a prayer for us, Sir. We do welcome death."

"Little else to do," Monro said later. "They were dead men walking. Maybe this'll teach the others a lesson."

"Aye! Better be killed clean by your fellows than rot in agony. What now, Bully Munro?"

"Now we raze that village, burn it to the ground and leave four people alive to go each way to spread the word. The boores must learn that to mutilate a highlander brings death just as our men will remember the punishment for looting."

"Those highlanders hold grudges longer even than we do in the borders." Armstrong accepted the annihilation of the village phlegmatically. "They're good people to have on your side though, Sir, and that's a fact."

CHAPTER 23
Breitenfeld

With their rear defended by treaty with the Dukes of Brandenburg, Pomerania and Mechlenburg, Gustavus Adolphus marched south with enthusiasm. They met the Elbe and turned south along its banks.

"Remember this road, Sir?" Sergeant Armstrong was delighted to know where he was for once. "We'd scarcely got used to not having leg irons on and ye were training us every evening."

Hepburn laughed. "How little we knew then, all of us. If we'd had this army at the White Mountain it would have been a different story."

Small citadels came and went. Most capitulated without a shot fired. The sight of Swedish cannon lining up was enough to precipitate a trumpeter with a white flag.

"I wish some of that money reached us!" Hepburn growled to Monro as he led his men into yet another city offering contribution.

"My Brigade is a disgrace. Oh aye, their muskets are clean and their pikes shine but there isn't one in uniform like his neighbour and they not only look hungry, they are hungry. As for your lot in their plaids, it's as if great moths have been busy for a month."

"But the King told me that what he calls our "Wild Highland Charge" won his battles. So there! The man's human after all."

"All too human! Plumb self centred most of the time." Hepburn thought for a bit. "But what King isn't? I've advised him to march into Saxony as if he means to stay and see what the Duke does."

The Duke of Saxony, brought to bay, simply caved in and summoning his full army met them as if he had always intended to put his men under Gustavus Adolphus's leadership.

The two armies were drawn up to face each other. Astride his sturdy chestnut Hepburn looked back at his Green Brigade, each sporting something green but sadly dusty and bedraggled.

Jamie Douglas moved up beside him.

"Very pretty manikins are they not, Colonel? See the shine on those cavalry boots and you could eat your meat off the pike-men's breast plates. Did we ever look like that? I'd not trust them to do anything that would dirty their bonny clothes though."

Hepburn looked at them thoughtfully. "Their numbers will give us superior manpower to the army Tilly is massing against us at Leipzig. The King likes that but I'd not trust them to stand. I'd better take that into my battle plan. Tilly has the rump of the Old Saxon Brigade that escaped from Landsberg and those bloody Spanish Tercios that hacked off old Halberstadt's arm. They'll not run."

"Smile at the nice new Saxon soldiers then, Sir!" Jamie Douglas wheeled his horse back into position as the Swedish King led the Duke of Saxony down the lines. "Look as dour as ye are and they'll run away at once."

Gustavus Adolphus was delighted to find his Scots officers in good humour. "Attend me tonight Colonel and I'll tell you my battle plan. We march for Leipzig at once with our new allies."

Catching Douglas's lifted eyebrow, Hepburn grinned and nodded. "I'll have a back-up strategy for the Greens."

General Tilly, old and tired but indomitable of will, had drawn up his fifty thousand men in the plain to the North of Leipzig which had surrendered to him by accord after one look at the huge hostile army round the town.

"We are for a pitched battle," he had told his officers. "Leipzig is not important. Today we must slaughter the army of the King of Sweden. He grows more powerful with each town he takes, powerful and rich. He may have more men in the field but we have better soldiers. We will win."

"God willing," said a voice.

"This battle is too important to trust completely to God." Tilly looked round the assembled officers. "I shall also be in charge."

"God's Acre this place translates as". Monro had organised his sentries and joined Sir John Hepburn and the other Scottish officers in his tent.

"Breitenfeld! So it does." John Hepburn had an air of excitement about him.

"You look as if you'll send out sparks soon," his friend told him.

"All the men are fizzing with excitement, Robert. This is going to be a right rammy and no mistake." Hepburn's red hair seemed almost incandescent as the rays of the setting sun caught his unguarded head. The men were in tents spread over the plain and the September weather was comfortable for once, little wind but the baking heat of summer lifted. Hepburn gathered his officers together after their evening meal.

"I've been with the King and this is how we go tomorrow." There was total silence as they concentrated on his words. These were battle-hardened veterans and they respected the man in front of them.

"Our highlanders will take the right flank." There was a growl of approval and Hepburn grinned. "Sir James Ramsay, Sir John Hamilton and you, Sir," he bowed towards Lord Reay, his friend's clan leader, "will lead the foot, both musketeers and pikes. You'll have artillery support to start the battle, four of the King's big cannon and eight small that you can use if the cavalry charge you. Once our big guns stop firing, we will attack as usual with what the King now calls his "Wild Highland Charge", a shattering double volley of shot, three lines of musketeers at a time, and then pikes and musketeers go through into attack. Outside you, Field Marshal Horne will have his cavalry roving to stop any incursions from the surrounding countryside as word is that Tilly has forces hidden in the villages around us."

"Horne's a good man!" That was James Ramsay the Dark, so called for his black hair to distinguish him from Colonel Ramsay the Fair, his namesake.

"Aye I like him well, Cousin!" Reay nodded at Robert Monro beside him and got a nod in return. "He's a gentleman, just. We'll be honoured to have him by."

"The Dutch and Swedes have the centre and are drawn up as you are. The Duke of Saxony holds the left wing and my Green Brigade is in reserve behind the right wing with the ammunition stores behind us as usual."

"An idle day for us then, Colonel?" Jamie Douglas was inclined to feel insulted.

His Colonel laughed. "I think not, Jamie. I want my lieutenant colonels to line their men up in the same order as the highlanders with instructions that they may need to wheel left and move very quickly on command. If we're idle I'll eat my morion for dinner tomorrow! Remember the Tercios hold Tilly's right wing. Now away to your coaches and get some sleep. I'll sleep here where the men know where I am. My coach is too small to stretch out in and anyway the surgeon has made it his own to bring him the casualties so its aye blood stained."

As the next day's sun lifted above the horizon Sir John Hepburn, already up and fully armed except for his headpiece, looked at the blinding light and swore.

"That crafty Tilly knows how to site his army. We'll be facing both sun and wind. God send a few clouds."

Their God seemed deaf for all that Gustavus Adolphus mounted his full army in order and led them in prayer. Then they ate.

Hepburn grunted as he attacked bread and meat with relish. "If it's my last meal I shall enjoy it, Robert. Here take my hand and good luck attend ye! This is what we trained for in France." Then they were off to see to the ordering of their men. The King was everywhere, leading companies forward to point out their positions, making sure they knew their orders. The men muttered proudly as he spoke to them.

Tilly wasn't waiting. His great cannon spoke as soon as his opponents came in range and for two hours they stood and took the fearful roaring rush of cannon ball that tore through ranks of men, scattering limbs and entrails and leaving gaping holes of death in their wake. The screaming started as men were terribly mutilated but the lines closed as if by magic and the officers walked calmly in front. Captains stood forward for lieutenant colonels; ensigns abandoned the colours to their sergeants and calmly unsheathing their swords moved to take their captain's place if he fell. The men rallied and stood firm as their drums steadied to a slow heart beat.

Then Tilly moved. His great squares, sixteen men thick, began to march forward to the quickening drum-beat.

"Musketeers hold your fire!" The highland officers' swords were raised and their drum beat steady. Field-Marshal Horne turned his cavalry towards the incursion in a graceful arc, raised his sword, pointed and they were off trot, canter, gallop, their pistols ready. Unlike their enemies' more traditional approach they performed no caracole, swerving to loose off their pistols at the last moment, but hit the approaching musketeers at full gallop and as they buried themselves in the opposing ranks, mowing men under steel shod hooves, their pistols spoke as one and more men screamed and fell. Then their swords were out creating chaos in the tight ranks that were unable to swing their long barrelled weapons into useful position. On command they wheeled out of the melee and as suddenly as they had struck they had gone. But ahead of the now chaotic musketeers, the highlanders on the right wing fired their eight small cannon loaded with spread shot and the front ranks went down screaming to join the struggling mass behind.

That was the signal for what Gustavus Adolphus called his "Wild Highland Charge". The musketeers loosed two shattering volleys of shot and then they and the highland pike-men were racing onto the shaken squares bursting through their musket cover to strike with awful accuracy. Robert Monro found himself humming a melody from his youth as his half-pike bit deep, turned and retired to strike with the pousse again.

Dust rose. The smoke from the cannon hovered and Monro found himself in a foggy blanket where sounds seemed far away and he could see little around him. The grunts of the men beside him as he toiled entered his ears. As they reached the last of the musketeer platoon and saw a gap he paused looking around. The dust swirled and glimpsing his drummer, he shouted, "Beat the Auld Scots March, lad! The men'll come to it!" As he spoke he heard the drum beat start its heartening roll, men shouted again and he heard orders to form up. Turning he saw musketeers approaching on his left. They looked smart enough to be the Duke of Saxony's lot but his grim smile at their dandyism disappeared as they settled to fire at him.

"My God, Saxony ran!" he shouted, "It's Tilly's bloody Tercios!"

About to order retreat before his men were cut off, he saw a giant of a man in close helmet, green plumes waving above, sweeping into the approaching square like an arrow, his pikemen hurling themselves forward behind him and in the moment before they engaged, their small cannon with exquisite timing hurled spread-shot into the massed men.

"John's at them." Monro was speaking to himself. "We'll be fine now." He turned to order his men to prepare for Tilly's next square, this time of pikes. "Musketeers forward! Fire at will as soon as they're in range! Cannon engage them!" His voice was hoarse but his drummer was beating out the orders as he spoke and he saw the cannon mouths belch fire and the front ranks fall and the ones behind falter as the musketeers found their mark. Then he was off again. "Pikes to the charge!" The drumbeat was urgent as his highlanders fell in behind him and started to run. Out of the corner of his eye he saw Horne's cavalry strike the back of the square causing chaos as the men tried to fight on two fronts but, hemmed in by their very numbers, were helpless to respond.

Tilly's great cannon came in sight and a growl of satisfaction rose as gunners died on highland pikes and the guns stood silent in the stourie air.

"Well done, lads! Our battle's won. Take prisoners where ye can and stop them escaping with their ammunition and baggage!"

"Trust a highland soldier to do that well, Sir!" His ensign appeared beside him, his pike still dripping blood.

"Where's our colours then?"

"Oh Sir, ye wouldna' have me miss masel? I passed them back some-wheres. They'll be safe enough. We won didn't we?"

Monro laughed and tried to see what was going on to his left.

"Did you see what happened on the left wing, lad?"

"Aye. I was still holding the colours then. The Saxony lot took one good look at Tilly and ran. They were shouting "All is lost, save yersels!" Then there was this whooshing sort o' sound and Colonel Hepburn was suddenly there with the Saxons running through their ranks like water in a burn and the Greens going the other way, their musketeers firing with great precision ain rank after another. It was right bonny to watch."

"I saw that bit." Monro nodded. "They're still at it. He's aye magnificent is my friend John Hepburn."

It had been touch and go, Hepburn accepted later. He had ridden out of the dust cloud to see Tilly's cavalry caracoling in front of the Duke of Saxony's equally traditionally formed squares. As he watched the front line shivered as if a strong wind had hit them.

"They'll never stand," he thought and wheeling, rode back to his men.

Swinging off his horse he gathered his half-pike and ordered, "Drummer beat for left wheel." Then raising his voice he shouted "Small cannon forward ahead of us. One volley on command, then step aside!" His men nodded. This was something they had practised again and again. They readied their cannon and moved left.

"Musketeers forward behind them! Pikes follow me!"

The Reserve, Sir John Hepburn's Green Brigade, was on the move.

The Tercio squares having stampeded the Duke of Saxony's men had swung round to attack the right flank of Gustav's men. They met the Green Brigade head on and perished.

This was a grim return for the damage they had wrought to the

Bishop of Halberstadt's cavalry on their road to Bergen op Zoom. Perhaps they remembered Fleurus. Hepburn certainly did. After their cannon's deadly shock his musketeers poured volley after volley into the opposing square then stepped aside to allow the pikes, led by Sir John Hepburn, to tear forward into the main body of already shaken Tercios.

Bannier's cavalry, bewildered by seeing the Saxon retreat, now returned to charge the Tercio left. Hepburn's musketeers infiltrated the right side of the square and turned to pour fire down those ranks.

The Tercio, Spain's crack troops, had never been seriously challenged. Their musketeers were well trained, proud and hardy. They did not run. They died. Trampling on bodies as they went down before him Sir John Hepburn was lost in a quiet world where only the next man existed, where he dealt out death unerringly time after time. He felt shot strike his breast-plate but it could not stop his forward rush. His close helmet guarded his face and the Spaniards who died at his hand saw only a metal mask on a giant that struck and struck again.

Tilly's wave of musketeers was annihilated and the pikes came forward. The old fashioned squares were no match for the new tactics that Gustavus Adolphus's army had adopted and that John Hepburn had drilled his men in until they no longer had to think what to do. Bannier's cavalry took them in the side again and again, charging deep into their ranks using their horses as battering rams so their swords could bite deep. The musketeers of the Green Brigade harried the other side firing accurately and low to miss their body armour.

"A soldier wi' a bullet in his gut disna' gang far." Sergeant Elliot's voice rose above the drum-beat ordering fire by ranks and his men responded. Menteith grinned as he moved forward ahead of his men, calm in the hail of bullets and then deadly as he got within sword length. But powering through the centre Sir John Hepburn led his men on. "A Hepburn! A Hepburn!" his shout rose above the drum-beat and the screams and his men followed, grunting with effort as they killed.

They poured through into the command centre behind the action looking for General Tilly.

"He's long gone!" Robert Monro grasped his friend's hand. "I'm that glad to see you John. Tilly was wounded and they took him away in his coach, so his colonels say. Field Marshal Fustenberg, the Duke of Holsten and the Count of Shoneberg are all dead and we've many, many prisoners."

Later Hepburn was to report to the King that they had lost about three thousand men in all.

"They were cut down by Tilly's cannon in the main, Sire. We must try to find a way to protect against that first cannonade. Perhaps a pitched battle is no longer the way and we need sconces to repel the first salvos."

"But our tactics worked, Sir John!"

"Indeed they did and brilliantly. In fact most of our dead are from the Duke of Saxony's lot. My Brigade is scarce touched. The worst thing is that when Saxony ran they came on our baggage and looted the lot. Could you ask the Duke if he would get his men to give us back our gear. My men would be right pleased to see it again."

Gustavus Adolphus laughed. "For my Scottish soldiers, anything! Without my Scots I would not have triumphed. How many did Tilly lose?"

"Near eight thousand, Sire, and the highlanders captured thirty two great cannon and three score wagons of ammunition to say nothing of hundreds of prisoners."

"We'll ransom the officers and I'll see you get rewarded, Sir John. You can tell Lieutenant Colonel Monro the same."

"I thank you, Sire." John Hepburn's tone was dry. "At least the men taken prisoner have all decided to join your army. Our losses are almost made up without replacements."

That evening the Scottish camp had an almost silent, peaceful air. Men moved slowly, quietly about. Friends shook hands or hugged each other, glad to be alive. No one was celebrating. The fleeing Saxons had stolen their baggage train. Food was in short supply though the cooks had tried their best with fresh horse meat. Of beer or wine there was none. There was little talk but smiles and sighs as they sat round small fires together and remembered friends who had fallen.

In the officers' tent John Hepburn sat with Monro and Jamie Douglas. Hector Menteith came to join them sitting quietly at their table. Looking over, Hepburn could see Lord Reay leaning back and nodding as the dark haired Colonel Ramsay made some remark to him. Colonel Hamilton beside him was smiling in agreement. There was an air of quiet satisfaction in duty done about them.

"By God they deserve to think well of themselves," he thought.

"Our Scots fought like demons," he said out loud. "But more than that they stood and took cannon without flinching. I'd not ask them to do that again if I was leading them."

"It's aye been that way." His friend Monro looked at him and smiled. "Last night it came to me that our life is but a story that we dinna' ken the end of but we must just follow our honourable duty to the end and when it comes welcome it."

"May be so but I'll not ask my men to stand as targets again if I can help it!"

"What else in a battle such as that?"

"I think the day has gone for pitched battles, Robert. I'd put men behind sconces and have wings with musketeers and cavalry and not let it be a formal business like it was. We stood because we had faced cannon before. The Duke of Saxony's lot hadn't. "

They thought about it. "It shows the men's mettle!" Menteith spoke unexpectedly.

"It scatters their brains and guts and limbs and all. I'd rather put them to better use than whistling through the air into purgatory."

Menteith nodded. "I'll give ye that, Colonel. We'll do what you say, anyway."

Hepburn grinned. "You're a good man, Hector. We'd have done poorly if you hadn't been raking those Tercio pikes with bullets." Menteith looked self-conscious but pleased. "The King said to tell you all he'd be rewarding us well for what it's worth!"

"He said the same to me." Monro nodded.

"Oh Robert. You'll believe anything the King says." Hepburn lowered his voice. "If we see any of the ransom money I'll be amazed. The men were not paid last month, nor this one though it's well due. I told mine to grab what they could off the field. At least Tercio armour is the best."

Monro rose. "Well I'm for my coach and bed. Your coach is no doubt shuttling our wounded to the villages round about. I heard our surgeons had set up shop in them once Horne had rid them of Tilly's men."

Hepburn nodded.

"You're welcome to share John."

His friend laughed. "You'd not get room to breathe. My men have set up a wee tent beside this one. I sleep there and well. The nights are still warm for all it is September."

As Monro turned to go he touched his arm. "They've laid out our dead beside yours, Robert, and tomorrow we'll bury them. The Blues are to dig the trenches for Tilly's lot. They'll be at it for days. The King looked at me but I shook my head and he said we deserved a respite."

"He's right there anyway." Monro turned away, his face sad. "I'll say good night to ye all. Tomorrow we'll say good-bye to the rest. This has been a day to remember."

As he went Jamie Douglas looked after him. "He's right holy for a highland-man, John."

"He always was, more like a dominie than a student sometimes." He grinned suddenly. "But when you've pulled him from all the scrapes I have it's hard to take his pontificating seriously. He's a right bonny fighter for a wee man and he's made of steel, mind and body. I'm right glad he's my friend."

Douglas laughed. "I'll remember! He's right one way. There is no man alive who fought today who will ever forget September the seventh and Breitenfeld."

CHAPTER 24
Frankfurt on Maine

The next day, Leipzig opened its gates to them and they marched in.

"Each brigade commandeer a district!" Gustavus Adolphus was heading off to the castle with his Swedes. "Settle in. Let the men relax. They deserve it."

That raised a cheer but Hepburn sighed. "I'd have been happier if he'd paid us as well. We deserve that too!" He turned to his sergeant but Armstrong already had the men in order and marching. "I ken the best district, Colonel. The rest of the Scots will join us. I sent the cooks on ahead."

"Trust a border reiver to look to his comforts." Robert Monro had wheeled his men to follow. "I've heard there's duck and goose and all sorts."

"We're bidden to the Castle to dinner with the King, Robert." Hepburn's shout followed him. "Don't get stuck in to the men's dinner."

"I'll manage fine, Colonel." The reply came back, raising laughter in the ranks. "I missed a meal yesterday, remember!"

That night Hepburn watched Gustavus Adolphus play the King.

"He does it right well," he murmured to Robert Monro beside him.

"Aye, he took me about the shoulders and told everyone that the Scots had won the day for him and begged me to drink with him."

"He did the same for me." Hepburn nodded. "That old General Ruthven who's come from Spruce was for drinking our health."

Monro chuckled. "Old Papa Rotwine, the locals call him! I said I couldn't help His Majesty entertain that one. I haven't got hollow legs."

Hepburn laughed. "I hope the Duke of Saxony has. They are all well in with each other. I couldn't spoil the party by asking for my baggage back."

"Wheesht, John." His friend was horrified at the thought. "They're great men."

"It's time we were as rich! We'll be lucky if we see any ransom money come our way. At least my men have decent armour and gear now, but that's it. It fair makes me mad."

"It'll come John. It'll come." Monro lowered his voice. "I hear the Duke of Saxony goes east with his army towards Bohemia and we are for Erfurt towards the Rhine. Austria should sleep less well I'm thinking."

Hepburn obediently lowered his voice, muttering, "At least that polished bit of uselessness brought us maps of lower Germany. The King had none south of the Oder and I was hard pressed remembering the towns we passed going west after Prague. Saxony gets Leipzig back when we leave and we can stop putting a guard on our baggage train when we're fighting!"

A week later they marched west to take Halle by accord and then turned south.

"We've got fifty well experienced Scots that were in Halle that want to join our brigade, John." Monro was cock-a-hoop. "The King said I could have them all."

"The King is keeping in with us." Hepburn's tone was cynical. "He was arm about neck with us at dinner last night so everyone could see how he loved us and he was making speeches to the men this morning so they cheered him to the echo but have you seen a pay packet yet?"

"Hush, John. Someone will hear you!"

"I'm getting past worrying. The Scots are the best soldiers he has and the worst treated."

"Just bide yersel' in patience, John. He's sent for the Rex Chancellor to come from Spruce to deal with all the foreign emissaries that are gathering. You'll get help when he comes."

Hepburn nodded. His hopes were already fixed on that arrival. "I hear that Duke William of Saxe-Weimar has come over to us. Perhaps his son Bernard accompanies him. You'll like him, Robert. We met in Prague."

In fact all the Dukes and Counts of the smaller Lutheran districts were swearing fealty to Gustavus Adolphus.

"They've little choice." Hepburn stood as yet another Princeling knelt to kiss the King's hand. "But they are hazarding their land, their lifestyle, everything. If things go wrong for us they've lost everything. We just go home. I am right sorry for their plight."

"I'm just glad to see them join us, Colonel." Jamie Douglas came up beside him. "We need men. Our numbers fade, even without a battle. There's aye one plague or another in barracks."

Erfurt, that stronghold of Catholicism, surrendered to the Duke of Saxe-Weimar. Wurzburg was taken by force, the Scots as usual to the fore when they stormed the walls. Then they were marching down by the river Maine on towards Frankfurt on Maine. The trees were bright with autumn colour and fruit hung ripe upon the branches. Wheat was plentiful, so dinner plates were full.

"This is the best part of the campaign so far." Monro managed to find his way to John Hepburn's tent most evenings. He was firm friends by now with Hepburn's lieutenant colonels and they welcomed him.

"Except for no pay." Jamie Douglas looked glum.

"My men are extracting contribution from the villages and I am not handing it on to that fellow Bauditz who the King made our General." Monro sniffed. "He takes everything we give him but doesn't share it out."

Douglas grinned. "We're doing the same. At least the men will have something to spend when we reach Frankfurt. I hear the town sent Commissioners to the King but the negotiations were inconclusive."

Hepburn nodded. "Aye, and Strasburg, Ulm and Nuremberg, forbye. We march against them as if to attack."

Next day they rode over a rise to find Frankfurt on Maine lying before them, grey walls circling the town, graceful bridges spanning the river and pale spires shining in the slanting sun of early winter.

John Hepburn rode up to where Gustavus Adolphus sat his great war horse.

"A pity to raze such beauty, Sire. See how the morning sun makes the buildings shine silver. I've sent Ramsay with a couple of companies to reconnoitre to the East where there are vineyards as cover but you'll mind that since Erfurt we have been invading the lands of the Catholic League."

"You keep your damned religion to yourself, Colonel! I have no pity for Catholics."

"Sire, these are the Catholic League lands you undertook never to invade when you signed that treaty with King Sigismund. We risk losing French support and money." His tone became urgent. "Count Oxenstierna would say the same, Sire, and my men have not been paid for months."

"They get their rations, don't they?" Gustavus Adolphus sounded tetchy "We'll need to set my cannon on this hill, Colonel. Give them a pounding and see if they wish accord."

Hepburn, loath to give an order that he knew would cause serious trouble with their allies, rode slowly towards his men. Suddenly he noticed defenders leaping over the walls and running every which way. By the time he reached his Brigade, Douglas was laughing fit to burst. His ensign and sergeant were pointing. "Look Colonel! They're fleeing. Ramsay sent a rider to say the East gate lay wide so he took his men in and they met nothing but burghers who set up a screech "The Scots are coming! The Scots are coming!", when they saw his plaids. Then everyone started to run. If we could just stop one of them long enough they'd parley!"

"Thank God! I thought I was losing control of that damned Viking!" Hepburn galloped back to the King shouting. "The city is yours, Sire. Who could stand against such a leader?" To himself he muttered, "The

Rex Chancellor should be proud of me for that untruth even if my confessor isn't."

They marched through Frankfurt on Maine flags flying and drums beating. The pipers skirled in front of the highlanders and the people of Frankfurt on Maine thanked their lucky stars that they had not resisted. The burghers brought presents to the King and promised co-operation.

Gustavus Adolphus, astride his great grey, was in an expansive mood. He waved Hepburn over. "Take your men right through, ensure that Tilly is beaten well back so we are safe from attack and then return here for winter quarters, Sir John. See to it!"

Returning to Frankfurt on Maine the Green Brigade found everything in train for celebration.

"The King has gone to escort the Queen on the last stage of her journey. At least I don't have to nursemaid him for that." Hepburn was happy to have peace for a short while. "I'm away to see if there's any books left from last Autumn's Frankfurter- Messe." He laughed at the bewildered faces looking at him. "It's the big book market they hold here. The King told them they could hold it just as usual even if we still hold the city. People come from all over to sell and buy."

"For God's sake, Sir John! Who needs books?" Jamie Douglas rolled his eyes at his colonel. "I'm away to get a new coat fitted. There'll be dancing and receptions and the like when the Queen gets here."

He was right. When the Queen rode in through the gates she found a stage set up in front of the Burgomaster's tall house. The big town square was full of soldiers in their best uniforms and local people in their Sunday best. Drums played, bagpipes skirled and the Queen ascended the stage on one side to meet her husband the King who climbed the steps on the other. They met in the middle and putting her arms around his neck Eleanor cried, "You are my prisoner now!"

Sir John controlled a curling lip but everyone else cheered. From then on the city partied.

King Frederick of Bohemia made the long journey from his court in exile at Brussels, arriving with an entourage of well dressed, penniless courtiers who intended to enjoy themselves at the expense of the burghers of Frankfurt on Maine. The tall terraced houses round the town square filled with lordly visitors who displaced their owners but used their servants and supplies to the full.

The Marquis of Hamilton rode into the town ahead of a small army he had recruited in Scotland.

Sir John Hepburn only knew about it when a Swedish captain arrived at his door one evening.

"The King asks that you see to their quartering, Sir." Clearly ill at ease to be giving orders to a superior officer he stood rigidly to attention and tried to pretend he was not there.

"At ease, Captain", Hepburn gave him the smile that made his own men stand easy but this one clearly wished to be gone. "Tell the King that it will be done." His visitor disappeared as if by magic.

"And no wonder", Hepburn said to Monro the next day. "He just didn't mention the numbers involved. A regiment of Scottish jail sweepings. How Hamilton hopes to get them to fight I know not. No discipline, no training and no wish to gain either. I just threatened them with death if they thieved here and hoped for the best. I'll need to talk with Hamilton and that right soon."

He got the opportunity two days later when, having asked for an urgent meeting, he was bidden to dinner.

The Marquis of Hamilton lived in great state in a suite of rooms in one of the tall houses fronting the city square.

"It's a good enough place for a short visit," he told Hepburn when he congratulated him on finding such a pleasant apartment. "I am, after all, cousin to our King Charles."

"The problem," Hepburn told Monro later. "The problem is that Gustavus Adolphus gave Hamilton's last regiment to Leslie and this time our Marquis wants to lead his own men into battle and become a hero."

"So why can't he?"

Hepburn laughed shortly. "Because he is a drunkard, a lecher, and too young and inexperienced to lead anyone, other than a court lady to bed."

"He's a great Lord, John!" Monro was horrified at his friend's levity.

"He's still all those other things. I offered to put my sergeants on to training his men and he gratefully accepted and even kindly wished to include me in the training process, "Just to make sure they were doing it right!""

"He never!"

"I tell you no lie. The man has no idea how to be a General. He has money and has learned to use a sword and feels he knows it all. He's well fed up with the "Lion of the North"! It was the only sentiment we had in common. So tomorrow, count me out of the hunt. I'll be training jail birds again, and what Sergeant Armstrong and Sergeant Elliot are going to say I really will not want to hear."

"The men are not fit, they've not enough brain to master simple orders and they are very dangerous with arms. They'll kill each other before they get within range of the enemy. Keep them away frae our Brigade, Sir." Armstrong was clear at the end of the day.

"Just let them stay back in their billets, Sir. They're that poorly, the half of them will be dead in a week or two." Sergeant Elliot was equally firm.

"March them back then, Sergeant Armstrong. I'll tell the Marquis they are as ready as they will ever be."

"March!" Armstrong's voice was scathing. "Shamble off in every direction is the best that lot can manage."

As the days passed Hepburn found himself the elected confidant of the Marquis of Hamilton. Respect from the hero of Breitenfeld was flattering to a spoiled young grandee. Even better, the huge red head with his charming smile had no interest in the women that Hamilton fancied.

It was a position Hepburn hoped he might use to escape from Gustavus Adolphus's stranglehold on his life.

"The King relies on me winning for him but he prefers his Swedish generals' fawning and he's never going to make me rich enough to become independent," he said to Monro one evening when they sat alone together, a beer in their hands.

"Had you thought he might be a kennan jealous of your size, John. He's aye more at ease with us smaller yins".

"Whatever! He makes me anxious when he becomes foolhardy because he feels he can't lose. I wish Oxenstierna was here to talk sense into the royal blockhead."

Jamie Douglas brought the news that his wish had been granted when he came to show off his new dark red, velvet coat with gold facings. "I'm thankful to hear it. You'll maybe get enough back pay to pay your tailor now. Half rations have fairly turned us into elegant courtiers!"

Douglas grinned. He knew when his colonel had mockery in his tone.

"Who knows? There may be a well-dowered Swedish lady-in-waiting would fancy a muckle great red-head."

"I'll aye be a war-horse beside you light cavalry." Hepburn sounded resigned. "I'll away to hunt with my friend Robert Monro. At least we're popular with the men if we bring in enough venison."

That evening as they were riding home he asked his friend. "Are you never tempted to attend the junketing, Robert?"

Monro shuddered. "Their kind of dancing is just wickedness, John. I went once and the women were that lustful with their hot breath in my face and the stink of scent was like the Devil's incense, a hateful temptation. I ran."

Hepburn laughed. "The only time I've heard you confess to being trounced. I'll take you round the book stores with me tomorrow. It'll give you something to do these long dark nights. At least Frankfurt has candles and to spare."

Most evenings Hepburn would retire to a tavern where he could sit and savour a tankard of Leipzig beer, his favourite. He seldom sat alone. Bernard of Saxe-Weimar appeared one evening to embrace Hepburn and throw himself into a chair beside him. "My family have declared for your King and here I am."

"Now it's just like Prague again only better because all the people I love best are here." Hepburn's smile was warm. "We'll make you an honorary member of the Green Brigade, Bernard. You'll like my friend Robert Monro and my officers. They'll be along soon and tomorrow we'll go hunting."

Then the weather changed.

"Thank God we are under cover, John." Jamie Douglas hated the cold. "Word is that the King intends to stay here till Spring. That will suit me fine."

He was to be disappointed.

That December of 1631 would be etched in Colonel Sir John Hepburn's consciousness as the worst month of the whole campaign.

CHAPTER 25
To Mainz

"John! Sir John! Colonel! Wake up!" Robert Monro's voice was loud enough to waken the whole district. "The King says mobilise the Green Brigade. We're away to war again! He's going to lead us to Mainz."

"Jesus wept!" John Hepburn rolled over under his warm covers and cursed comprehensively. "That damned Queen is giving him grief again and we've got to bear the brunt."

"How can ye say that?" By this time Monro was in his room, dragging his covers from his resisting fingers. "Get up, John! He came to my room, the king did. My, I was that proud!"

"He knew you were a suck-at-the-tit, Robert. He knew fine what I would have said so he didn't try my door!" He staggered to his feet as his orderly arrived breathless, and started to help him on with his armour. "Does Sergeant Armstrong know?"

"Aye, Sir!" his orderly answered smartly. "We all heard the lieutenant colonel, here. They'll be ready when ye are, Sir."

By this time his officers were crowding into his room, still buckling straps and settling their sword hangers.

"Great news!" Hepburn's tone was as acid as his state of mind. "We spend Christmas in the cold, slogging down-river to Mainz."

"You make it sound a treat, Colonel." Jamie Douglas sounded depressed. There had been dancing promised in Frankfurt, dancing and hunting and good dining.

"Oppenheim is well defended and we must take it first." Hepburn pointed their path on their new maps. "The only thing I can promise is that we will be the first into Mainz and the booty will be evenly divided amongst us."

Gustavus Adolphus, bright eyed and astride his great horse, was waiting impatiently at the South gate of the city with his entourage.

He led them west along the banks of the Maine. It was cold, very cold, as the men trudged, heads down, against a freezing wind. When the sun rose it sparkled on the heavy frost that silvered the trees whose branches drooped under loads of frozen snow. The drum beat kept their slogging steps in time and the activity at last began to warm their bodies inside their cloaks, corselets and as many shirts as they owned which they had piled on against the weather.

"It makes me proud to lead them," Hepburn said to Jamie Douglas, riding beside him. "Never a word of protest, and every one of them feeling just as resentful as I do!"

Douglas laughed. "I'll wager the King knows it too. That's why he's riding with the highlanders this morning. Lieutenant Colonel Monro leads them and is looking well pleased."

"The man's simple when it comes to Kings. Thinks they can do no wrong! I can't make him see straight. Never could. But he's a great man to have beside ye in battle, Jamie."

"Aye. I've seen him in action. Takes no prisoners, that one!"

Late that day they came in sight of the walls of Oppenheim and were greeted with cannon fire. Sir John Hepburn cursed the King in his heart, as he rode to where Gustavus Adolphus sat his horse peering into the distance in the short-sighted way that Hepburn was now used to.

"They have trenches before the walls, Sire, and musketeers well ensconced in them."

"You have hawk's eyes, Colonel. What do you propose?"

"We can't bivouac here or besiege the place while those musketeers lurk around the walls, Sire. Permission to clear the foreground?"

The King waved his hand in acceptance and Hepburn wheeled his horse to rejoin his brigade.

"Menteith! Take our musketeers and work your way round to one side of that great central sconce and start firing. Once they're well engaged with you, Douglas and I'll take the pikes in from the other side. For

God's sake stop firing when you see us come over the earthworks. I've no wish to be slaughtered by Sergeant Elliot's sharp shooters!"

Monro's highlanders stood in the foreground. "Keep your men on the move as if we're getting ready to charge, Robert," He ordered. "That way they'll not think of looking to their flanks."

Cannon continued to play on the highlanders but the cannon balls were largely falling short and though earth was being thrown up close to the men, there was no injury.

Hepburn's men knew their part. They melted into the freezing mist that gathered when the sun went down. As Monro and the King watched, muskets suddenly started to rattle and the trenches came alive with musketeers falling over themselves to turn on the flank where they were facing attack.

Monro looked to the other side and saw what looked like a brown wave break over the trench and disappear into it. Screams and shouts rent the air. The sound of musket fire ceased. Ahead of his men John Hepburn showed little quarter. His pike bit deep time after time and he heard his men grunting with effort as they wreaked havoc along the trench. Few survived and on the battlements horrified faces watched the carnage unable to help in any way.

"I knew they wouldn't fire on their own." Hepburn was panting as he strode up to the King, pulling off his casque. His pike and the front of his armour steamed as the life-blood of his enemies cooled on them. "Right, Sire. We can get the men to set up camp now. Where would you like your tent raised?"

"You did well there, Colonel." Gustavus Adolphus nodded graciously. "I shall assist you by returning to Frankfurt to bring reinforcements." He wheeled and galloped off, his personal entourage falling in around him.

"So we get to sleep in the cold and he finds a warm bed!" Hepburn snorted, but Monro shook his head in reproof. "He's the King, John!"

"He's a bloody nuisance, Robert. If he'd brought his whole army they'd have sued for accord. Now our only warmth will be Oppenheim's damned cannon. It's like treading on an ants' nest. He runs off and we're left to stand while they sting us."

"We'll need to make fires, Colonel. The men will never stand the cold otherwise." Armstrong appeared at his side.

"Aye do it, Sergeant. Heaven send my coach comes up sometime soon. Even if I have to curl into a ball I'll be in it the night."

There were few trees to take cover under and those that straggled by the river side were cut down for the small fires the men huddled round, eating what supplies they had brought with them. It was bread mostly and dried meat. Not much to fill hungry bellies but the Scots were used to privation and just huddled round the warmth. Later they would crawl into small shelters made of branches stuffed with dried grasses pulled from the banks. The earth was too hard to dig turf to make a roofing.

Hepburn sat with Monro gazing morosely at the tiny blaze in front of him. Cannon fire sounded periodically and they heard the "swoosh" of the ball but it was not close. Then suddenly a scream rang out.

"They've killed Sergeant Murdoch, Sir! That bloody cannoneer is shooting at our fires."

Hepburn sighed. "The ground is too hard to dig a sconce to shield the light. We'll just have to bear it."

"He's my senior sergeant and a good man." Monro was furious. But as he half rose, a cannon ball whistled between him and his friend and smashed into Hepburn's coach drawn up behind.

"Now that is the end. I'll be on the ground all night thanks to that damned Viking." Hepburn kicked their fire apart and went to grab what bedding he could salvage from the wreck of his coach. "Stay clear, Robert those bastards have our range. I shall have much pleasure in killing the lot of them tomorrow."

But when the sun rose it glinted on the pennants and armour of the rest of Gustavus Adolphus's army riding towards them.

A surrender party from Oppenheim arrived even before the larger force had reached their camp.

"I couldn't kill even one of them," Hepburn said to Monro later when, warm and well fed, they were preparing to retire to bed in the Castle. "They're Italians, the lot of them and have all begged to join the Green Brigade. I left them their clothes and baggage and removed their weapons pending my agreement."

"They're unreliable, John. Don't trust them!" Monro's tone was anxious.

"Teaching your grannie how to skin a rabbit, Robert?" Hepburn smiled. "Sergeant Armstrong has put them all on watch at the South gate with a couple of pikes that are well blunt and he'll keep an eye on them all night."

By next morning the South gate stood locked with a half company of Scots on watch.

"I was hard pressed not to laugh out loud at their cantrips, Sir." Armstrong's gnarled face was still creased with enjoyment. "The beggars canna' help but chatter for all the officers were hushing them and that so loud I was afraid the rest of the watch would give tongue. Then they were tip-toeing out the gate and running as fast as deer across the ground, slipping and falling and cursing and swearing. It was right comical. When they were gone I shut the gate and placed the guard like you ordered, Sir"

"Well done, Sergeant. Get the men victualled and ready. I want to be the first company into Mainz. There is no way that town of shopkeepers will resist."

He was wrong. They were met by blasts of cannon fire and as they neared, musket balls whizzed around their heads from the trenches in front of the walls.

"Jesus Christ!" Hepburn only swore when stressed. "Look at that flag, James. The Spanish Tercios hold Mainz and after Breitenfeld they have scores to settle with the Scots."

"I take it that'll be another night on the ground then, Colonel?"

"Aye. Tell the men to hold their positions as if we're going to besiege the place, bring up our cannon. They're light things and haven't their range or elevation. Still, they'll let them know we aren't running. Get the cooks to hand out what they have that we can eat without cooking. There's little wood for fires here." He turned to shout at a passing soldier, "You there, Rotmaster Kerr, have someone bring up a new coach for me. This night I'll enjoy the favours of being a colonel."

They took more care to shield their fires that evening but still the cannon played on them and the Scots took casualties.

"They're like frogspawn, those Spaniards." Monro came as usual to join Hepburn at his little fire. "They seem to produce huge numbers however many we kill."

"More like rock slime, Robert, treacherous on the surface and hard beneath."

"Good description, Colonel!" Out of the mist a slim older man appeared and settled himself beside them.

"Count Axeltilly! It's an honour to have you with us. I thought you were in attendance on the King." The two Scots made room for their visitor. John Hepburn had always called him the best of the Swedes and Monro had no reason to doubt his judgement.

"I find I have difficulty making conversation to the Queen's companions. They grow proud and insolent and it is hard to be patronised by a wizened creature up to my knee." Axeltilly sounded apologetic. "Sleeping out is no hardship to a Swede, Colonel Hepburn. We do it for fun some winters at home."

"Their cannon are keeping things warm here, Sir. It might be safer elsewhere."

"What comes will not be denied." He had scarcely spoken when they heard the scream of a cannon ball and there was an explosion of earth between the two Scots.

"My God. They've got Axeltilly." Monro's shout brought Scots soldiers round them gazing down to where the older officer lay, too shocked to even moan.

"His leg's gone!" Hepburn's tone was sharp. "Have you got my coach?"

"Aye Sir. We were just un-harnessing the horses." Rotmaster Kerr had come up behind him.

"Re-harness!" Hepburn tore off his armour and corselet and stripped his top shirt to wrap it firmly round the stump of leg that lay so horribly bare before them.

"Carry the colonel to the coach and put any other soldiers that are wounded in with him and get them back to the surgeon. Wake him if necessary and make him dress the lot of them. It's their only chance."

As he saw them go he turned muttering, "Another night on the ground to thank that damn King for!"

The morning light once more outlined Gustavus Adolphus, well slept and joyous, at the head of his full army. Again the Spaniards opted to treat and Hepburn grudgingly accepted.

"I'd have liked to kill the lot of those wicked wee men but I'll not take losses where I don't need to." He turned to Jamie Douglas beside him. "They can leave with their colours but no weapons. Line the men up, highlanders one side and Green Brigade the other to watch them march out and if you suspect they have booty hidden, search!"

"Aye, and if a man has a limp, look up his trews for his musket." Monro came up to hear his orders and turned away.

"No flies on that one, Colonel!" Douglas laughed as he turned to order his men. "On you neither, Sir! This way we'll be the first in to Mainz and any booty or gifts are ours for a change."

That forenoon the Green Brigade and Monro's highlanders marched into Mainz, colours flying and stomachs rumbling, and there they dined well and slept warm. They welcomed the King into the city the day after and by that time Hepburn had received contributions from the Burghers and had shared them with the Scots. But booty couldn't soften his fury as he went over his muster roles.

"We've buried more Scots than we needed to this day. I hold it against the King," he muttered but only Sergeant Armstrong heard him and he was not about to tell.

"The Queen is not a well woman," Gustavus Adolphus confided to Sir John Hepburn later that day. "Her mind has become diseased and she is not as she was. I fear she will never be normal again."

"I am sorry to hear that, Sire." Hepburn looked suitably impressed, though later he said to Douglas and Menteith. "It's just what I told you. That woman is giving him grief and he wants away. That's why we had to fight in mid-winter. However now we're here I'll do my uttermost to see we stay. It's as easy for envoys to come to Mainz as to Frankfurt so you'd better get that smart coat of yours back into working order, Jamie."

Their first visitor was the French Ambassador. Hepburn remembered him from the Polish truce negotiations.

"Monsieur Hercule de Charnace," Hepburn bowed and held out his hand. "I am honoured to make your acquaintance again."

The small dark Frenchman swept off his plumed hat and smiled. "I remember you Sir John Hebron, whose name I can never pronounce. You were ever the voice of calm. But I doubt you can work any magic here. My King is seriously unhappy about the inroads your master is making. Be in no doubt King Louis will not continue to fund this Vandal sweeping towards France!"

Hepburn laughed. "My sergeant in Paris called me, Hebron, just like you, Sir. It's like coming home to hear it again. I trained with the French King's Guard, you know."

"I did not know you were French trained, Colonel." The Frenchman's interest was caught.

"I did, Sir, and why should you know? You had weightier matters on your mind. But they were the happiest years of my life."

"Indeed!" A brightly intelligent dark eye assessed him. "Again I am here with things on my mind. Will you accompany me to audience with the King?"

They went together and Hepburn bowed before Gustavus Adolphus and begged leave to present the French ambassador, reminding the King that he had met him before.

Gustavus looked down at the small Frenchman in his ornate coat and his lip curled. He had not enjoyed the negotiations with his cousin of Poland and despite Oxenstierna's assurances that they had done as well as they could he still felt unhappy.

"So what has my cousin the King of France to say to me?"

"He is unhappy that your Majesty has seen fit to invade the territory of the Catholic Leagues in direct contravention of the treaty that you signed on the plains of Danzig only two short years ago."

The French envoy's abrupt tone stung Gustavus Adolphus to fury. Raising his fist he shook it at the smaller man. "You may tell your King that I know the way to Paris and if your king makes me angry I have hungry soldiers who will drink wine and eat with as good will in France as in Germany!"

Hepburn blenched. This was crazy talk and he wished the Rex Chancellor had been there to take control. Looking round he could see no help. The King's Swedish officers were all grinning approval, some even gesturing in triumph. The French Ambassador was red-faced and snorting like an enraged bull.

A hand on the Frenchman's shoulder welded him to the spot and Hepburn stepped between the furious men. "Sire. Monsieur Hercule de Charnace means no reproof. He merely begs your Majesty to deal gently with the Catholic League countries."

"Have I done other?"

Hepburn put all thoughts of Wurtzburg, Mainz and Oppenheim from his mind and turned a bland face to a very cross envoy.

"The King was invited into Mainz and Frankfurt as well as Strasbourg and Ulm, Sir. We merely pause to negotiate safety behind us when we make our real push south towards the enormous riches of Munich."

His voice was loud enough to engage the King's interest as well as the ambassador's.

For a moment peace hung in the balance. Blue eyes held the dark French ones, bright with warning. Then the Frenchman nodded. Turning to Gustavus he bowed deeply. "That is indeed what I meant, Sire. If I gave any other impression I beg your pardon most humbly."

Gustavus Adolphus turned on his heel and spoke over his shoulder. "Sir John here can show you our intention. My regards to your master in form if you please!"

He left the chamber, an arm about General Bauditz, pausing only to throw over his shoulder, "You'll attend me after you've escorted the ambassador out, Hepburn!"

The room emptied. Hepburn was left facing Hercule de Charnace

"My God!" The Frenchman wiped his brow. "That one is out of control, no?"

"He has been emboldened by conquest, Sir." Hepburn grinned at the other man's discomfort engagingly. "He's a different man from the wounded leader of a force that had just been trounced on the plains of Danzig. He's battle crazy now and I see to it that he wins."

"Count Oxenstierna?"

"Ah, he's still as sensible as ever and the only man whose advice the King will take."

De Charnace bowed. "I thank you for your intervention. You should be a diplomat."

"Never, Excellency! I am a soldier of fortune and an experienced one. I serve the master I am contracted to."

The ambassador's head came round to survey his huge companion thoughtfully. "Is that so? I think you are more subtle than you admit. Perhaps you would attend me tomorrow night for dinner?"

Hepburn's bow hid the deep satisfaction he felt as he turned away to find the King.

CHAPTER 26
Munich

"What did you mean by the riches of Munich, Colonel Hepburn?" Gustavus Adolphus looked round to make sure there was no one listening, "Get on with it! Tell me."

Sir John Hepburn's golden moustaches lifted in a grin. "We got the trumpeter who came out from Oppenheim to treat, right drunk."

"And?" The King was hanging on every word.

"He said that Munich was overflowing with gold, jewellery and pictures abandoned by their owners who flee south to safety. They've even buried the great Hapsburg cannon there to let them retreat faster."

"Gold, jewellery and pictures? You are sure?"

"Absolutely, Sire."

"We should march at once!"

Hepburn shuddered. "We'd march all the quicker once Spring warms the land and they'll have had time to hide their riches and get out."

"Wise words! Keep Munich to yourself, Colonel. I'll consult the Rex Chancellor and let you know when to mobilise."

Hepburn bowed. "Your Majesty's decision is my command, as always."

"We're billeted in Mainz for the duration of winter!" Hepburn told his officers that evening when they met for dinner. He was greeted with cheers.

"It gets better! The King is going to use the contribution from Frankfurt to pay the men up to date." Hepburn's voice held a chuckle. "He said if Hapsburg troops heard that he paid well they'd desert to us. So don't tell any silly lumps who enlist that it's likely the last money they'll see."

"My! The King is a clever one." Monro's tone was admiring.

"The King, nothing!" Douglas was scornful. "If you don't see our Colonel behind it, you're wanting sense."

Hepburn laughed and shook his head. "Paying the men was our gracious Monarch's own idea. I got him to let us stay for the Winter, however much the Catholic League countries hate us. It's a wonder we don't need tasters before we eat here!"

"We just take their contribution. The Spaniards were Catholic but they bled the burghers white and killed any that refused to pay." Douglas looked self satisfied. "We're better dancers besides."

"Enjoy it while you can. I'm away to dinner with the French ambassador. Happen I'll need a new coat too if this sort of revelling goes on."

Hercule de Charnace had been making enquiries and his despatch to Cardinal Richelieu was emphatic. "The Swedish King depends on Sir John Hepburn to win his battles but ridicules him for being Catholic and scorns his flamboyant dress. Lure him away and this Viking warrior King, who ravishes Catholic lands, will fall. Count Oxenstierna, the Rex Chancellor, will take his place and he is a sensible man with whom France may deal."

While he waited for an answer Charnace made Sir John his friend. Had he known how trapped his guest felt, he would have exulted.

"The King keeps me like a slave to win his battles and never claim a reward," Hepburn complained to Monro as they sat together one evening. "He knows I can't produce letters attesting to my nobility like Ramsay did, so he sighs and says that then he is unable to give me a Barony in Sweden, but still orders me to lead my Brigade to make the breach into any city he is attacking and then stand aside so his Swedes can march through and grab the booty." His misery was complete when news reached him of Cathy's death.

Sergeant Armstrong heard it first. "Once ye went away frae Frankfurt she went back to her friends in the baggage train. They're quartered by Hamilton's jail-fevered rabble, so my cousin says." He shook his head.

"Cathy just took the fever and was gone in three days."

"Thank you for telling me Sergeant." Hepburn as usual kept his thoughts to himself but he felt the loss deeply. When, two weeks later, Hercule de Charnace offered him a Colonelcy in the French army he accepted without hesitation.

"I'll need to stay with the King while he's pushing forward," he said. "But the Marquis of Hamilton means to return to London. I'll go with him. He has offered to introduce me to King Charles and I had it in mind to ask His Majesty for a recruiting warrant."

"You'll be welcome in Paris with or without men, Sir John Hebron." Ambassador Charnace was well content.

In the burgeoning warmth of the 6th of March 1632 the Scots marched out of Mainz in good fettle. Sir John Hepburn had a formal offer of a Colonelcy in the army of France, signed by Cardinal Richelieu under seal of King Louis XIII, in his pocket, Robert Monro had read himself to a standstill and Jamie Douglas had danced with every rich beauty in Mainz and found none he wished to marry.

Sergeant Armstrong spoke for all of them when he said, "It's time we were away, Colonel. The recruits are trained as far as I can make them. They need the real thing now to turn them into soldiers."

"This is the sort of marching for me!" Robert Monro had ridden over to overhear Armstrong. "Warm days without dust, decent camp sites and even though the Imperialists have raped the countryside, we've enough food coming from the north to give the men a decent ration."

"Thank Count Oxenstierna for that." Sir John Hepburn had been delighted to have had a long audience with the man he revered. "We discussed the problems and he is going to try to keep our supply lines open."

Thirty two thousand, horse and foot, followed King Gustavus Adolphus south. Their march, unimpeded by the orchards destroyed by the retreating Hapsburgs, still offered new grass for their cavalry horses and here and there a fruit tree was bursting into white blossom.

Oxenford on Maine fell, then Vinchen, then Furt on the river Pegnets that guarded the pass south into what had been Palatinate territory.

Nuremberg welcomed them, the two Kings riding in side by side. Their Elector Frederick had come home and brought the Lion of the North with him. The burghers brought them rich gifts.

Donauworth on the Danube proved a much harder nut to crack. As Gustavus Adolphus pounded the north walls with cannon shot, Sir John Hepburn, his green-plumed casque above his bright breastplate and a half pike in his hands, led his men into an army of escaping soldiers from the south gate. Towering over most of the men about him he powered into the now disorganised troops, pike biting deep.

"He's better than the colours to home in on!" Jamie Douglas led his men in pursuit of the huge killing machine.

Armstrong, ahead of him gave a grim nod. "No prisoners yet, men! These are all Spanish regulars who'll give us grief if they escape!"

They killed five hundred in that push and only bodies barred their entry to the town.

"Open the North gate, Sergeant Armstrong. We'll let the King in but tell the men to get their booty quick, as once he comes he'll take it all himself." Hepburn moved forward to greet a delighted Gustavus Adolphus.

When he returned Armstrong was waiting. "It's not right what the Swedes are doing, Sir! We just cleaned out the empty houses, and we've booty enough including a nice horse for yourself, Colonel. But that Swedish Colonel Worbane's men are hanging the burgers up by their balls to make them give up their money. It'll give us a bad name."

"The King appointed Worbane governor, Sergeant! But the burghers'll know fine whose orders those are. We'll leave them to it, savages that they are! Make camp up-stream by the river away from the stench of death."

That evening, as he sat in his tent, a young, sandy haired man in officer's uniform entered, a nervous look on his face and a letter held out. "Count Oxenstierna sent me,"

"James! For goodness sake! It's you lad!" John Hepburn, surprise and a growing concern in his face, leapt to his feet. "What are you doing here?"

"Same as you, John, er Colonel." James Hepburn was puzzled. He'd expected more warmth from his big brother. "When Count Oxenstierna heard who I was, he called me in, spoke right kindly and sent me to you. I used father's leavings to buy an ensignship and I've worked to better myself! I'm a captain now." His smile drooped. "Count Oxenstierna said he thought you'd be pleased."

John Hepburn recovered and enveloped his brother in a huge embrace. "I am James, I am. It's just such a shock. How's everyone at home?"

"As always, but once George married there was no place for me." His tone held resentment.

Sir John sighed. "Sit, James and listen, but tell no one or I'm a dead man. I'm sure Oxenstierna sent you to me to be a safe conduct for my letters to him. He thinks that way."

He held up his hand to stop his brother's intervention. "Aye, I'm Oxenstierna's man though I'm contracted to the King. The Rex Chancellor drew me in to calm the King when he wanted to walk out of the peace talks with Sigismund two, three years ago. I was the King's favourite then, and I kept him sweet. In return he got the King to send me as ambassador to the Danziggers, said I was better at negotiation than any Swede, but those days are well past. The King got wounded and he's in pain half the time and Oxenstierna trusts me to keep him safe and win his battles, but I've fair lost the King's favour. I'm whole and strong and tall and he's not. That King Frederick is his best friend now and he is a right self server. However Oxenstierna is content as Frederick never goes near the fighting and he keeps King Gustavus by him so he's doing my job. But once you're the Rex Chancellor's man you're that for life. He pays for my letters of information. Sometimes it's the only money I get as the King is right miserly."

He lowered his voice as he continued. "I'm getting out as soon as I've saved enough money. The King will have me killed in battle else. I know it. Having you here just puts you in jeopardy too so tell no one that you're my brother. While the King doesn't know, you're safe. Oxenstierna won't tell. He's a secretive spider with a web of informants that the King knows nothing of. But he's the King's man for all that and a Swede through and through so we can't annoy him either."

"Ye Gods, John! What a fankle." The younger man ran his hand through his curly hair. "But I'm well trained and I can look after myself and my men, John. You'll see!"

His brother laughed. "Blate as always, young man! But at least you now know the score and you'll be trained when my Sergeant Armstrong says so, not before!"

It was not many days before Armstrong reported the new company fit to fight. "Their captain's your brother, isn't he, Colonel? He doesna' look like ye. He's smaller but wiry like and tough and a bit of a firebrand but his men are for him so he must have something of ye."

"Aye, my younger brother. We were close when we were young."

"He doesna' make anything of it." Armstrong nodded approvingly. "When I asked him if he was related he just said, "All Hepburns are kin.""

"He's a good lad." John Hepburn nodded as he suddenly realised he was well content to have someone who he could talk to without reserve.

"The King becomes greedy for booty," he said one evening, when his brother, seeing him alone, had slipped into his tent. "Priests flee south ahead of us with their monasteries' treasures just as the Scots did when the Vikings came. But don't quote me or I'm a dead man."

His brother grinned. "There's no one knows we're close, John. I'm just another captain at the foot of the table." Then as he looked at the big red-headed brother he loved, his face sobered, "Take care, John. Being unco' grand has pitfalls."

But the King had no complaint while his army rolled south. Dillingen, Minchin and Neuberg opened their gates. Still Gustavus pressed on.

At the banks of the Lech river they finally met General Tilly, his army drawn up for battle. No longer battle-hardened veterans, his tightly packed squares were blasted into blood spattered shreds by Gustavus Adolphus's cannon.

Tilly himself received a small cannon ball in the knee and was carried off the field. The rest ran, leaving about a thousand dead, and three days later "the Monk in Armour" had joined them.

On and on they pressed. The Duke of Bavaria had no troops that could withstand the cannonade that Gustavus Adolphus launched. Augsburg accepted an accord. Besieged Ingolstadt surrendered.

As they went the King left troops behind to assume control of the towns they had taken. It meant their force was seriously diminished.

"This way our retreat will be secure, Sir John," he told his Scottish commander. "So long as my Green Brigade is there to fight we shall reach Munich."

Hepburn was less content. There was word that Wallenstein had recruited a huge army and was moving in their direction.

"Wallenstein marries for money and kills for pleasure. Saxony won't stand. They'll probably even give him our baggage that they stole when they ran at Breitenfeld. Our forces are thinned to danger point." He was sitting with his lieutenant colonels in his tent, a tankard at his hand, when Duke Bernard of Saxe-Weimar joined them.

"Why do we have to reach Munich, Sir John? The Kings talk of it as the Holy Grail."

Hepburn smiled and shook his head. "I'm their fighting dog, Bernard, not their confidant. I just want to stay alive while they show off their manhood."

Jamie Douglas chuckled. "I'm with you, Colonel. Thank God it's still early summer. I'd hate to be marching back in the snow with Wallenstein snapping at my heels."

It was the 6th of May before they saw the walls of Munich and Hepburn had become seriously anxious. He had reliable intelligence that Wallenstein was marching North and West to cut off their retreat. But the Lion of the North and the equally voracious King Frederick of Bohemia were blinded by greed.

"Surround the town with your Green Brigade, Colonel Hepburn. Let no one escape with their valuables!" Gustavus was in high spirits for the town had capitulated without a fight. "Tomorrow the Scots will take over the town and the rest of my army will make camp outside, ready to march when I give the word. See to it!" "Those orders have hardly made me popular with the Swedes," he muttered to Monro as they marched in together.

"It's an honour, John, and I am to be in sole charge of their Majesties' housing at the palace while ye govern the town from the castle."

"Oh, Robert, you're simple minded where Kings are concerned. He's chosen you because you're such a souk, man! You can see no wrong in the Kings but they are just reivers like the rest of us. You wait and see."

He did not have long to wait. King Gustavus Adolphus and King Frederick took over the palace, stripped its portraits and tapestries, looted anything worthwhile and ordered Robert Monro to pack them and send off the carts to Frankfurt on Maine where Oxenstierna had orders to see them shipped to Brussels and Sweden.

They hunted in the palace policies, killing deer and hares by the score and dining richly. Each day they played tennis together in pleasant accord before threatening the burghers to let the Scots loose upon them if the constant outpouring of gold, jewels and money faltered. Robert Monro, dazzled by their condescension, made their life as easy as possible and even found the great cache of cannon that the Duke of Bavaria had buried and arranged for it to be trundled north for later use.

The Marquis of Hamilton, already rich beyond avarice, retired to Hepburn's quarters in the castle to give dinners for any young and beautiful noblewomen foolish enough to have stayed.

But there were empty mansions that the two Kings missed and these the Scots from the castle looted quietly and efficiently and spread the booty amongst their companies in fair distribution. As usual Hepburn had his men under tight discipline and the townsfolk remained unmolested. However, affluent burghers included Sir John Hepburn in their outpouring of contribution in the hope that they and their families would remain safe. This money he kept. No one came out of Munich empty handed, except perhaps Robert Monro, who was too happy hobnobbing with royalty and the Marquis of Hamilton who was too rich to care.

By the first of June 1632 Hepburn had become seriously rich and seriously anxious about their retreat. The army outside had captured a messenger from Ferdinand that spoke of Wallenstein accepting the post of Generalissimus of the Imperial Army on the 26th of May. He found the two Kings at their tennis and waited impatiently until they came off court, arm about each other's shoulders, to give them this intelligence.

"He'll be heading West through Saxony to cut us off, Sire!"

"Time to go, hey?" Gustav was still in spirits.

King Frederick nodded. "We'll make for Nuremberg. I'll be safe there amongst my own subjects."

As they turned away, Gustavus threw a word over his shoulder. "That Lieutenant Colonel Douglas of yours! You'll find him in the common jail. We sent for him to partner us at tennis but he dared to appear casually dressed and thought to excuse himself by saying that he had just returned from leave."

Hepburn stood incandescent with wrath. "You put my officer in a common jail, Sire, and without consulting me! I gave him leave of absence. He has worked tirelessly for your Majesties. You have no right to behave so!"

Gustavus Adolphus turned, his face darkening, "You question my right to command, Colonel! This is mutiny and the punishment is death!"

Hepburn fought for control. "I am yours to command as you well know, Sire! But if you undermine my authority over men who have fought and risked death for you, I have no position. We need Douglas to mobilise his men so they can escort you safely north."

Turning away, Gustav Adolphus shrugged. "Find him then. We don't need him for tennis any more!"

CHAPTER 27
Escape from Gustavus Adolphus

They were on the march a couple of days later. Sir John Hepburn's fears had communicated themselves to the whole army. Regiments poured north, unit by unit, colours flying, cavalry jingling, musketeers with shouldered weapons and pike-men, their weapons at the trail, all marching in time to the drum-beat. Great trails of oxen pulling cannon rumbled behind them followed by ammunition wagons and last of all, the chaotic shambles that was the army of the camp followers.

Hepburn was thankful to be away. At the last moment Gustavus Adolphus had noticed that not all his prize wagons had been packed.

"Hold the army, Colonel! I'm not ready."

"As soon try to hold the sea back, Sire!" Hepburn was not going to even try. His King stared at him his face darkening in furious disbelief. Hepburn bowed to avert a tongue lashing.

"Order General Bannier to take over Munich, Sire, He'll dispatch your prize wagons, wrest a last contribution from the burghers and follow us. You are our lodestone and it is you I must make safe."

"Lost without me, hey? That is true, all true. Pass the order, Colonel!"

Sir John Hepburn sighed with relief. "And it's not true either," he muttered to Jamie Douglas later. "Count Oxenstierna would lead us just as safely and without all the bowing and scraping."

His lieutenant colonel looked sideways at him. "I'll consider I did not hear that, Colonel. Just be thankful we were the ones in Munich. I'm rich!"

"I too!" Hepburn shook his head. "Those two Kings, scrabbling for profit like greedy children in a feast day kitchen, scunnered me. It's not as if they've paid my men. The Swedes will hate us all the more for being the ones in Munich but I no longer care. I'm getting out when I can and if I'm still alive! I've had a bellyful of being taunted for my religion and my dress."

"My thoughts exactly, Colonel! As I lay in my filth in that bloody jail, and all for not turning up to play the pretty at a tennis match, I realised he thought I was a damned poodle to jump when he commanded and die at his pleasure. If you hadn't come for me I'd have perished."

Hepburn's face closed. "Just don't get me started, Jamie. The King never knew how close he was to death that day!"

They made long marches North, first to Donauworth, but supplies there were scanty. Sir John Hepburn used this as an excuse to push on.

"We have to make the pass at Weissenburg before Wallenstein knows our intention," he told Robert Monro when he asked why they were in such a rush. "My men have been abroad of an evening, scouting, and the villages round about are full of news that they will be saved by that Bohemian monster. Little do they know he'll take their all and, if they resist, their lives as well."

It was a close call. Wallenstein was hard on their heels when the last of the baggage train staggered through the hill bound road into the plains around Nuremberg.

"At last a city that is pleased to see us!" Douglas rode up to report his men present and correct.

"The joy is mutual." Sir John Hepburn felt a great sense of relief. "We need their supplies and they need our protection. Long may it last."

Gustavus Adolphus was in his element, giving out orders for his army to dig in all round the city, seeing each officer personally to explain their duties. Like magic the ground changed. Huge trenches gaped and walls of earth were thrown up to protect against cannon fire. Camp sites were set up in protected areas and the army settled down thankfully. Marching on increasingly empty stomachs had lost its charm.

They skirmished with the approaching forces. On one occasion Jamie Douglas appeared with fifty oxen.

"I've told the cooks to use them sparingly, Colonel. There's no need to tell the King is there?"

"None in the world! Finders keepers! Our men are muttering about back pay. Thank God they still have their Munich booty. The Swedes are ready to go home. I find the King's greed overweening. His men have done him well. I wouldn't treat them so. He'll need them yet."

Douglas nodded. "You're right there! Wallenstein has us well surrounded and though he makes no move I calculate that he has thirty thousand men to our sixteen. It's a wonder he doesn't attack."

More and more the Scots soldiers drew apart from the other units. They had their own camp outside the city walls. Gustavus Adolphus had been invited into Nuremberg with King Frederick and unless there were orders to be given, the Scottish officers tended to mess together in camp. If Sir John Hepburn went into Nuremberg it was to dine with the Marquis of Hamilton who now found himself entirely sidelined.

"The King treats me like a minor ambassador not a general! I shall not stay."

Hepburn could only agree with the King but he wasn't about to say so.

"I should be happy to accompany you back to London, my Lord. I have received a very flattering offer of a commission in the French army. "

"I could present you at court! The hero of Breitenfeld!" The dark haired young man's petulant face lit up. "I have the ear of King Charles. We are, after all, related."

"I should be grateful, Sir. In fact I shall lose no time in withdrawing myself from the Swedish army. The King will realise your true worth when we leave."

"He will, won't he!" Hamilton was delighted. To have the most prestigious colonel in the Swedish army begging his protection was a boost to his self esteem. "He'll wish he had paid me more regard!"

"The whole army will miss you, your Lordship. You brought men and supplies at a time when we badly needed them." Flattery, he thought with a sigh, was becoming second nature to him. Hamilton's jailbirds were long dead of fevers and plagues. "We could petition King Charles to grant me a recruiting warrant. The Scottish Privy Council would finance it and our King could send me and it as a good-will loan to Louis of France."

"Now this is something!" Hamilton was delighted with the idea. "We'll keep it between us, Sir John! King Gustavus Adolphus will learn what he has missed."

But the Swedish king was not wishful to learn unpalatable truths.

"I shall not miss the smell of incense at my war council, Colonel Hepburn," was his reply to Hepburn's formal request to be relieved of his command, and as he turned away added, nor a colonel who seeks to out-dress his betters."

The sheer ingratitude took Hepburn's breath away. Only the memory of Oxenstierna's sorrow at his leaving stopped hot words from bursting forth. But when Gustavus Adolphus, as if to prove how little he needed his Green Brigade colonel, launched an attack on a hill held by Wallenstein, his fury turned to dread. Hovering behind the King and his entourage his horror grew as he saw Robert Monro lead a company of Green Brigade pikemen over open ground to attack an enemy well entrenched on the upper slopes.

"But Wallenstein will have reserves behind the peak, Sire!" The warning was wrung out of him.

"Not your men, Sir John! I gave Monro your Green Brigade. He follows my orders to attack." Hepburn watched as the Scots turned and twisted and then were lost to view in the gathering dark. Above them musket flashes became ever more insistent.

"They're not winning the ground!" At last Gustavus Adolphus seemed to realise the danger. "Order retreat! There are Swedish troops with them." The Swedish generals around him looked at each other and shifted in their saddles.

"It's suicide, Sire."

"I am retired from your service but I will go if you permit?" Hepburn spoke quietly but his tone was urgent.

The King nodded. It was enough.

Sir John Hepburn was off, lying flat to his saddle as his horse streaked across the unguarded plain. Shot whistled over him but thankful for his steel corselet, he just lowered his head and rode. He came up with Menteith already in armour, his musketeers in battle order.

"They're being bloody mown down! The King says bring them off, all of them!"

Menteith just nodded. "Beat the advance, drummer. Tell the King we're on it. Heaven send we're in time. Douglas is there with Colonel Monro!"

"I'm with you, but you've command. Save the Scots. I'll sort those useless Swedes."

They parted at the killing ground. The disorganised Swedish musketeers found a huge officer amongst them shouting orders in a voice that brooked no delay. In minutes they were in ranks and retreating as if at drill, their rotmasters beginning to take command again as they staggered out of range of Wallenstein's guns.

Later Jamie Douglas came to his tent.

"Colonel Monro has got himself a ball in the side, John. Lucky for him it hit the clicket on his sword hanger before it seared him. Thank God you sent Menteith. In the dark it was anybody's guess who was who, but Elliot knew! He starts shouting, "The next yin o' you miserable vermin to try to get past me gets my musket up his bum!"

John Hepburn started to laugh and even Douglas smiled at the memory. "It fairly turned the tide. We all edged back up the hill where the Colonel was staggering about covered in blood, still trying to lead his men. I took over, sorted them out and we came off with few losses." He hesitated, and looked down. "Armstrong's not with us. He was watching Colonel Monro's back. I'm sorry, Colonel. I know you were fond of the man."

"Aye I'll miss him." Hepburn sighed. "It was going to be hard to bid him good-bye. You'll see him properly buried, Jamie?"

Douglas nodded. "The Colonel thinks the King is Lord God Almighty, John."

"He's a highland gentleman. They love royalty. Encourage him to recruit in Scotland. Go with him and stay. You'll be safe that way."

On the fifteenth of September 1632 he set off for the coast riding beside the Marquis of Hamilton. King Gustavus Adolphus remained in conference with his Swedish generals but all the Scottish soldiers turned out to wish them farewell. His drummers, now almost grown men, beat the old Scots March. Monro, still pale from blood loss, embraced his big friend.

"We were comrades in love before ever we were comrades at war, Jamie," Monro said sadly as his old friend rode out of sight. "I'll miss him sore. Catholic and opinionated he may be but he's magnificent! I'd follow him to Hell and back."

However, Sir John Hepburn, riding beside the Marquis of Hamilton, saw the Autumn berries spangling the briars by the roadside and felt the excitement of a new life beckoning as he had many years before on the road to St Andrews.

In London, King Charles nodded delighted approval at the idea to raise a regiment on loan to Louis XIII and confirmed Hepburn's knighthood. The Privy Council in Edinburgh were happy to offer him a secretary and the sweepings from their jails. Sir John Hepburn took the one and refused the other. "I'll recruit only Scottish veterans, my Lords."

Then he was away back to Monks Rig. At once he missed Sergeant Armstrong. The Privy Council secretary was no organiser.

Hepburn sighed as a cacophony of shouts rose from the chaotic mass outside his recruiting tent. It was going to be a long day. Suddenly quiet fell, then sharp orders and a regular tread began to overtake the milling about. A few curses rent the air.

"I know that voice," he shouted leaping to his feet. "Sergeant Wat

Elliot you great lummock, thank God for ye!"

A grinning face looked in the tent. "Aye, Colonel. After Andra Armstrong died it wasna' the same. The King pushed Swedish captains that he'd taken a shine to on to us and they couldna' speak English. Colonel Monro did nothing so I left. I'd made some booty in Munich and thought to settle, but I'm no farmer. When I heard ye were recruiting it was an answer to prayer."

"I'll not ask if you've any experience! Do you want a commission?"

"Na', Colonel. I'm aye happier with the sergeants and rotmasters and training the men."

"Sign here, then, and take charge. I'm recruiting experienced soldiers only, Wat. I've got messengers going all over Scotland so you'll have your work cut out welding them into a well trained regiment. We'll call you Sergeant Major. Doesn't maybe mean much but you'll get more pay!"

In the end Hepburn found enough seasoned captains to take over the companies made up by Elliot. Just his name, Sir John Hepburn, brought volunteers from all over Scotland. Most were Dutch trained. Many were Catholic and had been unhappy about remaining in that Reformed Church army. France would suit them fine, they said.

"Ye'll need a lieutenant colonel, Sir." Elliot said one morning.

"Which of the captains shall I choose then?"

Wat Elliot grinned. "It's in my mind ye should wait a wee while, Sir. It's amazing who may turn up."

"With prayer?" Hepburn laughed shortly.

"I dinna' think we need to go to those extremes!"

Next morning, he found a thin, sandy haired, young man bending over his lists, signing up, a grizzled looking soldier already accoutred in buff jacket.

"I'd made a bit o' booty so I came home with Sergeant Elliot, John. I thought I'd join George but he doesn't want me. Do you need another captain?" There was a half-shy half-pleading look to his face though he stood to attention.

"James!" His brother stood transfixed, his thoughts chaotic.

The silence between them grew. James Hepburn lowered his gaze, disappointed. He had hoped that the aloof brother he knew in Germany might have changed. It seemed not. But Sir John Hepburn was lost in his own homecoming disillusionment. "Drop your purse and leave is all my brothers wish me to do," he had said to Marie.

A widow now, her face had crumpled in sorrow. "Dearest John. You're always welcome here."

"I know, I know, Marie. I gave them what I could. George can buy a wee farm by Coldstream, and Andrew will settle his son as a burgess of Haddington. But it is you I'll name to look after my affairs, none other!"

As the truth struck him he blurted. "We're all that's left of family! And no! James, lad, I have your namesake and our cousin as my senior captain." His face split in a huge grin. "I don't need another captain, James. I need a lieutenant colonel. Will you sign on with me?"

"Lieutenant Colonel!" James Hepburn's face lit with delight. "I should think so!" Then he paused. "But you'll tell me what you want doing, John. Don't let me get it wrong."

"Sergeant Major Elliot will tell us both what to do, I make no doubt." Hepburn had his hand out but his younger brother hugged him fiercely, then stood back and saluted. "I'll be there to watch your back when he isn't."

CHAPTER 28
Marshal de Camp

Cardinal Richelieu, sitting hunched in his red robes behind his huge desk, was vexed. His vast Palais Cardinal, completed by architect le Mercier just three years before, gave him no pleasure. His pages slid away to find other duties. Their master frowned.

"Having survived a palace coup, planning a war should be simple," he muttered. "But I need trustworthy commanders and charismatic leaders who will give me victory and the only recruit I'm offered is a deserter from that blockhead Gustavus Adolphus's army; some Scottish thick-wit that Ambassador Charnace signed up, probably in a drunken stupor in Mainz. Oh God, send me a leader!"

He heard a disturbance at the far end of the room and kept his head down. Let the damn man wait.

Sir John Hepburn had dressed carefully for the interview. His chestnut-brown velvet coat was laced in gold and a gold chain of command glowed on his chest. Plumed hat in his right hand, he let the other lie on the pommel of his serviceable sword. Away from Swedish army rules at last, he had let his hair grow to his shoulders as other French officers did. Walking forward expecting a welcome he came to a halt faced with a resolutely lowered head.

At a loss, Hepburn stood, straight and soldierly, and at that minute the sun burst from behind the clouds outside and a great beam of light blazed through the long windows, enveloping him as he stood.

Richelieu looked up, transfixed. He saw a huge golden figure, a shining warrior outlined in light.

"A Golden Knight! Can God answer that quickly?" he muttered and scolded himself for blasphemy.

"He reminds me of Count Oxenstierna," thought Hepburn and smiled. "He's tiny and frail but his eyes are wise."

He moved forward to sink on one knee before the red robed churchman and automatically Richelieu put out his hand for Hepburn to kiss his cardinal's ring, but as he looked a sunbeam followed and turned the bowed head before him fiery red.

"A crown of glory for France!" he thought, "This is meant."

"Welcome, Sir John Hebron," his voice hesitated on the surname and Hepburn looked up and smiled, a smile so full of delight that the prelate found himself smiling back.

"To be Hebron again! At last I am home. Tell me how I can serve you, Eminence?"

Richelieu found himself pouring out his problems to an expert whose advice, though sparing, appeared based on experience.

"We must talk again, Colonel Hebron. You shall dine with me."

Hepburn bowed, stammering his thanks. "It will be an honour, Eminence."

"It was as if we had been meant to meet and work together," Sir John Hepburn told his brother later. "I would fight to the death for a commander like that."

"It's certainly a lot more welcoming than Germany. The barracks are cleaner, the food regular, and an official has already demanded a list of our numbers so he can pay us! When did King Gustavus Adolphus ever do that? What is more, they call us "Le Regiment d'Hebron", which is the best they can manage with Hepburn."

Sir John Hepburn nodded. "I know. It lets people know who leads them but I told His Eminence that my regiment will be called "The Royal Scots". They can manage that in French and, after all, we were raised by warrant of one King as a loan to another."

It was not long before Sir John Hepburn's own fluency in French returned. He was thankful. He had no wish to appear stupid before the Cardinal but now his occasional mispronunciations only seemed to amuse the great man.

"It was all the Emperor Charlemagne's fault." Richelieu had bidden Hepburn to dinner but when he arrived, flamboyant in gold embroidered scarlet velvet, he found himself the only guest except for a quiet man in the grey habit of Franciscan monks that the French called Capuchins.

"Father Joseph, here is my new Colonel. He brings a regiment of Scots as a loan from his King Charles."

Hepburn had no knowledge of the awe that monk, Father Joseph, engendered. To be reported to Richelieu by "l'Eminence Grise" was everyone's nightmare. Peasant or Marquis, they shuddered at the thought. But to Sir John Hepburn the name Father Joseph brought happy memories. He turned to him with a smile of such innocent charm that both men were startled.

"A Father Joseph showed me the true Church, Eminence. It will always be a name I revere. I am delighted to make your acquaintance, Father." He bowed and beamed down on the smaller man.

"Father Joseph, bearing the name Francois Leclerc du Tremblay, Baron de Mafflier, was once a fighting man like you, my son." Richelieu was half amused by Hepburn's innocence. "He will accompany your regiment."

"We have priests already." He bowed again. "But Father Joseph is very welcome. I shall arrange especially comfortable quarters for him if he is your special agent and as an old soldier I shall be happy to listen to his advice."

"And take it, my son?" The grey-clad monk's voice was sharp.

Hepburn's lazy smile enveloped him. "I shall always listen, Father."

Richelieu laughed. "Tonight you'll meet other commanders of my King's forces. Tonight we'll plan to push France's eastern boundaries to their rightful place."

Hepburn nodded. "The Imperialists in the Spanish Netherlands, Lorraine, Alsace and Savoy crowd in like crouched lions with all the danger of sudden attack."

"Not only sudden attack but with rich farm land that should be ours."

Richelieu was clearly repeating an old refrain. "When Charlemagne died he left this continent to his three sons, a Western kingdom which is now France, an Eastern one which has been broken into the Germanic states, and a middle kingdom which has been nothing but a curse and a danger to France."

"The Spanish Netherlands?" Hepburn's history lessons had only touched Europe fleetingly.

"Indeed, but also Lorraine where Duke Charles sides with the Hapsburgs, and uses Spanish troops to man his castles."

"So we take Lorraine again?" The man in the grey habit spoke.

"Indeed we do but we must also take the Spanish Netherlands. I wish to enlarge France to the East for King Louis, God give him grace, stabilise our boundaries with the Dutch and swell the coffers of my King with the taxes from those rich middle kingdom territories. So far the Dutch have kept the Spaniards too busy to turn on France. Now I need to show them that I am on their side."

Hepburn nodded. "A great enterprise, Eminence! How can I and my Scots help? The regiment I recruited are all experienced men and ready."

"You are for Lorraine, Colonel. You are the backbone of the army under Jacques-Nonpar de Caumont de la Force and you will meet him tonight. He is old now, but still honoured in France and I can get younger men like the Vicomte de Turenne to serve under him without complaint. Gaspard de Coligny, Marechal de Chatillon, will do the same in the North-east and a relative of mine, de Breze, goes with him to do the fighting."

They ate in a room off the great hall. The dinner was formal and Sir John Hepburn looked enviously at the gilded wine stoops and silver plate that shone in the twinkling light of golden candelabra standing with military precision down the middle of the table. The King of Sweden's dinners had been gargantuan but had never offered the elegance that he enjoyed that evening.

"I shall have the same," he said to his brother the next day. "The delight of drinking from things of such beauty was breathtaking. You wait James. You'll see."

"Happen it will have to be in your apartment, John." His brother grinned affectionately. "I doubt the Cardinal has me on his guest list."

Hepburn had found la Force a prickly old bear.

"You march under my banner. You'll do what I order!"

"It will be an honour to serve under you, Sir."

"It will, will it? Then you had best see to the quartering and feeding. I can't give time to petty things. I need to concentrate on strategy."

"My thoughts exactly, General!" Richelieu beamed at them down the table. "I have therefore promoted Colonel Sir John Hepburn to Marshal de Camp. With his experience from the Swedish campaign, he can take the organisational role that is so time consuming but necessary."

Hepburn found himself floundering for speech. Marshal de Camp was second only to Marshal of France, the highest rank.

"Eminence! I thank you." He pulled himself together. "I swear I shall serve you as best I can."

The Cardinal nodded. "I know it, Colonel. We have prayed for someone of your calibre and it seems God listens."

CHAPTER 29
Taking La Mothe

They marched in early Spring 1633. Mounted on a tall chestnut, his red hair flaming in the sun, Sir John Hepburn scarcely needed the regimental colours to show his men the way to go.

However his ensign, a younger son of a Hepburn cousin from a farm near Haddington, held their colours high. Beside him Sergeant Major Wat Elliot was trying to cool his exuberance.

"Ye'll be a smoking bag o' lard in no time, if ye wave the thing about like that, Sir."

"But I'm excited, Sergeant Major!"

"By the end o' the day, I reckon it'll be out o' your system."

Hepburn heard the growl and grinned. He was excited himself. But there was much to remember. Cardinal Richelieu had sent one of his pages to him with a letter. "Lord James Douglas is mad for the army. With his father's permission, I must bow to his desperation."

"Any experience?" Hepburn had asked as he looked at the dark haired, plump-faced young man before him.

"No Sir. But I can learn." His eagerness was almost palpable. Hepburn's golden moustaches curved up as he smiled and the face in front of him quivered with hope.

"You'll need to start as ensign and train under Sergeant Major Elliot. Will you accept his orders?"

"As if he was my father! Sir."

"You've a short enough time to train."

"I can shoot true and I've been taught to use my sword by a veteran from the Dutch army."

Hepburn nodded. "You'll do, Lord James Douglas. Work hard and show me your progress." He smiled. "I am used to a Douglas beside me as an officer. But you'll need to struggle hard for that."

"Sir!" The rather sallow face before him flushed pink with delight. "I'll not let you down. Not ever!"

"I like him," Lieutenant Colonel James Hepburn said to his older brother later in the week. "He's keen. He's desperate to please, and it's good to have officers who are on our side not their own."

"Leave him to get to know his company as an ensign, James. He'll show us when he is ready for more responsibility. I've no time for the well-born officer who only wants glory for himself."

He looked back now to where James Douglas rode proudly at the head of his musketeers. His sergeant, another dark haired Douglas, rode beside him and his men were in good order behind.

Seeing his Colonel's eye on him, Douglas straightened in the saddle and said something to his sergeant and as a word passed his soldiers straightened up and held their muskets at the same angle.

Hepburn grinned and waved.

"He's a keen enough pike-man, Colonel." Sergeant Major Elliot had reported, "but he's a rare marksman and I've never seen a better man with a sword. I'd leave him with the musketeers."

So Hepburn had offered him the ensignship and seen delight war with desire to excel in a way he remembered from the days when he followed Colonel Gray down the Elbe towards Prague. They seemed very far away and he sighed. Now he had rather more to prove to Richelieu and the French King. Now he had to win a war.

They travelled South and East. As Marshal de Camp, Sir John Hepburn had to organise quarters for the army each evening and it stretched his French and his organisational expertise to the uttermost.

"At least these French towns accept us," he said to his brother that first night. "Their Town Councils have agreed to becoming staging posts and the house owners know they have to produce a bed, a candle and an evening meal. In Germany we had to terrorise them into taking anyone and force them to make a contribution to Gustavus Adolphus's war chest. It makes a difference not having to threaten to kill them unless they co-operate."

James Hepburn chuckled. "My sergeant said it was great to go to sleep and not wake to find your throat slit."

"Aye, Sir." Sergeant Major Elliot, as always at his colonel's side, nodded. "I'd aye sleep with my dagger in my hand! We all did."

The first town in Lorraine, La Biche, capitulated after one look at the huge army that seemed to stretch to the horizon. Not so the next! La Mothe sat on a rocky peak and was well defended by the Duke of Lorraine's troops under Colonel Ische, a Spaniard. The high walls formed an oval frame to the small town protecting all the buildings except the church spire.

"Leave it! March on by." General la Force was quite clear. "We've never taken La Mothe."

"But then we leave a dangerous enemy in our rear, Sir." John Hepburn felt he could not let this order pass.

"So we won't retreat." The old Marshal was tired and irritated by having his orders questioned.

"God send we don't, but I am deeply unhappy about leaving a thorn to tread on."

General la Force was beginning to realise that he had competition. As the lion of Richelieu's army his word had been law. Over seventy and after a hard day's march he wanted his bed.

"You want it. You take it then, Colonel! Join me when and if you succeed."

A voice spoke from the back of the room. "I'll join my men with yours, Colonel, if you permit."

Hepburn looked over the heads crowding round him to a young man, his lean face framed in long dark curling hair, standing at the back of the room. His smile dawned. "Henri de la Tour d'Auvergne, Vicomte de Turenne! My Scots will be honoured to have you beside us. It was at Bergen op Zoom we met wasn't it?"

"You were mentioned in dispatches, Colonel. I saw you fight!" The young man's eyes brightened. "We'll take La Mothe, together!"

"And I too will join you, Colonel." Another shout brought heads round.

"La Vallee de Rarecourt-Pimodan!"

John Hepburn looked apprehensively at their leader.

"Oh take my damned son too. Take them all. Its time I retired to bed if I'm to lead what you've left me to subdue Lorraine!" General la Force stamped out of the room followed by his officers. Hepburn stood and looked at his two supporters, both young men, both full of pride and the wish to prove themselves.

"We'll need to keep an eye on more than the enemy this time, James," he muttered to his brother. "We'll need to take La Mothe after that."

"It's a place for a classic siege," he said later to his officers gathered round. "I've reconnoitred and we'll need to dig trenches and parapets right round the place so if they don't submit they'll starve."

"Draw maps of what you want, Colonel, apportion the work and I'll set my men to digging" Turenne stood ready.

"And I! And I!" La Vallee pushed between them. "My men will work faster than any, you'll see!"

Sir John Hepburn turned a calm gaze on the excited young man. "I thank you, La Vallee but remember this is a joint venture. We all work for each other in a siege."

The cool tone seemed to upset the recipient. "Of course I knew that, Colonel. I shall always follow your orders."

Later Hepburn said to his own officers, "What was that all about?"

Lieutenant Colonel James Hepburn shrugged, "Past my comprehension! Young hot-head that he is!"

Lord James Douglas gave a little cough to gain attention. "La Vallee was a page with me and he was aye like that, either "aux anges" or down in the dumps. He worshipped Richelieu for a while until he started giving him all the boring jobs. He needs a hero." He grinned sheepishly. "I fear he's found one."

"I hope to God there's no more like him then. I'll not have him rutting with Turenne and ruining my plans. I need La Mothe."

The next day he had the Vicomte deTurenne into his tent. "I'll have no vying with La Vallee, Henri." The younger man grinned and nodded. "We come from the same part of France, Colonel. My father and his both think themselves experts at war and he's always been jealous. Now that he hero-worships you, he's like a gadfly buzzing round my head."

"Do not swat him, Henri. He is General la Force's pride and joy. Put up with him. It may be that I'll find another hero for him."

"You'll be so lucky, Colonel! I could almost sympathise with the silly ass. Remember I saw you in action at Bergen!"

"Ah, but I have learned caution in old age."

Henri de Turenne chuckled. "I've been talking to Lieutenant Colonel Hepburn, Sir and somehow he didn't give me that impression."

But Hepburn was not going to make any mistakes at La Mothe. He reconnoitred, sometimes with his brother, sometimes with Turenne and, when he had to, with La Vallee riding close beside him chattering until he could have strangled his young companion.

"Easy to see why they bypassed this place," Sir John Hepburn had his officers around him and a map spread before him.

"The site is impregnable. Look!" He pointed on the map. "It's a small, oval, compact town, only one major road through the middle and only one heavily fortified gate. Furthermore it is built on a small rocky hill with slopes running away from the walls and they've had plenty time to build sconces with trenches to defend the walls."

"They've lots of cannon too, Colonel." Henri de Turenne nodded.

"They've mounted them in units round the walls so that those hills opposite that I thought we could mount ours on are wide open to be blasted to pieces."

"That is correct." Hepburn's golden moustaches lifted in a smile. "So we will dig an outer ring of trenches with high protective parapets. Then they can't see where our soldiers lurk and we will starve the bastards out."

"I could mount a charge on the gate if you are all afraid," La Vallee interrupted.

"I think not." Hepburn saw the young man pout and turn an angry shoulder. He sighed. It wouldn't do to have furious letters cascade on General la Force accusing Colonel Hepburn of incompetence and cowardice.

"When the time comes you will certainly lead a charge. I look forward to seeing it. But for now we should act in a military manner and dig trenches. It is what your father advised and I obey his orders."

"I'll get my men onto it," Turenne turned away smiling.

"Did the old buffer say that?" James Hepburn asked his brother when the others had gone.

"Of course not! He wants us to fail. La Vallee is going to be a cross to bear with his desire to shine and his father to complain to. However trenches are what we need, in a tight cordon round that sore tooth of a place. Once it weakens we'll pull it."

The Scots hated digging trenches. John Hepburn smiled as he remembered Robert Monro telling Gustavus Adolphus that if he wanted quick trenches he should have used the Dutch. The ground was as hostile as the Lorrainers in La Mothe. Cannon shot whizzed amongst them and they took losses until the parapets were high enough to screen the soldiers. After that the work went quickly and La Mothe was held in a vice. Sentries were on all day and all night. At first, food convoys tried to slip past by night, but Hepburn's seasoned troops became expert at trapping the convoys and appropriating the food and ammunition.

When he thought they might have had enough Hepburn sent in a trumpeter from Henri de Turenne's regiment. He wanted to make sure there was no misunderstanding. There was none. Colonel Ische had no intention of surrendering, ever.

"Right, then we mine! We'll go from the closest trench that is well screened."

"But Colonel it's solid rock!" De Turenne held up his hands in horror.

"Why do you think I left it so long?" He sighed. "My troops man the reach that is both best protected and close. I shall become the least popular Scotsman in France."

"I'll get cannon onto the hills yonder and screen them behind trees so we can drop shot into the town and keep their minds off what is going on down below."

"Good man." Hepburn patted him on the back. "We'll spend our summer here I fear."

Days passed, then weeks, then months. Nothing happened though Hepburn knew that within the town there would now be serious starvation. Men, women and children would be dying, not in battle but from hunger and the diseases that feed on weakness and accumulated dirt.

"I hope they get bloody plague!" he muttered to his brother one evening in mid July as they inspected the progress of his mine. "That would sort them out. I told the men to start filling the mine works with gunpowder. I'm getting tired of waiting. Brave defenders who are content to see their men die rather than live to fight another day are a curse. They may think it clever but mass suicide is a sin in my book."

"The girls of the town are beginning to get quite friendly with our men too, John." Lieutenant Colonel James Hepburn sounded worried. "They come out of the gate of an evening and cut grass, likely enough to stew up for themselves. They'll have eaten their horses long since. Our men just let them go."

"Aye! I'll not order them to kill women, James, but warn them that they might plan some trick."

His advice was well placed. Not a fortnight later Hepburn saw a large group of girls slip out of the great door and come singing down the slope to within a few yards from the trenches where the grass grew lush. He gave a sigh as he saw his pikemen call to the girls and then lay down their weapons and approach.

"Lunatics!" he shouted. "Ensign, get those men back!"

Too late! Bemused by welcoming smiles and gestures the Scots joined the ladies and as he watched half of them turned and ran and half tore off their skirts revealing their true sex as well as the swords they had concealed under their skirts. Armed only with their daggers the Scots were hard pressed and Hepburn watched helpless as they fell. Then from the next door trench he saw Douglas lead his musketeers in open order, firing as they came on. Some Lorrainers fell, the rest turned and ran for safety but the musketeers were reloading and firing as fast as they could and few made it back to the gates.

"Well done, Douglas!" Hepburn shouted, half laughing now the crisis was over. "Those horny bastards have learned a lesson."

The ensign waved and led his men forward to pull their wounded and dead comrades back to the safety of their trenches as cannon from the ramparts started to roar and cannon balls scattered parapets, body parts and earth in all directions.

Hepburn was never quite sure what happened next. Had a musketeer dropped his match? Did a cannon ball strike a flinty rock and cause a spark. No one was ready to talk. All he did know was that there was a rumble and the ground under his feet began to shudder.

"Oh God! They've set the mine off!" The roar that followed amply confirmed his shout. A huge chunk of wall and bastion beside the gate seemed to shiver and disintegrate in a great cloud of dust.

Henri de Turenne had been organising his troops for the evening sentry duty. "Mon Dieu! Colonel!" He looked across where Hepburn stood alone. "Vite, mes braves. Sound the attack!" Drums rattling he led what men followed into the breach. The townsmen were pouring in to resist and the two forces met in a frantic action that was hampered by the dust clouds as much as by surprise on everyone's part.

Standing helpless, Hepburn saw Turenne's white plumes on the rampart and cheered. His own men were forming up under Sergeant Major Elliot's imprecations and he yelled for the cannon to follow as he made for a corner under the wall where he was sheltered. It was a dreadful mess but training told. Some at least of his cannon appeared beside him and were trained down the trenches outside the wall.

"Fire at will! Clear those defences or Turenne will not be able to retire."

Well trained, the cannoneers responded, cursing as they worked. The outworks cleared as if by magic and Hepburn shouted for scaling ladders.

"Aye Sir!" Elliot passed the order.

"I was as amazed to see them appear as ye were, Sir!" He said later. "It's fair wonderful what a bit o' training does."

This time when the dust cleared the Lorrainers saw little more to fight for. Their commander had been killed. His son had taken over and rallied the townspeople to support his troops with pitchforks and old guns that scarcely fired but they were dying on their feet. The white flag flew and slowly as men saw it the sound of gunfire and the screams of the dying ceased.

A terrible dusty silence took over as Hepburn's troops were put in order by their officers and joined with those under Turenne to take over the city. Men women and children lay dead in the streets, some killed by musket-fire, most by starvation.

Hepburn exiled the few inhabitants who still lived and razed the walls and ramparts. La Mothe, so long a flag of rebellion to French rule, was no more. There was no booty, no celebration.

"This was grim necessity." Sir John Hepburn told his officers later. "And

I have learned two things, first to train my Scots not to fall for pretty French faces and second never to let a musketeer near a mine shaft."

"I led my men to the walls, Colonel." La Vallee had escaped without a scratch having led his men to the protection of a bastion and then attacked any survivors who tried to leave the city.

"You did extremely well, La Vallee, and I am writing tonight to tell your father of your competence and bravery." He turned to the others. "I think that is all now. Dismiss."

They turned to shuffle out, Turenne at the end looked a little downcast but was not going to show that he had hoped for a mention.

"Oh, Henri!" Hepburn's voice stopped him. "Without your quick thinking we would never have taken La Mothe." The young man's face split in a grin. "I thought you had not seen us."

"I saw you and gave thanks for such a commander. I've written to Richelieu describing the battle and requesting promotion for you. I said I thought Marshal de Camp would be nice. Its time you helped me put all those men to bed every night!"

"Marshal de Camp! I thank you Colonel. I had no expectation!" He was stuttering with the joy of it.

"You were a pupil to be proud of today, Turenne. Keep it up."

He watched as the young man left, his step light and bouncy as if his tiredness had disappeared. The Scottish officers, remaining, looked at each other.

"Not quite as I planned, but successful just the same. Well done Douglas. You led your musketeers well. I think it is time you took on more responsibility. I have reported to Richelieu that I have promoted you to Captain as from today. Your men will be increased to give you a full company."

The senior Captain, another James Hepburn and Sir John's cousin, turned to wring Douglas's hand. "Now we're getting somewhere, Captain Lord James Douglas. The Colonel and his brother won't need to bother getting up in the morning. We'll have it all sorted between us!"

CHAPTER 30
Onwards into Lorraine

They caught up with the slow moving army of General la Force in the Barrois and moved east to occupy the villages round Nancy in preparation for a siege. It was not to be. Sir John Hepburn came late to join his lieutenant colonel who was sitting with their cousin Captain James Hepburn and Lord James Douglas in the shadow of a great tree that hung over the small bar that they frequented of an evening.

"We can stop digging trenches. That damned two-faced Duke Charles of Lorraine has caved in again and agreed to let French troops man Nancy for thirty years."

"Thank God! We're almost done then, aren't we? Another six months and it'll be damned cold sitting here in the wilderness." Captain Lord James Douglas raised his beer glass and sipped. "Trier is ours. The Elector, Archbishop von Sotern, begged protection last year."

Hepburn nodded. "Aye, Sotern's always looked to be part of France, not like that Canon Metternich, his second in command. He would throw his lot in with Spain any day. These middle countries are like quicksilver, hard to contain. La Force has been ordered to stay West of the Rhine but he's like an old war horse pawing the ground as he looks at Mannheim so close and poor old Heidelberg still under siege with the Swedes inside down to their last crusts."

"I heard he'd written to Duke Bernard of Saxe-Weimar to ask him to relieve Heidelberg," his brother broke in.

"Aye, and that idle so and so refused." Douglas's tone was scathing.

"I remember Bernard so well from Prague days." Sir John Hepburn sounded regretful. "He was a great friend then, and ready to have a go at anything. He has changed." He stroked his moustache into place as memories jostled. "I reckon we all have. The Swedish campaign knocked any principles out of us young men. The greed of our leaders, their incompetence, their neglect of their soldiers and their callous disregard for their safety when they ordered men to risk their lives for a whim, turns a man grim. Bernard did well to turn Lutzen into a victory. He shot the general ordering retreat, rallied my Green Brigade, and my Scots won it for him. I think he changed then. He's a hard man now."

"He still has the remnants of the Green Brigade. He's kept them." Lieutenant Colonel James Hepburn spoke.

"Sensible fellow! They're the salt of the earth." Sir John Hepburn grinned wickedly. "I have to say that I'm encouraging our leader as hard as I can to forget King Louis's orders and go for it. I'd just love to meet up with those men again."

His blandishments worked. That Autumn they took Mannheim and pushed on to relieve the siege of Heidelberg. The Swedish troops, starved to skeletons and all but defeated were thankful to see them. Then in the cold December winds and early snow they pushed on to link up with Saxe-Weimar.

Expecting nothing, Sir John Hepburn was moved to tears by his welcome. Ignoring their officers, the Scottish soldiers lined up to greet his regiment as they marched in. The last of the Mackay pipers played a march and Hepburn's well ordered troops melted into a mass of men hugging each other and talking and laughing so that the noise drowned any attempt of their officers to sort them out.

"I don't know where we end and they begin, Colonel!" Captain Lord James Douglas was laughing and had his arm round a dark haired ensign. "He's a cousin of my mother's, Sir. She'll be happy to have word of him."

But Sir John Hepburn had enveloped a small wiry man in his embrace and was lifting him off his feet and shaking him. "Rotmaster Tod Armstrong you old thief! I'm right glad to see you!"

"Sergeant Armstrong, Sir! I'd have ye ken! You'll be wanting another sergeant to sort this lot, Colonel. You'll not get rid of us this time!"

Celebrations continued all night to the bemusement of the French soldiers.

Next morning General la Force called his senior officers to his tent.

"What is all this partying, Colonel Sir John Hebron? Saxe-Weimar, these are your troops making an affray!"

"Alas, General, they were my troops until yesterday and ones to be proud of. Today they are Colonel Sir John Hepburn's. My tents lie empty. His barracks are full to overflowing."

Hepburn looked across at his old friend with a rueful smile that hid a delight that Saxe-Weimar didn't miss. "It is true, General. These were my men when I fought under the Swedish banner. Now they have recruited themselves under King Louis in my regiment."

"You should make them return."

"I don't think I could, Sir, even if I wanted to."

"Believe me, General. He doesn't want to either!" Saxe-Weimar sounded huffed. "I've led them as well as any commander but one look at that great red head and they follow him like homing pigeons."

"Bernard, they're my men!"

"I know, John, I know! In my heart I understand, but in my head I hate you!"

"We'll go and have a beer and you'll feel better. They're noisy, argumentative, insolent dastards. You know they are!"

"But great fighters, John!"

"Aye but they're better together. And I'm right pleased to get them. By joining with us, they make the Royal Scots the oldest Regiment of Foot in the army and we can now claim the right wing in any battle! Just think of the service you've done me."

"Well you can buy the beer then." Saxe-Weimar capitulated. "I'll just have to join you as well!"

"Duke Bernard of Saxe-Weimar is a commander whom I can recommend," Hepburn wrote to Richelieu that evening. "Promise him land in Alsace or somewhere that he needs to fight for and you will have a great leader who will recruit his own men and lead them."

A few weeks later Father Joseph appeared at his side in the magical way Hepburn had got used to.

"My Cardinal was pleased with your recommendation, Colonel. We are sorely in need of allies now. The Swedish loss at Nordlingen has given the Spaniards new heart." He turned his cowled head towards Hepburn so no one could hear and continued. "France lies open on many fronts and my Cardinal fears a sea attack to the South-West. He has written Nicholas de l'Hospital, the Governor of Provence, urging him to raise defences on his coast. With no need to fear the Swedes and the German Catholic states rallying to their support, the Spanish can plunge the whole of their ill-gotten gold from the Americas into an attack on France. Cardinal Richelieu depends on you."

It was a timely warning and Sir John Hepburn caused cries of misery when he demanded that his officers put their troops into good fighting order despite the grip of winter.

"What on earth do you think will happen, John?" His brother looked at him as if he was mad. "The Spanish are tucked up warm at Worms. Why would they mobilise?"

"Wait and see, James and for God's sake have the men well drilled and ready to move. I'm taking a unit back to headquarters to collect the pay-chest for the regiment but when I return I want my troops ready to fight."

Father Joseph's warnings had substance. Hepburn could sense unrest as he returned to Lorraine leading the train of eight pack-mules that carried bullion in bags slung on either side of their saddles. Lodging house keepers were less willing, less smiling, but much more interested in the pack-mules.

"Double the night watch on the bullion," Hepburn ordered a grim faced Sergeant Major Elliot.

"Already done, Sir! I'm sleeping wi' those baggies, myself. There's a nasty feeling about. Ah dinna' trust these Lorrainers further than I could throw them and they're that fat they'd go no distance!"

As the flat lands gave way to wooded hills their task grew harder. John Hepburn put scouts out almost a day's march ahead to sit on the heights and look for unusual activity. It was a job that he knew Scots from the Borders were good at but he found that many of the highlanders, especially those veterans who had come over to him from Saxe-Weimar, were even better scouts. They seemed to melt into the trees and just disappear.

It was a Mackay from his friend Monro's old regiment that brought word of trouble.

"Dinna' doubt him, Sir." Elliot had brought him straight to his colonel.

"As if I would, Sergeant Major! He's probably got the second sight as well!"

Elliot grinned. "I'd not go as far as that, Colonel, but we'll need to shift for there's a strong force well entrenched above our path down by the river and that's the way we must go. There's no other pass."

"I'm not for open war against an ambush." Hepburn unrolled his maps, such as they were, and looked at the terrain. Elliot appeared right. There was only one pass, a deep valley with steep wooded hills on either side. "Can you find me a reliable local scout, Sergeant Major?"

"There's none of the locals would give us the time of day, Sir." He rubbed the side of his head. "But I'm thinking that your inn-keeper's daughter has a soft spot for me. She's aye bringing me extra to eat and we've been chatting."

"Chatting is it! Sergeant you are incorrigible! But ask her if there is another way through these hills as if it were just idle interest."

That evening Elliot appeared at his supper table in the inn. "There's a wee path frae the end of the village goes to another village to the south but once ye're up on the heights you can run along the ridge almost all the way to above the plain. If we're quiet the Spanish would never even hear us pass because we'd be the other side of the ridge."

"Can we muffle the mules?"

"No bother! We'll take half the number of animals and move slow and easy and they'll have a man to each headband to gentle them along. They'll not ken we've gone if ye stay in the village for another day, Sir, and then slip out by night with the rest of the men. They'll keep ye right."

"Won't your lady love notice you've gone?"

"Aye. She will, but if ye give me a bawling out, Sir, and confine me to the mule watch she'll not see me go."

"I'll pay the inn keeper for two nights more and he'll not expect me to leave either. It's just as well we've left the men on watch or sleeping by the mules."

Their plan appeared to work though Hepburn suspected that paying for two more nights at the inn had more success in lulling suspicion than all their play-acting.

On the second night he let himself out of his window to the grim delight of a plaid-clad soldier waiting. "It'll not be your first escape frae a lady's window, Sir." He chuckled softly and slid away before Hepburn could damn him for insolence.

That night he appreciated Elliot's confidence. His highlanders moved quietly and so quickly that John Hepburn, hardy though he was, had difficulty keeping up. His breathing rasped in his throat. His men appeared not out of breath at all and they did not stop. A full moon reflected cold and white from the snow-laden pines and the frost turned their breath into steam clouds. Their boots bit silently into untrodden snow that gave each step purchase as they climbed. Half way up the hill, they turned to move along its shoulder parallel to the valley on the other side of the ridge. Now his men moved more slowly, spreading out and disappearing amongst the trees. John Hepburn followed, picking his way carefully and just following one set of tracks. Suddenly a soldier rose from the underbrush before him, his musket at the challenge. Hepburn simply bent to the charge but before he could launch himself at the threatening barrel a shadow rose behind the man, a knife sparkled in the moonlight and the sentry was lowered silently to the ground his lifeblood dark on the snow. "I'm hoping the mules dinna' make as much noise as ye, Sir!" muttered the same plaid-clad soldier who had helped him from his window before disappearing again.

By next morning they were all through and away from the pass and moving quickly eastwards across the plain. In two days they saw their camp and safety ahead.

"A nice little sortie, Sir." Sergeant Major Elliot was well pleased with himself. "We can look forward to pay day as well."

CHAPTER 31
Metternich of Trier seized

There was only bad news in the camp.

"Things are hotting up, John." His brother, Lieutenant Colonel James Hepburn, looked anxious and his captains stood silent about him awaiting orders.

"La Force is pulling back over the Rhine. The Spanish are massing for an attack, he says."

"He may be right." Hepburn stroked his moustache. "I wish the Swedes had stood at Nordlingen. Now the Imperialists don't fear a rearguard attack and will push west. Wallenstein has gone but Galas is twice the commander and his men respect him." He grinned. "You pay the men and I'll go to confession." And he was off.

"What will that do?" Lord James Douglas was bewildered.

Captain James Hepburn, standing beside him, laughed. "He's away to Father Joseph. Me? I'd rather break my fast with a serpent."

"You don't know the half! When I was a page if I did the slightest wrong I'd look round to see that fiend in a grey habit just standing looking at me and I knew Richelieu would have the whole within the hour!" Douglas shuddered. "The Colonel just doesn't know how dangerously he lives."

The Capuchin was pleased to see Hepburn though his greeting was austere. "You left when we needed you, Colonel!"

"But I return bearing gifts, Father Joseph! My men will die paid up to date!"

The old priest shook his head. "It's no laughing matter. While you were away Galas attacked Philipsburg and Speyer. He holds Philipsburg still. It's a bridgehead into Lorraine and his troops are massing there day on day."

"That will be his riposte to our relief of Heidelburg." Hepburn nodded. "He couldn't let his masters see him worsted."

The priest nodded. "That's what that Saxe-Weimar said, and to do him credit he mounted an attack on Speyer with the help of young Turenne."

"They took it?"

"Under my instruction, of course!"

"Not a bit priestly, Father, but very satisfying!" Hepburn was openly laughing.

His Grey Eminence shook his head ruefully. " I have done penance for my savage thoughts, my son."

"But when France is in peril, the old warrior surfaces, does he not?" The honest sympathy in the younger man's voice stopped any resentment. The older man nodded. "We are in great danger now, my son. Scarcely had we won Speyer when a Spanish force in the North took Archbishop Sotern who is Elector of Trier and now holds him to ransom."

"So how bad is that? Trier will pay."

"They will pay but in the meantime his deputy Canon Metternich has taken charge and asked Spain to enter Trier! I suspect he organised Sotern's capture."

"Cardinal Richelieu, my master is unhappy?" Hepburn grinned but his mind was working furiously.

"France is unhappy, stupid boy! Trier is an arrowhead pointing at the heart of Paris."

Hepburn shrugged. "Tell my master not to worry, Father. I shall see his sleep is not disturbed."

He left on the word and the older man was left muttering to himself.

"I am off again, James," he was saying to his brother ten minutes later. "You, Cousin James and Douglas keep the regiment in good order. When I get back I suspect we'll have to fight, so keep them exercising.

I'll need a half company of musketeers and pikemen with an ensign. Whom do you suggest?"

"Get some sleep, John. I'll have them ready by daybreak tomorrow."

Sir John Hepburn nodded. His brother was right. It seemed weeks since he'd had a quiet night. "I need good men that are also good horsemen!"

"Go to bed, John." His brother shook his head at him and left.

"And that's insubordination!" His shout merely brought a smile to his brother's face.

Sleep was welcome and Sir John Hepburn emerged from his tent late the next morning stretching and ravenous. He found a half company on horseback ready for inspection. Lord James Douglas at its head swung off his horse and saluted.

"I said an ensign, Captain Lord James Douglas!"

"If you can be captain I can be ensign, Sir. Lieutenant Colonel Hepburn says he'll manage fine." He paused. "Father Joseph came by with this huge package which he said you should take. Must we, Colonel?"

"Beware Greeks bearing gifts, eh James? Did you look inside?"

"Didn't dare. He was standing there."

Hepburn cut the twine that held the burlap wrapping together and the parcel collapsed into a heap of black monks habits.

"Benedictine robes!" Douglas stood with his mouth open. "That would clothe a small monastery!"

Sir John Hepburn shook his head. "It will cover a half company of Scotsmen I'm thinking. The crafty old devil!"

"Oh hush!" Douglas looked round nervously. "If he heard that you'd be excommunicated or worse!" But Sir John Hepburn was handing the habits to each man. "Pack it in your saddle bags, lads. You're about to turn holy, you lot."

They rode North and West, resting their horses as best they could but pushing on through the largely flat lands of the Middle Kingdom as fast as they were able. The weather remained fine and cold with a sharp frost by night but his men were used to worse and they had money for lodgings so they slept warmer than if they had been in the fields. At both their stops Hepburn took care to tell their hosts that they were headed for Paris but having met the Moselle they followed it up its East bank to see at last the great Roman "Porta Nigra", the black gate that dominated the approach to the city of Trier.

"We'd need an army to get through that." Lord James Douglas looked stunned.

"We need the aura of holiness to waft us through!" Sir John Hepburn was laughing. "Get the men off their horses. We'll leave the animals with two troopers to rest and feed them. Everyone else into your black habits, now!"

"I aye fancied being a black beetle." Tod Armstrong appeared beside his Colonel unrecognisable in his black hood.

Hepburn looked down the lines of black-cowled figures. "Oh dear! Oh dear! March up in ranks like that and we'll be shot before we reach the gates. Douglas, you take one line and I'll take the other and get them shuffling along as if they've walked miles and need their beds. Stick your weapons through your belts at the back, lads, so the habit covers all. Thank God I ordered short pikes."

Even though they seemed rather upright and stiff, Hepburn thought they might just pass distant inspection and once the guards had written them off as a danger he hoped they would let them by.

It was not to be. The gate guards were Canon Metternich's men and very much on edge as they waited for Spanish reinforcements. They had imprisoned the Elector's soldiers the moment they heard of Archbishop Sotern's capture as he repelled a Spanish incursion.

The towns-people were afraid to confront their Canon. He was after all the Elector's deputy. His troops were few but they were harsh. They kept the great gates of the Porta Nigra closed.

"God send they didn't have bright enough eyes to see us change into monks," Douglas muttered as with lowered head he shuffled ahead of his men.

"We were far enough away behind the trees. Just keep your head swinging as if you are right weary and I'll think of something to get us through."

"Benedictines are great book men, Colonel. They copy all the holy works and illuminate the psalters. The Cardinal had a clutch of them, all ink-stained fingers and peering eyes. We could be coming to copy something in St Matthias's Abbey."

"You know a lot about them?" Hepburn was interested.

"I was the Cardinal's page forever. Everyone knows about St Matthias Abbey in Trier. It is so bloody old and pilgrims used to throng to it before this war started."

"Bloodier soon, I hope and not ours. Right, here we go!" Hepburn raised his voice and called quaveringly in German. "We are from Cologne and for St Matthias Abbey, my sons. Of a goodness open the gates for we are weary."

He saw heads peering at him and muttered, "Heads down men and droop a bit."

"On what business, Father?" A soldier's head appeared at the wicket gate.

"We come to copy the great bible for our monastery. We will be with you for many months." His voice fell with a sigh. "It is a duty that we have undertaken."

"Only Canon Metternich is in residence." The soldier sounded hostile.

"We are glad of that. Canon Metternich is our Father Abbot's friend and our Spanish brothers gave us free passage to Trier."

The wicket gate closed and the main gate creaked open. One by one the cowled figures drifted through, heads bowed but eyes darting from side to side. There was a duty room on their left with sounds of men beginning their evening meal. The shadows here were enormous and the few lanterns cast little light. As the last man came through one of the others moved behind the sentry and he subsided without a sound. Hepburn pointed to the door of the guard room and throwing off their habits and dropping their pikes they freed their swords. Tod Armstrong led his rot inside. There was one shout, quickly muffled and a table went over with a crash but nothing more.

Douglas now led the musketeers and Hepburn the pikes and they slid out of the inner gate to reconnoitre.

"His sentries seem thinly spaced like the man said." Hepburn pointed. "You take that side and I'll go this. Use your swords and we'll free this whole gate of guards. That way we can get clear in a hurry. Meet you back here."

Neither took much time. Hepburn heard muffled curses and a few squeaks but there was nothing to arouse interest.

"We'll need to be out before the next guard change." Douglas was breathing hard but his eyes were shining with excitement.

"Let's go." Hepburn led the way to the cathedral. With its huge bulk dominating the town, it was easy to find. Not so easy was the door into Metternich's apartments. The men drifted along the side of the building. In the darkness they were almost invisible, Hepburn thought, invisible death for anyone stupid enough to challenge them. They came to a door that lay half open and Hepburn peered inside. Unmistakable sounds of cooks working greeted his ears.

"Don't kill unless you have to," he whispered. "Line them up at one side of the kitchen and we'll see who's with us. They can't all be for Metternich."

There was no resistance. Four fat cooks and two young scullions clung together in a terrified group.

"We are for Archbishop Sotern," Hepburn said, thankful for his German now. "We've come for Canon Metternich."

"Don't kill him, Sirs. It would be unholy." The chief cook had his cowl pushed back from his face and was sweating with fear as much as the heat of the ovens.

"The Spanish hold your Archbishop to ransom. We'll do the same for his Canon." Hepburn had rapidly rethought his simple assassination plan.

"We have sent money for our Archbishop already, Sirs." The second cook looked anxious. "He will return soon."

"Your Canon may find that his ransom is not so swiftly found." Hepburn's tone was grim.

This seemed to cheer all of them and John Hepburn laughed. "Hate him do you? Just show us where he lies and we'll rid you of his presence. Tell your Archbishop that he will find him in Paris under the care of Cardinal Richelieu. He will teach him better ways no doubt. Now where does he lie?"

"He complains about our work all the time," muttered the head cook as he wheezed up the stair ahead of them. Hepburn had left Douglas in charge of the kitchen and led Tod Armstrong with his rot to take the Canon. "We spend more time in penance than at bread making and God needs help to make the dough rise." He indicated a door. "He's by himself praying for strength to complain about the dinner. The Elector, God bless him, said we had an angel's touch with his pastries."

Hepburn motioned for the older man to return and sent a soldier with him. The rest of them burst into the room. Hepburn embraced the dark little man in his monk's habit who rose angrily from his knees to demand, "How dare you!" Lifting him off his feet with one arm he clapped the other hand over his mouth. Tod Armstrong swept a scarf about his throat and twisted. The Canon subsided, his mouth opening and a gag was slipped in and secured. Arms pinioned behind his back and legs hobbled, Hepburn picked him up like a bag of hay and they were tip-toeing down the stair again within minutes.

The kitchen was a-bustle.

"The cooks you left thought to summon the Canon's coach," Douglas explained. "The coachman is a cousin of the scullion and they swear he's for Sotern. They thought it would excite less notice. No one will approach Canon Metternich's coach without his permission. They all hate him in Trier. If we look like his bodyguard we can all pour straight out the Porta Nigra and no one the wiser. We're to tie these fellows up as if they tried to resist. That way no one will slaughter them later."

"It sounds too easy," Hepburn laughed. "Let's do it."

They almost made it to the gate before a sentry on one of the walls challenged them. "Run for it!" Hepburn increased his pace and the coachman whipped his horses. Then they were out and running, a hail of bullets following. A trooper swore.

"Who's wounded?" Hepburn turned to see a man fall, picked him up and continued running. Then they were out of musket shot but he heard rather than saw the sounds of pursuit. The Canon's men were after them. Panting the men ran on waiting for the order to turn and stand. It never came.

"Mount, damn you! Mount and ride. Follow the coach!" Hepburn had glimpsed the horses half hidden by the trees but ready and waiting.

"Good man!" He swung into his saddle, grabbed the reins from the soldier holding them, laid his burden before him on his saddle front and rode.

They were behind trees in no time and he heard the pursuit slacken. The men from Trier had no idea of how many men waited on them in the dark, behind the wood. They stood muttering amongst themselves then turned back. The Scots pushed on until they came to a bridge across the Moselle. Here Hepburn reined up, still breathless.

"Right, here we part! Douglas you'll accompany the coach to Paris with my pikes as guardsmen. Tell his Eminence that Metternich is a present from me and get back to us as soon as you can. We could be in retreat so keep your ears and eyes open. I think things are going to hot up this Spring."

He turned. "I'm afraid we've lost one man. But we'll bury him decently ourselves before we push on."

A voice from below him muttered, "Dinna' be in such a hurry, Sir. I'm not wanting to be below ground yet!"

"Tod Armstrong! For God's sake why didn't you speak?"

"Ah didna' want ye dropping me, Sir! Your horse is awfy big and it's a long way down."

Hepburn picked him up, and slid him to his feet where he stood rocking slightly. Another pikeman came beside him and scarves were loosened and wrapped round the rotmasters arm where a bullet had lodged.

"We'll get him home, Sir, dinna' worry."

"Take him straight to the surgeons."

"Aye, Sir." His rot formed round him and they were away. Hepburn watched them go and then gathered up Douglas's musketeers. "We'll ride slowly so if they come after us, it's us they'll follow and we'll show them some un-monkish musket ball."

CHAPTER 32
The Retreat of 1635

"Thank God you're back!" Lieutenant Colonel James Hepburn hugged his brother careless of who watched. "We're in a right pickle. Galas has massed huge forces from his German front and is about to attack. Turenne is running about like a headless chicken asking where you've got to, Duke Bernard of Saxe-Weimar is having shouting matches with General la Force who just turns his face to the wall and that bloody Grey Eminence goes flitting round giving useless orders and threatening excommunication. Do something, John! It's a haemorrhage of disaster."

Tired though he was, John Hepburn laughed. "I'll away to plug the leak, starting with his Wee Greyness. But I'll need a decent meal when I get back and a beer." He was away and his brother sighed thankfully.

"He makes it all sound easy doesn't he?" A Captain Hume had come up to listen to the end of the conversation. "I'll get the cooks going, but you'll need to press for the beer. We're short the now, and that Father Joseph would raise a thirst in anyone."

His Grey Eminence was thankful to see Sir John Hepburn enter his tent though he did not let it show. Rising from his knees he turned to grunt, "About time too! Leaving just when sage counsel is required is a bad habit, my son."

"Talking about habits," John Hepburn was laughing at his grumpy face, "your gift was mighty useful and you'll be pleased to hear that Canon Metternich is on his way to stay with His Eminence the Cardinal in Paris until such time as Trier will pay to have him back. My impression was that that might be some time in happening and certainly well after the return of the Elector."

"God be thanked!" The small capuchin sat down and allowed a small smile to cross his face. "I was just praying for your return and here you are."

"I'm away to see our General la Force. I'll take Saxe-Weimar with me and Turenne and we'll get some sense knocked into him, eh Father? Do you want to come?"

Father Joseph shook his head, an impish grin beginning to appear. "You'll report to me after, my son." He hesitated. "Sometimes I think my mind moves too quick for those blockheads, though Turenne has done well to mould his regiment on yours as I told him to. I seem to cause him alarm."

"Indeed, Father! I'd be terrified myself if I didn't keep remembering that you were once a soldier like me."

He was waved away and collecting the other commanders they descended on la Force who was sitting in his tent with only his son La Vallee for company.

The young man leapt to his feet as they entered. "You are back Colonel! How I have looked for you. Why did you not take me with you?"

His eyes shone with hero worship and Hepburn heard Turenne click his tongue in disgust beside him.

"Your duty is to your father, La Vallee, as is mine. Now shall we make a plan, Sir? We need your advice." He turned to bow courteously to the old commander. "I fear there is little hope of winning a pitched battle against Galas here. His force is overwhelming. He took Phillipsburg scarcely losing a man just to show us his strength."

"But Saxe-Weimar replied by taking Speyer," Turenne broke in. "It was a great boost to our army's morale."

"Well done, Bernard!" Hepburn slapped him on the back and the grizzled soldier grinned.

"Turenne was with me with a unit of his troops. We mined the wall and spread all over the city. That huge Roman cross-shaped Cathedral is remarkable John. We made sure French Catholic Bishops were in charge of it and left with a huge contribution to our war chest."

Hepburn gave a short laugh. "They would be surprised and grateful to be saved by two unbelievers, no doubt." He turned. "That's where you should have been young La Vallee if you wanted action. These two could have hid their reforming tendencies behind you."

The young man shrugged and turned away.

"He hates to be teased by his hero," whispered Turenne.

"The sooner he hates me the better. I'll not suffer fawning puppies."

"I hope you do not call me a puppy. I looked for you too, John."

"For God's sake, Turenne! You're a soldier. You seek to learn. We all learn from watching someone and then improving on it. I'm delighted to share all my tricks with you. One day you will eclipse anything I have ever done."

Turenne was young enough to blush with pleasure and seeing it La Vallee pouted even more and went to stand behind his father looking away.

Hepburn raised his voice and stepped forward. "Sir I believe we should ask Duke Bernard of Saxe-Weimar for his advice. He has made reconnaissance of Galas's position."

His old friend came forward to face them all. "We should stand and try to repel the incursions that Galas throws across the Rhine. It will be more and more difficult as his force grows larger. But the Rhine is a bulwark that he cannot mine or scale with ladders. If we can hold position this summer, God willing something may happen to interest him elsewhere."

It appeared that God was disinterested. Galas was not. France had signed a treaty with the States General of the United Provinces and de Breze and Chatillon were fighting their corner to the North, always praying that the Dutch would do more. After Trier or because of it in that year of 1635, France finally declared formal war against Spain on the 19th of May.

The declaration precipitated an avalanche of attacks from Galas.

"We need Oxenstierna to do more," Hepburn was standing in the sunshine, his maps before him spread over a spare cannon carriage, studying the terrain with His Grey Eminence. "I wrote him, Father Joseph, but I hear nothing. Of course he too is short of money because the levy from the Hanseatic ports must have dried up this year. He will depend solely on France."

"My Cardinal does not have unlimited means. France bleeds with taxation already."

"I know, Father. I know! He has sent us military replacements time after time to save us. I'm not ungrateful."

The little priest bent to look at the maps and pointed. "We could perhaps take this castle and this." His finger strayed on. "If we were in here and here we would be difficult to dislodge."

Hepburn laughed and shook a finger at him. "Don't go so fast, Father Joseph. I assure you castles are not taken with the point of a finger."

The officers round him turned away to hide their smiles. Some slipped off to pass on the exchange. In no time it became the army's stock answer for any problem and caused laughter every time it was uttered.

That summer there was little else to laugh about. Lorraine behind them was hostile. Food had to be brought in from France and was often late and rotten by the time it arrived. Men looked gaunt and tired. Some fell down as they mounted guard. They were not fainting: they had fallen asleep. Hepburn doubled the sentries. That only made them all more tired. Long hours on watch followed by brisk skirmishes where an apparently tireless red haired giant led counter attack after counter attack became a never-ending misery.

By late autumn they were all exhausted and if anything Galas had massed even more troops.

Hepburn limped in to his officer's tent one morning and announced. "I think it is time to take stock again. We don't want to be caught here all winter."

James Hepburn looked up. His brother only limped when he was so tired that his old knee wound gave trouble. "Whatever you decide,

Colonel! We'll back you."

"I think we should get out while the weather is still with us." Sir John Hepburn was off to gather the other senior commanders.

"We retreat!" Saxe-Weimar seconded his decision. "No ifs, no buts. He has upward of twelve thousand horse and fifteen thousand foot."

"Nasty!" John Hepburn looked impressed. "I wouldn't want that lot descending on us. Have we time?"

"I hope so."

His hope was misplaced. Fully reinforced, Galas pushed his cannon forwards and from dawn to dusk laid waste the country over the Rhine. That night he brought up boats and making them into a bridge he poured his infantry into Lorraine, the musketeers taking up a forward position and raining shot on to any resistance while his pikes fell in behind them ready for the charge.

"Have we a chance of holding them, Bernard?" Hepburn looked to the next most senior commander as la Force just sat with his head in his hands.

"None!" Saxe-Weimar's tone was urgent. "We must go and go fast. My men are burning our baggage as we speak but I am having difficulty with the general in charge of ordinance. He will not leave his cannon, John, and they will slow us down. The Spaniards will be all over us. Our only hope is to steal away fast until we reach the passes at the edge of Lorraine and once there perhaps Galas won't follow. If we can make it back to winter quarters we'll be lucky. He won't follow so far. Galas prefers to winter in barracks. King Gustavus Adolphus never allowed him but I should be delighted to see him tuck his soldiers up for a month or two."

John Hepburn nodded and turned to la Force. "With your permission, General, we will follow Bernard's lead. May I talk with the artillery general?"

The old man shrugged. "I've had enough. I've done all that Cardinal Richelieu asked of me and it has come to naught! Do what you will."

"You led a glorious campaign, General, and we are all proud to be your officers. This is a minor set-back at the end of a splendid season. Let us make sure it remains so and is not annihilation."

The old man looked slightly mollified and waved him away. "Burn anything you want. La Vallee will tell my men."

"Get going fast before he changes his mind. I'm off to bury the cannons. I'm damned if Galas shall have them." Hepburn's long stride took him to where cannon were being harnessed to mule trains. One look at the big red head and the officer in charge shouted, "No! and a thousand times, no! Sir John. We will not give up our cannon."

"You have a choice, Sir," Hepburn's tone was deadly earnest. "Galas will take them and kill you, or you bury them, burn the gun carriages and when we return next year as we will do, I promise, you may dig them up again."

"We don't spike them?"

"Never! Wrap them well and dig a great pit. Once they are covered burn your gun carriages above them so the ground looks ordinary and no one will think to dig. Let their spies see you getting the mules ready and they'll think the guns are with you. Take the mules, we may need to eat them!"

"For you, Colonel Hepburn, for you I will do it; but if they are not here next year, for you I shall conceive a terrible fate!"

Hepburn laughed and shook his hand. "Thank you, General. I want to save every man to fight again next Spring." He was gone on the word and found his own men complaining loudly but almost ready to move.

"Let the others go first, James. We'll form the rear guard. I'll ask Turenne to help. Saxe-Weimar has already moved out."

"Aye his bonfires were going from dawn," Lieutenant Colonel James Hepburn looked exhausted. "I don't know how you look so fresh, John. It feels like failure."

"Never believe that. I've a trick or two to show General Galas."

Hepburn was off again. Soon the whole camp was deserted. Only fires raged and the heavy smoke pouring east kept the Spaniards from seeing what was happening. Galas was not about to walk into a trap. He waited until the next day and by then his quarry was long gone and moving quickly towards the hilly area to the west.

It was on this retreat that John Hepburn came to depend on his highland veterans from the Swedish campaign. Sergeant Major Elliot had organised them into scouting parties and Hepburn was kept aware of Galas's forces at all times. They seemed to have the eyes of eagles and the ability to run all day without tiring. As for invisibility, they appeared only to have to stand still and they disappeared.

"We reivers are good, Sir, but they lot are fair amazing," Sergeant Major Elliot said one time when they were out on the hill together and a plaid-clad soldier materialised beside them. "They'd cut your throat without ye noticing."

"They'll get their chance at that soon." Hepburn sounded grim.

"Aye, Sir." The kilted man beside him pointed. "The first of the scoundrels are just over that hill yonder. I can hear their horses. It's cavalry likely."

"Make for the valley behind us and await me, Sergeant Major Elliot. Take the men with you." The grizzled Borderer who seemed to have taken Andrew Armstrong's place as of right, saluted and turned away. Hepburn spurred his horse ahead of them to catch up with Turenne who was leading his men into the valley already.

"Henri. They are up on us!"

The French man held up his hand. "Halt men. We turn to fight to the death." There was no fear on his face and no doubts in his voice.

Hepburn laughed.

"You wanted to learn from me? Now pay attention! Send your pikemen on making plenty of noise. My pikes will join them. Make them pretend to mill about in terror. There is a regiment of cavalry coming up fast and they'll hope to mow them down in a charge. You take your musketeers up that side of the hill and spread them out in line but under cover of the trees. Mine are massing this side. Wait for my men to fire and follow suit at once. Pour ball into them. I even have small leather cannon that we used in Germany that will spread grapeshot and we'll unroll our chevaux de frise in the grass of the valley and that will slow the bastards down."

Turenne stood with his mouth open. "We fight?"

"We fight with our brains, Henri. Now hurry! Do exactly as I say and see what happens!" His voice sounded grim. "I am going to make Galas remember this retreat."

When the cavalry entered the valley they saw a milling mob of soldiers staggering about at the far end apparently all trying to get ahead of each other. A smile lit their commander's face. "They run like rabbits in Spring. We shall hunt them down. Form your lines men, trot, canter, charge!" He drew his sword and pointed it and they were off, a hurtling wall of screaming death.

Hepburn, above them on the hillside, was unaffected. "Ready men!" His shout was unheard by the horsemen but the front rank of his musketeers blew on their matches. He waited until he saw the front rank founder on the metal teeth of the chevaux de frise and shouted "Fire!"

The volley was answered almost immediately from the hill opposite and then as the men changed places, primed, loaded and fired in order the sound of musketry was non-stop.

In the valley the whole mounted unit had piled up on each other and were being massacred by the shot pouring into them. The rear men were inextricably tangled with fallen horses. They died as musket ball took them. Few escaped. The disordered pike-men suddenly formed an attacking force, mopping up the escapees. They all died. By the time Turenne and Hepburn met, the action had finished.

"Magnificent, Colonel. You were magnificent!" The Frenchman could scarcely speak for emotion.

"It's just the beginning, Henri. Galas will be more careful next time but we've won some time. Let's make the most of it and get on after the army."

From then on they fought a rear-guard action against superior fire-power and numbers. It was a running battle where John Hepburn took on trust the information his highland scouts brought him and never once were they wrong. Henri, Vicomte de Turenne obeyed him to the letter however unhappy he might be with his orders.

"I thought you were asking me to die, today, Colonel," he admitted after one particularly close call where Turenne had played the lure, marching as if unaware into a trap. But Hepburn had it all in hand. As the Frenchmen entered the narrow valley he cut the pursuers off behind and before and Galas lost a whole unit of pike-men.

"We must play different tunes for them, Henri. Then they will not get bored."

"Bored! I am terrified, excited, exhausted! What they must feel I cannot imagine. But bored? I think not!"

Gradually the great mass of their army swept away from them and they were on their own.

"A band of ruffians led by a genius, that's us," Lieutenant Colonel James Hepburn said after one long miserable day of hiding and firing and running to turn and fire again. "It reminds me of playing soldiers on the farm, John. You always beat me."

"Heaven send I beat them." Sir John Hepburn looked thin and grey about the face but his eyes still sparkled blue excitement. "My reckoning is that we've killed about a thousand of them already and how many Scots have fallen?"

"Nine all told. We buried nine anyway and I don't think anyone is missing. Turenne has had a few run off in the hope the opposition will feed them but as you never do the same thing twice there's nothing they can tell Galas that will help."

"It is true, Colonel. Every night I write your plan down so one day I shall remember. My father never taught me this sort of warfare and he has the best training school in France, so they say."

"He trained you well Henri. You fight with your heart and you obey orders. What more can a leader want." Hepburn smiled at the young man opposite and was amused by the blush that rose in his sallow cheeks.

"We'd all be better for a decent meal. My highlanders tell me that they can scent winter weather. God send they are right and that it is a severe one. Galas must give up soon or he'll be on French soil and that I do not want. For one thing it is as flat as a pancake and we'd stand no chance."

It was a close run thing. The snow began its gentle cascade one evening when Hepburn had climbed to the top of a hill and was appalled to see flat farm land to the west. But by morning everything was white amongst the pine clad hills and a sharp wind had risen to make marching a misery as sleet was hammered into nervous faces looking always for attack out of no-where.

"We've got Galas terrified at last, I'm thinking." Hepburn had joined his officers after talking to his scouts. "They haven't moved out of camp since the snow started."

By the next day it appeared that the Spanish had given up. The scouts reported that they were retreating but carefully with scouts of their own out in case of attack.

"They just don't know how unlikely that is." Hepburn was beaming. "Get your kit together and let's be off to winter quarters, a decent meal and a warm bed."

CHAPTER 33
Paris. Winter 1635

Leaving his brother, Lieutenant Colonel James Hepburn, in charge of the regiment in its winter quarters, Sir John Hepburn rode to Paris. His small apartment was an oasis of delight. All the rich furnishings he had ordered had arrived and he dined on plate and drank from gilded silver beakers, his initials entwined on their base. That winter he learned what it was like to live like a nobleman. He breakfasted late, had his hair, beard and moustaches trimmed and curled a la mode, then sauntered out to meet friends.

It seemed every man was keen to be his comrade and take his arm and ask how the war was going. At receptions beautifully painted and dressed ladies pressed his hands with scented fingers and promised even more with dancing eyes. He was a hero.

Hepburn revelled in luxurious living, ordering and wearing elegant suits laced with gold and silver. The one he favoured most, a vermilion cloth edged in gold with a great white lace collar, pleased him so much that he had his portrait painted in it.

"I have a sister," he told the artist. "She would love to see me thus."

"Then remove that great sword, Sir. Your dress is superb, your small cane elegant, but that sword is, is," he hesitated for the word and then blurted, "It is workmanlike!"

Hepburn looked down at the well worn handle. "It is part of me, Sir. It stays." So shrugging, the limner turned to his brushes. None of his other sitters wore such a weapon.

At first Hepburn enjoyed the dinners, musical evenings and poetry readings he was asked to. It was such a different life and so exciting to be one with the nobility of Paris, part of the scene that he had only glimpsed as a soldier in training in Paris, so many years ago. Now he was parading with the officers of the Kings Scottish Guard and they listened to him, admired him and were proud to call him friend. But after some weeks of it, the triviality suddenly hit him. Their fawning was unreal. He was merely a passing fad to be taken up and then forgotten as a child forgets its toy.

One evening at a men's dinner thrown by Lord James Douglas he was delighted to find himself sitting opposite Bernard of Saxe-Weimar.

His old friend leaned across the table to murmur in a low voice, "I came to talk to Cardinal Richelieu, John. We have come to a good agreement. I am for France now."

Hepburn's long rather stern face dissolved in a beaming smile. "I told him you were the salt of the earth, Bernard. He is lucky to get you." He lowered his voice. "France needs young leaders." He paused, "and I need comrades."

Saxe-Weimar nodded and gestured at the table. "This is what I was brought up to, John, but now it seems unreal. They talk like rooks cackling in a tree. It is time we were back in barracks with a real job."

"Lord James Douglas is entirely at home here," Hepburn sighed and looked up the table to where his second most senior Captain sat in deep consultation with one of the King's Scottish Guards. "I wasn't brought up to it, Bernard. I thought I should revel in it but the emptiness now bores me. I need something more."

They were interrupted by a loud challenge to their host from an officer whom Hepburn knew was a lieutenant colonel in the regiment of Picardie.

"One of de Breze's lot isn't he?" he whispered. Saxe-Weimar nodded. "Great lands, great titles and a great opinion of themselves. They trace their regimental history back to a Roman legion, on duty at the time of the Crucifixion, no less!"

Sir John Hepburn choked back a laugh but he was heard. The officer turned to him, sneering, "It is all very well to laugh but being granted the Right of the Line is too much. You lot will be claiming to be Pontius Pilate's Bodyguard next, so long established as you are."

His hostility was palpable and there were drawn breaths as the guests waited to see if Hepburn would rise to the challenge. But Douglas spoke from the top of the table. "No, no, my dear Sir! Had we been the guard on the Holy Sepulchre I assure you the sacred body would not have disappeared!"

Universal laughter greeted the riposte but by the next day Hepburn was amused to hear his Royal Scots called Pontius Pilate's bodyguard.

"It's a name that will stick, I have no doubt," he said to Cardinal Richelieu one evening some days later when he amused him with the story. The Cardinal had bidden him to dinner and when he got there, dressed in his favourite brown and gold coat, his gold officer's chain glinting on his chest, he found only Father Joseph as a fellow guest.

They discussed the war and Richelieu pressed him for ideas. "I can not hide the fact that last year ended disastrously for France, my son. Declaring war was inevitable but the Spanish response was overwhelming."

"The Swedish sector did not function when we needed it and the Dutch were war-weary." Hepburn nodded. "But France is mobilising in earnest now, Eminence, and I hear from Count Oxenstierna that the Swedes will mount an attack on a more limited front, this Spring. That will require the Imperialists to carve off troops to face them." He grinned. "I have told him how much he should be beholden to yourself, but I am sure Father Joseph keeps an eye on my letters. I leave them out now in case his spies are interested."

The priest shook a finger at him but Richelieu chuckled and Hepburn continued. "What I hear is that the Dutch appear to have poured money into their navy and are interrupting the bullion ships from America. Each one sunk or captured is as good as us slaughtering a battalion of Spaniards and saves French lives."

"I fear they may attack France where we have no resistance."

"The Southern and Western ports? Maybe. It was worth alerting those who guard them. But England has learned its lesson since you, Eminence, beat them out of La Rochelle, and is too busy vying with the

Dutch navy for Spanish gold. It is my feeling that our Spring offensive will go well and you will be proud of us!"

"Proud, I already am, my son. Father Joseph has told me of your retreat from the Rhine."

"It is a retreat that Galas will regret all his life." John Hepburn sounded satisfied. "He lost many more than if we had beaten him in pitched battle and he has gone back beyond the Rhine. Those few towns he left fortified in Lorraine will be easily taken this Spring and we'll push on into Alsace to give France a solid outline that I expect to hold on to."

"Too good to be true!" A growl came from Father Joseph.

Hepburn's smile encompassed him. "With you beside us, Father, how can we lose? No. Don't berate me." He held up his hands in submission. "I seriously think that Galas finds Lorraine one step too far. That last push was only possible because he massed all his men. This Spring he will have to fight in the North against both the Dutch and de Breze, us in Lorraine and Rohan to the South. With dwindling resources he is stretched. Besides, Lorrainers hate him even more than they hate us. They adore that swine the Duke of Lorraine but he will die and then I believe they will look to France as their protector. They speak French and are married to French men and women. It's a natural progression."

"But what about Sir John Hebron? What does he want from such a success?" Cardinal Richelieu was smiling at him as he sat at the shining table the candle-light making a golden glory of his hair and glinting off the great gold chain that hung on his chest.

"You have promised me Metternich's ransom. I will be a rich man and well satisfied, Eminence. Fighting for France is my reward. My heart is here."

"Perhaps a kindly widow with a chateau and a vineyard when you retire, my son? It could be arranged."

Hepburn looked at the two men he revered most and the colour rose in his face. "You are very good to me, Eminence." He hesitated, then took a deep breath. "I have enjoyed playing the nobleman this winter but it is an empty life and I am no farmer. I had thought," he hesitated then continued in a rush, "I had thought of following Baron de Mafflier here, and in a small way you too, Eminence. I wondered if you would allow me to study for the Church when France no longer needs my sword."

Both churchmen sat back astonished. But then Richelieu nodded. "Of course, my son! Without doubt! How stupid of me not to have seen such an obvious desire. You would never have turned to the true Church as a young man if you had not had a true calling. To stand firm in your faith all the time you fought with Sweden must have been hard. When the time comes, I will stand as your sponsor with pleasure."

Later when they were alone Father Joseph muttered to Richelieu. "He'll want a Bishopric!"

"Why not? Settle him in a border Bishopric and we could sleep easy. He would defend it with his life and he'd look magnificent in the robes, Joseph."

"He'll need to become a great deal more respectful, Eminence. He teases me all the time and makes people laugh at me."

"He loves you, Joseph."

"Well, it doesn't show!" Clearly the thought startled him.

"Get used to the idea. You may be his tutor. My guess is that he sees you as his temporal father and me as his spiritual one. His heart is France's because it is ours. His intelligence is enormous, my Golden Knight, and his soul is ardent. There are times when those blue, blue eyes seem to blaze into my soul and then when I see their reverence I hope that, overlaid as it is by temporal cares, my soul still stands a chance of heaven. He would make a great churchman, Joseph."

"Humph." His Grey Eminence shrugged, but he did not look unpleased.

CHAPTER 34
Return to Winter Quarters from Paris

Duke Bernard of Saxe-Weimar accompanied Sir John Hepburn and Lord James Douglas south to headquarters at Pont a Mousson. Then Hepburn and Douglas continued on to join their regiment which had been in winter quarters at Moyenvie. Of them all, only the younger man had seemed sorry to leave.

"I miss the life in Paris, Colonel. It's because I was brought up as Richelieu's page, I expect," Douglas answered when Hepburn took exception to his Captain's long face. "My older brother, Archibald, is still in his household, though he's desperate to join the army too. But your nephew joined the Cardinal's household as a page recently, Colonel. Don't you miss him?"

"No!" Hepburn's tone was sharp. "George Hepburn turned up out of the blue with a letter from my eldest brother begging my assistance for him and I hadn't the slightest idea what to do with him. He's a right wastrel in the making in my opinion. I guess my brother hoped to get rid of him."

"He takes to court life like a duck to water." Lord James Douglas looked curiously at his Colonel. "You meet him everywhere and the ladies adore him."

"Oh yes! Puppy that he is! He had the cheek to tell me that he would take care of my apartment while I was away and moved in before I could think of an excuse. I offered him an ensignship and you should have seen his lip curl. His Eminence was listening to our exchange and offered him a place in his household before I could warn him not to. Now I'll never get rid of him, I doubt."

Douglas laughed. "He'll get too old to be a page eventually."

His Colonel shrugged. "It can't come soon enough for me. I just know he will make Hepburn a bad name in Paris. My brother would never have sent him out of Scotland else."

The irritation his nephew George caused him was quickly forgotten on their arrival at headquarters.

"I've suddenly realised that getting back to the Royal Scots is coming home to you, Colonel." Douglas was shaking his head at the delight in Sir John Hepburn's face as their colours came in to view outside their barracks.

His Colonel's stern face softened as a happy smile lifted the ends of his luxuriant golden moustache. "Aye. I recruited our men from all over Scotland and from every walk of life, veterans all, and good at what they do. I've trained them to work and fight together and for one another and they are all the family I'll ever need. I'd lose even one with sorrow. In fact we only needed sixty to make up strength so I sent Captain Alexander Gordon, that's grandson of the Earl of Sutherland, to recruit. He'll bring experienced soldiers of highland stock likely, and West coast men as well. Next time we'll seek men from the East coast. It keeps the regiment balanced."

Their arrival had been spotted and the city gates were wide, saluting soldiers beside them. Sir John Hepburn turned a joyous face to his companion, "Right, Captain Lord James Douglas. If you are ready we'll report to our new General. This year Lorraine will belong to France."

Richelieu had offered command to Cardinal Duke la Valette and he had already arrived.

"Just as well I've kept the men in training all winter, John." His brother greeted him with a hug. "La Valette was much impressed when we paraded for him. Told me we had a well drilled force. You'd have been proud of them."

"I'm proud of you, James." John Hepburn's voice was warm. "You've been so much more than a brother to me."

"I've learned so much from you."

"I've learned to love and depend on you, little brother!"

His brother blushed and turned away. "I always thought you great,

John, even when you beat me at the Battle of Athelstaneford."

That made them both laugh and they went out together to review Hepburn's troops, where Lord James Douglas was waiting.

Later that evening his two senior Captains joined Hepburn and his brother in his quarters where he sat contentedly, a stoup of Leipzig beer at his hand. "Help yourselves," he gestured to bottles and tankards and the others fortified themselves and joined him.

"We'll never make that lot into a really smart regiment while the highlanders insist on wearing those ragged kilts and hose or tartan trews and the borderers keep to their boots and jerkins and the rest wear anything they've looted." Douglas set his tankard down and sat back, looking questioningly at his Colonel.

"I don't think it matters." Sir John Hepburn was unworried.

His younger brother nodded. "That was my conclusion. I made no regulations about their garments so long as they all had decent breast plates and well kept weapons. They all own morions too, though I know your musketeers prefer those hats with sweeping brims and plumes, James."

Douglas grinned. "Devils aren't they! But we shoot faster than any other unit in the French army or, I bet, any musketeer in the damned Imperialists."

Lieutenant Colonel James Hepburn grinned back. "They're not too keen on hip boots either but I've persuaded most of them into them and so we know who they are I issued great green sashes for everyone to wear across one shoulder. I've issued green plumes for officers' head gear and huge ones for you John, though big lump that you are, no one's going to miss whom to follow."

"I thought they looked great, James. People will certainly recognise my men, call them what they will."

"Pontius Pilate's Bodyguard! The Green Brigade! First of the Line! Hebron's Regiment! The Royal Scots!" Douglas chanted the names like a battle cry.

"For heaven's sake what's all that about?"

"Long story!" His older brother was laughing. "Get Douglas to tell you. Most of it was his doing."

But that Spring, Sir John Hepburn felt a warm pride as he led his men out of winter quarters and away towards the Lorraine border. Ahead of him he was amused to see Cardinal la Valette in scarlet robes topped by a shining breastplate, a sword by his side, riding companionably with that confirmed Calvinist, Duke Bernard of Saxe-Weimar, and obviously in deep agreement.

"We are all for France," he said to Turenne who had spurred up to ride beside him. "This is not a religious war but a fight for freedom."

Turenne laughed as he saw the two ahead. "Just like you and me, Colonel!"

Hepburn smiled. "I suppose so. Had you never thought of becoming Catholic, Henri?"

"I think more of becoming a great general. I couldn't change while my father lives. It would pain him. I'll put it on my list of things to consider in retirement. Cardinal Richelieu is always at me. Don't you start!"

Hepburn laughed. The two of them had slipped into a master and pupil relationship, the older man recognising his own tactical talent latent in Turenne and happy to pass his experience on.

He had been called to interview with la Valette last of all the commanders and his slight pique at this was stifled when the Cardinal greeted him with, "I kept you till last Sir John Hebron because I see you as the real leader of this army."

He held up his hand as Hepburn was about to disclaim. "Cardinal Richelieu and I had many discussions and we both agree on this. The King himself is in full knowledge of it."

"I shall do nothing without your permission then, Eminence." Hepburn bowed, both delighted and terrified. But the more he thought about it, the better he liked the idea. He knew the terrain best. He knew what his men could do and he was well aware of Turenne and Saxe-Weimar's capabilities.

"It will be an honour and a pleasure to enable France to live in peace, free from fear of Spanish incursion, but with your permission this arrangement will be between us so that you will have the men's obedience as you should."

"As you wish." Well pleased, the churchman nodded. "I should mention that we will naturally have the advice of Father Joseph whom Cardinal Richelieu has seconded to my household."

Hepburn laughed out loud. "Eminence, I would not have it otherwise."

"Well you're the only one of that opinion, my son!" La Valette's dour tones followed him out of the door.

CHAPTER 35
Retaking Lorraine and Siege of Saverne 1636

Lorraine surrendered before them, la Mothe and its destruction still fresh in their minds. Walled cities took one look at the size of Sir John Hepburn's army and capitulated, offering contribution to Louis XIII and food to his soldiers.

"It's very different this time," Henri de Turenne spoke at a meeting of the commanders. "Remember that retreat last winter, Colonel Hepburn?"

"The important thing is that Galas remembers. He's retreated East of the Rhine and left Lorraine to defend itself. He can stay there forever as far as I am concerned. We'll strengthen the West bank fortifications and move South into Alsace."

"We'll need to take Saverne."

"We will, Bernard," Hepburn nodded to Saxe-Weimar. "It's the door to Alsace and what should rightly be the South East of France."

"Did you know that the name comes from the Latin, "tres taverna?" Cardinal la Valette spoke and Hepburn turned to him, interested.

"I didn't, Eminence."

The older man nodded. "It was the only pass from Rome into Gaul. The Romans required three taverns or resting places for their mules on their way from the wide lush lands of Alsace into Gaul. Saverne was the third and last. It's different for us. Once Saverne falls the country to the south lies open. How will we take it, Colonel?"

"Besiege it, Eminence. Saverne is a tough nut to crack. There is a well trained Spanish garrison inside under Colonel Mulhern and they will look to Galas to come to their aid. Myself I think he won't, but they will learn that the hard way, as we will do."

"You think Mulhern won't negotiate?" Turenne was interested.

"Not a chance! I'd wager money on it." Hepburn's voice was grim. "I hate the aftermath of a besieged city taken eventually by force. The carnage is dreadful."

He had been proved right, he thought as he sat by the river in the little village of Phalsburg, where Cardinal la Valette's army were quartered that hot July evening. Saverne had resisted tooth and nail and losses on both sides had been severe. Only that day he had despatched Captain Robert Tours, the son of Sir George of Innerleithen, to approach the Privy Council in Edinburgh for another sixty recruits, this time from the East of Scotland as he had told his young Captain on their journey back to quarters from Paris. His Royal Scots, his family of veteran soldiers, would always represent the whole of Scotland and it was time to bring a halt to further losses, on his side anyway.

That night he slept sound, as the mental picture of the blue and gold baton of a Marshal of France brought contentment and delight to his dreams. Even the irritation he had felt when the bearer of Richelieu's dispatch with its good news had been his young nephew George, was dissipated by his joy at reading of his promotion. Young George had no desire to be a soldier, he thought with a sigh. He'd been delighted to be dispatched to a tent on the outskirts of the camp where he could maintain his elegant clothes. Why his eldest brother had sent the boy to him in Paris was a mystery. If Cardinal Richelieu had not taken him into his household as a page, John Hepburn would have sent him home. At least this time he had been useful. He had carried the greatest accolade a soldier could want.

The next morning Sir John Hepburn was up early and, shrugging on his breast plate, called for his horse. The heat was already making him pour with sweat so instead of his visor he donned a soldier's morion. It would give him better all round vision anyway. His thoughts were on his brother James. His death a month ago had been a sore loss and despite his outward calm he missed him sadly. Lieutenant Colonel James Hepburn had become his right hand and a safe and secret conduit to Oxenstierna. He knew he would not find another he could trust as he had the younger brother he had learned to love.

There was no one stirring in the tents when he set off. Sergeant Major Elliot materialised as he mounted his horse but Hepburn waved him away.

"I'm just going for a quick look, Wat. No need to come. Away and break your fast."

But Elliot watched as his Colonel rode off and when he saw him fall his shout brought Scots tumbling from their tents to run forward, unarmed and uncaring, to lift their Colonel and carry him swiftly to the surgeon's tent.

On the battlements of Saverne that morning, no one stirred either, all except one musketeer who with one lucky shot at a casual rider was responsible for the deaths of everyone in Saverne and the destruction of every edifice except the red sandstone church of the Virgin Mary.

Hepburn had been assessing the work his men had put in during the night clearing a path through the bodies that lay strewn in already stinking heaps right up to the walls. The sandstone walls themselves shone blood-red in the morning sunrise and as he saw the path they should attack on he was dazzled for a moment and missed the musket flash.

His men worked desperately, unbuckling his armour, stripping his shirt off and pushing the surgeon, still undressed, in beside him. They waited breathless as he moved gently about his patient. At last, stone faced he bent over so that Hepburn could see his face.

"Well, Surgeon?" Hepburn's voice had lost power.

He shook his head. "The ball has gone in by your neck, Colonel, and has travelled down, how far I know not. I cannot reach it. You are in God's hands, Sir. I would I could say different." He turned away and the watching men saw tears running down his cheeks. They had never seen their Surgeon cry before and they knew the meaning of it. Their heads drooped.

Captain James Hepburn rushed in half dressed to hold his cousin's hand as if he could pour life into those paling cheeks. "John! John! For

God's sake John, don't die!"

They heard Sir John Hepburn sigh and his whisper came again.

"We're a long way from home, James-lad, but you'll take my regiment on and do it well." His head turned slightly to find Sergeant Major Elliot. "Go to Turenne, Wat. Tell him to attack in a narrow line between the bodies right up the steps to the gate below the church. Take rams for the gate. Once in, the battlement runs straight along and his men will be in the town. Tell him to go now while they sleep!"

The effort of concentration to get the words out left him exhausted and for a moment he lay still. The regiment's Chaplain, Thomas Cammerarius, appeared at his side, putting his bands round his neck as he came.

Hepburn managed a half smile. "Tom Chalmers, I need to make my peace."

"I am here for you, my son." The Borderer who had become a priest took his other hand in a steady grip. A gesture cleared the room. Even his cousin moved outside to be taken and held in a comforting embrace by Lord James Douglas who had just heard the news.

They stood together in their grief, realising what a rock of stability Sir John Hepburn had been in their lives. Behind them the Scots gathered, silent. Tod Armstrong, that grizzled veteran, stood with tears falling unchecked as his men gathered about him, helpless in their own grief.

"He is in God's hands now." The priest came out of the tent, his face white and strained. Putting a comforting hand on Captain James Hepburn's shoulder he added, "He made a good confession and his time in Purgatory will be short before he is restored to his God and maker. You may go in to him now."

James Hepburn, tears still coursing down his face, went back to sit beside his cousin holding his hand. At one point he looked up at the Surgeon who stood ready but helpless. The man shook his head sadly and whispered, "He bears his pain bravely. I can do no more. There is internal bleeding that I can not stop."

James Hepburn returned his gaze to his cousin's white face and dashed his tears away.

"Remember when we played soldiers by the burn, John?"

The pale face softened and the watchers heard their Colonel sigh. "A long while back, James. Young James was with us then. We've come a far way since."

James Hepburn felt his cousin's grip tighten and then his hand lay lax in his clasp and they sat that way quietly as the tent emptied of men who had lost their lode star. Far away on the red battlements of Saverne they heard the sounds of war and Turenne's white plumes waved from the walls where they had made a breach just as Sir John Hepburn had told them to.

Captain Lord James Douglas watching, growled in his throat and shouted for his men to stand to arms. Willing, they were right behind him as he followed the path Turenne had taken. The French regiment felt a warm growling wind behind them and suddenly they were being forced forward as if a tornado was tearing into them.

"Stand aside, men! We hold by the church. Let the Scot's go through!" Turenne was shouting and pulling his men out of the way. Powered by fury and blood lust Lord James Douglas led Sir John Hepburn's Scots through into the town to exact vengeance. They killed indiscriminately and thoroughly. Few survived and most of Saverne was in flames when, exhausted, they dragged themselves back to camp. Only the church of the Virgin Mary where Turenne had gathered his men still stood. Palaces, city chambers, monasteries, and ordinary houses burned to the ground, their inhabitants dead within them.

"Sir John Hepburn's funeral pyre!" Turenne murmured as he ordered his men out. "Oh God, but I shall miss him so!"

Somewhat after the chaos in the camp had lessened, George Hepburn emerged from his tent, fully dressed and fed, to be told that his uncle had died. His face blanched. "Did he have time to make a will?"

The soldier who told him turned away and spat on the ground. Had he known it young Hepburn had just had a close call with death. But George Hepburn bustled on to find his cousin in his tent his head in his hands.

"Did he make a will, Cousin James?"

Captain James Hepburn made a sound so hostile that his relative blanched. "I'll just get off then. I'll be the first to tell Cardinal Richelieu. We need to be sure of Metternich's ransom and I'll get a message to my father too. We should all share his leavings."

His master in Paris, Cardinal Richelieu was overwhelmed by sorrow and assuaged it by pouring largesse on Sir John Hepburn's now apparently grief stricken nephew.

"I cannot express to you, my Lord, my great concern at the death of poor Colonel Hepburn," he wrote to Cardinal la Valette, "not only for the great esteem I have for his character but for the affection and zeal he has always testified for His Majesty's service. His loss has so touched me in so sensible and lively a manner that it is impossible for me to receive any comfort."

Once alone, he put his head in his hands, "My Golden Knight! Oh God why take my Golden Knight when France has such need of him!"

It took much prayer before he could bring himself to say, "Saverne has cost us very dear but we must bend our wills to what God pleases."

A year or so later Lord James Douglas's elder brother, Lord Archibald, joined him in the regiment and spoke of that time.

"That ninny, George Hepburn, paraded a damp eye around every party currying sympathy until I could have struck him down. He was for grabbing everything but an older uncle, a burgess from Haddington, arrived and taking Hepburn's testament he insisted on packing everything named as well as Metternich's ransom. George Hepburn was as mad as a wet hen but he got away with plenty and is still fighting for a return from all the pistols that your Colonel Sir John Hepburn sent to that armourer in Paris."

"He'll get no where with that one!" Lord James Douglas gave a grim smile. "That armour dealer's as crafty as a fox and he'll be saying they are all out of date and of no value. Serve George Hepburn right. I know because James Hepburn tried when he was Colonel and he failed. By God, brother, I miss Colonel Sir John. I didn't want the Colonelcy yet. I still feel I'm inexperienced."

Lord Archibald nodded. "Richelieu wanted you to have it after Sir John. He wrote to Cardinal la Valette and ordered it but la Valette wrote back saying the Scottish soldiers wouldn't stand for it. They had their own method of choosing and they'd not follow another. Captain James Hepburn was senior captain and that was that!"

His brother nodded. "I told him that too. I was too young anyway. But he wanted a Catholic colonel. With Turenne still Huguenot it gives a poor image for France to have two reformist colonels against the Spanish Catholics. Colonel James Hepburn was great, though. He led us into Alsace as if a high wind was with us." He sighed and plucked at a lip. "Trouble was I think he was trying to live up to Colonel Sir John and no one could do that. He was right wild in the charge and we lost men. He had to send Captain Tours back to apply for a recruiting order for a thousand men as well as drummers. Sir John would have hated that. He saw the men as his family. It was that recklessness that did for James in the end. He got a bullet in the chest as he hurled himself into a Spanish square with his men desperately trying to keep up with him."

"So now it is you, Colonel Lord James Douglas!"

"Aye and it's a great regiment to lead, with a fine history already and experienced committed men. You'd better learn quickly, brother. I'll not be promoting you to be my lieutenant colonel until you get a lot more experience."

"Just teach me, James. I'll learn." His elder brother nodded enthusiastically.

"At least you aren't a wastrel like George Hepburn," James Douglas grinned at his brother. "Now go and sort the men's quarters for the night, Archie."

His brother grinned. "They call us "Le Regiment de Douglas" now. I like that"

His younger brother gave a short laugh. "Never believe it, brother. They can call it what they like but this is "Le regiment d'Hebron", "Hepburn's Regiment", and always will be. You ask the men!"

Andrew Hepburn returned to Haddington with both his brothers' leavings. His elder brother George had alerted his siblings of John's death as soon as he had received the news from France. Marie had wept the inconsolable tears of a mother who has lost a child. A widow now, she had no one to console her. George, however, was more alarmed than grief stricken. He had set off to see his younger brother in Haddington.

"I canna' leave the farm, Andra, and anyway I'm no hand at the figuring. Get away up to Edinburgh to petition the Privy Council to let you go to Paris to collect John's leavings and whatever young James had. John's testament dative lists silver plates, silver-gilt beakers and much more. Go quickly or young George will have everything away!"

He knew his son, thought Andrew Hepburn. He had not been a moment too soon in reaching Paris. His youngest brother James's leavings were few, but it had taken all his threats of exposure to gather the things Sir John Hepburn had mentioned in his retour. The only thing not mentioned in the testament that young George didn't quibble over was Sir John Hepburn's portrait. "Take the thing. I'm not for having that ugly face louring at me," he spat. "Father and you don't realise how much money I need to live here!"

With their youngest brother dead, George, Andrew and Marie were the only siblings left.

"Andra and I'll split the whole," George told the other two. "Marie's just a woman and that doesn't count. You can have John's portrait, sister."

Marie looked at her grasping younger brothers and simply shook her head.

"I'll take the portrait and thank you, George. I'm the only one that loved him so that is no loss to ye. But John named me as his executor, and only me. That means he wanted me to share his leavings."

"But ye're but a woman!"

"I'm a woman as has a lawyer for son-in-law, George Hepburn, and he and I will take ye both to court for my rightful share."

The men looked at her in alarm. "No need for that Marie!" Andrew had been thinking. "No point putting gowd into lawyers' pockets! Would you agree to the old feudal way where we ask the head of the family to make the judgement?"

" Hepburn of Waughton?" Marie considered. "Aye I'll abide by that, Andra."

Her brothers' hopes were dashed, however, when Waughton ruled a three way split and though Marie became rich, it was always the portrait of her brother John that she valued most.

CHAPTER 36
Burial in Toul Cathedral

Leaving the smoking, stinking, deserted ruins of Saverne, the Green Brigade, Pontius Pilate's Bodyguard, Right of the Line and First of Foot, the Royal Scots, Hepburn's Regiment, buried their colonel in the great cathedral at Toul with all the splendour they could manage.

A blinding blanket of heat enveloped low lying Toul, embraced though it was by two rivers. Sun reflected painfully off breastplates polished to honour their colonel. Even the gawping residents of Toul turned away from the brightness. Men staggered and fainted as they marched but their fellow soldiers picked them up and the whole shambling river of mirrored steel pushed their way through the great doors of the cathedral.

Inside their sweat lay in beads across their brows as the cold of the sombre grey stone walls bit. Men shivered, feeling the chill of the grave as great waves of song from the choir poured up and up into the high vaulted roof. The Bishop of Toul, clad in white ornamented only with jet bands, rose from his white marble throne to await the long cortege filing up the wide aisle of that great grey solemn cathedral. Embalmed and encased in a lead lined coffin, Sir John Hepburn lay beneath his sword and armour. The baton signifying his promotion to Marshal of France lay atop all.

His fellow officers were there. The new Colonel, Sir John's cousin, James Hepburn, and Lord James Douglas, white faced and grim, toiled with their own emotions as they led their men. Beside them Duke Bernard of Saxe-Weimar had tears on his rough cheeks and did not bother to wipe them away. Behind them Cardinal la Valette and a cowled Father Joseph walked with Henri, Vicomte de Turenne who was crying unashamedly. The old priest attempted to comfort him with little success.

"He was so much my tutor, my mentor. He taught me almost as if he knew time was short for him," Turenne whispered.

"Time is short for all of us, Henri. We bury La Vallee beside Colonel Hepburn. De la Force is devastated but at least Colonel Hepburn will have an ensign to guide him into heaven."

Turenne gave a watery chuckle. "Poor Sir John will be so cross when he wakes to find La Vallee still fawning on him for all eternity. When I die I shall put a stop to it for him."

Somewhere in the crowd George Hepburn, dressed immaculately in black, tried to insert himself amongst the officers with little success. The Scottish troops crowded on their leaders and the French officers had no time for him. He found himself standing in the mass of soldiery at the back of the church and felt ill-used amongst the stench of sweating bodies. However he contented himself by going over in his mind the possessions that he knew his uncle owned and pictured them bringing lustre to his own apartments.

They buried him in the South, the Notre Dame, transept opposite the choir and against two arches with beautiful murals. Cardinal Richelieu had asked his page if he wished his uncle buried in Paris but George had blanched and disclaimed any such desire.

"With your permission, we shall bury him in Toul, Sire." Richelieu had told his king. "He will lie at the heart of Lorraine which he more than anyone has secured to France. His tomb will be magnificent and, as he would have in life, so in death, he will remind Lorraine that it is part of France for ever."

"I agree." Louis XIII nodded. "Give orders for a monument of suitable proportions. Those Lorrainers must never forget the power France can unleash."

Sir John Hepburn's tomb was indeed magnificent. Twenty-five feet high and eighteen feet broad it was made in the form of a great white stone altar table, on which two slaves supported the warrior's bier. Upon it, his right elbow on a stone cushion, reclined a statue of Colonel Sir John Hepburn in armour, booted and spurred, with a plain square collar and a belt from which a sword hung along the top of his thigh, his left hand resting on its hilt. Under his right hand his helmet and gauntlets were portrayed. His real armour was displayed to one side with a gilded copper sword and spurs on the other. At the top a resurrection with angels arose from the head of another angel and beside it a statue of the Virgin Mary cradled the infant Jesus in one arm and held a sceptre in the other hand.

At the top and bottom of the plinth saints approached; St Mansuy, the Scot from Ireland who was the patron saint of Toul led St Palladius. On the other side Sir John himself, accompanied by angels and a torchbearer, was portrayed with St Andrew and St John, Hepburn's own patron saint.

On the long sides of the plinth the thirty two shields of families with whom Sir John Hepburn had claimed connection on being knighted proclaimed his lineage, amongst them the arms of Oxenford, Scrimgeour, Chambers, Pitfodels, Blebo, Garden, Smeaton, Dunbar and Monteith; Marquis of Huntly; Count of Livingstone; Wigtown, Hume, Douglas, Ogilvy, Errol, Grey, Kinghorn and Perth: Lord of the Isles. His epitaph was inscribed in gold on a great black marble tablet standing in front. It was said to have been written by Thomas Cammerarius, born Tom Chalmers from the Scottish borders, who went to Rome to become a priest and who was with Sir John at his death.

This is an excerpt from the longer original:

"To the immortal memory of Sir John Hepburn, Golden Knight of Scotland and Marshal de Camp in the French army, who fell, struck by a bullet, at the siege of Saverne on the 8th of July in the year 1636...

You would need eyes of stone to contemplate without sadness the features of the fiery Hepburn now set in marble!

And you, oh town of Toul...when so many different nationalities surround you, French, English, Italian and German, you can display Hepburn to them all equally as each remembers him as they follow the fortunes of war. Sometimes for his enthusiasm in friendship, sometimes for the terror he inspired as a redoubtable enemy, but always great and always invincible."

To make sure that no one was in any doubt that this was a piece of sacred French soil the whole was surrounded by a great grille of iron shaped into foliage surmounted by fleurs de lis separated by flaming urns.

Alas, during the French Revolution the monument was totally destroyed. However the grave of Sir John Hepburn, "the best Soldier in Christendom and therefore in the World," as Richelieu wrote about him, is still cared for lovingly by Cathedral staff. It is marked by a simple tablet.

"This stone covers the body of the Scot, Sir John Hepburn, Golden Knight, Marshal de Camp in the French army, who, shot by a leaden ball at Saverne, fell gloriously on 8th July 1636. Wayfarer, of your kindness, pray for him. Scotland has his birthplace, the world his fame, Toul his ashes, Heaven his soul."

My thanks and enormous gratitude to Colonel (Retd) R.P.Mason, Lieutenant Colonel (Retd) W.J.Blythe, Regimental Secretaries, The Royal Scots, and Mrs H. Spence, Historical Researcher, who encouraged me with archive material and read and corrected my script with unfailing tact, and equally to Professor Steve Murdoch of St Andrews University who gave me an indispensible bibliography and knew the answer to all my questions.

Thank you too, my kind brother, Sir Alastair Buchan-Hepburn, for introducing me to Sir John Hepburn, first Colonel and founder of the Royal Scots, and for finding the one known portrait of him, and as always, my thanks to my husband, James, whose knowledge of Scottish history and English grammar far exceeds mine.

Without your help I should not have written this book.

Elizabeth Scott

Printed by Richardson & Son Printers

Unit 7 Lochpark Industrial Estate
Hawick   TD9 9JA

01450 372656

www.richardsonprinters.com

Published by Buchan-Hepburn Publishers
ISBN: 978-0-9569516-0-1
© Elizabeth Scott 2011

THE BEST SOLDIER
by Elizabeth Scott